AF423370

To my husband, my parents, my sister, my family, and my friends — Thank you for standing by me, for lifting me up, and for helping me gather the pieces when everything seemed to fall apart. Your unwavering support made this book possible.

To the flight attendants and pilots at my airline — Your constant encouragement gave me strength when I needed it most. Thank you for your patience, input, and for your willingness to provide feed-back throughout all the stages of this book's development. Most importantly, thank you for being my family in the sky, always cheering me on from the jumpseat and beyond.

To all the teachers and coaches who challenged me to think bigger, push harder, and dream bigger — Your lessons left a mark deeper than you'll ever know.

And to you, the reader — Thank you for giving this story a chance. "Welcome Aboard" — I'm grateful you're here.

FLIGHT 987

STACY GOODMAN

FLIGHT 987
by Stacy Goodman

©2026, Relevant Edge Publications
Bellevue, Washington

Print ISBN: 979-8-218-90312-1
eBook ISBN: 979-8-31780-169-4

The plane jolted, snapping flight attendant Stephanie Pratt from the book in her hands. It was 1 a.m., and her break was still an hour away. She shivered, pulling her sweater tighter, and set the book aside. Just one more hour, she thought, holding onto the thought like a lifeline.

Rising from her jump seat at the front of the aircraft, she stretched her arms overhead, stifling a yawn. Peering into the first-class cabin, she saw passengers asleep, their faces peaceful, unaware of the chill creeping into the cabin. She decided to walk through coach, hoping movement would wake her up. The faint glow from the aft galley was the only light, a small, comforting beacon in the darkened plane.

As she walked, her eyes swept the floor for hazards. Near seat 3D, she spotted a stuffed rabbit, worn and missing an eye. She picked it up, tucking it gently beside a little girl curled up in her seat, tiny fingers clutching the edge of a blanket. One day, Levi and I will have kids, she thought, feeling a smile tug at her lips. Maybe then my parents will finally accept him.

In the back, three of the five crew members were asleep in the last row. Another flight attendant sat in her jump seat, knitting, her needles flashing in the dim light. Stephanie left her to her work and slipped into the bathroom, locking the door behind her.

She caught sight of her reflection in the mirror. Shadows lined her eyes, and her eyeliner had smudged beneath them. I look like hell, she thought, rubbing at the smears. Reapplying her lipstick, she glanced at her phone, smiling as Levi's message glowed on the screen:

"I love you. I'm a better person because of you. I can't wait to marry you. Call me when you land. PS: The cake tasting didn't go as planned. I'll tell you later."

She brushed her thumb over his picture, envisioning his familiar smile. But before she could savor the moment, a sharp pain knifed through her ears, and the cabin plunged into darkness. Oxygen masks dropped from the ceiling, swinging like pendulums.

Decompression.

Her heart leapt, each beat thundering in her chest. She lunged for the mask, but it swung out of reach, taunting her. Come on, come on! At last, her fingers closed around it, and she yanked it over her face as air flooded her lungs. Her training kicked in: mask first, then the PA, then brace for the dive to 10,000 feet. But the plane didn't dive. It stayed eerily level.

Why aren't we descending? Minutes dragged by, thick with silence. Panic tightened its grip. *The pilots . . . they must be unconscious.*

Swinging the bathroom door open, she expected chaos—masks hang-ing, passengers panicking. But the cabin was dead quiet. She hurried to the other attendant, shaking her shoulder, but her head lolled to the side, unresponsive. Dread clawed at her chest as she ripped open an overhead compartment, then another. No masks.

Her breath hitched. Six minutes. That's all it takes for brain damage . . . then death. And it's already been more than six.

The bathroom oxygen wouldn't last. She knew there were spare tanks near the back row of coach. Stretching the mask's tube as far as she could, she reached for a tank, her fingers brushing the cold metal. I'll have to take it off. Holding her breath, she tore the mask from her face, fumbled with the bracket, and finally freed the tank. She rushed back into the bathroom, connected the mask, and inhaled deeply. Thirty more minutes.

In the galley, her heart dropped. The other attendant lay crumpled on the floor, eyes glassy. Please, no. Kneeling beside her, Stephanie rolled her over and gave two rescue breaths, pressing on her chest. No response. She was gone. Hysteria clawed at her throat as she backed away, pressing herself against the wall.

I don't want to die.

Then her ears popped. The plane was finally descending. Relief surged through her, shaky but enough to push her forward. She stumbled toward the cockpit but tripped over something—a body. A woman's lifeless eyes stared up from the aisle.Stephanie stifled a scream, pulling herself up, her hands fumbling for the interphone. She hit the captain call button. No response. She pounded on the cockpit door. "Captain! Are you okay?" Silence.

Pressing her face to the peephole, she saw movement inside. "I can see you! Are you okay?" she shouted, banging harder. The door suddenly swung open, and she staggered backward, catching herself against the closet.

The captain stood there, his gaze vacant, as if he didn't recognize her. Then she saw the axe, gripped tightly in his hand.

He swung, and she barely managed to lift the oxygen tank, blocking the blow with a metallic clang that reverberated through her arms. She staggered, her muscles trembling under the force.

She turned to run, slowed by bodies slumped into the aisle. Her heart hammered. This is it. There's no way out.

Before she could move, the captain swung again. The axe met her skull in a sickening crunch. Pain exploded, her vision fading. Her last thoughts drifted to Levi. I'm sorry.

As the world dissolved, her gaze fell on the stuffed rabbit in seat 3D. Then—silence.

CHAPTER 1

NJ NEWS COURIER

OBITUARIES

Danielle Lynn Wheeler (Danni), 14, of Bridgewater, NJ, passed away at Somerset Medical Center on December 18. Danni is survived by her parents, Abby and Evan Wheeler, and her sister, Jennifer. Her Grandparents, Jack and Margaret Douglas. Aunts, uncles, and cousins. Danni will be remembered as an All-County soccer player and an avid fan of Taylor Smith. All her classmates at Adamsville Junior High School will miss her sorely. A viewing will be held at Bridgewater Funeral Home, 707 Main Street, Bridgewater, NJ. The service will be at Blessed Sacrament Church, 1890 Washington Valley Road, Martinsville, NJ. In place of flowers, the family requests that donations be made to the Organ & Transplant Alliance.

Evan Wheeler

Bound Brook, New Jersey

"Mommy!" The scream from over a year ago echoed in Evan Wheeler's mind, piercing the December chill as he helped his wife, Abby, out of the limo. Memories of his fourteen-year-old daughter, Danni, crowded his mind, each one sharper than the last. Now, Jennifer their 12-year-old was all they had left. Thankfully Jennifer had driven over to the church with her grandparents. She waited inside, out of the wind.

He pulled Abby close as they followed the uniformed pilots who carried Danni's coffin into the stone church. The clack of the gurney wheels on the marble floor jolted him back to the ER: the sterile lights, doctors shouting, helplessness pressing down on him as he watched them try to bring her back. She was so frail; they must be breaking her bones.

For a year, they'd chased a cure going from hospital to hospital. He remembered that final drive—Danni limp in the back seat, Abby's sobs filling the car. He'd run every red light, but it hadn't mattered. She never opened her eyes again.

The funeral director patted his back, and "Amazing Grace" began to play. Evan barely registered the people around him, the room a blur of incense and flowers. Jennifer took hold of their hands in the middle.

As the priest stretched his arms heavenward, Evan's mind drifted to the endless doctors and diagnoses, each more hopeless than the last. Dysmotility. Intestinal Dysmotility the disease taking his family. Only one in 100,000 survived at the end stage. He'd waited for a call that would bring a transplant, some miracle to save her. It never came.

He glanced at Abby, her figure so thin and fragile it hurt to look. She wore her clothes like a little girl dressing in her mother's outfits. Grief had hollowed her, but the disease had her now, stage 3. Jennifer was showing symptoms too. He tried not to think of their funerals.

The priest lifted his arms to the heavens. Evan's phone rang out, startling him. The whole congregation let out a gasp.

"Dad, you promised," Jennifer cried out, breaking into tears.

Abby's glare burned into him. She'd made him promise that he would leave his phone off today, but his habit was too ingrained. "You missed her last days," she'd said, her voice cutting like glass. "Consumed with your search for a cure. You were on your phone when you could have been with her. You're like an addict." He was chasing the dragon like any addiction. Gripping him with thoughts of being seconds away from the answers he was seeking, a cure or at least a liver transplant which could have bought her more time, bring them more time.

The priest took pity and moved on with the service.

When the mass ended, and as they followed Danni's coffin out. Inside Danny wore her first high heel shoes and lipstick, it's what she wanted for Christmas.

At the cemetery, Abby whimpered, her face twisted with grief. "We can do this," he whispered.

Jennifer sitting between them stretched to see what was about to happen. She spotted the astro turf draped hole and broke down sobbing. "I can't do it," she whimpered. An old friend, the babysitter they used when the girls were young, stepped up to the car.

"I'll get in with her," she said.

"Jen, are you going to be ok if Julie sits with you?" Evan asked.

Jennifer nodded her head.

At the end Abby kissed the coffin, patting it like you would rub someone's back when they're sick. Evan awkwardly hugged the coffin wanting one last embrace.

Back home, strangers filled the rooms, murmuring condolences he barely heard. People approached him like waves on a beach. Someone handed him a glass of water and a plate of food he never touched it. Eventually he drifted through the house, numb, past the unlit Christmas tree looming in the corner—a painful reminder of what they'd lost.

Without thinking, he found himself in his office, typing "Regeneration of the liver" into his computer.

CHAPTER 2

THE NEW YORK CHRONICLE

ONE YEAR LATER—CORRESPONDENT YAZMIN DA SILVA REFLECTS ON IRAQ KIDNAPPING

By Michael Carter

A year after her harrowing kidnapping in Iraq, correspondent Yazmin Da Silva has returned to journalism with renewed vigor. Da Silva, who was held captive for several weeks while covering conflict in the region, has bravely shared her story of resilience and survival.

Her ordeal, which gripped the nation, highlighted the dangers journalists face in war zones. Now, Da Silva is back, using her platform to advocate for press freedom and the safety of reporters worldwide.

Her experiences have not only shaped her career but have also inspired many, as she continues to pursue the truth with unwavering determination.

Levi Mathews

New York, New York

Levi took a deep breath, steadying himself in the cramped office of Reuters' chief editor, Sydney Upton. The room felt smaller than he remembered, cluttered with papers and food wrappers, a faint, sour smell of dill pickles lingering.

The news ticker scrolling on a muted monitor read, "Worldwide Airlines stock falls with expectations of flight attendant strike." Stephanie, a flight attendant for WWA, had dismissed the strike rumors. "Flight attendants tell me it's not going to happen," she'd said, her optimism almost naive. Ignorance is bliss, he thought.

Her words echoed as he repeated them to himself, his leg bouncing—a nervous habit he couldn't shake. Memories of past failures haunted him. This was his last shot. If he didn't land this job, he would have no choice but to settle for something small-time, a far cry from the prestige he'd once held.

When Sid finally entered, Levi stood, extending a hand. "Mr. Upton, thank you for meeting with me."

Sidney sighed, waving a hand dismissively as he squeezed behind his cluttered desk, moving a half-eaten bagel aside. "Sit down, Levi. No need to be so formal. What can I do for you?"

Levi swallowed, feeling his heart pounding in his chest. *Wasn't it obvious?* "I . . . I need a job."

Sidney's expression hardened. "Levi, you know I can't hire you." His voice was firm, almost impatient, as if they'd already had this conversation a hundred times. Levi's stomach tightened. Sidney wasn't pulling any punches. "You caused an international incident."

Levi winced, feeling each word hit like a blow. Sidney didn't stop. He recounted the details Levi wanted to forget—the drunken rant in Iraq, the passport debacle, the scandal that had cost NCC millions. Levi felt his face burn with shame as Sidney listed each offense. He'd been trying to move past it, but hearing it laid out like this made it all feel raw and fresh again.

"I've been sober for seventy days," Levi said, his voice barely above a whisper. He cleared his throat, willing himself to sound more confident. "I've changed. Stephanie's been helping me stay on track . . . I know I messed up, but I'm turning my life around."

Sidney's expression softened, just for a moment. Levi thought he saw a flicker of sympathy there, but then Sidney shook his head. "Levi, it's not just about you. The risks are too high. The insurance alone would be outrageous. I'm going to frank with you, no one wants to work with you. We can't afford the risk."

Levi's shoulders slumped. The words stung more than he'd expected. He'd hoped that Sidney would repay him for an editorial award he had won from Levi's expose on the Airline employees' drug and gun smuggling operation and the dirty bomb working out of JFK.

"Look, stay sober, earn the AA chip and we'll talk again," Sidney finished the conversation.

Levi left Sidney's office in a daze, his thoughts swirling. His thoughts mingled with disappointment, bills to be paid and his looming wedding. This wasn't going to help with Stephanie's parents who already didn't like him.

Out on the street, the winter air bit at his cheeks, sharp and unforgiving. His thoughts drifted to Dino's bar, just down the block. The neon sign flickered in the dim evening light, casting a glow that felt oddly comforting, like an old friend waiting to welcome him back. Just one drink, he thought, just to take the edge off. Stephanie would never have to know. He could almost taste it, the familiar warmth of whiskey easing the tension in his shoulders, numbing the shame and fear, if only for a little while.

But then Stephanie's face filled his mind—her warm smile, her crystal-blue eyes filled with hope. She'd changed his life in ways he hadn't thought possible. She was his reason to change, his new addiction. The thought of letting her down stopped him in his tracks. She believed in him, and that belief was the one thing that kept him going. If he gave in now, he knew he'd lose her trust, and maybe even lose her altogether.

Taking a deep breath, Levi turned away from Dino's bar, his gaze falling instead on Ray's Pizza across the street. It wasn't much, but he figured a slice might be enough to distract him. He could almost hear Stephanie's voice cheering him on, telling him he'd made the right choice.

Tomorrow, he'd accept the midnight anchor position at one of the last independent TV stations he could find. It was far from the dream job he'd envisioned, but it was something. And for now, something was enough to keep him moving forward—for himself, and for Stephanie.

CHAPTER 3

THE JOURNAL

Flight Attendant Strike Looms at Worldwide Airlines

By Morgan Jones

Flight attendants at Worldwide Airlines are preparing for a potential strike amid escalating tensions with management over pay, scheduling, and workplace safety concerns. The union representing the airline's cabin crew has announced that contract negotiations have stalled, citing insufficient progress on key demands, including better compensation and protections against fatigue from extended flight schedules.

Union leaders have set a strike date for next week if no agreement is reached, threatening to disrupt operations at one of the country's largest carriers during a peak travel period. The airline has acknowledged the talks but has yet to release a public statement about contingency plans.

Passengers with upcoming flights are being advised to monitor updates closely as the potential strike could lead to widespread cancellations and delays. Stay tuned for developments as negotiations continue in the coming days.

Robert Thomas Alexander III
New York, New York

The hotel phone rang, slicing through the pre-dawn silence. Robert Thomas Alexander groaned, reaching for the receiver and silencing it before the second ring. He rubbed his eyes, remnants of a fitful sleep clinging to him like cobwebs. His notes for the morning's meeting with Casey Cleary, the president of the flight attendants' union, lay strewn across the desk. He'd spent most of the night perfecting them.

Meetings like this one usually took place at headquarters, but Robert had orchestrated it here at the hotel to avoid leaks and keep Cleary off balance. The room was quiet, save for the low hum of the heater kicking in. He glanced at the clock. He'll be here soon.

Robert paced the room, feeling the weight of the tension press against him. The last time the airline had been in this kind of trouble—back in the '90s—it had barely survived the strike. But I've learned from that, he reminded himself, a faint smile tugging at his lips. He'd spent years slowly eroding the unions' influence. This time, they wouldn't have the upper hand. Piece by piece, the flight attendants, the pilots, and eventually, the mechanics—he'd bring them all to heel. It was only a matter of time.

But the unions were just one headache in a long list. The board, stockholders, lawsuits, airplane manufacturing issues, the volatile market—it all pressed down on him, like the recycled air of the hotel room closing in around him. Viral videos of customer complaints spread like wildfire, fueling public outrage and complicating his tightrope act of leadership. Robert exhaled slowly, letting his mind drift to his side venture, the one that would secure his place in the world far beyond the airline. He and Jose Santiago were on the brink of something monumental, something that would change medicine forever. And make us untouchable.

A sharp knock interrupted his thoughts. Cleary.

Robert took a moment, composing his expression into an unreadable mask before opening the door. "Come in," he said, turning his back as Cleary entered.

Casey Cleary stepped inside, his flight attendant uniform that fit a little too snug, his reddish-blond hair neatly combed. Robert gestured toward the sofa and took his seat opposite, studying Cleary's movements with a practiced eye. The man's shoulders were tense, his eyes darting around the room as though searching for an escape.

"We both know why you're here," Robert said evenly. "Why don't you start?"

Cleary nodded, pulling papers from his briefcase. "Eight years ago, we took concessions to avoid bankruptcy," he began, spreading documents across the table. "We kept this airline afloat, while executives continued to receive bonuses."

Robert leaned back, his face impassive. *Same speech, different day.*

Cleary's frustration was visible, his jaw tightening as he met Robert's gaze. "We were promised that once the airline recovered, we'd get a fair contract. The financial reports show we reached that point two years ago, but since then, you've delayed negotiations, dodged every meeting, and used lawsuits to stall the process. It's time for WWA to honor its commitments."

Cleary wiped sweat from his brow, pushing more documents across the table. Robert watched him, letting the silence stretch, savoring the man's discomfort. He could practically feel the seconds ticking bye, each one amplifying Cleary's tension.

"The mediation board has indicated a decision to release us next week," Cleary continued, his voice strained. "We will begin work actions if you don't return to the negotiating table. We will strike."

Robert allowed himself a small, satisfied smile. The national mediation board had accepted the bribe.

Cleary spoke again, his voice wavering. "How do you look yourself in the mirror, knowing you earn the largest bonus ever recorded at this airline while flight attendants live below the poverty line?"

Robert's smile vanished, his expression hardening. He leaned forward, his voice turning cold. "They don't have to work here. They're lucky to have a job." He let the words settle, watching the anger flare in Cleary's eyes before continuing. "The airline is not in a position to negotiate right now. We can discuss a new contract after the next two quarters."

Cleary shook his head. "Even if the last quarter fails, this year will yield the largest executive bonuses in five years. Other major US airlines have paid employees thousands in profit-sharing. This needs to be resolved now."

Robert felt a surge of irritation but kept his voice measured. "Casey, the airline won't negotiate before the next two quarters. Once the last quarter is over, we'll talk."

He reached into his briefcase and pulled out a green folder. "Laura Johnson, your vice-president, has agreed to take over as president when you step down. She understands the big picture."

Cleary's face fell as he opened the folder and saw Laura's endorsement on a check. His hands shook slightly. Clearly surprised the amount of the check.

"And here's proof of your treasurer, Bruce Childs, embezzling from the strike fund," Robert continued, sliding another folder across the table. "The account is nearly empty. A lawsuit over this would cripple the union."

Robert delivered the coup d'etat. 8x12 black and white photos of Cleary in a compromised position in a hotel room with a man who was not his wife.

Cleary stared at the photos and documents, visibly shaken. When he finally spoke, his voice was barely a whisper. "What do you want from me? What can I do?" His voice cracked, tears pooling in his eyes. "Please, I need this to go away. My wife will be devastated."

Robert's smile turned predatory. "Step down. Let Laura take over. Tell the membership you're having a mental breakdown. Make it happen quickly."

He showed Cleary to the door. "You will tell the membership you're stepping down for health reasons. Laura knows what to do. I expect this done by the end of the month."

Shutting the door, Robert returned to his coffee, savoring his victory. He picked up his phone, scrolling through an obituary.

"Hola," Doctor Santiago flatly said.

"I found someone," Robert said.

"You've said that before; why is this different?"

"He's desperate. You need to begin setting up, I think I can get him to sign on in a couple of weeks," Robert said.

"You know I need at least a month. I can't set up until he is ready."

"He will be. Trust me," Robert said as he hung up the phone.

CHAPTER 4

THE WASHINGTON TRIBUNE

VENEZUELA GOVT. CRISIS FORCES US STATE DEPT.

TRAVEL WARNING

Travelers planning to visit Caracas, Venezuela, should be aware of the current instability within the government, which has led to heightened political tension and unrest. The situation remains unpredictable, with frequent protests and a significant military presence in the capital. Visitors are advised to exercise extreme caution, stay informed about local developments, and avoid large gatherings. The U.S. State Department has issued a travel advisory, recommending that non-essential travel be postponed. Travelers should ensure they have a reliable means of communication and stay in touch with their country's embassy for the latest updates and safety guidelines.

Evan Wheeler

Caracas, Venezuela

Evan eased the 757 onto the runway, the low growl of the landing gear resonating through the cabin as the aircraft rumbled over the tarmac. His hands gripped the yoke a little too tightly, his fingers tense. Usually, the rhythmic hum of the engines brought him a sense of calm, but today it barely cut through the static of his thoughts. The faint bitterness of stale coffee lingered on his tongue, a reminder that he hadn't eaten anything since that dry muffin hours ago.

The past six weeks had blurred into one long nightmare, every day laced with the cold sterility of hospitals and the antiseptic tang of death. Danni's passing had shattered them, but it was Jennifer's worsening health—and Abby's quiet suffering—that haunted him now. His chest tightened as he thought of Abby's pale face, the way her hands had trembled when she'd pushed him out the door, insisting he take this flight. "You need a break, Ev. Just twenty-four hours." He could still hear her voice, soft but insistent, even as guilt clawed at him.

As soon as the post-flight checklist was complete, Evan bolted from the cockpit, barely registering the low hum of the airport. His phone was already in his hand, dialing home.

"Hi, Honey! We just got here. I'll try your cell," he said, his voice sounding hollow in the echo of the voicemail.

No answer.

A cold prickle ran down his spine as he dialed again—Abby's cell, then Jennifer's. The sound of the call connecting seemed too loud against the buzz of the terminal, but still, no one picked up. Abby had mentioned errands, maybe picking Jennifer up from school, but they should've answered by now.

Evan's pace quickened, his shoes squeaking against the polished floor. Each unanswered ring pressed tighter against his chest, the weight of dread sinking into his stomach like a stone. The fluorescent lights cast a harsh glare across the white tiles, and the scent of disinfectant filled his nose, sharp and unforgiving.

"Still no answer?" the first officer asked, noticing Evan's tight grip on his phone.

Evan shook his head, barely able to form words. "Something's wrong," he muttered, his thumb pressing redial almost reflexively, the screen's glow burning into his eyes.

The first officer exchanged glances with the flight attendants, whispering softly. Evan didn't care. He could feel the panic building, his mind leaping from one worst-case scenario to another. Where were they? Why weren't they answering?

By the time he reached the hotel, he was practically sprinting through the lobby, the rich scent of leather and polished wood barely registering. He dialed his in-laws next, his fingers slick with sweat, knowing that if they weren't answering either, there was only one place they could be: the hospital.

He called the hospital directly, barely keeping his voice steady. "My name is Evan Wheeler. I'm trying to reach my wife, Abby, and my daughter, Jennifer. They're both sick, and I need to know if they're there."

"I'm sorry, Sir, but we can't give out patient information over the phone," the operator said, her voice muffled through the line's static.

Desperation surged through him. "Please, I'm a pilot calling from Caracas. I just need to know if they're there. Can you help me?"

"Sir, it's against policy. I'm sorry."

"Can I speak to a supervisor?" His voice cracked, frustration spilling over. His palms were damp, his grip slipping on the phone.

"Please hold."

Evan paced the hotel room, his undershirt clinging to his chest, damp and cold against his skin. He could barely breathe. Finally, a voice crackled through the line.

"This is Regina, the supervisor. How can I help you?"

"My wife and daughter—can you page Mrs. Abby Wheeler?" His words tumbled out, frantic, every syllable scraping against the dryness in his throat.

Silence. Then more waiting. His fingers curled into fists, nails digging into his palms.

"I'm sorry, sir, no one answered," Regina said, her voice impassive.

His legs nearly gave out as he sagged against the bed. "Can you page Mr. and Mrs. Douglas, please?" he asked, his voice barely a whisper.

The line went quiet, and then a familiar voice, soft and trembling, broke through.

"Evan?"

He froze. It was his mother-in-law's voice.

"We didn't know how to reach you, Evan," she said, her voice heavy with grief. "Abby's in liver failure. Jennifer found her passed out in the kitchen."

The room spun, his vision blurring. His mother-in-law's words sliced through him, every syllable a fresh wound.

"You need to come home, Evan," she continued, her voice breaking. "We're at the hospital. Jennifer's with us."

"I'm coming," he choked out. "I'll be home in a few hours."

Evan dialed Crew Schedule; his voice tight with barely contained panic. "This is Captain Wheeler. My wife is in the hospital. I need to get home immediately."

CHAPTER 5

THE NJ STAR

LOCAL JERSEY STATION HIRES "STORIED" TV NEWS CORRESPONDENT

In a surprising career move, a former national correspondent, who left his previous role amid controversy, has taken a new position at a local television station in New Jersey. The journalist, known for his hard-hitting reports and a career marked by high-profile stories, will now bring his experience to the Garden State's news scene. The local station hopes his expertise will enhance their coverage, despite his tarnished reputation. Viewers are eager to see how he adapts to the new role and whether he can rebuild his career on a local platform

Levi Matthews

Edison, New Jersey

Levi sat in the small dressing room, staring at his reflection in the mirror lined with dim, flickering bulbs. His leg bounced with nervous energy. The last time he'd been in a chair like this, he was in a private green room, waiting for his segment on NCC. The memory felt surreal, like it belonged to someone else—a person who hadn't yet fallen so far.

He barely recognized the face staring back at him—lines deeper, eyes hollower. He checked his watch, waiting for the makeup artist, though he knew by now she probably wasn't coming. The smell of cheap hairspray filled the room as he quickly spruced up his hair himself, trying to maintain some shred of professionalism.

A knock at the door made him jump. "You ready?" the NJ12 producer asked, stepping inside. Levi had already forgotten his name—Peter? Maybe Pete? It hardly mattered.

"Is someone going to do my makeup?" Levi asked, clinging to a sliver of hope. He was too old to go bare faced, especially under the harsh studio lights.

"What do you think this is, NCC?" The producer chuckled. "If you want makeup, you have to do it yourself. Let's go."

Levi blinked, momentarily speechless. The past year had been one humiliation after another, but this felt like the final blow. Wow, he thought, a faint sting of resentment building. A bitter taste rose in the back of his throat—familiar and unwelcome. He had once drowned that taste with whiskey, and his mind betrayed him with the memory of its warmth, its ability to dull moments just like this. Shaking his head, he forced himself to focus. He couldn't go down that road again. Not now. Not ever.

Nevertheless, he scrambled to keep up with the producer, who moved with the speed of a man on a mission. Out of breath, Levi was introduced to the staff in rapid-fire succession, their names blurring together as he struggled to keep up. The fluorescent-lit hallways cast a sickly green tone over everything, and he caught a faint whiff of chlorine as they passed the janitor's closet.

The producer pushed open the studio door, and Levi nearly collided with a man in a baseball hat and T-shirt.

"Levi, this is Scott, our cameraman," the producer said casually.

Scott grinned, extending a hand. "Do you remember me? We worked together at WPFJ in Trenton. Your meltdown was epic, dude."

Levi's cheeks flushed, a forced smile stretching across his face. "Your dad still running the station?"

The producer interrupted before Scott could respond. "You're on in five minutes. Let's go."

Levi hurried after him, trying to regain some composure. "I need a week or two off in August. I'm getting married."

The producer barely paused. "You might not need to take off. This week is a test. Next week, we'll have your numbers and can put you on the permanent schedule," he said, clipping a microphone onto Levi's expensive silk tie.

"A test?" Levi asked, his heart sinking. "I thought I had the job."

The producer gave him a pointed look. "Everybody has to test. Plus, we'll have the results of your drug test by then."

The word "drug" hit him hard, sending a faint, familiar tremor through his body. Levi swallowed, forcing himself to remain calm. "I don't drink anymore," he said, his voice tight with frustration and pride. Stephanie had helped him through the hardest days, reminding him that he could rebuild his life. *Just don't mess this up.*

But as he took his seat at the desk—a flimsy folding table with 1970s wood paneling stapled to hide his legs—he could feel that old itch in his veins, whispering to him. Back in his NCC days, this would've been a moment to "take the edge off." He'd come to rely on that ritual, letting the burn of a drink smooth over any frustration or shame. But tonight, he only had himself and the camera in front of him. He clenched his fists under the table, grounding himself with the sensation of his nails pressing into his palms. His legged bounced uncontrollably. This isn't who you are anymore, he reminded himself.

The producer smirked. "Right. If you do that and stay sober, you'll have a great career at NJ12. Just read it exactly as you see it. Guess how the last guy got fired?"

"He didn't read the teleprompter verbatim," Levi said, mimicking the producer's cadence, a faint smile breaking through his nerves.

The producer clapped him on the shoulder. "Exactly. So, if you keep it together, we're golden. We're on in ten . . . nine . . .can you stop that with your leg…" He continued the count down, waving his arm dramatically. At three, he pointed directly at Levi.

The newsman in Levi instinctively sat up straighter, his voice settling into the practiced cadence he'd spent years honing. "Good evening, I'm Levi Mathews, and I'll be your NJ12 guest midnight anchor for this week. Our top story tonight . . ."

As he read, he felt a familiar rhythm settle in, a comfort he hadn't felt in months. The studio's harsh lights faded into the background, replaced by the steady scroll of the teleprompter. For those few minutes, it felt like he was back where he belonged, back in control. The desk may have been a cheap folding table, and the set a far cry from NCC, but for a moment, it didn't matter.

Yet, even as he delivered each line with poise, he could feel the faint urge lurking in the back of his mind, a reminder of how close he'd come to slipping back. The teleprompter rolled on, and he forced his focus back to the script, grounding himself in the rhythm of the words, refusing to let his past dictate his present.

When the broadcast ended, the producer gave him a nod. "Not bad, Mathews. We'll see how the week goes."

Levi managed a smile, though inside, he felt hollow. This job was a shadow of what he'd once had, a bitter pill he'd have to swallow every night. As he left the studio, he allowed himself a moment of reflection, thinking of Stephanie. She had stood by him, even when he'd been at his lowest, even when he hadn't deserved it. Her faith was the one thing that kept him moving forward, the spark that kept him fighting.

For her, he thought, glancing back at the cheap, worn set behind him. I can do this for her.

As he exited the building, the cold night air stung his cheeks, grounding him. He took a deep breath, letting the chill sharpen his focus. It wasn't the life he'd imagined, but it was a second chance. And for now, that was enough.

CHAPTER 6

Evan scratched his head, feeling his unwashed hair clinging in matted clumps. Days had passed since his last shower, and his lower back throbbed from the endless hours spent slumped in the waiting room chairs. He stretched, wincing at the pain, and glanced around the empty ICU waiting room. Abby's condition weighed heavily on his mind. If she showed any improvement, maybe he'd go home for a quick shower.

With a sigh, Evan typed "liver regeneration" into his laptop's search engine. The hospital Wi-Fi was painfully slow. "Come on," he muttered, watching the loading bar crawl across the screen.

This sterile space had become both a comfort and a prison. The waiting room, now like a second home, offered little distraction. The usual crowd of grieving families was absent; no one was there to offer words of encouragement or solidarity. Just him, his laptop, and the silent weight of waiting.

Finally, the doctor swept into the room, her lab coat billowing behind her.

"How is she?" Evan asked, standing up quickly.

"Please, sit down, Mr. Wheeler," she said, settling beside him. Evan placed his laptop on the empty chair next to him, giving her his full attention.

"She hasn't improved as far as her liver damage is concerned," the doctor said, her tone grave.

Evan exhaled, shaking his head. "I see."

"Blood tests indicate her kidneys are beginning to show the effects of the feeding tube. The good news is that her internal seizures have reduced to three or fewer a day, so the drug cocktail is working. If we can stop the seizures completely, she'll have a better chance of recovery after the transplant."

"Transplant?" Evan's voice cracked. "I mean I knew this was coming but I thought the feeding tube and medicine would be enough to hold it off. You know allowing her liver regenerate? I thought Danni died because we didn't get her the drugs fast enough."

The doctor's expression softened. "It helps, but it can't replace real food. Abby's body is breaking down, though she's better off than Danni was. The meds are buying time, but . . ."

Evan rubbed his eyes with his palms. "Why is this happening so fast? Even Jennifer's disease is progressing way faster than Danni's did."

"It's mutated," the doctor explained, her voice calm yet clinical. "Diseases mutate to survive. We'll need an MRI to see how much damage has been done."

Evan nodded numbly. "Can I see her before the test?"

"Yes, but just for a few minutes. Go on in," the doctor said, rising and leading him to the nursing station.

He entered Abby's critical care room, greeted by the familiar sounds of beeping machines and the steady rhythm of the respirator. A nurse stood beside her, adjusting the monitors.

"Hi, Evan. Abby, Evan's here," the nurse said cheerfully, though Abby remained unresponsive.

"Remember, she can hear you, so be positive," the nurse added with a gentle smile.

She can't hear me. Evan took Abby's ice-cold hand and brought it to his lips. She was literally disappearing before his eyes. He traced his thumb along her yellowed knuckles, trying to push away the memory of Danni looking this way just before the end.

He touched her face, his fingers trembling. He was losing her. Despite everything he'd done to keep her alive, the cure felt more elusive than ever. He rested his head on her hand and let his tears flow silently, raw with grief and helplessness.

"Evan." The nurse had returned. He sat up quickly, wiping his cheeks. "They're ready to take her. I'll let you know when she's back."

He kissed Abby's forehead before returning to the family waiting area. To his surprise, it was no longer empty. A tall man in an expensive suit stood in the middle of the room, talking on his phone.

The man turned, noticing Evan. "I'll call you back in about fifteen minutes," he said, ending the call and slipping his phone into his jacket pocket. He extended his hand. "Hi, Evan, I'm Robert Alexander. Please call me Robert."

Evan blinked, trying to place the familiar face.

"I'm the chief executive officer of the WWA," Robert explained.

My boss. Evan straightened, acutely aware of how disheveled he looked.

"We met a few months back at the donor event," Robert continued. "I'm sorry for your loss."

Evan swallowed, the memory stirring a hollow ache in his chest. "Thank you."

"I sit on the board at this hospital. Someone told me your wife was here, so I thought I'd stop by to see how things were going."

Evan averted his gaze, the tears still fresh in his eyes. He nodded. "Thank you."

"Is your wife waiting for an organ as well?"

"We're not sure yet, but it looks like she will need a liver," Evan replied, staring at the floor. The conversation felt invasive, like a stranger rifling through your medicine cabinet.

"My wife was here some years ago for a similar situation," Robert said. "Her kidneys and pancreas were failing from diabetes."

Evan tilted his head. "I'm sorry to hear that."

"The doctors here were great, but . . . they saved her in Venezuela."

Evan frowned. "Venezuela? What happened there?"

Robert hesitated, a small smile playing at his lips. "It's . . . complicated. But they did what needed to be done."

Evan's heart quickened. "How did they save her?"

"That's a long story, one I think you'd find very interesting. How about you come to my house tomorrow for lunch? I don't live far. I can send a car."

Wait. What? Evan hesitated, the invitation strange and unexpected. "I really can't leave the hospital for that long."

"You look like you could use a break, and the information I have could save your wife," Robert said.

Save? The word echoed in Evan's mind, filled with unspoken promise. "What information?" he asked, leaning forward. "Can't you tell me now?"

"I'd rather not get into it here. I'll tell you over lunch tomorrow, in private. The car will pick you up. Noon?" Robert extended his hand for a confirmation shake.

Evan looked at the outstretched hand, torn. Every instinct told him to be wary, but desperation clawed at him. "Okay. Sure," he agreed, shaking Robert's hand.

Robert nodded and strode out of the waiting room.

What just happened? Evan slumped into a chair, the weight of Robert's words pressing on him as he drifted into an uneasy sleep.

CHAPTER 7

SCIENCE TODAY

REVOLUTIONARY ADVANCEMENT: SUCCESSFUL HUMAN ORGAN CLONING MARKS A NEW ERA IN MEDICINE

By Randy Parr

In a groundbreaking achievement, scientists have successfully cloned fully functional human organs, heralding a potential revolution in the future of medical transplants. This milestone offers new hope to patients awaiting transplants, with the promise of significantly reducing the waiting time for donor organs. Conducted by a leading team of biologists and geneticists, this research aims to address the critical shortage of transplantable organs, potentially improving survival rates for countless individuals. While ethical and regulatory challenges remain, this advancement represents a significant leap forward in regenerative medicine, with the potential to save countless lives in the years to come.

Dr. José Santiago

Santiago Hospital de Clínicas, Caracas, Venezuela

Dr. José Santiago paced in front of the only bench in the sterile hallway of Hospital de Clínicas, Caracas's public hospital. His fists clenched and unclenched, the familiar weight of his ambitions pressing down on him. Three years of fighting Dr. Jorge Perez—three years of watching his vision stifled by a man too focused on outdated morals. "The Frankenstein of Caracas"—a nickname Perez had helped spread, but José had long stopped caring. Perez couldn't see the big picture; he would have to explain it once again.

Santiago glanced at Raoul Ortiz, the five-star general of the Venezuelan armed forces, and Tito Sanchez, the Venezuelan Secretary of State, sitting behind him. Their presence wasn't just symbolic; they were here to show Perez that this was no longer about hospital politics. The president had seen what others refused to—what Venezuela could become the saviors of the world. Where people could come to Venezuela to live longer, healthier lives by replacing failing organs, one by one. A future where doubling the human lifespan wasn't a dream but a reality.

When Perez emerged from the critical care ward, irritation flickered in José's chest. This man—this relic—had stalled progress for far too long.

Perez sneered, "So now you need the military to push your agenda? Even for the Butcher of Caracas, that's a new low."

José's smile was cold, his tone measured. "You still don't understand, do you? This isn't about control. It's about something far bigger. Something you can't see."

Perez crossed his arms, his expression hard. "Progress? You want to turn hospitals into organ stores in strip malls, where people come in to swap their organs like car parts. Face it, José. You're low on bodies, and you'll say whatever you need to get them."

José stepped closer, his voice dropping. "It's about time, Perez. Time people wouldn't have to lose. Imagine it. People living twice as long because we replace what fails. But every time you slow me down, more people die waiting for something I can already give them." His gaze flickered with a quiet intensity. "And when they start living longer—healthier—you'll just be a footnote. A man who stood in the way."

Perez's disgust was palpable. "You're no visionary. You're just a murderer who thinks he's playing God."

José's jaw tightened, but he kept his voice level. "You think this is a choice I enjoy? It isn't. But I'm willing to make it because it's necessary. This isn't about ego. It's about changing what medicine can do. About giving people, a future—more of it."

He turned sharply, motioning toward the critical care ward. "I'll do the rounds. If the patients meet my criteria, my ambulance is downstairs. You can't stop what's already in motion."

Perez followed, his voice rising with anger. "This isn't progress, Santiago. This is madness."

José didn't respond, his eyes already scanning the chart of the first patient. "Too old." He tossed it back without a second glance. He moved on to the second bed, studying the chart. Severe head trauma. "Two weeks in a coma. A perfect candidate." The inside source hadn't disappointed.

"He's not going to make it," José said calmly. "His body's still alive, but his mind is gone."

Perez's fists clenched. "He has brainwaves. He could recover."

José glanced at Perez, his gaze steady. "Recover into what? A body that can't survive on its own? A life tethered to machines, draining his family for years? You want that for him? For them?" He shook his head slowly. "We have the chance to do something better. To give people more than just survival. To give them time."

Perez glared at him. "You're building your future on the backs of the dead."

José's voice was calm, almost tired. "I'm building a future where people don't have to fear their bodies breaking down. Where we replace what's broken so they can keep living. But you—you'd rather keep clinging to something that's already gone." His eyes narrowed. "I won't waste time convincing you."

He turned to leave, his voice colder. "Tell the boy's family to come to my clinic this afternoon. They'll understand."

Perez's voice, thick with revulsion, echoed down the hall. "You're a monster, Santiago."

José didn't pause. "I'm a visionary. And one day, they'll thank me."

Later that afternoon, José stood in his private clinic, watching through the glass as the young man's parents sat slumped in the waiting room. Their clothes were worn, their faces lined with exhaustion and grief. He'd seen it before—families clinging to a sliver of hope, too desperate to see the truth.

They didn't need the truth, though. What they needed was belief. And José was ready to give it to them.

The video he would play for them was a trick made to look like a real scenario of a young man coming out of a coma alluding that his brain had been restored. The film offering the reassurance they were desperate for. It would convince them their son wasn't beyond saving—that with the right treatment, his treatment, there might still be a chance. They wouldn't understand the reality, but they didn't need to. They just needed to sign the release.

Once they did, it would all be over quickly. A clean dose of fentanyl, and their son's organs would go on to help others. They would believe they'd saved him. In reality, they were making the only choice that mattered.

José opened the door to his office, his expression calm, professional. "Please, come in. I know this is difficult, but I'm here to help. There are still options we can explore."

The parents entered slowly, their faces etched with hope and desperation, searching for anything to hold on to. And José knew exactly how to give it to them.

As he closed the door quietly behind them, his mind was already moving forward. The paperwork would be signed. They would leave, convinced they had done everything possible.

CHAPTER 8

**Day One, Done Right: How to Nail Your First Impression
at a New Job**

By Emily Parker

*Starting a new job can feel like walking a tightrope—you're
excited to shine but nervous about every little detail. The good
news? Making a stellar first impression isn't as hard as it seems.*

*With these expert-backed tips, you'll be ready to walk into your
new workplace with confidence and leave a lasting mark on
your first day.*

Dana Billings

WWA Headquarters, New York, New York

The receptionist, a model of runway-style elegance, guided Dana through the
bustling, modern office. Every passing colleague seemed to fit the same sleek
mold—sharp, polished, efficient. The quiet click of the receptionist's heels
echoed on the glossy floor, contrasting with Dana's hesitant steps. A faint,
clean scent lingered in the air, maybe eucalyptus or lavender, mixed with the
sterile undertones of polished glass and steel, amplifying the office's precise,
clinical feel. She suddenly felt hyperaware of the weight of this opportunity.

The two reached a door marked "Olivia Jennings." The receptionist knocked softly, her knuckles making a controlled, polite sound against the frosted glass. "Olivia, Dana's here."

The door opened, and Dana took in Olivia Jennings—blonde hair swept back, her expression warm but commanding. Though clearly in her final weeks of pregnancy, Olivia moved with an energy that offset her physical exhaustion, the faint scent of vanilla wafting from her as she waved Dana in.

"Come in, Dana. I'm Olivia. Welcome to WWA."

Dana took a seat, adjusting as the leather creaked faintly beneath her. A chill from the air conditioning prickled her arms, and she clasped her hands tightly in her lap, willing herself to look confident. "Thank you, Ms. Jennings. I'm really excited to be here."

"Please, call me Olivia. And how was your commute this morning?"

"Smooth enough," Dana replied, easing a bit. "I live with my parents in Queens, so the train's usually quick when it's on time," she added with a light laugh, willing her nerves to settle.

"Good habit," Olivia nodded approvingly, flipping open a file with a crisp snap. "So, your dad works as a mechanic at JFK, right?"

"Yes, ma'am," Dana replied, a hint of pride coloring her voice. "He helped me get this job."

Olivia's gaze softened. "Well, he got you the interview, but you got the job. Graduating summa cum laude from Howard University a semester early—that's not something just anyone does."

Dana felt her shoulders relax slightly, pride filling her chest. "First in my family to go to college."

"That's fantastic. Your parents must be proud."

"They are." She smiled, her hands unclasping as her nerves began to settle. But the momentary comfort reminded her why she was here. She'd worked too hard to let herself get derailed by a case of first-day nerves. She took a breath, catching the faint, comforting smell of coffee as it mingled with the sharp tang of the office's disinfectant.

"All right," Olivia said, her tone shifting into business mode. "Let's get you settled."

Dana straightened in her chair, feeling the cold, smooth surface of the desk as she prepared herself. Her hands felt like ice, but she focused on Olivia's words.

"Your main responsibility will be analyzing passenger lists and trends to catch things our automated systems miss. You'll be working closely with the revenue team. Only you, me, and my boss have access to this data—it's sensitive." Olivia's voice grew serious, her gaze intent. "Are you familiar with MATLAB?"

Dana's heart skipped a beat. MATLAB? She hadn't worked with that software before. In college, she'd learned SAS VIYA, and she hadn't expected this curveball on day one. But she couldn't let the panic show.

"I thought you used SAS VIYA?" Dana asked, keeping her voice steady, despite the knot forming in her stomach.

"We did, until last month," Olivia said, noticing Dana's hesitation and offering a reassuring smile. "Don't worry. We're all adjusting to the new system. There are plenty of tutorials, and Jared in revenue loves this stuff. He'll show you a few shortcuts."

Relief washed over Dana, though she kept her expression neutral. "I'm a fast learner. I'll go through the tutorials tonight."

Olivia chuckled as she rose to her feet, the polished leather of her chair creaking slightly. "Relax, you've got time. Follow me—I'll show you your workspace."

Dana followed her down the hall, her nerves ebbing slightly with each step. This was it—her first real job, her foot in the door at one of the top airlines. She could practically feel the weight of her family's expectations on her shoulders. She was determined not to let them down.

"Here we are," Olivia said, gesturing to a modest office stall with partial glass walls. "It's all yours."

Dana took in the small desk, her first personal office space, the hum of her computer quietly filling the background as she powered it up. She felt a strange mix of pride and responsibility. This was her chance, her own little corner in one of the biggest airlines in the country.

"In the top drawer, you'll find your employee credentials and temporary network passcode. Change it once you log in," Olivia said as Dana powered up the computer. The screen filled with icons, and for a moment, she felt overwhelmed.

Olivia pointed to a few icons on the screen. "You'll only need these to get started, plus this one for tutorials. And this green S icon," she added, pointing to another, "is for any aircraft incidents involving fatalities. I'm part of the senior Care Team, and you'll step in for me while I'm on leave, but don't worry—it's rare. I'll get you signed up for full training when I'm back."

The word "fatalities" sent a chill through Dana, and she tried to keep her face composed, even as her nerves flared. "That sounds . . . intense."

Olivia smiled warmly. "It's not as scary as it sounds. We're ranked one of the safest airlines, and as your dad probably told you, our maintenance program is top-notch. You'll be ready by the time I go on leave."

Dana felt herself relax a bit more. She had two weeks to settle in, to familiarize herself with the data systems. "Congratulations, by the way," she said, nodding toward Olivia's belly. "Do you know if it's a boy or girl?"

Olivia's face softened. "It's a girl—our third. My husband's outnumbered by women, even the pets."

Dana laughed, feeling her nerves ease. "Have you picked a name yet?"

"Franky," Olivia said with a grin. "He wanted something masculine to balance it out. I think it's cute."

"I love it," Dana replied, feeling a genuine smile spread across her face. The conversation felt easy now, her earlier nervousness fading into the background. She could see herself here, fitting in, making a difference. This job was her chance to prove herself—not just to her new coworkers but to her parents and, maybe most importantly, to herself.

As Olivia left, Dana looked back at the green S icon on her computer screen. It felt strange that her new role, seemingly centered around numbers and data, could touch something as serious as loss. She made a mental note to look into it later, not wanting to get too caught off guard by anything she might have to handle on her own.

Her fingers hovered over the keyboard, and she took a steadying breath, feeling a renewed sense of purpose. The faint hum of the office around her—the phones ringing, colleagues tapping away at their keyboards, muffled conversations drifting in from beyond the glass—felt like the background music to a new chapter. She was here, ready, and determined to make this work.

CHAPTER 9

THE CONTINENTAL

EXCLUSIVE: A Dark Market for Organs?

In a world where medical advancements promise hope, a chilling reality lurks beneath the surface—an underground industry where life-saving organs are bought and sold at astronomical prices. Sources within international medical communities' whisper of a Venezuelan doctor, hailed as a "miracle worker," who has reportedly developed a method to clone human organs with zero risk of rejection. But there's a catch.

With prices soaring into the millions, these procedures are accessible only to the ultra-wealthy. And when demand outstrips supply, what happens next? Disturbing allegations suggest that certain high-profile figures have found alternative methods— methods that require tragedy to strike in just the right way.

Could "unforeseeable accidents" be more than coincidence? Some whistleblowers believe so. Investigators are now questioning whether medical ethics can stand against the weight of unchecked power and unimaginable desperation.

How far would someone go to save the ones they love? And more importantly—how far have they already gone?

—The Atlantic Investigations Team

Evan Wheeler
Somerville, NJ

Evan sat in the ICU room, holding his wife's frail hand. The oxygen machine's rhythmic whoosh was like a lullaby, dragging him into the edges of sleep. He rested his forehead against their entwined fingers, exhaustion weighing on him. *Just a few minutes.* That's all he needed.

A gentle shake pulled him back. "Evan?"

He blinked, disoriented, until the nurse's face sharpened in front of him. "Someone from downstairs called. Your ride is here."

His stomach twisted. He kissed Abby's cool cheek, guilt clawing at him. "I love you," he whispered. "I'll be back soon."

Walking toward the nursing station, his chest tightened. A nurse looked up and gave him a small, practiced smile. "We'll call you if there are any changes."

Evan nodded and forced himself forward.

Through the sliding glass doors of the hospital lobby, he spotted a black sedan idling at the curb. A heavyset older man leaned against the side, watching him approach. "Evan Wheeler?"

Evan nodded. The man opened the back door, and Evan slid in without another word.

The drive was thankfully quiet, the silence broken by the occasional turn signal. Evan's hands typed words in the search engine without any help from his brain. His fingers twitched against his thigh, a nervous habit he couldn't seem to shake.

Too soon, the sedan pulled under a covered entrance in front of a stately late-eighteenth-century mansion. Before the driver could open the door, Evan had already stepped out.

"Sorry," he muttered, feeling his cheeks warm.

"Happens all the time," the driver replied, giving him a knowing look.

The front door swung open before he reached it. Robert Alexander stood in the doorway, smiling. "Evan," he said, extending his hand. "Come in."

The air inside was crisp and scented with something rich—polished wood, maybe leather. The sheer scale of the house made Evan pause. A massive crystal chandelier hung from a cathedral ceiling, sending shards of light across the polished marble floors. A grand stairway curled toward the second floor like something out of a movie.

"So glad you could make it," Robert said, leading the way. "We're having lunch on the patio. My great-great-grandfather built this house in 1875. We updated it last year."

Evan followed through a series of impeccably furnished rooms, past a sleek, modern kitchen, and out onto a sprawling stone patio. The New Jersey valley stretched endlessly below.

"We added the infinity pool last year," Robert said, gesturing before leading Evan to a vine-covered pergola. A stone fireplace stood at one end; its hearth flanked by two sofas.

"Sit," Robert urged, settling onto the opposite sofa and stretching an arm along the backrest.

Evan perched forward, his elbows on his knees. He didn't want small talk. He needed answers.

"Mr. Alexander, you have a beautiful home," he offered, just to push things along.

"Please, call me Robert," he said smoothly. The maid arrived with two glasses of iced tea. "Before we get started, would you mind giving Masha your phone?"

Evan tensed. His fingers instinctively curled around the device in his pocket. "My phone?"

Robert smiled, reassuring. "What I'm about to tell you is very controversial. Masha will let you know if the hospital calls."

Evan hesitated before slowly pulling his phone from his pocket. His hands trembled as he handed it over. His throat was dry.

"Now, tell me about your wife and little girl," Robert said. "What is their diagnosis?"

Evan exhaled, his shoulders stiff. "They have intestinal dysmotility. Their intestines seize every few minutes, cutting off blood, oxygen, and nutrients. The medications have slowed the process, but some of the damage is irreversible." He swallowed hard. "My wife, Abby—her liver is shutting down. My daughter, Danni… we caught it too late. She needed a five-organ transplant. There was nothing we could do."

Robert's expression was unreadable. "I'm truly sorry for your loss. And your younger daughter?"

"She's diabetic now. She has grand mal seizures from low blood sugar. Eventually, she might need a pancreas." Evan rubbed at his temples, feeling a dull headache forming.

Robert took a measured sip of his tea. "I may have a solution."

Evan's breath hitched. His stomach twisted. "What solution?"

"My wife, Alexis—we call her Button—she almost died." Robert leaned forward. "She was adopted from a remote Romanian village as a baby. Right away, her parents knew something was wrong. Juvenile diabetes. She nearly didn't make it."

Evan nodded, but his chest felt tight. Where was this going?

"They spared no expense—took her to every specialist, tried every treatment. But when I met her, she had just graduated from Princeton. The disease had ravaged her body. By the time we married, both of her kidneys were failing." He sighed. "I was shattered. I couldn't lose her."

A maid appeared. "Mr. Alexander, lunch is ready."

Robert stood. "Come, Evan. Let's eat."

They walked through an ivy-covered stone archway into a garden where a bistro table was set for two. The maid placed shrimp salad in front of Evan, then offered wine.

"No, thank you," he said quickly. His focus was on Robert, his fingers gripping the edge of the table.

Robert continued, "Button needed a kidney and a pancreas, but her rare blood type made a transplant nearly impossible."

Evan's pulse quickened. His hands curled into fists on his lap. "So, what happened?"

Robert smirked. "I met a man at a fundraiser. He introduced me to a doctor in Venezuela. A genius. His name is Dr. José Santiago." He took another sip of wine. "He changed everything."

Evan leaned in; his stomach coiled tight. "What do you mean?"

"Santiago developed a way to clone human organs," Robert said, pausing for effect. "Organs that aren't blood-type specific. No chance of rejection."

Evan's heart pounded. He felt his hands go clammy. "That's… not possible."

"Oh, it's very possible," Robert said. "Button had her transplants. Seventeen years later, she's thriving."

Evan barely heard him. His ears buzzed. "How do I get these organs?"

Robert's smile turned sharp. "One pays a lot of money. A kidney? A million dollars. A pancreas? Two million."

Evan's stomach churned. His breathing quickened. "Does he allow payments?"

"No," Robert said simply. "It's all cash."

Evan's nails dug into his palms. "Then why am I here?"

Robert leaned in. "Because there's another way."

Evan stilled. His mouth went dry. "What are you saying?"

"All the doctor needs are a large group of people, say, a hundred and eighty, from an unforeseeable accident."

Evan frowned, his fingers going numb. "I don't—what do you mean, a supply?"

"A decompression," Robert said coolly. "All you would have to do is turn off the oxygen."

"Murder?" Evan's voice broke. "You want me to commit mass murder?"

Robert leaned back in his chair. "It would be a painless death."

Evan reeled back, shaking his head his jaw ajar. "You're serious? You're actually serious?"

Robert swirled his wine glass, unconcerned. "Think about it, Evan." "You're insane," Evan proclaimed, "I'm not killing a plane full of people - I need my phone."

Meesha came running out of the house with Evan's phone. Evan stared at Robert for a moment, mouth agape from what he just heard. "The answer is no," Evan said.

Evan turned, walking away fast, his mind spinning. Then, for one terrible moment, he stopped. And for one terrible moment, he had almost listened.

CHAPTER 10

Psychology Monthly Online

Potentially Dangerous Behaviors Resulting from Caregiver Overload

By PM Online Staff

Providing care for a loved one can feel like a natural responsibility—but also overwhelming and potentially dangerous: at times leading to extreme behavior stemming from desperation and panic. Caregiver exhaustion is a state of emotional, physical, and mental exhaustion, often marked by fatigue, irritability, anxiety, and withdrawal. It comes from prolonged stress, lack of support, and trying to do too much without self-care. Over time, it can harm both the caregiver and the person receiving care. Experts strongly recommend family caregivers to recognize warning signs, take time for self-care, and seek help—whether through relaxing activities, support groups, or mental health professionals. Caring for yourself isn't selfish—it's a must for sustaining care long-term.

Evan Wheeler

Martinsville, New Jersey

A loud thump jolted Evan awake, sending him leaping out of bed. His heart hammered as he dashed to Jennifer's room, throwing open the door and flicking on the light. She lay sprawled on the floor, her small body convulsing, foam gathering at the corners of her mouth. He dropped to his knees beside her, hands shaking. "Jen? Jen!"

The seizure finally eased, her body going limp. Evan leaned close, straining to hear her shallow breaths, his mind racing. "Come on, come back to me." Her tiny chest rose in a weak, fragile rhythm, and he pressed his fingers to her wrist, relief flooding over him as he found a faint pulse.

The clock read 3:00 a.m. In this quiet New Jersey town, emergency services took precious minutes. Evan knew he couldn't wait. He wrapped Jennifer in a blanket and lifted her, nearly stumbling under her slight weight as he rushed down the stairs.

In the car, he laid her in the backseat, turning to check her lips—no blue tint yet. He punched his mother-in-law's number, letting it ring twice before hanging up—their signal. His grip tightened on the steering wheel as he sped down the winding road, the shadowed trees blurring past. A soft moan came from the backseat, and relief surged through him. "Hold on, honey. We're almost there."

But memories of Danni surfaced, clouding his mind with fear. The night he and Abby had raced her to the hospital, the same terror filling him now.

He pulled up to the emergency room entrance, tires screeching as he threw the car into park. He ran to the backseat, lifting Jennifer in his arms. "You're going to be okay, baby," he murmured, but the words tasted hollow.

Inside, he called out, his voice echoing through the empty reception area. "Hello?!"

No one came. He gently laid Jennifer on the floor, pounding on the locked doors leading to the emergency bay. "Help! Somebody!"

Desperate he pulled the fire alarm.

A security guard, fire extinguisher in hand, rushed around the corner, a mix of confusion and concern in his eyes. Evan had used this tactic once before in an emergency with Danni, knowing the chaos would bring help.

"Evan?" Dr. Miller, familiar with Evan from past visits, appeared, shaking his head. "You scared the hell out of us."

"I couldn't get anyone to respond," Evan panted, casting an anxious look at Jennifer. "She had a seizure. She was foaming at the mouth."

"Come on, we'll take care of her," Dr. Miller said, guiding Evan to the waiting area. "You know the drill. Let us do our job."

Evan followed mechanically, the sterile smell of the hospital filling his senses, familiar and sickeningly comforting. The nurse's office was cluttered with old furniture, a strange contrast to the high-tech monitors around them. The nurse sighed, beginning to type. "Everything the same as last time? Address, insurance?"

He nodded absently, his mind far from the routine details.

"Your wife's still in ICU?"

He forced out a "yes," his voice breaking. "Can I check on Jennifer?"

She gave him a knowing look. "You know you can't until they're done with her. If they haven't called for you, she's stable. Sit tight."

Minutes later, Dr. Miller reappeared, motioning for Evan to follow. "She's stable—no brain damage as far as I can tell. But her pancreas is shutting down. Her kidneys may be next."

The words hit him like a punch. He felt his legs weaken. "Why is this happening faster than it did with Danni? Wasn't the medication supposed to help?"

Dr. Miller's face was grim. "It could be a mutation of the disease. The right balance of meds might buy us some time, but a pancreatic transplant is looking necessary soon."

The word "transplant" stung, as if bringing back all the helplessness he'd felt with Danni. His little girl was lying in that hospital bed, and now his wife was fighting the same battle.

Inside Jennifer's room, her eyelids fluttered weakly. He leaned down, brushing a kiss on her forehead. "I love you, my potato," he whispered, a name she'd loved since she was a toddler. His heart ached as he let them take her away to be stabilized in ICU, beside Abby.

When he returned to the waiting area, he saw his mother-in-law Margret's tear-streaked face. "What happened?" she asked, her voice trembling.

"She had another seizure. Dr. Miller thinks she may need a pancreas soon," he said, pulling her into a tight hug.

Margret broke down, clinging to him as her husband Jack steadied her. Minutes passed in thick silence until Dr. Miller returned.

"Jennifer's pancreas is barely functioning. She's now fully diabetic, and her kidneys are showing signs of distress. And as you know, Abby's liver could fail at any time. Both need transplants soon."

Margret collapsed into Jack's arms, sobbing uncontrollably. Evan sank into a nearby chair, burying his face in his hands. The weight of it all seemed to press the air from his lungs. How much more could he take? How much more could they lose?

"You look exhausted, Evan," Dr. Miller said softly. "Go home, get some rest. We'll call if there's any change."

He nodded, collecting his jacket and laptop. But instead of heading home, Evan found himself driving toward the cemetery. An unseen force pulled him there, the memories too strong to resist.

He parked and made his way to Danni's grave, his footsteps heavy as he neared. The flowers they'd left weeks ago had withered; their once-bright colors faded. He knelt beside her headstone, the cool surface grounding him. "Hey, baby," he whispered, his voice breaking. "I'm sorry I haven't been here. I just . . . I don't know what to do."

He lay beside her grave marker, pressing his cheek to the earth, letting the cold ground absorb his pain. "I'm failing, Danni," he murmured, his eyes closing. "I couldn't save you, and now Jen . . . Abby . . ." His voice trailed off, the words suffocating him.

Images of Danni's bright smile and her laugh floated through his mind, a bittersweet reminder of everything he'd lost. He thought of her first soccer game, her excitement over Christmas, her resilience. Her absence cut into him, sharp and relentless.

And then there was Abby, his steadfast partner, now wasting away in the same hospital bed. And Jennifer, growing weaker every day. Despite everything he'd done, he was losing them too.

For a moment, lying beside Danni's grave, he wished he could stay. The thought of staying here, surrounded by his memories, felt easier than facing his helplessness.

But the image of Jennifer's frail form lying in the hospital jolted him awake. He couldn't let this happen again. He wouldn't. But he couldn't save them on his own. His family needed a miracle, and there was only one person who might have answers. *Robert.*

A voice broke his thoughts. "Hey, man, you can't stay here. The cemetery's closed."

Evan blinked up at the groundskeeper, disoriented and stiff from lying on the damp ground. He pushed himself to his feet, apologizing softly.

"You're lucky I didn't call the cops," the groundskeeper grumbled, his voice tinged with irritation. "But if I catch you here again, I will."

Evan gave a slight nod, casting a final glance at Danni's headstone. He felt a strange resolve harden within him. He knew what he had to do.

As he walked back to his car, he knew he was driving to Robert's house. He was going to beg, to plead, for anything Robert could offer to save his family. But deep down, he understood something darker. He wasn't just going there to ask for help; he was prepared to do whatever it took.

CHAPTER 11

MEDICAL MAGAZINE

The Soaring Costs of Organ Transplants: A Financial Burden on Patients and Healthcare

The financial burden associated with organ transplants remains a significant concern for patients and their families across the nation. The average cost for a single organ transplant can range from $250,000 to over $1 million, depending on the type of organ and the related medical care required. These expenses encompass surgery, hospitalization, post-operative care, and lifelong immunosuppressive medications. Even with insurance coverage, many patients are left with substantial out-of-pocket expenses, leading to financial strain and challenging decisions regarding their healthcare. This growing issue underscores the urgent need for improved support systems and funding mechanisms to ensure that life-saving transplants are accessible to everyone in need.

Evan Wheeler

Sommerset County, New Jersey

Evan's car skidded along the slick road, the tires fighting for traction as rain battered the windshield in relentless sheets. The storm was deafening, drowning out everything but his panicked thoughts: Help me save my family. I'll do anything. The wipers struggled to keep up, barely making a dent in his view as he pressed on through the downpour.

He finally pulled up under the dimly lit porch of Robert's mansion, the headlights briefly illuminating the ornate door before darkness swallowed it again. Drenched as he dashed up the steps, he pounded on the door, his heart racing and his mind swirling with desperation. The door creaked open, revealing the maid in a floral housecoat, her eyes widening at the sight of him.

Before she could say anything, Robert appeared, wrapped in a white terrycloth robe, his face impassive. "Go back to bed. I got this," he said to the maid, dismissing her with a flick of his hand. He gestured for Evan to follow him down a long, silent hallway into his office, where the faint scent of leather and scotch hung in the air.

Inside, Evan dropped to his knees, his hands shaking as he pressed them together, feeling the cool, unyielding wood floor beneath him. "I'm begging you," he choked out, the words catching in his throat. "I'll do anything. They're dying, and I don't know what else to do."

Robert extended a hand, pulling him up with a firm grip and guiding him to a brown leather sofa. Evan's heart hammered as he slumped back, feeling the rich leather press against his tense shoulders. Robert poured two glasses of scotch, the amber liquid glowing under the dim desk lamp, casting eerie shadows across his face.

"Just . . . please get that doctor to give my family a chance," Evan stammered, gripping his glass so tightly he could feel his pulse in his fingers. The burn of the scotch was a fleeting relief, distracting him from the terror gnawing at his insides.

Robert set his glass down, leaning forward, his gaze unwavering and predatory. "There's a reason the cost is so high," he began, his voice smooth yet chilling. "We need more organs to save more lives."

Evan nodded, though unease coiled tighter in his gut. The scotch turned sour on his tongue. How could he live with himself if they got caught? How could he reconcile this with his conscience?

"There's a way to secure a large surplus," Robert continued, his voice dropping to a conspiratorial whisper. "It involves a decompression. If the pilot cuts the cabin oxygen, the passengers will slip into unconsciousness. No pain, no fear. A hundred and fifty lives could save hundreds, thousands."

Evan felt his stomach twist. He set the glass down, his hands shaking. "There must be another way. I can't . . . I can't do that! This is insane!" He felt his voice crack, the weight of Robert's words settling over him like a shroud.

Robert's face remained calm; his voice almost soothing. "Think about it, Evan. You could save your family. It's humane, really. This is the only option, and it all rests on you."

Evan forced himself to stand, his legs trembling. "You want me to kill a hundred and fifty people? I've never hurt anyone! I was a cargo pilot in the military! I transported lives—I didn't take them!"

"Keep your voice down," Robert whispered sharply, pressing a finger to his lips as a dark anticipation glinted in his eyes. "This isn't about murder. It's about survival—yours, your family's."

Evan sank back, his mind racing. He forced himself to breathe, to steady his voice. "But . . . how would I even do it?"

Robert leaned back, his tone calculating. "Since 9/11, pilots are trained to cut cabin oxygen if there's a hijacking. Everyone would be unconscious in minutes, giving you time to land." He walked to his antique walnut desk, retrieving an item from the drawer. "You're the pilot for this operation."

"What do you mean?" Evan asked, his voice barely a whisper, as if speaking louder would make the nightmare real.

"After a stop in Venezuela, you'll poison the first officer. Then you can create the decompression. It'll look like a malfunction." Robert's voice was level, clinical, as if discussing the weather.

"Poison?" Evan felt bile rise in his throat. Every word was a fresh nightmare.

"In the air. It's all in the checklist." Robert handed him an iPhone, the screen glowing in the dim room. "It's in the 'Pilot Checklist' app."

Evan hesitated, his mind screaming questions and doubts. "And then?"

"You'll don your oxygen mask and turn off the cabin oxygen. The masks are removed; it's the only way to guarantee success of the decompression."

A cold sweat broke over Evan's body as he absorbed the horrifying simplicity of it all. "So, I poison the first officer and asphyxiate everyone. Then what?"

"Land the plane near the doctor's hospital in Brazil. It's simple."

"And I just . . . walk away? There will be an investigation."

"Brazil will shut its borders. The FAA and NTSB won't be allowed in. Your name will be sealed from the public."

Evan's throat was dry as he croaked, "When does my wife get her operation? It must be before I leave."

"After you land," Robert replied, his tone final. "Take it or leave it."

Evan's mind was a whirl of terror and desperation as he paced the room. The weight of the decision bore down on him like a lead blanket. He felt himself nod, almost involuntarily, the gravity of it all settling in. "Okay, when?"

"The day after tomorrow. Are you saying yes?" Robert's gaze was piercing, a hint of triumph in his eyes.

"Yes," Evan whispered, the words sealing his fate. His hands trembled as he pocketed the phone and stumbled out to his car, icy resolve battling against crushing guilt. He pulled over, gripping the steering wheel tightly as a scream tore from his throat, lost in the storm outside.

The sterile scent of antiseptic clung to the humid air inside the surgical tent, fighting a losing battle against the relentless jungle dampness. Dr. José Santiago pressed his fists into his lower back, stretching the knots that had formed from hours—days—of hunching over organ cultures, cell samples, and intake reports.

His eyes burned from lack of sleep. His fingers ached from the delicate work required to prepare for what would be the most ambitious operation of his career. Thankful that the chemicals had arrived and were almost balanced, he only needed one more week. That's all he needed. A few more days to refine the final tissue stabilization process, run the rejection suppression tests, and ensure everything was perfect.

The sat phone on the counter buzzed, the vibration rattling against a steel tray of instruments. He closed his eyes, exhaling before answering.

"José, good news. The plane arrives the day after tomorrow."

Robert's voice was slick, casual—as if he had just ordered wine for dinner instead of demanding the impossible.

José's grip tightened on the phone. He pressed it harder against his ear, as if he had misheard. "What did you just say?"

"I said the plane lands at dawn. Forty-eight hours from now."

Heat flooded José's face. His pulse thundered in his ears. "That is out of the question. We are not ready. If we rush this, the transplants could fail! Do you understand what that means? We could be sitting on a pile of useless flesh!"

On the other end, Robert sighed. "I understand, but I need you to understand something: the pilot is committed now. If we wait, he might get cold feet." His tone darkened. "We will not get another chance like this."

José turned, bracing his palm against the edge of the steel table. He could barely keep his anger from boiling over. He forced himself to breathe, but his body betrayed him—his hand shook. "Robert, listen to me. If we do this before we're ready, I cannot guarantee viability. The rejection buffers—"

"Will be fine."

"They are not fine!" José shouted, his composure cracking. "The glucose cell integrity on the pancreatic cultures is still unstable. If we implant those organs too soon, they'll collapse in the recipient's body like a rotting fruit. Do you want your miracle to fail?"

A long pause.

Then, Robert's voice, low and firm: "I also need a liver flown to the U.S. Two days from now."

José closed his eyes. The world around him tilted, nausea rising. He had sacrificed everything for his career, reputation, and life's work—and now Robert was gambling with it like a drunk at a poker table.

His breath came fast, his fingers white against the metal.

"I'll make it work," he said through clenched teeth.

"I knew you'd come through."

The line went dead.

José slammed the phone onto the tray, sending instruments **clattering** across the table. He took a shuddering breath, then grabbed the sat phone again, fingers dialing with urgency.

The line rang once. Twice. Then—

"Sí?"

"El Diablo. Get to the hospital. Now."

A pause. Then a wary, "Why?"

José's throat was dry. He squeezed the bridge of his nose, willing his head to clear. "Because everything has changed. The American found a pilot. The plane lands in two days."

Silence.

"El Diablo?"

A sharp breath on the other end, but still, silence. José could feel the weight of his disbelief through the receiver, even without seeing his face.

Finally—a low, hard curse.

"You just told me about this a few weeks ago; that is not enough time," El Diablo said, voice clipped. "My team is not ready. We were expecting a week."

"We are not using your team," José said. He wiped the sweat from his forehead, his other hand still gripping the counter. "The Brazilians will handle it."

El Diablo's silence turned frigid.

Then, quietly: "You're putting this in their hands? Then I cannot guarantee the campaign will be a success like I usually do."

José exhaled. "We don't have a choice."

El Diablo muttered another curse, something harsh and guttural. When he spoke again, his voice was lower, laced with something José rarely heard from him—uncertainty.

"We've never completed a job that I didn't use my team," El Diablo said. "Because if this goes wrong, it is outside of my control."

The line went dead.

José let the phone slip from his fingers onto the tray. The cold, calculated weight of reality settled in his chest.

He stared at the cooling vats holding his samples, his organs—the culmination of three decades of work.

CHAPTER 12

THE NEW YORK CHRONICAL

Wedding Announcements – Sunday Edition

Stephanie Pratt & Levi Mathews

Mr. and Mrs. Steven Pratt of Bridgewater, NJ, are delighted to announce the upcoming wedding of their daughter, Stephanie Pratt, to Levi Mathews, son of Mr. and Mrs. Robert Mathews of New York, NY.

The wedding will take place at Blessed Sacrament Church in Martinsville, NJ. The ceremony is scheduled for June 7 and will be followed by a reception at Fiddler's Elbow, Bedminster, NJ.

Stephanie and Levi look forward to celebrating their special day with family and friends.

Stephanie Pratt and Levi Mathews

Fiddler's Elbow Golf Club, Bedminster, New Jersey

"Turn here! Turn here!" Steph twisted in her seat, pointing urgently at the road they had just passed.

Levi slammed on the brakes, the tires screeching in protest as they missed the turn. The car behind them honked furiously.

"Sorry!" Lev waved apologetically, his heart racing.

"It was back there!" Steph pointed over her shoulder, a mix of frustration and laughter in her voice.

"Dude, really?" Lev shot back her laughter filling the car. "You said you knew where this place was!"

"I do—when I'm driving!" Steph said through her laughing.

Levi couldn't help but smile at her laughter, even as his nerves began to simmer again. They had only just pulled into the driveway of Fiddler's Elbow, but he could feel the weight of the impending interaction with her parents pressing on him. He lifted his arm, glancing at his shirt. "Do I have pit stains?"

Steph looked, a faint smile on her face. "You're fine," she said not wanting to alarm him.

"You're not saying no, that means I have pit stains. Great."

"You're fine, it's just a very little. You can't see it."

Levi took a deep breath, attempting to shake off his jitters. "Your parents hate me," he muttered under his breath.

"They don't hate you," Steph said, her hand resting briefly on his shoulder, a grounding gesture. "They're just . . . concerned."

"Concerned?" Levi's voice held a hint of exasperation. "You told me last week they don't like me."

"My dad doesn't, but my mom's warming up to you," she replied, focused on her phone.

He parked under the portico, catching the eye of the valet as he stepped out. As they approached the entrance, Steph's phone rang, and she glanced at him apologetically before answering.

"Hi, this is Flight Attendant Pratt," she said. A moment later, her eyes widened. "JFK? Now? Are you serious? Ok I'm on my way."

"You have to go to JFK?" Lev asked, his frustration rising. "We just got here."

"I know. But I must go, I have no choice." Her face fell, disappointment flickering across it. "We were supposed to choose the cake together."

"And now I'm supposed to face your parents alone?" Levi's voice cracked a little, the thought of a solo cake tasting with her father tightening the knots in his stomach.

She looked at him, regret filling her eyes. "I'm so sorry. This was the only time the baker had for this appointment. But maybe this can be a chance for you to get to know them better?"

He exhaled sharply, unsure whether to laugh or groan. "Right. A chance to bond with Steve over buttercream frosting. Perfect."

"Hey." She stopped, leaning up to kiss him softly. "My dad doesn't hate you. He hates the idea of his daughter marrying someone, anyone."

"Yeah, well, that doesn't make this any easier," he muttered, running a hand through his hair.

She took his hand, squeezing it. "You're my everything, Levi. If I had to go through all the hardships and heartbreaks just to meet you, I would do it all over again."

They shared a long kiss, and he picked her up, twirling her around, trying to let her words ease his tension. But as she walked away, he felt a familiar heaviness settle back in his chest. He forced a smile, determined not to let her see his nerves.

Inside, her father Steve was already seated, his country-club chic outfit complete with plaid pants and a bright-pink polo shirt. Beside him, her mother Barb wore a twin set with flamingo-dotted pants and a Botox smile that barely moved.

"Sorry we're late," Steph said as they approached. "But I've got some bad news. Crew scheduling called; I have a trip that signs in a couple of hours. So . . . Levi will be the cake tester."

Barb's mouth opened, "oh no."

Steve's eyes narrowed. "Can't you tell them you're busy?"

She shook her head. "I wish I could, Dad. But traffic's brutal on the Belt Parkway. I have to leave now."

After Steph kissed her parents' goodbye, Levi walked her out to the car, savoring a last private moment. "You owe me big for this one, princess."

She smiled, a mix of warmth and worry in her gaze. "I know. Thank you. I love you."

"What's your favorite cake again?" he asked, half-joking, trying to lighten the mood.

"Cheesecake. I love cheesecake!" She laughed.

"Won't that melt?"

She shrugged her shoulders as she got in the car. "That's what I want." She blew him a kiss and pulled away.

Levi returned to the table, his leg bouncing under the table as he tried to brace himself. A sidelong glance from Steve was all it took for him to still it, though the tension remained coiled in his gut.

"Can I get you another round?" the waiter asked.

Steve nodded. "Yes. Levi? Scotch neat and a beer back?" His tone was casual, but Levi sensed the challenge beneath it.

"Club soda with lime," Levi replied, keeping his voice steady, meeting Steve's gaze.

Steve raised an eyebrow, almost as if he were disappointed. "How long is her trip?" Barb asked, trying to ease the tension.

"Three days—Brazil, São Paulo," Levi replied. "She loves her job, but being on call can be hard."

"I hate her job," Steve muttered. "Four years of college, and for what?"

"I jump whenever her phone rings," Levi offered, hoping to find common ground, but Steve just kept his gaze steady, piercing.

The awkward silence lingered, stretching longer until Barb finally asked, "So . . . Levi, what was it like in all those war zones? It must have been terrifying."

"Being in the middle of an active battle? Yeah," he said, hoping the conversation wouldn't drift toward his recent troubles.

Barb looked genuinely interested, but Steven cut her off. "Do you plan on returning to the combat zone after marrying my daughter?"

Levi looked at Barb to see if her expression had changed. Nope. "Well, I would like to get back into the action one day, but many things would have to happen."

"Like what?" Steven asked in a rapid-fire sort of way.

The tension was building. Levi could feel it. "As you know, I have had some issues that I am working hard on. Currently, I am the anchor at a local television station. I started a few weeks ago."

"The midnight shift, right? You're not going to get rich doing that," Steven said, sipping his drink.

"It's less than what I used to make, but it's a living," Levi said. "It's doable."

"Doable?" Steven said with another sip. He was getting louder, causing the other diners to look in their direction.

Barb's head snapped toward her husband. "Keep your voice down. People are trying to enjoy their lunch."

The waiter brought the food, but Levi was no longer hungry, his leg pulsing at 100 mph. Steven began to eat his salad. Barb started removing things from hers that Levi guessed weren't on her diet.

Levi took a bite of his burger and waited for the next verbal assault from his future father-in-law.

"How many different news outlets did you get fired from?" Steven asked.

Wow! "Four," Levi said.

Silence.

Levi felt he needed to say something before it went too far. "With all due respect, Mr. Pratt—Steven—I feel like you have an issue with me marrying your daughter."

Steven froze, his fork raised midway to his lips. He smiled, putting it back down.

Levi continued, "I would like the opportunity to get to know you, and maybe you could get to know me before you make your final judgment. I have made many mistakes over the years and take full responsibility for them. I am on a new path now, and I hope to continue living a healthy lifestyle to make Steph as happy as possible. All I ask is that you give me a chance."

Steven looked at his wife. His wife looked at her plate.

"I don't think you have the faintest idea how I…" Steve waved his finger between Barb and himself, "How we feel. Let's start from the beginning. You came from a broken household at a very young age. Your mother, a heroin addict, overdosed, leaving you to your father, an alcoholic, and a heroin abuser, who dropped you off at Child Services when you were six. You ran away from several foster homes, living on the street. Later, a pimp took you in and forced you to sell drugs."

Levi kept eating his French fries, trying not to show any emotion.

"Once the police got hold of you, you were sent to juvenile detention until you were eighteen. After a few more years of being pulled in for petty crimes, a small TV station owner hired you as a stagehand, and later, you were the anchor for the midnight shift, which I believe is where you are working now." Steven took another sip.

"Did you hire a detective or something? Had my background checked?" Levi asked as his leg bounced harder. This time, he turned in his chair so it wouldn't move the table.

"I did a web search," Steven said. "My favorite part of the article was when you said you love women, love variety, and could never choose just one. You enjoy the run-of-the-mill one-night stand. Keeping track of them was hard, and you had trouble remembering their names."

"*Rolling Stone*," Levi said, nodding.

"Yeah, the *Rolling Stone* interview," Steven said. "How are we supposed to believe that you've changed? I believe you said your vices fill that vacancy created by your parents. Is my daughter a vice? Is she a run-of-the-mill one-night stand? I still haven't addressed the stunt you pulled last year on live network news."

"Levi," Barb said, "we are unsure if you are the right fit for our daughter."

"You're right. I keep telling her the same thing," Levi said.

"Oh, is that so," Steven said. "What happens if you fall off the wagon? Sobriety can be fleeting."

"To be clear, I'm fully entrenched and working the AA steps. My current goal is to stay sober and make Steph happy. It's a process," Levi said.

"It's a *process*?" Steven asked. "Why does my daughter have to be a part of your process?"

"Look, every day, your gorgeous, smart daughter has one endearing trait that makes me feel like this conversation will have minimal effect on our relationship," Levi said. He placed his napkin on the table. "She is stubborn, and she'll never give up on us. How do you think I got this far? I tell her every day she can do better."

"My beautiful, stubborn daughter is too young and naïve to see that the man she is about to marry is a selfish, self-centered narcissist, a man too damaged ever to put her first. When she finally realizes it, you will have ruined her," Steven said, raising his voice again.

Levi said nothing.

"I guess we are going to have to work something out then," Steven said, reaching into his jacket pocket, hanging on the back of his seat, and pulling out a checkbook.

"Work something out?" Levi asked, looking at his future father-in-law, mouth open, shaking his head. His leg stopped pulsing, which usually signaled that he had hit his wall and was ready to blow.

"How much?" Steven said without blinking, putting the pen to the check.

Levi shook his head. "Wow. Do you think I need money?"

"Everybody needs money," Steven said, glowering.

"I don't need money. I may be cash-poor, but through all my stunts and mistakes, I was smart enough to invest my money in real estate. I will be able to provide your daughter with the life she deserves," Levi said as he got up, placing his napkin on the table. "Rest easy. I will take excellent care of her. Enjoy your meal.

"And Barb, it was nice seeing you again," Levi said, taking some money out of his pocket and laying it on the table. "Lunch is on me. Steven." He nodded and strode away.

He waited on the pristine lawn for his Uber. He'd come back another day to choose a wedding cake because it wasn't happening that day.

The door opened behind him. He looked back and saw Steven, his hands in his pockets. "Barb sent me out here to get you," Steven said, looking past Levi. "Out of everything you just said, the one thing that couldn't have been truer is my daughter's stubbornness. I don't think either of us would have a chance ever to change her mind about anything. I've tried her whole life."

Levi nodded.

"Well," Steven paused. "Yeah."

Levi's ride pulled up. He turned to shake Steven's hand.

Steven paused and took Levi's hand. "We'll see you soon."

"Yeah," Levi said, getting into the car, hesitating. "Cheesecake is her favorite," he told Steph's father.

"Won't it melt?" Steven said.

"I already told her, she still wants cheesecake," Levi said, closing the door.

CHAPTER 13

******ATTENTION******

From: Worldwide Airlines Customer Care

Re: Adjustment to your flight itinerary

Flight 987 Schedule Update - Important

Dear Guest,

We would like to inform you of a change to your travel itinerary. Worldwide Airlines Flight 987 will now include a brief operational stop in Caracas, Venezuela.

Updated Schedule:

- Departure: JFK - New York John F. Kennedy Airport
- Intermediate Stop: CCS - Caracas, Venezuela
- Arrival: GRU - Sao Paulo Guarulhos International Airport

Please ensure you adjust your plans accordingly. We apologize for any inconvenience this may cause and appreciate your understanding. For further assistance or to make any necessary changes to your booking, please contact our customer service team or visit our website.

Thank you for choosing Worldwide Airlines. We look forward to serving you.

Evan Wheeler

John F. Kennedy Airport, Queens, New York

Evan's knuckles were bone-white on the steering wheel, his pulse thudding painfully in his temples. He tried to release his grip, shake out his hands, but they wouldn't relax. Dark thoughts curled around him, thick as smoke, the same one pounding through his mind like a drumbeat: I can't sit and watch her die. He could barely make out the honk of an oncoming truck until it was nearly too late. Swerving just in time, he checked his speedometer—45 in a 60. He forced himself into the slow lane.

As if on cue, his phone buzzed in the cupholder. He snatched it up, barely glancing at the caller ID. Shit, his father in-law. He knew this moment was coming.

"Hello?" he said, forcing his voice steady.

"Evan, it's Dad. Where are you? Are you on your way to the hospital?" Jack's voice crackled over the line, each word a stone dropped in the pit of Evan's stomach.

"I'm on my way to Kennedy. Crew scheduling assigned me a trip." He braced himself for the reaction he knew was coming.

"You were there when the doctor said she might not last the week! And you're leaving?" Jack's anger burned, raw and immediate.

Evan squeezed his eyes shut, letting the rage roll over him, trying to hold onto his own unraveling calm. "I don't have a choice. If I don't go, I get fired. No insurance. No benefits." The words felt empty even to him.

A tense silence hung on the other end. "I'll pay for your insurance," Jack finally replied, voice colder. "You need to be here."

"I can't let you do that." He hesitated, knowing what he was about to admit would only make things worse. "I can't watch her die, Dad." It was the truth, a knot he couldn't untangle. "If I'm gone . . . if I can finish this . . ." He trailed off, unable to say more.

Another silence, filled with bitter understanding. Finally, his mother's voice filtered through. "Evan, honey, where are you?"

He took a breath. "I'm on my way to the airport. They say if I don't take this trip, I could be grounded for months." It was flimsy, and he knew it, but it was all he had.

"Then take a deep breath," she replied. "Focus on your job. Abby would want you safe, too."

He bit his lip, nodding as tears welled up, hot and unrelenting. "I'm sorry, Mom. I'll call as soon as I land."

"It's okay, sweetheart. Just . . . come home safe."

When the line went silent, he pulled onto the shoulder and pressed his head to the steering wheel, letting himself cry, just for a moment. He flipped on his hazard lights, listening to the rhythmic clicks that calmed him. Eventually, he took a shuddering breath, wiped his face, and picked up the burner phone Robert had given him. The voice on the other end was cold and clinical, stepping him through each step of the checklist.

"Step one: the poison," Robert's voice instructed, detached as though reading from a manual. "You'll find it on the plane in a brown paper bag. Inside, there's a sealed vial. The poison is hazardous. Use gloves and apply it to the first officer's oxygen mask."

Evan's stomach clenched. The instructions made murder sound as routine as a pre-flight check. He thought of Abby, still and pale in a hospital bed, and forced himself to absorb the details. He could do this. He had to do this.

By the time he reached the airport, the air was thick with the smell of jet fuel and fried food. As he scanned the gate area, he saw a mother with two kids struggling to corral them. His throat tightened, his gaze dropping to the ticket counter for support. You haven't done anything yet, he told himself. *Breathe. In and out.*

"Captain Wheeler?" The voice startled him, and he looked up into the eyes of a man in his late thirties, clean-cut and with an easy smile.

Evan's pulse quickened. *This is him. The man I'm going to kill.*

"Didn't mean to scare you. I'm Lucas, your first officer." Lucas's face creased with concern. "Are you okay?"

"Yeah. Sorry. Traffic was a nightmare," Evan lied, feeling the bile rise in his throat.

Lucas nodded, sympathy coloring his face. "Happens to the best of us. They flew me up from Miami to cover this trip—they said they needed a Portuguese speaker. Still not sure why they'd swap the usual 767 with a 757 on an international route." He glanced back toward the gate area, looking faintly puzzled. "I mean, a 767 could make it without a stop. Now we'll need a refuel in Venezuela."

Evan forced a tight smile, his gut twisting. This wasn't an accident. He thought of the checklist, the poison waiting on board, and how deliberately every piece was falling into place.

"Captain?" He jumped, turning to see the gate agent holding out the flight plan. "Here's your paperwork. You left it on the printer."

Lucas laughed softly. "Everything okay?"

"Yeah, just a little on edge," Evan admitted, a hint of the truth slipping through. "My wife is . . . sick." He forced the words, feeling a pang of guilt.

Lucas's expression softened. "I'm sorry. Is it serious?"

"Yeah." His throat felt tight.

Evan moved past Lucas into the plane, leaving his bag at the cockpit door. Closing it behind him, he took a shaky breath, scanning the area. The poison. His eyes roamed the cabin, but the brown bag was nowhere in sight. Relief washed over him, but it was short-lived as a soft knock came at the door.

CHAPTER 14

THE NEW YORK CHRONICLE

BLACK MARKET HUMAN ORGAN TRADING

By Caroline Clapp

Authorities worldwide are intensifying efforts to combat this black market, but the demand for organs continues to drive this dark and dangerous industry. Public awareness and stringent regulations are crucial in addressing and curbing this alarming issue.

The illegal trade of human organs on the black market is a growing global concern, posing serious ethical, health, and legal challenges. Desperate patients facing long wait times for legitimate transplants are often exploited by criminal networks that harvest and sell organs under dangerous and unethical conditions. This illicit trade not only jeopardizes the lives of donors and recipients, but also undermines trust in legitimate medical practices.

Margret and Jack Douglas

Somerset Medical Center, Somerville, New Jersey

Margret's fingers worked through her rosary beads, her whisper-soft prayers blending into the steady hum of hospital machinery. The scent of antiseptic stung her nostrils, a constant reminder of where they were. She glanced at Jack, who paced by the window, nursing a cup of bitter, lukewarm coffee. The faint sounds of a baseball game crackled from his earbuds, his usual ritual when nerves took hold.

It had been hours since Evan told them he was leaving, vanishing on a flight to Brazil just as the hospital called with unexpected news: a liver had been found for Abby. Margret's attempts to reach Evan had gone unanswered, the silence pressing on her chest like a weight.

Jack pulled out an earbud, sensing her movement. "What's up?"

"It's been over three hours. No word yet. Don't you think they'd tell us something by now?" Her voice was brittle, edged with exhaustion.

Jack's face darkened, his brows knitting. "Yeah. Has Evan called?"

Margret shook her head and rose, her muscles stiff from sitting. She approached the nurse's station, keeping her voice low but urgent. "My daughter, Abby Wheeler, is waiting for a liver transplant. Do you have any updates?"

The nurse frowned, her fingers moving swiftly across the keyboard. "She's still in pre-op. Surgery's been postponed."

Margret's stomach twisted. "Why didn't anyone tell us?"

The nurse offered an apologetic shrug. "Sometimes it happens. We keep patients prepped, expecting the surgery to start soon."

Margret bit back a retort, her frustration clawing up. "Can we talk to someone in charge? We've been waiting here for hours."

The nurse picked up the phone. "I'll have the charge nurse meet you in the lounge."

Margret returned to Jack; her hands clenched tightly. "They haven't started. She's been in pre-op this whole time."

Jack's face flushed with anger. "What? Why wouldn't they tell us that?"

Just then, a frazzled-looking charge nurse hurried in, her voice soft but hurried. "I'm so sorry for the delay. I've been on the phone, trying to get a clear answer. The liver is still at Newark Airport, held up in customs."

"Customs?" Jack's voice rose, incredulous. "We thought it was coming from the Midwest."

The nurse's face tightened. "It's coming from Venezuela. It seems there may be some . . . unusual circumstances."

Margret's hand flew to her mouth. "What? Are you saying it's from . . . the black market?"

The nurse's gaze softened but remained steady. "It's possible. This isn't unheard of, and as long as it's a match, hospitals tend to look the other way. But customs issues can complicate things."

Jack's voice was rough, barely controlled. "How do we know it's safe?"

"Once it arrives, the doctors will evaluate it carefully," the nurse assured them.

Margret swallowed hard, feeling the weight of each passing second. "So . . . what do we do?"

The nurse handed them a memo pad with a hastily scrawled number. "The legal department is working on it. It seems a tax payment is required to release the organ."

Jack's jaw tightened as he took the phone and made the call. Moments later, he returned, his face etched with frustration. "They need $2,500 now and another $7,500 on delivery, plus $1,000 to expedite."

Margret slumped, a wave of helplessness washing over her. "We have no choice, do we?"

Jack punched in his credit card numbers, the tension in his face deepening with every tap. As he finished, he shook his head. "Evan bought a liver off the black market. Maybe that's why he left—afraid he'd get in trouble if it went wrong."

Margret's voice dropped to a whisper. "He should have told us. But if he'd asked, what would you have said?"

Jack's shoulders sagged as he stared out the window, lost in thought. "I'd have wanted a chance to weigh the risks. This is . . . dangerous."

Margret's fingers resumed their path along the rosary, the beads cool and familiar against her skin. "We're not saying anything to Abby when she wakes up. If it works . . . let Evan tell her."

Jack sighed heavily, giving her hand a squeeze. "Agreed. We don't know what he went through to make this happen."

As silence settled between them, Margret leaned back, closing her eyes. The sterile scent of antiseptic filled her lungs, mixing with the unyielding tick of the wall clock—a countdown that gnawed at her patience, each second tightening the grip of uncertainty.

CHAPTER 15

THE TEXAS MORNING NEWS

THE TEXAS MORNING NEWS

EXHAUSTED AT 36,000 FEET

FLIGHT ATTENDANT FATIGUE ON RED-EYE FLIGHTS

Flight attendants face significant challenges when working overnight flights, often known as "all-nighters." The demanding schedule disrupts their natural sleep patterns, leading to fatigue and increased stress. Balancing safety, passenger needs, and personal well-being becomes particularly tough during these hours. Despite their professionalism and dedication, the physical and mental toll of all-night flights is substantial. Airlines are being urged to provide better support and rest opportunities to ensure that flight attendants can perform their duties safely and effectively, even during the most exhausting shifts.

Stephanie Pratt

John F. Kennedy Airport, Queens, New York

Steph slipped her bags into the narrow closet by the entryway just as the captain brushed past her. He didn't offer a word, didn't even glance her way. His face was set in a hard line, his eyes fixed ahead, almost like she didn't exist.

"Hi, I'm Steph," she offered softly, but he disappeared into the cockpit, the door shutting with a cold, metallic click. Nice, she thought, feeling a prickling heat rise up her neck.

She turned her attention to her paperwork, flipping through it with quick, practiced fingers. Her brow furrowed as she noticed something odd—all the other flight attendants were based in São Paulo. *I thought I wasn't supposed to fly with foreign nationals. Her grip tightened on the papers. Guess that wasn't accurate.*

Looking down the aisle, she saw the crew already busy with pre-flight tasks, their movements quick and synchronized. She picked up the PA system, heart thumping. "Hi, everyone. I'm Steph. Could we do a quick briefing in first class?"

No one looked up. Her chest tightened. *Maybe they don't do briefings on their trips . . . or maybe they don't speak English.* She fumbled for words, trying to remember a basic phrase. "Uh . . . por favor?" She cringed at the awkwardness, certain her high-school Spanish had failed her.

A few snickers drifted up from the back of the plane, and one by one, the crew drifted forward, wearing amused smiles. *At least they're coming.*

She cleared her throat as they gathered around, forcing a smile. "Hi, my name is Steph." She kept her tone friendly, but the crew's blank stares made her falter. One attendant muttered something in what she thought was Spanish, her words laced with amusement. Steph felt heat creep up her cheeks. She repeated herself louder, hoping somehow the volume might bridge the language gap.

Just then, the first officer, Lucas, stepped onto the plane. The crew's demeanor shifted instantly, their faces brightening as they greeted him warmly. "Hi, I'm Lucas," he introduced himself first in Portuguese, then switched to English. The crew responded to him with ease, their voices filling the space.

Steph felt a rush of relief. "I'm Steph. Sorry, I don't speak . . . Spanish."

Lucas's gentle smile softened her embarrassment. "They're Brazilian," he explained, keeping his voice low. "They speak Portuguese, not Spanish." he added with a twinkle of humor, "and they also want you to know they're not deaf."

Steph's face burned as the crew chuckled again. "Oh, right . . . I'm definitely the new one here," she muttered, laughing nervously.

Lucas's expression grew understanding. "What do you need to tell them?"

She took a steadying breath. "Just that the first leg to Venezuela is four hours, and to São Paulo is eight. We'll have two breaks. If they need anything, they can tell you, and you can pass it on to me."

"I'll relay that," Lucas nodded, turning back to the crew and translating her instructions into Portuguese. As he spoke, Steph noticed how the crew listened attentively, nodding along with his words.

Lucas finished and cast a quick glance toward the cockpit. "I'm going to do the outside inspection. I'll put my things away when I'm done."

Just then, the cockpit door swung open, and the captain's voice interrupted the moment. "Sorry, I didn't realize I had shut the door," he muttered, though his gaze remained distant.

Lucas left to begin the inspection, leaving Steph with a strange feeling that gnawed at her. She shook it off, returning her focus to the cabin preparations.

Not long after, a mother approached, her two young children in tow. Steph knelt to their eye level, offering them a warm smile. "Welcome aboard! What's your name?"

The little girl pressed her face shyly against her mother's leg. "Anya," she whispered.

Steph beamed. "That's such a pretty name. And how old are you?" She looked between the children, her eyes softening.

"I'm Billy, and I'm eight! She's four," the boy announced, his excitement infectious. "I want to be a pilot when I grow up!"

"Me too!" Anya's voice broke through her shyness, her face lighting up.

The mother looked at Steph with a hopeful smile. "Would it be all right if they peeked into the cockpit?"

"Of course," Steph replied warmly, though a hint of hesitation crept in as she approached the cockpit door. She knocked softly. "Captain? We have two future pilots here who'd love to see the cockpit."

There was a pause, then the captain's voice snapped back, tense and dismissive. "No." The door closed with a resounding finality.

Steph's smile faltered, embarrassment creeping into her cheeks as she turned back to the family. "I'm so sorry," she whispered. "Maybe we can try again in Venezuela?"

The mother's smile turned brittle, but she nodded. "Thank you anyway."

Steph watched them walk away, a mixture of irritation and confusion churning inside her. *What's his problem?*

Just then, Lucas returned from his inspection, weaving through the boarding passengers. Steph caught his eye, lowering her voice. "Do you know what's going on with the captain?" she whispered. "He hasn't introduced himself, and he just snapped at me—and at two little kids."

Lucas's expression shifted, a flicker of sympathy crossing his face. "He found out his wife's having surgery—right before we boarded."

Steph's irritation softened, though it didn't disappear entirely. "That explains it . . . but still, it's no excuse to be so rude."

Lucas nodded, accepting the water bottles she handed him. "I'll check in on him," he murmured, disappearing into the cockpit.

* * *

Once in the cockpit, Lucas stowed his vest and bag in the tight compartment behind the right seat. He cast a quick glance at the captain, hoping to lift the tension. "So . . . do you have kids?" he asked, his tone conversational. "I've got three back home in São Paulo. If we're on schedule, I'll see them tomorrow."

The captain's eyes remained fixed ahead, his face unreadable, barely registering Lucas's presence.

Lucas tried again, pushing past the awkwardness. "My wife and I used to do the São Paulo–Miami commute, but she's American, and it got to be too much for her. We're settled in Miami now, hoping for more kids soon."

The captain's voice sliced through the moment, low and impatient. "Can you shut up? I can't even hear myself think."

Lucas fell silent, taken aback. He shot a glance at Steph, who was watching from the galley with a sympathetic look. *It's going to be a long flight.*

CHAPTER 16

THE MIAMI

VENEZUELAN MILITARY INTENSIFIES CHECKS ON LUGGAGE FOR OUTBOUND FLIGHTS

By Nicole Rodriguez

Travelers flying out of Venezuela are facing increasing scrutiny and concerns regarding loaded luggage. Reports indicate that unauthorized items, including contraband and illicit goods, are being secretly placed in passengers' luggage by criminal networks. These incidents pose serious risks to passengers and highlight the broader security challenges within the country's aviation system. Authorities are intensifying efforts to crack down on these illegal activities, but travelers are advised to remain vigilant. It is recommended to keep a close watch on your luggage and report any suspicious activities to airline officials immediately.

Evan Wheeler

Simon Bolivar International Airport, Caracas, Venezuela

Evan eased the airplane to a stop as the ground crewman made an X with his wands. Every nerve was taut, his hands gripping the armrests tightly. This was it. If the poison was going to be delivered, it would happen here. His palms were damp, and he rubbed them against his thighs, attempting to calm his fraying nerves.

He glanced at Lucas, who was absorbed in his phone, oblivious to the turmoil swirling inside Evan.

As the jet bridge connected, Evan practically jumped from his seat, throwing open the cockpit door. The sudden movement sent his stomach churning, but he forced himself to keep steady. The flight attendant standing nearby took a startled step back.

"Whoa!" she exclaimed.

An agent approached, handing Evan a revised flight plan. The paper felt dry and gritty in his clammy hands, his grip tightening as he scanned the details.

"Next gate, leaving in twenty minutes," the agent informed him, though her voice seemed distant, almost drowned out by the thundering in his ears.

"Wait, we're switching planes?" he asked, his voice sounding strained.

The agent nodded absently. "That's the plan." She turned away to make announcements in Spanish, her words blurring into background noise.

Evan swallowed, fighting the rising anxiety. He hurried back to the cockpit, his hands shaking as he shoved his belongings into his bag.

"Where are you going?" Lucas's voice broke through the fog, tinged with surprise.

"We're switching planes. I'll meet you over there," Evan replied, barely holding back the edge of panic. He swung his bag over his shoulder, nearly tripping in his haste to exit.

Lucas raised an eyebrow, watching him with mild curiosity but simply shrugged. "See you there," he murmured, returning to his phone.

Evan stepped into the new jet and froze. On the captain's seat sat a brown paper bag. His heart skipped a beat. He had secretly hoped the poison would never be delivered, but there it was, waiting for him. What he really hoped was that Abby's liver transplant happen before he had to make his final decision.

Lucas stumbled in behind him, almost tripping over Evan's bag. "Sorry," Evan muttered, gesturing vaguely toward the door. "I need to make a call to my wife. Leave your bags there I'll put them away. Just do your walk-around inspection."

Lucas's brow furrowed. "I was just about to stow my bags—"

"I'll do it later," Evan cut him off, his voice sharper than he intended. "Please, it's urgent."

Lucas hesitated, his gaze lingering, but finally gave a reluctant nod. "Sure, no problem," he said, grabbing his safety vest and heading outside.

Left alone in the cockpit, Evan's breath came shallow and quick. His fingers trembled as he pulled out his checklist. Gloves on. Cotton balls. Poison.

His hands shook as he prepared the first officer's oxygen mask. Just as he was about to finish, a knock at the door startled him, and a few drops of poison splattered onto the floor. He forced himself to stay composed.

"One second!" Evan called, sealing the poison and stashing the supplies before opening the cockpit door.

Lucas appeared, brow furrowed in concern noticing his bags were where he left them, "How's your wife?"

Evan blinked. "My . . . my wife?"

"You said you needed to call the hospital—everything okay?"

"Oh, uh . . . yeah, she's fine," he managed, his voice hollow. Did he see anything?

Evan sank into his seat, realizing they were running behind schedule.

"What time were we supposed to leave?" he asked, his voice strained.

Lucas glanced up from his phone. "Ten minutes ago."

A surge of urgency shot through him. "We need to go now," he said, turning to Lucas with barely concealed anxiety. "What's the purser's name?"

"Steph," Lucas replied, giving him a cautious look. "Delays happen all the time here, especially with random security checks. Relax."

Evan's mind raced. A random security check? Are they looking for the poison? His thoughts spiraled, each one more consuming than the last.

"Steph!" he called, stepping into the cabin. The flight attendant appeared almost immediately.

"Yes, Captain?" she asked.

"What's going on? Why are we still here?"

She offered a practiced, reassuring smile. "It's just a random security check. They're inspecting the luggage. Happens all the time here in Caracas."

Random? Evan's skin prickled with unease. He clenched his hands to steady them. "Where's the supervisor?" he demanded, sharper than he intended.

The security agent by the door responded in Spanish, but her words barely registered as he pushed past her, stepping into the jet bridge. She followed him up to the gate repeating words in Spanish he didn't understand. He pushed the door open, an alarm shrilled into the terminal.

"Captain, please, you need to knock," the agent said, her tone cautious but polite.

"I don't care about the alarm," he replied. "Why wasn't I informed about this check sooner?"

"It's random," the agent repeated calmly. "They should be done in five minutes."

Five minutes. His stomach clenched as he struggled to keep his composure. *We'll never make the rendezvous on time.*

"Captain, are you okay?" the agent asked, her gaze flicking over him with concern.

"I'm fine," he muttered. "I just want to get going."

The phone at the agent's desk rang. She answered briefly before looking up. "They're done. The luggage needs to be loaded."

"Loaded? Come on! Are you kidding me right now?"

"It'll be done in five minutes," the agent said eyebrows raised.

Evan returned to the cockpit, his legs feeling like lead. He slipped into his seat; his gaze fixed on the controls.

"We're good," he mumbled to Lucas, his voice hollow. "Start the checklist."

As Lucas began working, Evan stared at the throttle, his fingers hovering over it. He closed his eyes for a moment, gripping the armrest tightly. *I've already crossed the line. There's no going back.*

Opening his eyes, he steadied his breath, focusing on Abby and Jen. *For them.* He tightened his grip on the controls.

"I can do this," he whispered. And with that, he leaned forward, the finality of his choice settling over him. There was no turning back now.

CHAPTER 17

THE NEW YORK CHRONICLE

Deadly Poison VX Nerve Agent Used in Assassination of Kim Jong-Nam

By Lilly Choo

In a shocking revelation, Malaysian authorities confirmed today that VX nerve agent—a highly lethal chemical classified as a weapon of mass destruction by the United Nations—was used to assassinate Kim Jong-Nam, the estranged half-brother of North Korean leader Kim Jong-un. The attack, which took place at Kuala Lumpur International Airport in 2017, has drawn international attention and raised concerns over the use of chemical weapons in high-profile assassinations.

Evan Wheeler

Brazilian Airspace, Brazil

Evan fixed his gaze on the horizon, blocking out the agonizing wheezes from the seat beside him. The cockpit seemed to shrink around him, the air dense and stifling. Lucas's breathing rasped, each breath labored and uneven.

"Help . . . me . . ." Lucas's whisper broke the silence, raw with pain.

Evan's eyes flicked over. Lucas's face had lost all color, his skin slick with sweat. A froth had formed at the corners of his mouth. His glassy eyes met Evan's, pleading. The raw terror in his expression was unmistakable—the fear of a man staring death in the face.

Evan's chest tightened. His hands clenched involuntarily, torn between instinct and obligation. Every part of him screamed to act, to reach out, to save Lucas. But it was too late. Lucas was too far gone. The decision had been made; he couldn't afford to waver now. Images of Abby and Jen flickered through his mind, and he held onto them like a lifeline. He wasn't a killer, but for them, he'd crossed this line. He had no choice now.

Lucas gripped Evan's arm with surprising strength, his fingers digging in. "Evan . . . please . . ." His body convulsed, fighting for air. Evan forced himself to stay still, ignoring the burn of guilt twisting in his stomach. Lucas's breath hitched, his hand slackening as he lost his battle. His eyes rolled back, and his head slumped forward onto the yoke, sending the plane into a sudden dip.

Evan snapped into action, grabbing Lucas and pulling him upright, securing his limp body in the seat and fastening his seatbelt. He stared at Lucas's vacant face; a life slipped away. The full weight of his choice settling over him. But he couldn't linger on it—not now.

Robert's voice crackled through his earpiece, snapping him back. "Put on your face mask, located in its bracket to your left. Take a few deep breaths."

Evan pulled the mask free, inhaling deeply, trying to push down the nausea churning inside him. The cold rubber pressed against his skin, grounding him. He felt like a puppet, going through the motions, his actions detached from his conscience.

As his hand hovered over the switch on the instrument panel, he hesitated, his pulse pounding in his ears. One flick of his finger and dozens of lives would end. He'd seen these people before takeoff, laughing, relaxed people who'd trusted him with their lives.

"I'm doing this for my family," he muttered under his breath, though the words felt hollow. His finger brushed the switch, but he jerked back as if it had burned him. Could he really go through with it? Could he justify trading their lives for the chance to save his loved ones? Every instinct screamed at him to stop.

Robert's voice droned on, but it was background noise now. His own heartbeat drowned everything else, relentless, hammering in time with his doubts.

With a shaky hand, he cut the transponder, silencing the aircraft's data feed. There was no going back now. The bile rose in his throat, and he forced it down. His fingers hovered over the knob that would raise the cabin altitude. Hypoxia would be peaceful, he told himself—a way for them to fall asleep and never wake up. But the reassurance offered little comfort.

For a moment, he just stared, paralyzed by the gravity of what he was about to do. Tears pricked his eyes, but he blinked them back. Then, with a deep breath, he turned the knob and flipped the switch. The deed was done.

The interior altitude alarm blared, shattering the silence. Panicked someone would hear it. He silenced it quickly, focusing on his breathing, counting each exhale to stay steady. Outside, rain lashed the windshield, obscuring his view. The wipers swung back and forth, futile against the downpour.

Roberts count down was accompanied by music. He must have thought music would calm his nerves and pass the time faster. Like music would make mass murder easier. "Everyone should be dead by now, it's safe to make the descent to 10,000," Roberts voiced instructed.

Minutes later four chimes sounded from the passenger cabin, piercing the tension. Evan's breath hitched. Impossible. His eyes darted to the control panel. Four more chimes. A surge of dread clenched his gut. A flight attendant. Someone had survived.

Pounding erupted on the cockpit door, frantic and desperate. Evan's heart raced as he set the plane on autopilot and rose to peer through the small peephole. There she was, her yellow oxygen mask clinging to her face, her eyes wide with fear.

"I can see you!" she shouted; her voice muffled through the door. "Are you okay? They're dead. I think they're all dead."

Evan's mind whirled. She wasn't supposed to be here. She was a complication, a witness. If she made it out, everything would fall apart. His gaze fell on the crash ax mounted beside the door, cold metal gleaming ominously.

For a moment, he froze. He could lock her out. Walk away. Leave her there. But she knew.

His hand wrapped around the ax handle, the cold metal biting into his palm. Anger surged—a twisted fury that she had survived while he had already damned them all. This was her fault. She shouldn't have been there.

For Abby. For Jen. He had no choice.

With a burst of adrenaline, he ripped open the door. The flight attendant's eyes widened in terror. For a heartbeat, they locked gazes. His grip tightened on the ax.

She backed away, panic flickering across her face. He swung, the ax glancing off the oxygen tank she used to shield herself. Her scream tore through the cockpit, a sound filled with raw fear as she tried to turn, seeking escape. There was nowhere to go.

"Stop!" she begged, but her voice barely registered. Evan was beyond hearing. He swung again, striking her head. Blood sprayed, warm and metallic, coating his face.

She collapsed, she was dead, but he couldn't stop. The fury consumed him, blinding him to everything else. Again and again, he brought the ax down, each blow severing another thread of his humanity.

When it was finally over, he stood over her mangled form, blood dripping from his hands. Everything felt distant, surreal. The ax slipped from his grasp, clattering to the floor.

The cockpit was silent now, save for the hum of the engines. Evan took a step back, wiping his face and hands on the galley curtain. The metallic tang of blood lingered on his lips, a grim reminder of what he'd become.

For a brief moment, the weight of everything crashed down—Lucas's death, the flight attendant's, the passengers. His stomach roiled, and he fought back the urge to vomit.

But there was no time for that. No time for guilt or regret. He had to finish this. He had to land the plane.

CHAPTER 18

THE GLOBAL TIMES

Mercenaries Expand Skillset to Include Remote Runway Construction

By Richard Blackwell

In a surprising shift of capabilities, private mercenary groups are increasingly being tapped for their expertise in building airstrips and runways in remote, hard-to-reach areas. Often working under extreme conditions, these specialized teams are now deploying sophisticated construction equipment and utilizing rapid-deployment techniques to establish makeshift runways in locations ranging from dense jungles to remote deserts.

El Diablo

Fordlândia, Brazil

El Diablo crushed his cigarette into the mud, then slipped it into his pocket—leave nothing behind. The mantra had once meant something, a remnant from a time when every mission was sharp, each move deliberate. Now, the stakes were high, but he felt a dull numbness. The thrill was gone, replaced by a creeping sense of doubt.

He touched his scar, running a rough thumb over the deep line under his beard. Not every problem has a simple solution, he reminded himself, feeling the faint tremor in his fingers. The scar was a reminder of lessons learned, of times when he'd fought for something that mattered.

Fifty yards ahead, a cluster of teenage soldiers from the Exército Brasileiro laughed, oblivious to the gravity of the moment. Barely more than kids, they had no idea what real violence looked like. Santiago's idea to use them had grated on him from the start. El Diablo scanned the rough line of trucks parked along the rutted street, doubt gnawing at him. Is this street even long enough for a 757?

He strained waiting to hear the whine of the plane overhead. Static-filled radio and the omnipresent hum of the jungle drowned out their banter. He decided to wake them up, get their attention. "Truck Alpha, respond," he barked in halting Portuguese.

"Truck Alpha, check," came the reply, barely audible through the static. The radios he was given to use for this mission was crap.

"Truck Beta?" Silence. He slammed the radio against his palm, his patience unraveling. Typical. Santiago's fancy office was stocked with every luxury, yet they were stuck with outdated equipment in the field.

Then he heard it—a high-pitched whine slicing through the heavy clouds. Here we go. The plane was coming in, but it was too high. His pulse quickened. This landing is going to be tight.

"Turn on the lights!" he shouted. The soldiers, lost in conversation, didn't react. His temper snapped.

El Diablo stormed toward the nearest one, yanking the radio from the kid's hands. "Las luces! Turn on the lights!" he barked, sharp in Spanish before switching to Portuguese. The boy flinched, scrambling to obey, his eyes wide with fear.

At last, the trucks' headlights flickered to life, cutting jagged lines through the rain and darkness. But it was too late—the plane's engines roared as the pilot aborted the landing, vanishing into the mist. El Diablo's fury boiled over. No control. No respect. He hurled the useless radio to the ground, watching it shatter.

"Turn them off," he ordered, his voice a deadly calm. The young soldier fumbled to obey, stealing nervous glances at him. The lights were to come on when the plane held a precise position to guide the pilot.

El Diablo stood alone, rain mingling with sweat on his face, staring into the thick darkness where the plane had disappeared. His hands still trembled—a fact that enraged him even more. He clenched his fists, steadying himself. You're losing it. Get a grip.

The silence was broken by the buzz of his cellphone. Santiago. The text was brief, clinical: Did the plane land?

"No. Missed the runway. Radio's out," he typed back, jaw tight.

The phone rang seconds later, Santiago's voice crackling through. "Are the lights off?"

El Diablo bit back his irritation, his voice clipped. "They're off. The plane wasn't lined up. Low cloud cover." He paused, then added, almost involuntarily, "This wasn't my plan."

A tense silence stretched over the line. "I know. Turn the lights back on when it returns," Santiago replied, his tone as detached as ever.

The casual command was the last straw. "Maybe if we had better equipment, we'd have control over this operation," El Diablo shot back, a rare edge in his tone.

Santiago's response was calm, dismissive. "Make do with what you have. That's what you're good at."

The line went dead, leaving El Diablo seething, gripping the phone so tightly his knuckles turned white. Santiago, safe in his dry tent, could issue commands without understanding the chaos on the ground. They'd known each other for forty years, since the orphanage, but Santiago had always been the calculating one, the one who kept his hands clean. El Diablo, he thought bitterly. He'd been given the nickname, the devil, because he was the one who fought, who protected.

He glanced back at the soldiers, now quiet, stealing glances at him as if afraid he'd snap again. Let them be afraid. Maybe they'll finally pay attention.

The faint whine of the plane cut through the rain once more. El Diablo took a steadying breath. The plane was coming in lower this time, lined up better. His anger settled into cold focus. This has to work.

"Stand by for lights," he called out in Spanish, correcting himself in Portuguese, his voice steady, controlled. The mission depended on him, even if everything around him was falling apart.

CHAPTER 19

AVIATION WEEKLY & TECHNOLOGY

Emergency Malfunction: The High-Stakes Race to Find a Runway

By Wess Anders

When an in-flight emergency malfunction strikes, pilots are thrust into a high-stakes race against time to locate a safe runway for an emergency landing. As tension rises, they must expertly navigate complex systems, maintain clear communication with air traffic control, and prioritize passenger safety, all while scanning for the nearest viable airport. This scenario highlights the critical importance of rigorous training and preparation. Recent incidents have showcased the heroic efforts of flight crews who, despite severe mechanical failures, skillfully identified and reached safe landing sites, averting disaster and saving countless lives.

Evan Wheeler

Brazilian Airspace

Evan's hands trembled, foreign and clumsy. The sensation barely registered—everything felt dulled, like he was moving underwater. He just had to land the plane, and it would be over, everything back to normal.

Stumbling back into the cockpit, he caught sight of the first officer, slumped across the controls, his weight pressing the plane into a slight, uncontrolled bank. Evan hesitated, staring at the lifeless body sprawled before him. He had to get him off the controls. He tried to lift him out of the seat. Why does he feel so heavy? The thought flickered before slipping away. Mechanically, he gripped the man's shoulders, hoisting the slackened form and securing it upright, with his belt. He re-engaged the autopilot with a sharp breath, hands slipping on the blood-streaked controls.

The cockpit was awash in dim, pulsing warnings. The plane was off course. He forced himself to focus, narrowing his vision to the instruments. Clouds stretched out below, thick and unyielding. Where's the runway? The question hung like a lifeline, tethering him to the task. He adjusted the altitude, searching desperately for a break in the mist.

Finally, through a thin veil of fog, he caught a glimpse of faint lights—runway lights. Relief flickered briefly, but his hands remained unsteady. He made a slow, banking turn, aligning for descent, only for the lights to vanish again, swallowed by the darkness. Panic prickled his spine, momentarily piercing the numbness. "What the . . .?" he muttered, gripping the yoke so tightly his knuckles blanched. He had to go around but at least he knew the general position of the runway.

The lights flashed back on, then flickered off, as if taunting him. The runway faded, leaving only the pitch-black jungle. Evan clenched his jaw, dropping altitude by instinct, his mind blank but for the overwhelming need to land. Please . . . just let me see it.

The lights returned. He seized the moment, deploying the landing gear, angling the nose, forcing the plane down through turbulence and fog. Impact jarred him—the wheels hit the ground with a bone-rattling force. "Jesus Christ!" The words were guttural, ripped from him involuntarily as the nose slammed down, the plane skidding and lurching forward. Trees loomed ahead, closer, closer—he yanked the throttles to full reverse, desperately willing the aircraft to stop.

Branches clawed at the windshield as the plane plunged into the jungle, finally grinding to a jarring halt. Silence followed, thick and stifling. Evan sat frozen, hands still clutching the controls, sweat mingling with the blood on his skin. Is it over? He could barely process it. The silence rang in his ears, deafening.

Then came the faint, rhythmic pounding. Distant voices reached him, muffled by the haze in his mind. Get up. The command was faint but insistent. He pushed himself up, unsteady, and stumbled down the aisle, past lifeless forms slumped in their seats and the girl, eyes fixed and empty. His stomach twisted, but his body moved of its own accord, autopilot guiding each step.

He reached the exit door and fumbled at the handle, his hands numb and unfamiliar. He knew how to open the door, but it seemed so foreign now. He followed the instruction detail placard on the door. The door burst open; the slide inflated a breakneck speed. Gunfire ripped through the air. Bullets tore into the cabin, shredding seats, corpses. Evan flinched, ducking instinctively. "Stop! Hold your fire!" The words sounded raw, barely his own, rasping through the thick air. Laughter responded, cold and mocking, and the shooting ceased.

A man appeared at the door, dressed in camouflage, his expression calm and assessing. Soldiers followed in his wake; weapons lowered but ready. "My name is El Diablo. I'm in charge of the ground operation." His tone was indifferent, as if this were routine. "Let's step away from the door, yes?" He motioned for the soldiers to begin deplaning the passengers.

Evan moved, numb and obedient, not noticing his measured steps over the girl. She lay still, blood pooling beneath her. *I did this*. The realization hovered, just out of reach, detached from feeling.

El Diablo crouched, briefly checking her pulse before standing, unfazed. "Good landing," he said coolly. "Now, you'll come with me. We'll take you to the hospital."

Evan's mouth felt dry. "The . . . hospital?" The word sounded foreign, almost absurd.

"It's also a hotel," El Diablo clarified with an air of indifference. "Where the doctor works. Do you have the phone Señor Alexander gave you?"

Evan nodded vaguely. "In the cockpit." Exhaustion pulled at him, dragging him down like an undertow.

"Retrieve it, along with anything else you need." El Diablo's voice was distant, a faint directive. Numbly, Evan obeyed, his movements slow and mechanical. He retrieved his suitcase, made his way to the waiting catering truck. He tried to avoid stepping on the bodies in a heap on the truck.

"Call Señor Robert," El Diablo commanded as he helped Evan off the truck.

The line connected with a single ring. "Is it done?" Robert's tone was impassive.

"Yes." Evan's voice barely registered. "My wife ... she'll get the liver?"

"She's in surgery. Five hours," Robert replied, cold and clinical.

"When ... when can I see her?" The words slipped out, barely audible.

"In three days. The army will find you, evacuate the bodies. Stick to the plan. You remember?"

"Yes." The response felt scripted, practiced. "I was checking my oxygen mask. When I woke up ... they were all dead."

"Good. And the last thing?"

"I destroy the phone," Evan said.

Robert's reply was swift and final. The line went dead.

Evan dropped the phone, smashing it into the ground. Then picked up the pieces throwing them into the jungle. *It's over.*

El Diablo handed him a small vial. "Take this once you're in your room. It will help you sleep."

Evan took the vial mechanically, his fingers closing around it. Climbing into the jeep, he barely registered the tremor in his hands. Everything around him blurred, fading into the edges of his vision. *I did this.* The thought whispered through his mind, as distant and detached as the world around him.

CHAPTER 20

MEDICAL PRACTICE JOURNAL

Doctors and the God Complex: A Growing Concern

By Dr. Shane Johnson

The "God complex"—a troubling attitude where some doctors perceive themselves as infallible due to their life-saving skills—is sparking concern within the medical community. While confidence is crucial in medicine, an inflated sense of superiority can lead to poor patient communication, a lack of collaboration in care, and a higher risk of medical errors. To combat this, medical institutions are increasingly focusing on fostering humility, empathy, and a commitment to continuous learning. The goal is to ensure that patient care remains the top priority, and that the well-being of patients is always at the forefront of medical practice.

Dr. José Santiago

Fordlândia, Brazil

A scream tore through the operating tent just as Santiago made his second incision. His hand froze, a flash of anger and dread clenching his chest. The glare of the floodlights bore down relentlessly, casting stark, clinical shadows over the blood-slicked floor. He watched, helpless, as a nurse lost her footing, the heart she'd been carrying skidding across the tarp covering the floor. Two interns scrambled after it, their wide, pale faces mirrored in the surgical lights.

"Not in the solution!" Santiago's voice cut through the commotion. "It's contaminated ice it now!" But he could feel dread coiling tighter within him. He wasn't used to this chaos. Years of precise, sterile procedure, all shattered by a single rushed order. Robert's fault, he thought bitterly. This whole mess—*his fault*.

The heat in the tent was suffocating, sweat trickling down Santiago's back, mixing with the humidity that hung thick in the air. His team wasn't equipped for this—not these students, pulled in like cannon fodder for Robert's ambition. Santiago's eyes locked on a young nurse whose hands shook as she gripped another organ, her face glistening with fear and perspiration in the relentless light. He stepped closer, his voice low but cold. "Drop it, and it's useless. Steady yourself."

From the corner of his eye, Santiago saw an intern falter, his face flushed, and in a moment, he collapsed, dropping to the floor. Santiago's patience finally broke. "Get him out of here!" he barked, his frustration spilling over.

The storm outside beat at the tent walls, the blood mixing with the water pooling at their feet. He needed to breathe, to clear his head. The heat was unbearable, and the air, thick with antiseptic and rot, was choking him. Crossing the tent, he yanked out his scalpel and slashed the canvas, creating an opening for ventilation. It offered barely any relief, but it was something. "Here," he snapped to a nearby nurse, thrusting the scalpel into her hand. "Cut more slits in the tent."

Outside, he forced himself through the mud toward Tent A. Bodies lay in heaps, stark in the harsh light, the lower layers submerged in muddy water. The rain poured in relentless sheets, plastering his hair to his forehead, but he welcomed it—a brief, biting reprieve from the swelter inside. As he entered, the stark reality hit him like a blow: soldiers tossed in more bodies, the heaps of limbs and torsos growing higher, bleeding into the swamp beneath them.

"Stop!" he shouted; voice hoarse. He repeated himself in Portuguese, raising a hand. "No more bodies!" The soldiers paused, exchanging glances before backing off, visibly uncertain.

Raking a hand through his wet hair, Santiago dug out his phone, hands slick with rain and sweat. El Diablo, he thought, grinding his teeth as he dialed. "Where are you?" he demanded when the line clicked.

"El Diablo here. I'm at the plane, overseeing the cargo."

Santiago's grip tightened on the phone. "Get back here," he hissed. "Your men have dumped more than we can handle. We're knee-deep in corpses, and the tent is flooding."

Santiago ended the call, his blood pressure pounding in his temples. This wasn't how it was supposed to go. He thought of the sterile operating rooms, the symphony of coordinated hands, the clean efficiency that had once defined his work. All replaced by a madhouse—a bloody, chaotic spectacle under an unrelenting sky.

As he trudged back, his thoughts sharpened. This was not the revolution he had envisioned, not the way to usher in his grand vision of medicine. He had let Robert push him, coax him, into compromising every principle he once held sacred. Years of surgical precision and self-sacrifice, wasted here in a forgotten jungle, lost to the same raw, elemental mess he'd once escaped.

He glanced at the rows of organs, watching his team as they scrambled, hands slick and slippery, faces taut with panic. A nurse's hand slipped, an organ nearly dropping before she steadied it. His stomach clenched. Every failure felt like a visceral blow, yet he knew it wasn't entirely their fault. They were simply unprepared, forced into this brutal initiation by his own acquiescence.

Stepping outside, the rain felt colder, harsher. He dialed Robert, each ring amplifying his fury until the line clicked.

"José. How are things progressing?"

"Progressing?" Santiago's voice cracked; his tone barely controlled. "We're losing organs, Robert. You forced this pace, and we're hemorrhaging the very things we need." His voice held a bitterness that felt foreign to him, a man who once believed in reasoned discussions, not accusations.

Robert's voice was maddeningly calm. "José, I understand your frustration, but there was no choice. The pilot was ready. This was our only window."

Santiago's grip on the phone tightened, his pulse thrumming in his temple. He spoke through clenched teeth. "If we can't preserve the organs, this entire endeavor is for nothing. You never listen, Robert. You see only your ends, never the cost." Blood-soaked rain pooled around his feet, lapping at his boots, yet he stood rooted, glaring at the indifferent sky as if it, too, were complicit in this tragedy.

Robert's reply was almost condescending. "There was no other way, José. We had to act now, or we'd have lost everything."

Santiago's breath was shallow, his fury dangerously close to breaking through. He could feel the divide—the chasm that had always existed between them, widening with every syllable from Robert's mouth.

"Have you considered that you're losing everything now?" he managed, his voice a cold whisper before he disconnected. He let the phone drop back into his pocket, his head tipping back as he took in the sheets of rain.

This wasn't the legacy he wanted. He had built his career on saving lives, pushing medicine beyond its limits for the sake of progress. Now, he was drowning in blood and mud, his ideals twisted into something unrecognizable. He closed his eyes, letting the rain wash over him, trying to strip away the layers of regret and compromise that weighed on him.

For the first time, he wondered if all he had built was doomed from the start—if his grand vision had only ever been a mirage, shattered by the harsh, unyielding realities he had once thought himself above.

CHAPTER 21

MERCENARY MONTHLY
Behind the Shadows
By Gus Slemski

Living in the shadows, mercenaries face a world of constant danger and secrecy. These soldiers-for-hire navigate some of the most volatile regions on the globe, often accepting high-risk missions from private clients or governments. The daily life of a mercenary involves relentless training, meticulous strategic planning, and the execution of operations that span from security assignments to direct combat. While the financial rewards can be substantial, the job is steeped in ethical challenges and the perpetual risk of injury or death. In this shadowy profession, where loyalty can be bought, survival hinges on a mercenary's skill, discretion, and ability to adapt to ever-changing threats.

El Diablo

Fordlândia, Brazil

El Diablo steadied himself as the truck lurched along the muddy road, gripping the woman's lifeless body tightly. Her head, wrapped in an airplane blanket to contain the mangled skull, felt unsettlingly fragile in his hands. When the truck jolted to a stop, he braced himself against the wall, tightening his grip. Handling the dead was routine for him—he'd seen countless bodies in countless places. But this was different. These weren't soldiers or enemies. They were civilians, discarded in someone else's game. He looked down at her covered face, the faint outline haunting him. This isn't a battlefield. This isn't justice. It's slaughter.

Stepping out of the truck and into the tented area, El Diablo paused, taken aback by the scene before him. Bodies were stacked haphazardly, lying in puddles of rainwater and mud and bodily fluids. Workers moved in robotic efficiency, stripping corpses, tagging them, and bagging belongings without so much as a flicker of emotion. Each corpse felt like a life betrayed. The dead deserve better.

Pushing through the flap of the operating tent, he was hit by the harsh smell of chemicals. Workers scrambled around tables, carrying organs like grim trophies. He'd seen battlefields and makeshift hospitals, but nothing as bleak as this.

Is this what we've become?

He spotted Santiago in the center, drenched in sweat and barking orders, his hand passing an organ to a nurse who nearly slipped in the muck. Navigating the chaos, El Diablo forced his way through, his boots sticking to the ground with each step.

"José!" he called, his voice slicing through the din.

Santiago's head snapped up, irritation flashing across his face. "Where the hell have you been? Tent A and Tent C are falling apart!"

Ignoring the question, El Diablo gently laid the flight attendant's body on an empty gurney. Unwrapping the blanket from her head, he revealed the crushed skull, the grotesque injury made more jarring by the sterile lights.

"We've got a problem," he said quietly.

Santiago leaned over, his gaze narrowing as he examined the wounds. "What now?"

"The pilot did this," El Diablo murmured. "She was alive when he found her. He's in shock. Says he can't explain it."

Santiago's expression hardened, his attention shifting back to the organ tables. "I'll deal with it later. Get her to the freezer. And clean up the rest—this chaos is costing us."

El Diablo felt a surge of anger at Santiago's indifference but kept his face neutral. Rewrapping what was left of the woman's head, he signaled for it to be taken away. Without another word to Santiago, he left the tent, heading toward Tent A, where the frenzy had only intensified.

The noise hit him first—panicked shouts, the clang of metal against metal, the relentless hum of machinery. The mixed liquids on the ground, turned each step into a slippery challenge. He paused at the entrance, watching as workers stumbled over each other, their faces etched with fear and exhaustion.

"Slow down!" he called; his voice steady but with a gentleness he rarely used. "One task at a time. Breathe."

At first, no one seemed to hear him. The chaos continued unabated. For a moment, he felt the familiar sting of helplessness. *Is any of this even worth it?* He clenched his fists, forcing the thought aside. He couldn't let the mission consume him. Not completely.

He stepped forward, catching the arm of a young worker struggling to push a gurney that had snagged on something. "Easy," El Diablo said, his hand firm but reassuring. "There's no need to rush. They deserve dignity."

The worker looked up, blinking through a haze of panic. Something in El Diablo's voice seemed to reach him, his movements slowing as he nodded. One by one, El Diablo moved through the tent, his touch a quiet reminder to each frenzied worker. Gradually, the manic energy began to subside, replaced by a slower, more deliberate pace.

The noise dimmed to a murmur, the once-chaotic scene transforming into something more human. For the first time that night, the fear in their eyes softened, replaced by a shared understanding—these were lives, not just bodies.

El Diablo stood at the center, observing as the workers moved with newfound care. The anger still simmered within him, a steady burn he couldn't extinguish, but he held it back, channeling it into this small sense of order. This wasn't what he had signed up for. None of this was. Yet, in this moment, he felt a flicker of purpose.

What are we really doing here?

The question lingered, heavy in his mind. This wasn't the life he'd envisioned—stacking bodies, calming terrified workers, facilitating a harvest of human lives. He thought of Santiago's cold efficiency, the way he'd dismissed the flight attendant as just another part of the operation. They were supposed to be partners in changing the world, but now? They were just pawns, pieces on the American's board.

As the tent settled into silence, El Diablo's resolve hardened. He had spent his life being the weapon, the executor of others' wills, believing it was for a cause he could trust. But now, he wasn't sure if that cause even existed. Perhaps Santiago had crossed a line that could never be uncrossed, and by following, so had he.

He looked around at the still bodies, each one a testament to choices made far from here, decisions by men like Robert, untouched by the blood and mud.

In this moment, amid the silence and order he had created, El Diablo knew one thing with cold clarity: if he walked away from this mission, from Santiago, he would leave behind more than bodies—he would be leaving behind what was left of his own humanity.

And maybe, just maybe, it was time to walk away.

CHAPTER 22

THE NEW YORK MAG – PAGE SEVEN

LEVI'S GOT A NEW GIG: FROM FALLEN INTERNATIONAL STAR TO LOCAL NEWS GUY

Disgraced news correspondent Levi Mathews is making a comeback as the midnight anchor for News12 Edison in New Jersey. After a high-profile scandal derailed his career, Mathews is now reporting to a much smaller audience of night owls and insomniacs.

Sources say Mathews is adjusting to his new role, grateful for the chance to rebuild his career. While it's a far cry from his glory days, he remains determined to make the most of this opportunity.

Stay tuned to Page Six for more on Levi Mathews' journey back into the news world.

Levi Mathews

The News 12 Studio, Edison, New Jersey

"Can you give the news with a little more enthusiasm? Our viewers are already half asleep; they don't need your help," the producer's voice was sharp, a reminder of Levi's strained place here. He was used to the jabs but felt them sinking deeper lately, his leg bouncing restlessly under the desk.

The stale studio air weighed on him, tinged with the metallic bitterness of cold coffee. He took a sip, grimacing as it went down. Each time he spoke, his words felt hollow, and today, he found himself asking into the empty space, *"how long have I been here, anyway?"*

"Three weeks," a bored voice crackled from the control room. Levi could almost feel the indifference seep through his earpiece.

He glanced at his notes, flipping through them. "A potluck dinner segment?" he muttered to himself, half-smiling with bitter disbelief. "This is what my career has come to?"

The producer's voice cut in, loud and nasal. "Okay, Levi, reel it in. You're on in forty-five seconds. And remember, your ratings aren't exactly stellar."

Levi swallowed, glancing at the control room window. His tie felt tight around his neck, almost like a noose. "I'm just stating the obvious," he muttered, voice barely above a whisper, not really caring if anyone heard.

"Ten, nine . . ."

"Fuck this," Levi whispered to himself, his heart not in it. But as the countdown hit three, he forced the old plastic smile back onto his face. "Now, for the news on the hour," he intoned, his voice devoid of life. "Breaking news from the Associated Press: The Brazilian government has lost contact with WWA Flight 987 approximately two hours ago over Para in the Brazilian rainforest."

The words hit like a sucker punch, chilling his blood. He froze, the world around him shrinking to a pinprick. Stephanie's flight. No, it can't be.

His heart raced, pounding so hard he could barely hear the control room's frantic chatter. His hand instinctively reached for his phone, his fingers trembling as he scrolled to her flight details. 987. The red light of the camera blinked at him, a relentless reminder he was live, but he didn't care.

The producer's voice crackled in his ear. "Levi! Stay on script!"

Ignoring him, Levi ripped off his earpiece and threw down his mic. His pulse hammered in his ears, drowning out everything else as he dialed Steph's number. Voicemail. "Hi, honey. It's Levi. Call me back as soon as you get this." His voice cracked, raw fear bleeding through.

"What is he doing?" Muffled yelling came through the glass of the control room. "Go to a commercial."

Behind him, the studio team stared, slack-jawed, as he stood and began pacing, desperately seeking something solid. The floor beneath his feet grounded him, but just barely. He could feel his world teetering, about to topple over the edge.

The producer was now in front of him, "What are you doing? You're live. God dammit, what's wrong with you!"

"My fiancée is on that flight!" Levi's voice broke, raw and desperate. The producer's eyes widened, softening for a flicker of a second before hardening again.

"Planes go off radar all the time. Now, get it together and do your job," the producer snapped, his mask of indifference slipping back on, but Levi saw the hint of discomfort in his eyes.

"You're not listening. My fiancée is on that flight. She's not 'off radar.' She's missing," Levi whispered, his voice filled with disbelief. He couldn't process it. It felt too big, too immediate. Is this really happening? He brought NCC on his phone. Large letters: "Breaking News: Flight 987 is missing over the Brazilian Amazon."

The producer's expression hardened. "Get back on the air!"

Levi turned his phone screen toward the producer. "The flight is missing! You're not hearing me!"

Levi stared after him for a moment, the weight of the decision settling on him. "I have to go," he muttered, his voice gaining strength as he turned and strode out of the studio.

"You can't go! Get back here!"

The morning air was cold and biting as he stepped outside. Levi barely noticed it as he climbed into his car, fingers fumbling with the ignition. His knuckles were white against the steering wheel as he sped through empty streets, NCC's crackling coverage filling the silence.

His mind spun with the possibility. This can't be her flight. He barely noticed the red lights he ran, barely felt the bite of his nails digging into his palm. It felt like he was drowning in his own heartbeat, each thump louder than the last.

When he reached the Pratts' gated community, he fumbled for their name, his voice hoarse. The guard's polite detachment only sharpened his sense of urgency.

He barely registered the familiar sight of the Pratts' house as he parked. The house blazed with light, every window casting an eerie glow against the dark sky. Levi's heart pounded in his chest as he stepped out of the car, his mind reeling with dread.

Before he could reach the door, it swung open, revealing Steven Pratt, his face ashen, his robe barely fastened. His eyes met Levi's, a raw desperation in them that Levi had never seen before. Steven's voice was rough, strained. "You're here, good, good," he said, gripping Levi's shoulder tightly, his hand trembling.

"I didn't know where else to go," Levi said. The cold tension between them melted away, replaced by a shared, unspeakable dread.

CHAPTER 23

NCC

BREAKING NEWS * BREAKING NEWS * BREAKING NEWS *

Missing Jet: Flight 987 Disappears Over Brazil

Kassie Cambell, Anchor

"We have breaking news to report. Worldwide Airlines Flight 987 has been reported as missing over Brazil. The passenger jet, operated by Worldwide Airlines (WWA), was in route from New York's JFK airport to São Paulo, Brazil, when it lost contact with air traffic control. The aircraft's last known position was somewhere over the dense Brazilian rainforest. Search and rescue operations have been launched. Families of the passengers and crew are anxiously awaiting news, as the world watches and hopes for a safe resolution to this alarming situation. Stay tuned to NCC for the latest updates on this developing story."

Evan Wheeler

Fordlândia, Brazil

The high-pitched whine cut through the roar of the jet engines. Evan's eyes dropped to the woman beneath him, sprawled on the first-class floor, his hands still clamped around her neck. Her scream pierced through him, sharp and grating. But it wasn't an engine sound—it was her.

Evan jolted awake, drenched in sweat, his heart pounding against his ribcage. His breath came in ragged gasps, chest heaving as he fought to pull himself out of the nightmare's grip. For a few disorienting moments, he couldn't tell where he was. The memory of her scream echoed in his mind, but it blurred with fragments of other sounds—muffled cries, the scrape of metal, his own voice yelling. *What did I do?* His mind scrambled, unable to piece together the details.

He sat up slowly, the weight of exhaustion pressing him down as if gravity had doubled. His body ached, a bone-deep fatigue that went beyond sleeplessness. He looked around, trying to remember how he'd gotten here, but the events of the previous hours were a chaotic mess. Images of blood-stained uniforms, the pilot's yoke, and a vague sensation of falling flickered through his mind. It all felt like pieces of a puzzle he couldn't fit together.

His crumpled uniform shirt lay on the floor, stained with blood, the sight of it pulling him into the cold reality of what he'd done. He tried to stand, but his legs wobbled, muscles drained of strength, as though he'd been carrying an invisible weight all night. Every movement was sluggish, like his body was reluctant to follow his commands.

The buzz of his phone cut through the fog of his thoughts, jolting him back to the present. He picked it up with trembling hands, struggling to focus on the screen. His father-in-law's name flashed across it.

"Where are you?" Jack's voice was thick with fury, each word biting through Evan's hazy awareness.

Evan swallowed, the dryness in his throat making it difficult to speak. "I . . . I'm in São Paulo. How's Abby?"

"You'd know if you hadn't skipped town and left her to die!" Jack's words hit like a slap. "They found a liver for Abby, in case you even care."

Evan blinked, struggling to process the news. His pulse quickened. "They found a liver. When? How?"

"They've been trying to reach you all night. The hospital called at 10:00 p.m. The liver got stuck in customs for hours. We paid $12,000 to get it through. We're waiting for the doctor now."

Evan's head spun, the words blurring together. He struggled to keep up, his mind sluggish as if it were wading through mud. His grip tightened around the phone. "When does the surgery start?"

"No idea," Jack's tone was icy. "You should've been here, Evan. Instead, you ran off. Is there anything you want to tell me?"

"No," Evan muttered, his voice barely above a whisper. "I'll try to get an earlier flight back."

"Just get back here. And get your shit together."

The line went dead, the silence pressing down on him. He dropped the phone onto the bed, his hands still shaking. His eyes fell to the stained shirt on the floor, bile rising in his throat as the memory of those final moments flashed briefly. He remembered hands clenching, the scrape of the cockpit door . . . and then nothing. His stomach churned. How much had he forgotten? What else had he done?

He barely noticed his surroundings as he wandered, a dull throb behind his eyes. His legs felt leaden, each step an effort as he made his way to the lobby, hoping for some answer, some clarity. By the time he reached the front desk, the exhaustion had sunk deep into his bones.

The front desk clerk looked up, recognizing him immediately. "May I help you, Captain Wheeler?"

"Yes," Evan said, his voice barely steady. "I need to contact Robert Alexander."

The clerk's brow furrowed. "I don't believe we have a guest by that name."

"He's . . . an owner, I think," Evan stammered. "Can you help me reach him?"

The clerk nodded, offering a polite smile. "Perhaps Dr. Santiago could help. He's busy, but he may know how to reach Mr. Alexander."

Back in his room, he collapsed onto the bed, every muscle aching as he tried to make sense of the past hours. The fatigue was relentless, pulling him down, blurring his thoughts. For a long while, he just lay there, trying to remember details that slipped further with each passing second.

CHAPTER 24

NCC

Breaking News * Breaking News * Breaking News

Still Missing: Flight 987 Disappears Over Brazil

Kassie Cambell, Anchor

"Worldwide Airlines Flight 987 has disappeared in route from Caracas, Venezuela, to São Paulo, Brazil. The Boeing 757 passenger jet, carrying 188 passengers and crew, lost contact with air traffic control in the early hours of the morning. As search and rescue operations are launched in the Amazon Rainforest, aviation experts and authorities are scrambling to understand what led to the sudden disappearance. Families of those on board are anxiously awaiting news, while the global community watches in shock and hopes for answers. We are waiting for the press conference at Worldwide Airlines, which could start at any minute. Stay with NCC for the latest development, as we get them, on this unfolding crisis."

Robert Alexander

War Room, Undisclosed Location

The clock struck the hour, and every screen in the war room flickered with a stark, chilling message: WWA Flight 987 Missing. NCC's bold red banner flashed like an alarm, filling the room with a heavy, pulsing tension. Robert's gaze locked onto the screen, his face a mask of calm authority, though a subtle tightness around his eyes betrayed the storm brewing inside.

"Turn that one up," he commanded, his voice a sharp slice through the murmurs of the room.

The makeup artist standing beside him jolted at his tone, hastily backing away, her hands hovering nervously as if unsure what to do next. Robert grabbed a tissue, wiping away the thick layer of powder she had applied, the heavy mask feeling stifling on his skin. He scrutinized his reflection in the mirror, noting the faint lines of strain creeping around his eyes. Not now, he thought, forcing a deep, steady breath. *Not in front of them.*

The room buzzed with low murmurs and the rhythmic hum of computers, the air thick with the sterile scent of electronics and faint traces of stale coffee. Around the long, sleek conference table, departments huddled like tactical teams, faces set in concentration, their conversations muted but intense.

"Jessica!" Robert's voice sliced through the noise, drawing the gaze of the entire room.

A young woman in a sharply tailored suit hurried over, her heels clicking crisply on the tiled floor. "Yes, Sir?" Her cheeks flushed as she stopped beside him, clutching a clipboard tightly, knuckles white against the polished surface.

"Is the media all here? Who's missing?" His gaze darted across the room, then zeroed in on her, sharp and unyielding.

Jessica's eyes skimmed her notes, a faint tremor in her fingers as she flipped through the pages. "Everyone except some foreign press and the Brazilian agency," she replied, her voice betraying a hint of nervousness under his scrutiny. "Agencia Brazil isn't here yet. Should we wait?"

"No." His tone was final, unyielding, his fingers tapping a rhythmic beat on the edge of the clipboard she held. He glanced back at the screen, the red banner flashing like a countdown in his mind. "The NTSB?"

"They're all in place," she confirmed, trying to keep her voice steady amid the pressure that seemed to press down from every corner of the room.

His gaze narrowed. "Where's the other lady—the one who's pregnant?" he demanded, a flicker of irritation breaking through his usually composed facade.

"She's on maternity leave," Jessica replied quickly. "Dana's covering for her."

Robert's lips pressed into a thin line. A new face, right now. Just what we need. He gestured curtly for Jessica to bring her in.

Dana approached moments later, the click of her heels softer, hesitant, her eyes darting nervously around the room as if seeking reassurance. She stopped before Robert, her fingers gripping the edges of her notebook, knuckles pale against the dark leather. "Mr. Alexander, you wanted to see me?"

Robert's gaze bore into her, his voice low and deliberate. "You need to be ready," he said, each word dropping like a stone in the silence. He could see the slight quiver in her stance, the way her breathing quickened just a fraction. "Has anyone briefed you on your role?"

She nodded, though the rapid motion betrayed her uncertainty.

"You're in charge of the families' information control," he continued, his tone cutting through any veneer of comfort. "Do not give them anything that hasn't been approved by this room. Understand?" He leaned in, his presence pressing, dominating. "One mistake, and we lose millions."

Dana's throat bobbed as she swallowed, her voice barely more than a whisper. "Yes, Sir."

His eyes narrowed, watching her carefully, gauging every micro-expression. "The family room is being monitored. Every word you say is recorded. Follow the script exactly—no deviations. It's also very important that the family members watch the news brief. We all need to be on the same page." He let the words hang in the air, the weight of them settling heavily on her shoulders. "And make sure every family member signs a nondisclosure agreement before they leave."

"Yes, Sir," she whispered, her grip tightening on her notebook as though it were a lifeline.

He dismissed her with a sharp wave, watching her retreating figure. The soft click of her heels was drowned out by the low hum of conversations resuming, but Robert could feel the tension creeping back into the room like a living thing. His own pulse pounded in his ears, a steady reminder that even his carefully controlled world was vulnerable.

Just then, Jessica returned, a hesitant look in her eyes. "Sir, there's . . . there's one more thing."

"What is it?" His voice was icy, the impatience barely contained.

Jessica shifted, clearly uncomfortable. "There are rumors circulating . . . speculations about the delay in notifying the families. It's making people . . . uneasy."

Robert's jaw clenched. Of course, there were always whispers, especially when things didn't go according to plan. He forced himself to smile, though it felt like a foreign motion. "Jessica," he said, his tone smooth, almost comforting. "People thrive on speculation. Let them have their stories. We control the narrative."

Jessica nodded, though he could see the flicker of doubt in her eyes. She hesitated, then stepped back, leaving him alone in the pulsing tension of the room.

Robert's gaze drifted back to the screen. The red banner continued to flash, an incessant reminder of the growing pressure. This was more than a crisis; it was a test of his control, his ability to bend reality to his will. His fingers tightened around the edges of the clipboard, his mind already spinning the next steps, the next cover story.

But deep in the recesses of his mind, a single, unwelcome thought.

CHAPTER 25

*****BREAKING NEWS*****

NCC

Breaking News * Breaking News * Breaking News

Airline Assists Grieving Families Amid Flight 987 Mystery

Walt Booker, Anchor

"Good evening, I'm Walt Booker, and you're in the Situation Room. Tonight, as the investigation into the disappearance of Flight 987 continues, attention has turned to the families of the passengers, enduring an agonizing wait for answers.

Worldwide Airlines has announced measures to support the families, including grief counselors, temporary housing near its headquarters, and daily briefings on the investigation. Despite these efforts, frustration is mounting, as the airline has yet to make the manifest public.

In Sao Paulo, where the plane was due to land twelve hours ago, families huddle together in waiting areas, many clutching photos of loved ones. In New York, only a handful of relatives have gathered. One distraught family member told NCC, 'We just want to know what happened. Why don't we have answers yet?'

With growing calls for accountability, Worldwide Airlines has vowed to spare no resources in assisting the investigation and grieving families. We'll bring you updates on this developing story. Stay with NCC. We now go to Worldwide Headquarters for a briefing from the airline."

Dana Billings

Worldwide Airline Briefing Room, New York, New York

Dana splashed cold water on her face, letting the icy droplets hit her skin like a wake-up call. She gripped the edges of the sink, staring into her own reflection. Her tear-streaked face, red-rimmed eyes, and barely masked anxiety stared back. You have to hold it together. They're counting on you, she reminded herself, forcing her breathing to slow. With a steadying sigh, she dabbed at her eyes and reapplied her lipstick, each careful stroke restoring a sense of control.

She walked back into the hallway, holding her ID badge a little tighter as she passed the security guard outside the conference room. Stepping inside, the room's freezing air hit her. The lack of windows, the fluorescent lights, and the pitiful snack table in the corner did little to ease her and the families' obvious distress. It was a sterile space for delivering life-shattering news, and she could feel the weight of it pressing on her.

Dana glanced down at the packet in her hand, a stark reminder of the task ahead. There should be nine people, one was still missing. *Only nine family members on a full plane, there should be so much more.* They're here for answers, she thought. And I need to be the one who gives them something to hold on to.

As she moved toward the podium, her gaze swept over the families seated before her. Levi Mathews, face tight with worry, sat beside an older couple, likely his fiancée's parents. Their eyes were fixed on Dana, a mix of hope and fear etched deeply into their faces. They've been here for hours, waiting for any word, she realized, her heart clenching.

CeCe, a gate agent whose husband was the first officer, sat alone. Her eyes darted around the room, never settling, as if she could somehow anchor herself by absorbing every detail. The tissue twisted in her hands was crumpled and torn.

Paulo, an older man, sat in silence, his brother's fate lay waiting. Even though he didn't understand the language, his posture—the hunch of his shoulders, his clasped hands—told her he understood enough. His fear was palpable, yet his face remained blank, like he was waiting for the world to make sense again.

Three young women, a little younger than Dana, huddled together, whispering in hushed tones. They looked fragile, glancing at each other with pleading eyes, as if drawing strength from each other for news they weren't prepared to face. They were exchange students, roommates. The one girl missing was the one going home for a wedding. The last participant was Billy Meyers, her wife and two small children most likely on the way to see family.

Now, every eye in the room was on her, heavy with expectation and desperation. Dana's pulse quickened, her heartbeat loud in her ears, but she forced herself to exhale slowly, grounding herself. The conversation she had with her mother cemented her to the earth. *They need you to be steady. They need you to be strong,* her mother had said. She glammed onto the words her mother had drilled into her.

As she reached the podium, she gripped its edges firmly, feeling the solidity beneath her hands. She straightened her shoulders and let her gaze travel around the room, meeting the eyes of each person. The thin, cold air felt like it barely filled her lungs, but she knew she couldn't let it show. Not now.

Her thoughts steadied. This isn't about you, Dana. It's about them. Give them something—anything—to hold on to. Wisdom her mother shared was the only thing holding her up.

With one last deep breath, Dana began. "Good afternoon. My name is Dana Billings, and I'm here to ensure you are kept informed and supported. I understand that you're going through something unimaginable, and while I can't provide the answers you seek just yet, please know that we're doing everything in our power to bring you the latest information." Her voice was calm, carrying a quiet strength. She knew there was nothing she could say that would ease their worries, but they needed her to be a lifeline, and she was determined to be exactly that.

CHAPTER 26

******BREAKING NEWS*****

NCC

Rumors Swirl About Brazil Restricting Access to Flight 987 Search Zone

Jason Sawyer, Anchor

"Good evening, I'm Jason Sawyer, and you're in the Situation Room. We have breaking developments regarding the search for Flight 987. Unconfirmed reports are circulating that Brazil may have closed its borders to foreign assistance in the ongoing efforts to locate the missing aircraft.

The Brazilian government has yet to release an official statement addressing these rumors. If true, such restrictions could severely limit the involvement of international teams, including the US National Transportation Safety Board and other global aviation agencies.

Sources close to the investigation have expressed concerns about the challenges of conducting a comprehensive search in the dense Amazon rainforest without international collaboration. Critics argue that this could delay critical progress in uncovering what happened to Flight 987, which disappeared with 188 passengers and crew aboard.

We go now to Worldwide Airlines headquarters for a press conference."

Robert Alexander III
Worldwide Airlines, Press Room, New York, New York

Jessica stepped up to the podium, her heart hammering in her chest. She gripped the edges tightly, hoping no one noticed the slight tremor in her hands. Her body felt like it might float away. The lights overhead were too bright, the air too thick and humid from the overcrowded space. She glanced back at Robert.

He stood behind her, his posture perfect, his expression unreadable. The sight of him steadied her. Robert always knew how to take control, how to fill a room with his presence. Even now, in the middle of this crisis, he looked completely unshaken. She drew strength from that, from him, though she knew she shouldn't rely on him so much. It was dangerous—for a lot of reasons.

"Good morning, ladies and gentlemen," she began, her voice even. "My name is Jessica Brock, PR director for Worldwide Airlines. I'll be providing a brief update before our CEO, Robert Alexander, addresses you."

She outlined the facts: Flight 987, a Boeing 757 from JFK to São Paulo, had disappeared over the Brazilian rainforest at 2:00 a.m., carrying 188 passengers, three pilots, and a crew of five. The words felt hollow as she spoke to them, as if they belonged to someone else. But she delivered them with the calm professionalism Robert expected of her.

Jessica stepped aside, relieved, as Robert moved to the podium with the same calm authority, she'd seen him wield countless times. Her breath caught slightly as she watched him. He was magnetic—always had been. She had no regrets of their tryst, he assured her that no one would find out, her husband would never know the passion she felt when she was with him. The room shifted immediately, the hum of reporters quieting under his commanding presence.

"Good afternoon. I want to start by saying we are doing everything in our power to locate the missing aircraft," Robert said, his voice deep and steady. Jessica marveled at how he made every word sound like the undeniable truth.

"The rainforest has many remote landing strips," he continued. "We ask that speculation about a crash be avoided at this time. We remain focused on finding Flight 987 and will provide updates as they become available."

She found herself watching him too closely, catching the way his hand rested on the podium, the measured cadence of his words. He was flawless. Even with the weight of 188 lives and a room full of cameras pressing down on him, he didn't falter.

"I'll let the experts provide the specifics regarding Flight 987. This is the COO of Worldwide Airlines, Jeffery Teller," Robert said, stepping back with a nod.

Jeffery approached the podium, his crisp voice cutting through the room. "The Brazilian government is leading the search and has restricted foreign involvement. We are in active negotiations to gain access to the search area where they are looking. But as of right now no one has been allowed to help in the response."

Jessica stiffened at his words. No one had told her the Brazilians had cut off foreign help. *When did that happen? How had she missed it?* She glanced at Robert, who stood rigid and unfazed. The press loudly shifted in their seats. Across the room, a reporter adjusted her glasses and scribbled furiously in her notebook. Another leaned forward, his pen poised mid-air as murmurs to rippled through the crowd.

Marsha Beamer, from the NTSB, took the podium next. Adjusting her glasses with shaky hands, her voice was measured but brittle. "We have prepared investigation teams, pending permission to deploy," Marsha said, her voice cracking slightly. "Documentation about the aircraft, crew, and passengers has been provided. There was a minor pressurization issue three weeks ago, but it was resolved per standard procedures. At this time, there is no evidence that it contributed to the current situation. We are considering all possibilities."

The press lit up as Marsha stepped back, instinctively knowing they would get their questions answered. Their voices loud trying to get the attention of Jessica as she resumed the meeting coordinator. "We will take questions now."

"Mr. Alexander," a reporter called, her voice cutting through the noise. "Has the airline considered the possibility that NARC, the Brazilian terrorist group, could have taken the plane down?"

Jessica saw it—the slight tightening of Robert's jaw, the subtle tension that flickered through his expression. For the first time, he hesitated. It was brief, a fraction of a second, but she noticed.

"There is no evidence to support that theory," he said, his tone even, but his fingers gripped the podium a little tighter. "Our focus remains on the mechanical aspects and coordinating with the Brazilian government to expand the search. Speculation about terrorism is premature and unproductive."

Another reporter pressed him. "But doesn't NARC operate near the region where the plane disappeared? Have there been any communications from the group?"

Jessica's stomach knotted as she watched him. His hand brushed the edge of his suit jacket, a subtle habit she recognized as frustration.

"I'll reiterate—there is no evidence at this time to suggest terrorist involvement. Our priority is finding the plane and providing answers to the families. We will not engage in baseless speculation."

After several more questions Robert ended the conference with a firm, "This is all we have at this time. We will hold another news briefing as soon as new information comes in. Thank you." With deliberate steps, he walked out of the room causing a burst of energetic questions to follow after him.

Jessica exhaled quietly, relieved but still on edge. How had she not known about the Brazilians' decision to close their borders? Jeffery should have told her.

She stepped to the podium one last time. "We'll let you know when the next news brief will be," she said, her voice steady but tight.

Robert had already left the room. Jessica followed a few paces behind, her pulse quickening as she caught the faintest glance he threw her way. It was fleeting, unreadable to anyone but her, but it tightened her chest all the same. She swallowed hard, anger simmering beneath her nerves. Next time, she thought, I'll be ready.

CHAPTER 27

NCC

Could a Terrorist Group Have Taken Down Flight 987?

Amy Cohen, Anchor

"Good evening, I'm Walt Booker with NCC. We have new and potentially alarming information around the disappearance of Worldwide Airlines Flight 987 over the Amazon rainforest. Authorities say they are not ruling out the possibility of a terrorist action as the cause behind the sudden loss of contact with the aircraft.

The flight, which was en route from Caracas, Venezuela, to São Paulo, Brazil, has 188 passengers and crew. Sources within the investigation have revealed that intelligence agencies are examining if there are any potential links to extremist groups operating in the region.

The Brazilian government, which is now essentially blocking foreign investigators from participating in the probe, has yet to comment on these new developments. Families of those on board are anxiously awaiting answers, as the world watches and hopes for good news in this distressing situation.

Stay with NCC for the latest updates on this developing story."

Dana Billings

Worldwide Airlines, Family Support Center, New York, New York

Dana's focus snapped to a commotion in the hallway. The door flew open, and a security guard—a heavyset woman—struggled to support the limp body of a woman. "She fainted. Help me sit her down on a chair."

The room stirred as families and staff quickly cleared a space, settling the woman into a chair. The security guard brought a cup of water to her lips, murmuring, "You're okay. You're okay. Here, take a sip."

Instinctively Dana turned off the live feed from the press conference. Her heart pounded as she watched the woman slowly regain consciousness. Her eyes opened, disoriented, and she choked out, "Where's my wife? Where are my children? I was supposed to be with them." The words spilled over in sobs. "I should be with them. They can't be gone . . ."

The guard kept her voice calm, steady. "We don't know yet, but we're going to find them. You just need to stay strong."

The woman's gaze locked onto Dana, raw and pleading. "I was supposed to be with them . . . on that plane. It should be me. I can't lose them."

The room let out a painful sigh, more tears.

Dana's throat tightened, tears threatening to spill as CeCe, the gate agent, crossed the room and placed a gentle hand on Dana's shoulder. "Are you okay? It's okay."

Dana blinked, trying to gather herself. "I'm so sorry," she whispered, voice trembling. "I've only been here a few weeks. My boss is on maternity leave. I don't think I can do this."

CeCe squeezed her hand, her gaze warm and steady. "Yes, you can. We need you. Just start again."

Dana inhaled sharply, amazed by this woman's strength. These people needed someone strong, someone who could hold it together. She squared her shoulders, took a deep breath, and began reading from her clipboard. "My name is Dana Billings. I'm here to assist you in any way possible.

Worldwide Airlines is committed to keeping you comfortable and informed. We've reserved a floor of rooms at the hotel across the street for you and your families."

She glanced around, careful with her words. "We believe the plane and passengers will be found safe."

The TV screen caught her eye, and dread knotted her stomach. The press conference was already in progress possibly ended. She quickly flipped the monitor on, catching the room's attention. As the CEO's words filled the space, Dana's gaze darted to Billy, the woman who had fainted. Billy's face drained of color as a reporter asked about the possibility of a terrorist attack from a local separatist's militias.

Dana's pulse quickened as fear ignited panic in the room. All eyes turned to her, seeking answers she didn't have.

Desperation clawed at her, but she forced herself to stick to the script. It was the only anchor she had. "Let's start with introductions and any immediate questions," she said, her voice steadier than she felt. "Please tell us your name and any questions you have. Ma'am." She gestured to CeCe, trying to offer a reassuring smile that barely masked her own unease.

Billy's voice cut through the tense silence. "What do they mean, a terrorist attack? Are they saying someone shot down the plane?"

Questions erupted from all sides, English and Portuguese blending in a chaotic mix. Dana's hands shook as she looked around, trying to absorb the mounting panic. "We don't have any confirmation of that," she replied, keeping her voice as steady as she could. "The airline and authorities are doing everything they can to locate the plane and bring everyone home safely."

"But why haven't they found anything yet?" Billy demanded; her voice edged with panic. "It's been hours!"

"Please," Dana's voice cracked, "we need to stay calm. The search teams are working tirelessly. The terrain is difficult, but they're doing everything possible."

"What search teams? They just said that Brazil is not letting any foreigners in to help with the search. We don't even know if the Brazilians are searching with teams," Billy shrieked. "She's pregnant." The man beside her rubbed her back, whispering reassurances.

Dana's heart ached under the weight of her responsibility. She wanted so badly to promise them that everything would be fine, but the words felt hollow. "I know this is incredibly hard. We're all hoping for the best. We have to support each other through this."

As the room fell into a strained silence, Dana took a steadying breath. "Let's go around the room. Please share your name and any immediate questions or concerns. We'll do our best to address them."

She gestured to CeCe, who nodded and began speaking softly. Dana listened, grounding herself in the rhythm of their introductions. With each person's story, the weight grew heavier, but she held herself together, praying that the next call would bring good news.

Yet even as she listened and reassured, a tiny voice in the back of her mind whispered of uncertainties, lingering dread, and the fear that she wasn't nearly prepared for what lay ahead.

CHAPTER 28

NCC

DEVELOPING STORY

Panel: Why Are Investigators Barred from Plane Search?

Walt Booker Anchor

"Good afternoon, I'm Walt Booker in the NCC Situation Room. We continue to follow the developing story of Worldwide Airlines Flight 987, missing over the Amazon rainforest for over three days now. The Brazilian government has controversially barred both the airline and the National Transportation Safety Board (NTSB) from entering the area to investigate, citing dangerous conditions. Families of the passengers are demanding answers as frustration mounts over the lack of progress. Joining me to discuss this are journalists David Green, Sarah Thompson, and John Miller."

David Green:

"Thanks, Walt. The Brazilian government's decision is raising a lot of eyebrows. Typically, international cooperation is essential in incidents like this. The NTSB and the airline's investigative teams bring unparalleled expertise in determining what happened. Shutting them out is not only unusual but could delay critical answers for the families. It suggests there may be more going on behind the scenes than just safety concerns."

Sarah Thompson:

"Absolutely, David. One possibility is that Brazil is worried about sovereignty and maintaining control over the investigation. The

Amazon is a politically sensitive region, and there's always tension when foreign entities step in. Brazil may be trying to avoid potential backlash, especially if the investigation uncovers factors that reflect poorly on their government or infrastructure. But this decision is only fueling speculation, which isn't helping anyone."

John Miller:

"Let's not forget the political ramifications here, Walt. The Brazilian government may fear that a full investigation could reveal lapses in their security or aviation protocols. By barring foreign investigators, they can control the narrative—for now, at least. But it's a double-edged sword. If this delays the discovery of the wreckage or any survivors, the backlash could be even worse."

Walt Booker:

"Those are valid concerns, but we've also heard from some sources that the region has seen an uptick in dangerous activity—illegal logging, trafficking, and even armed groups. David, could this decision be about protecting sensitive interests in the Amazon, or possibly even shielding information Brazil isn't ready to share?"

David Green:

"It's certainly possible. The Amazon is not just a vast jungle; it's a hub for illicit activities. There might be fears that an investigation could expose more than just the cause of this incident. However, barring experienced investigators could hinder the chances of uncovering the truth quickly, which is critical for both the families and the airline."

Sarah Thompson:

"While I agree Walt, we also have to acknowledge the logistical challenges here. The Amazon is incredibly hostile terrain—dense, remote, and difficult to navigate. Brazil might genuinely be concerned about the safety of managing multiple international teams in such an environment. But the question remains: why not accept their expertise? This is what these teams are trained for."

John Miller:

"To offer a counterpoint, Brazilian officials have defended their decision, stating that the region is currently facing severe weather, flooding, and a rise in dangerous wildlife activity. These are real threats to anyone involved in the search. While we don't know if that fully justifies excluding foreign investigators, it does highlight the complexity of the situation."

Walt Booker:

"Sarah, you mentioned the families earlier. How do you think they're reacting to this decision?"

Sarah Thompson:

"Walt, the families are desperate for answers. They've been very vocal, with many calling the lack of international involvement unacceptable. Some have even accused the Brazilian government of dragging its feet. This frustration is compounded by the lack of updates. Every moment of delay is agonizing for them."

Walt Booker:

"Thank you, Sarah, David, and John. Worldwide Airlines is about to hold it's a press conference, let's go live."

Robert Alexander
War Room, WWA Headquarters

Robert strode into the war room, the cool blast of air conditioning brushing over him, yet it did nothing to alleviate the suffocating tension coiled tightly in his chest. The adrenaline from the press conference still coursed through his veins, his heart thudding with a relentless beat. As he surveyed the room, he sensed the apprehension rolling off his team—an undercurrent of silent fear that fed into his simmering frustration.

Around the long conference table, his employees sat in tense silence, their faces pale and eyes darting nervously between him and one another. The ambient hum of computers and muted beeps from monitoring systems filled the space, but even those sounds felt subdued, as if the machines, too, recognized the fragile line Robert was walking.

Finally, a young employee near the far end of the table cleared his throat. His voice, barely above a whisper, trembled as he asked, "Sir, is . . . is anyone actually looking for the plane? There's been no recorded anomaly from the aircraft or any distress signal."

Robert's jaw tightened, and he spun around to face the man, his gaze sharp enough to cut. "Yes, of course they're looking," he replied, the words crisp, each syllable laced with irritation. "Do you think this airline is incapable of handling a situation like this?"

He tried to keep his voice steady, but the edge was unmistakable, and he could see his team flinch. Inside, a part of him reveled in their discomfort—he thrived on being the smartest, most composed person in any room. But beneath that satisfaction, a flicker of doubt gnawed at him. The questions were getting sharper, more probing. He could feel control slipping, as if sand were trickling through his fingers.

A quiet voice from across the table dared to speak. "But . . . no one has confirmed the status of the search. The Brazilian authorities haven't exactly been forthcoming."

A pulse of anger surged within him. *They're undermining me.* His patience hanging by a thread, he took a breath, forcing his hands to unclench. "I'm certain it will be confirmed soon," he said, his tone softer but his voice brittle. But even as he spoke, he felt a prickle of unease at the back of his mind—a whisper that he had lost the tiniest of threads of this narrative. A gnawing fear that a minute detail could bring this whole thing down. He wasn't used to these kinds of emotions.

Silence settled over the room again, heavy and oppressive. His team shifted uncomfortably in their seats, some avoiding his gaze, others casting furtive glances at one another. They could sense it too—the thin cracks in his control, the fraying edges of his composure. And he hated them for it.

Another employee, her voice almost apologetic, ventured, "Sir, if . . . if this were a security threat—like, possibly, terrorism—would we be informed? The media is starting to speculate, and it's—"

"Terrorism?" Robert cut her off, the word like venom on his tongue. He felt a tremor ripple through his chest, but he forced it down, his jaw tightening. "Do you honestly think terrorists are hiding in the Amazon, waiting for a commercial plane to wander overhead? Don't be ridiculous."

The denial was swift, almost reflexive, but a cold bead of sweat trickled down the back of his neck. He brushed it off quickly, adjusting his tie with an attempt at nonchalance. This line of questioning was beneath him—beneath all of them. Yet, as his team exchanged worried glances, he saw the doubt spreading. They weren't convinced. Worse, they didn't trust his assurances.

His hand twitched involuntarily, a tremor that betrayed the tightening anxiety in his gut. The silence grew, suffocating, pressing down on him like a weight he hadn't anticipated. The walls of the war room felt closer, the air too thin. *How dare they question me?* He was the one in control, the one who saw all the pieces of this chessboard. But for the first time, he felt a fissure of fear split open, raw and undeniable.

The young employee from before cleared his throat again, his voice barely audible. "Sir, maybe we should . . . consider preparing a response in case the media continues down this line. We don't want to appear unprepared."

Robert's gaze snapped to him, icy and unforgiving. "I know exactly what I'm doing," he said, his voice a low, dangerous growl. He scanned the faces around him, daring any one of them to challenge him further. "Remember who is in charge here."

The employee recoiled slightly, murmuring a quiet, "Yes, Sir," as he looked down, cowed.

Robert straightened, adjusting his jacket as if it could somehow shield him from the unease coiling in his chest. He gave the room one last sweeping glance, his gaze lingering on each of his team members. "We stick to the story. Remote area, no known contact. This is under control." His voice held a hard edge, but inside, he felt the truth gnawing at him, a silent predator circling closer.

Without another word, he turned on his heel and walked out, the cool detachment in his stride masking the storm raging beneath the surface.

CHAPTER 29

Airlines Under Pressure: Financial Fallout Looms Over Flight 987's Disappearance

Tom Buckley, Anchor

"Good evening, I'm Tom Buckley and you're in the Situation Room. Tonight, we delve into the financial and legal challenges facing Worldwide Airlines as the mystery of Flight 987's disappearance deepens.

Aviation experts note that incidents like this can cost airlines hundreds of millions of dollars, with lawsuits, compensation claims, and a damaged reputation often leading to long-term financial instability. For example, in 2009, Air France Flight 447 crashed en route from Rio de Janeiro to Paris. The airline faced years of lawsuits from grieving families, massive payouts, and increasing scrutiny over operational practices.

Sources suggest Worldwide Airlines is already taking steps to curb potential losses. Reports indicate that family members of Flight 987 passengers have been asked to sign legal agreements, such as nondisclosure forms, before receiving updates or assistance. Critics claim these measures aim to control the narrative and reduce the risk of lawsuits rather than prioritize transparency and accountability.

With grieving families voicing frustration and public pressure mounting, the stakes for Worldwide Airlines are higher than ever. As the search for Flight 987 continues, questions remain

*about how airlines manage crises and whether stronger regu-
lations are needed to ensure accountability and compassion
during such tragic events.*

Stay with NCC for continuing coverage of this developing story."

Robert Alexander III

Worldwide Airlines Headquarters, Crisis Command Center, New York, New York

Jessica hurried to catch up with Robert, her heels clicking sharply against the tile as she tried to match his brisk pace. "Mr. Alexander, Dana . . . she lost control of the room," Jessica managed, her voice catching as she struggled to keep up.

Robert stopped abruptly, turning with an intensity that made Jessica flinch. His gaze was cold, piercing. "What do you mean, 'lost control'?" His words were clipped, each one laced with barely restrained anger.

Jessica hesitated, hands tightening around her clipboard. "She—she turned off the news conference. And one of the families . . . there was an issue." She winced, knowing the explanation would only fan the flames of his anger.

"Goddammit!" Robert's face darkened, his jaw tightening as his hand raked roughly through his hair, disheveling it. The pounding in his temples was almost audible, a tangible reflection of his frustration. How had it come to this? He clenched his fists, trying to force his pulse back to a steady beat. "Get her up here. Now."

Jessica nodded and stepped back, fumbling with her phone as she rushed to call Dana. The knot in her stomach tightened with every ring, her own fear mirroring what she imagined Dana must be feeling.

Moments later, the elevator doors opened, and Dana stepped in cautiously, her shoulders drawn inward as if she were trying to make herself as small as possible. The sight made Robert's frustration twist into something sharper, more unforgiving.

"Stop," he barked, freezing her in her tracks halfway to his desk. "Right there." His gaze was a cold, dissecting glare. "What. Happened. In. That. Room?" He spat each word; his voice razor-sharp.

Dana's mouth went dry, and she swallowed, her hands clenched tightly at her sides. "I—I'm sorry, Sir. I didn't mean for it to—"

"What do you mean, you didn't mean for it to happen?" Robert cut her off, his tone rising. He stood abruptly, his chair scraping against the floor with a harsh screech, making Dana flinch. "You had ONE job!" His hand sliced through the air, punctuating his words with a menacing force.

Dana's voice was barely a whisper. "I just . . . one of the family members came late . . . and she . . . fainted . . . and there were questions about terrorism, and . . . I couldn't hold the room together," she admitted, her voice thick with barely contained emotion.

Robert's face contorted, a mix of fury and disbelief. "And did you at least get the cease-and-desist forms signed?" He was pacing now, each step a release of his anger, his movements taut with frustration.

Dana's mind scrambled, her vision blurring. Her thoughts felt disjointed, jumbled, as she struggled to recall if all the forms had been signed. Her voice trembled. "Y-yes, Sir, I mean . . . no . . . I passed them out; I'm not sure if they signed them," she stammered, her throat tight as she fought to keep her composure. "It didn't feel like the appropriate time."

"Look at me when you speak," Robert barked, his voice slicing through her thoughts like a knife. Her eyes snapped up to meet his, but the intensity of his gaze made her look away just as quickly. She felt small, exposed, as if every flaw, every misstep, was laid bare.

"Yes, Sir," she said, louder this time, though her voice shook.

Robert stopped his pacing, standing directly in front of her, casting a shadow that seemed to swallow her whole. His chest rose and fell with each shallow breath, a testament to the fury boiling beneath his calm exterior. "You're going to make sure every single one of those family members signs that damn form. I don't care if it's the right time. Who are you to make that decision? Do you understand?"

"Yes, Sir," Dana whispered, her voice barely holding together. She felt the prickle of tears behind her eyes, but she forced them back. She couldn't afford to break here—not now, not in front of him.

"Repeat it back to me," Robert demanded, his voice low, lethal.

Dana blinked; her mind blank for a moment as she tried to find her words. "I—I need to get every family member to sign the cease-and-desist form," she managed, the words tumbling out in a rush, her voice tight with suppressed emotion.

"Louder," he snapped, his voice echoing off the walls.

"I need to get every family member to sign the cease-and-desist form," she repeated, the words escaping as a desperate plea. Her vision blurred as she blinked rapidly, trying to stave off the tears that threatened to fall.

Robert's jaw tightened as he gave a sharp nod, his gaze never leaving her. His own fists remained clenched at his sides, the muscles in his neck taut, his entire frame radiating frustration and impatience. "If you fail to do that, Dana, you're fired. Do you understand me?"

"Yes, Sir." Her voice was a hollow echo, a shell of the confidence she'd once felt.

"Now get out." His tone was final, dismissive. He turned away, heading to the window, his shoulders still tense, fists clenched as if he were holding onto the last remnants of his control.

Dana stumbled toward the door, her heart pounding so loudly it drowned out everything else. The room tilted slightly as she walked, her legs shaky beneath her, every step feeling like a test of her own strength. She fought the urge to run, forcing herself to walk with what little dignity she could salvage as she exited, leaving Robert alone with his simmering rage.

CHAPTER 30

NCC

PANEL DISCUSSION

Flight 987: The Mystery Deepens

Alison Chambers, Anchor

"Good evening, I'm Alison Chambers, and you're in the Situation Room. Tonight, new developments in the disappearance of Flight 987. Authorities have confirmed there were only seven Americans on board the plane, and their families have already been notified. This is unusual for a flight that departed from JFK Airport. Joining me to discuss are former FAA investigator John Drake, aviation analyst Rachel Cole, and international affairs expert Dr. Marcus Evers.

John how uncommon is it to have so few Americans on a flight leaving the US?"

John Drake (Former FAA Investigator):

"It's certainly uncommon, Alison. JFK is one of the busiest airports in the world, and flights departing from there usually have a significant percentage of American passengers. The fact that only seven Americans were on board suggests the flight likely had a large number of international travelers, possibly connecting through JFK from other countries."

Alison Chambers:

"Rachel, what does the composition of the manifest tell us, and why is it so important?"

Rachel Cole (Aviation Analyst):

"The manifest is critical, Walt, because it provides a detailed snapshot of everyone on board: names, nationalities, and travel patterns. This information helps investigators understand who the passengers were and whether any of them might have been targets or involved in unusual activities.

In this case, the low number of Americans hints at an international demographic. São Paulo is a major business and tourism hub, so many passengers could have been foreign nationals connecting through JFK."

Alison Chambers:

"Marcus, could the makeup of the manifest affect the investigation?"

Dr. Marcus Evers (International Affairs Expert):

"Absolutely, Alison. If most passengers were from countries with strong ties to Brazil, it might encourage cooperation. On the other hand, if the passengers were from nations with strained relations, it could complicate things.

Also, with so few Americans involved, US authorities might take a more supportive role rather than leading the investigation. That could frustrate the families here who are waiting for answers."

Alison Chambers:

"John, why hasn't the full manifest been released yet?"

John Drake:

"Typically, airlines delay releasing the manifest until all families are notified, which can take time. But in this case, the delay might be longer due to international regulations or concerns about inaccuracies. Investigators may also want to ensure the list is verified against customs and immigration records to rule out any irregularities, like passengers who missed the flight but remain listed."

Alison Chambers:

"Rachel, what role does the manifest play in the broader investigation?"

Rachel Cole:

"It's a roadmap, Walt. It can reveal key details about the passengers, including whether anyone onboard had a controversial background or connections that could point investigators in a new direction. The manifest isn't just about names — it's a tool for unraveling what might have happened."

Alison Chambers:

"Thank you, John, Rachel, and Marcus. As the investigation into Flight 987 continues, we'll stay on this story and bring you updates as they come in. Stay with NCC for the latest developments."

Dana Billings

Worldwide Airlines, Family Support Center, New York, New York

Dana stood at the head of the room, her gaze sweeping over the weary, anxious faces of the families before her. She felt the tremble in her hands but forced herself to still them, taking a breath to ground herself. *These people need me to be strong*, her new mantra. silently repeating it over and over. Her voice and her mother's voice willing herself to be strong. With a small, controlled smile, she cleared her throat, hoping it conveyed more confidence than she actually felt.

"We'll be moving to the hotel across the street now," she announced. "They've prepared rooms for all of you to stay in until we have more information about the plane."

A soft murmur rose as the families gathered their things, their exhausted movements matching the weight of the uncertainty that hung in the air. Just then, Dana's phone buzzed in her pocket. She glanced at the screen, and a chill crept down her spine. The message was from her boss's boss, Mr. Langston, summoning her to his office immediately. Shit! She swallowed hard. This is it; I'm going to be fired? Mr. Alexander probably told him to fire me over the mix-up this morning?

A bead of sweat trickled down her temple. She quickly turned to her colleague, Cammy, struggling to keep her voice steady. "Cammy, can you take over and escort everyone to the hotel? I've been called upstairs."

Cammy gave her an encouraging nod, her eyes full of understanding. "I've got this. Don't worry about it."

Dana offered a tight-lipped smile, grateful but hardly reassured. As she made her way through the building, her heart pounded, each step heavy with apprehension. She barely noticed the maze of corridors leading to Mr. Langston's office, her mind racing with every possible outcome of this impromptu meeting. It's not the first time I've made a mistake. But he's never called me in like this before.

The door was open, she hesitated for a split second, took a deep breath, and knocked lightly.

"Come in, close the door," came the cold, detached voice from within.

She pushed the door open and stepped inside. The room was oppressively quiet, the kind of silence that pressed against her eardrums. Mr. Langston's office was dimly lit, the blinds half-closed, allowing only thin slivers of light to filter in, casting sharp, angular shadows on the dark wood furniture. His desk, massive and imposing, dominated the room, and the air smelled faintly of leather and something sterile, like an antiseptic hidden beneath the polished surface.

Mr. Langston sat behind his desk, his back ramrod straight, his gaze flicking over her with an almost clinical disinterest before settling back on a document in front of him. The corners of his mouth turned down in the slightest hint of displeasure, and Dana had the unnerving feeling of being under a microscope.

"Sit down," he said, not bothering with pleasantries, "I need you to make some changes to the official passenger manifest of Flight 987."

The request landed like a slap. She blinked, momentarily thrown off balance. "Changes?" she echoed, a frown creasing her brow.

"Yes." He slid the document across the desk toward her, his expression hardening. "I need you to alter the nationalities of 30 percent of the passengers. Change them from Brazilian to other South American nationalities."

Her mind stuttered over the instruction, a quiet alarm beginning to sound. "But . . . why would we need to do that?" she asked, forcing herself to keep her tone neutral.

"Just do it," he snapped, his voice as sharp as a knife. The look in his eyes told her this was not up for debate. "This is not a discussion. If you don't do it, you will no longer work here. Don't tell anyone, you could go to prison for something like this."

A prickle of fear crept up her spine, mingling with anger she dared not show. She swallowed, nodded, and took the document, feeling as if she'd been handed something radioactive. "Yes, Sir," she whispered, throat tight.

Back at her cubicle, Dana sat motionless for a moment, staring at the manifest on her screen. Her fingers hovered above the keyboard, shaking. She knew what she was being asked to do was wrong—illegal. Getting fired over a small mistake earlier seemed laughable now compared to the enormity of what she was about to do. This wasn't just about her job anymore; this was about her integrity.

A burst of nerves pushed her to reach for her phone. After glancing over her shoulder, she quickly snapped a photo of the original document. She saved the image, her mind racing. If this all goes sideways, I'll need proof. *Before and after.*

Her fingers were unsteady as she began making the changes, each keystroke heavy with a sense of betrayal. The weight of her actions pressed down on her, knotting her stomach. With a final click, and a quick picture she saved and submitted the altered document, feeling a dark unease settle over her.

Later that evening, Dana sat at her father's kitchen table, gripping a warm mug of tea with both hands. The house smelled of coffee grounds and motor oil, familiar scents that brought a strange comfort after the sterile chill of Worldwide Airlines headquarters. Her father, a seasoned mechanic at Worldwide Airlines, sat across from her, the worn lines on this face deepened as he listened intently to her story. The hum of the refrigerator punctuated the silence, while distant sounds from nearby JFK airport filled the air, grounding her in a world that felt far removed from the tension she'd been swimming in all day. She had spent the last 30 minutes discussing the where-abouts of the jet, and the possibilities of what happened. Then it was time to tell him.

"They made me change the manifest," she whispered, her voice shaking. She pulled out her phone and showed him the document she'd saved. "I know it's illegal."

Her father's face hardened, his eyes narrowing. "What exactly did they have you change?"

She scrolled to the altered document, showing him. "They made me change 30 percent of the passengers' nationalities from Brazilian to other South American countries."

His brow furrowed, his lips pressing into a thin line. "Why would they do that? It doesn't make sense."

Dana shook her head, frustration lacing her words. "It's highly unusual, Dad. Even on a chartered flight, it'd be rare to have passengers from only one nationality, but this . . . this feels wrong. I can't shake the feeling that something's off."

Her father leaned back, crossing his arms, his gaze distant as he considered her words. The low light in the kitchen cast shadows across his face, making his usually calm expression look almost grave. "There's more to this than we know. That flight always uses a wide-body airplane, and it never stops in Venezuela for fuel. Something's not adding up."

The gravity of his words settled over her, amplifying the dread she'd felt all day. Why would the airline go to such lengths to falsify the manifest? What are they hiding?

"Keep that copy," he finally said, his tone resolute. "Don't let anyone know you have it. I'll look into a few things on my end."

As Dana left her parents' house, the cool evening air hit her face, offering little relief from the storm of fear swirling within her. The city lights flickered in the distance, but their familiar glow felt foreign tonight, tainted by the secrets she now carried. Clutching her phone with the incriminating evidence, she made a quiet vow to herself: Whatever this is, I'll find out the truth. No matter what it costs.

CHAPTER 31

Levi Mathews
Hilton Midtown, New York, New York
Levi sat on the edge of his hotel bed, feeling the familiar throb in his leg. His gaze drifted to the mini bar, half empty after three days. "I'll stop as soon as they locate the plane," he muttered, as if the promise could justify each little bottle of liquor he'd downed. The days blurred together, spent glued to NCC as panelists debated the plane's fate. Meals were a brief respite, shared with the others in the Worldwide Airlines conference room, a place where each update felt like both hope and torment.

With about an hour before lunch, he grabbed another bottle, downing the vodka quickly—the scotch had disappeared on the first day. The group had become a small, supportive family, sharing intimate stories about their loved ones, helping one another hold on.

CeCe, a Worldwide Airlines gate agent, had quickly become a key figure. Her husband, Lucas Cordoso, was the first officer on Flight 987. She had lived in São Paulo for years to be near Lucas's children from a previous relationship. Fluent in Portuguese, she became the group's unofficial spokesperson, her knowledge of the airline invaluable for answering technical questions. People naturally gravitated to her.

Among them were three college-aged kids from Brazil, here in the United States to learn English. Their roommate was on the flight, heading home for a family wedding. They clung to CeCe for comfort. An older man from New York City, who had a brother on the flight, sat quietly in the corner most days, absorbing the details in silence. Steve and Barb, meanwhile, were barely holding on, Barb's tears flowing almost constantly, her husband by her side, struggling to comfort her while also fearing for their daughter.

Billy, whose wife and two children were on the flight, teetered on the brink of a mental breakdown. Her erratic behavior unsettled the group—she seemed convinced the airline's CEO had the answers and demanded to speak with him over and over.

Levi and CeCe had formed a fast friendship, bonded by the shared connection of their partners working for Worldwide Airlines. Talking to her brought him a sliver of comfort—a connection to Steph, his fiancée.

NCC BREAKING NEWS

"We have breaking news to share with you about the missing plane. Officials report that they have found the passenger jet, Flight 987, and its pilot. Sources say the airplane landed, not crashed, in a remote area called Fordlândia, in Brazil, near the city of Manaus. There is no confirmed information about the state of the plane or its passengers, but we can report that it has, in fact, landed. This is a quickly evolving story, and we will bring you more updates as they come in."

Levi shot off the bed, grabbing his jacket and gum then sprinted down the hall to CeCe's room. He pounded on the door, heart racing.

She opened it already wearing her coat, her face breaking into a wide smile. "They're alive! Let's go!" She didn't hesitate, linking her arm through his as they rushed toward the elevators.

In the hallway, others were emerging, eyes wide, faces alight with hope. They embraced, exchanged hurried, joyful words, the air thick with relief.

"I need to call Steph's parents," Levi said, fumbling for his phone. They had gone home the day before to grab fresh clothes.

Steven answered on the first ring. "Levi! We saw the news! They found them—thank God."

"Are you coming back to the city?" Levi asked, barely able to keep the tremor out of his voice.

"Yes! It'll take about forty-five minutes, but we're on our way."

"Good," Levi replied, voice thick with emotion. "See you in the conference room."

In the conference room, the group gathered, taking their seats and glancing at each other with expressions of cautious optimism. A light hum of whispered conversations filled the air. Everyone assumed their loved ones were alive since the pilot had survived. Billy, who usually radiated anxiety, sat smiling beside her brother Frank, rocking slightly with her hands rubbing against his legs. For the first time, she looked almost calm.

Then Dana entered, her shoulders slumped, her eyes red and downcast. The whispers faded, replaced by an uneasy silence as everyone turned to look at her. Levi's stomach dropped. Dana's face, ashen and tense, betrayed what her words hadn't yet said.

She stepped to the front of the room, took a deep breath, and lifted her gaze. "We have located the pilot," she began, her voice barely above a whisper. Her fingers trembled as she clutched the papers in her hands. "He's alive." Her voice broke slightly, and she took a moment to steady herself. "However . . . I'm so sorry to tell you . . . the rest of the passengers and crew of Flight 987 did not survive."

"Are you sure?" someone called out.

Dana just nodded her head, tears streaming down her face.

A collective cry of anguish filled the room, grief cascading like a wave. Hands grasped for each other; sobs echoed against the walls. Billy started hyperventilating, Frank's hands firmly on her shoulders as he whispered, "Breathe, Billy . . . just breathe . . ."

CeCe's hand tightened around Levi's arm, her fingers trembling as she dissolved into tears. Levi held her close, his own tears spilling down his face, the news an unbearable weight pressing down on him.

Dana closed her eyes, wiping away her tears, willing herself to withstand the intensity of their grief. She continued; her voice fragile but determined. "The pilot reported that he believes the passengers and crew asphyxiated due to decompression. He said . . . he said they likely passed away before he could land."

The words hung in the air, heavy and incomprehensible.

Billy shot to her feet; her face twisted in disbelief. "What do you mean he's alive and no one else is? How could that happen?" She moved toward Dana, fists clenched, but Frank quickly pulled her back, holding her close as she fought against him, sobbing and screaming, "My babies."

Dana looked at her, eyes wide, and then back down at her papers. Her voice wavered, thick with emotion. "The pilot said . . . when he woke up, his supplemental oxygen mask was hanging loosely by his face. He saw that his first officer was unconscious and couldn't get any response from the flight attendants. Realizing they'd experienced decompression, he put the plane into a dive to reach breathable altitude. He spotted an airstrip in the jungle, lit up by the moon and landing lights, and managed to land, hoping he could get help. But . . . when the military arrived, they found no other survivors. That's all the information we have from Brazil right now. We'll provide updates as we receive them."

The room erupted again, families clutching each other in shared agony. Dana held up a stack of business cards, her hands shaking. "We have grief counselors available," she said softly, voice barely audible over the wailing. "Please . . . if you need support."

Billy clutched her head, her face a mask of despair. "I need a ticket to São Paulo now!" she cried, storming up to Dana. "They're not dead—they cannot be dead!"

Dana held her ground, reaching out to Billy despite her own grief. "We'll arrange a flight for you as soon as possible," she said, wrapping her arms around Billy as the woman broke down, sobbing into her shoulder.

Levi and CeCe sat numbly, holding each other's hands as the world crumbled around them. They didn't speak—there were no words.

"What are you going to do now?" Levi finally whispered, his voice hollow.

CeCe blinked; her eyes distant. "I need to call his kids in Brazil. They'll want him buried there, I'm sure." Her words were barely audible. "What about you?"

"I . . . I don't know," Levi replied, feeling lost. It was the truest statement he'd ever spoken.

A scream pierced the hallway—Barb, who had collapsed in the elevator upon hearing the news. The group rushed to her aid, a tangle of grief-stricken bodies.

"Give her some air," Steven said, his voice thick with exhaustion and heartbreak.

Levi and Steven gently lifted Barb, guiding her to a chair in the family room. Around them, the families clung to each other, broken but together, sharing a grief too deep for words.

CHAPTER 32

NCC TV NETWORK: DEVELOPING STORY

Final Body from Flight 987 Returned to U.S. After Six-Week Delay

Jason Sawyer:

The final body from Worldwide Airlines Flight 987 has been returned to the United States after a six-week delay, offering some closure to grieving families. While most of the victims—primarily Brazilian nationals—were buried within twenty-four hours of recovery, in line with local customs, this has complicated forensic efforts due to the lack of autopsies.

Experts say the delays in repatriating remains have raised questions about procedural issues and transparency. "Without thorough forensic examinations, key evidence may be lost," says Dr. Carol Benson, a forensic consultant.

As families of the victims continue to seek answers, the mystery surrounding Flight 987 remains unresolved.

Decker Funeral Home,
Sommerville, New Jersey

Lev had received a call earlier in the day from the director at the Decker Family Funeral Home, letting him know that Stephanie's body had been delivered and would soon be prepared for viewing. When his phone rang again late that evening, displaying the same number, he felt a twinge of unease.

He paid his tab and stepped outside the bar, away from the loud music and chatter, then dialed the number.

"Decker Funeral Home, this is Jim. How can I help you?"

"This is Lev Mathews. I just missed a call from you," Lev said, working hard not to slur his words.

"Hi, Mr. Mathews," Jim replied. "I'm calling because your number is listed as a contact on the service agreement."

"Yes, how can I help?" Lev asked, his nerves prickling.

"Just to clarify, you're the deceased's husband?"

"Actually, we never got the chance to marry," Lev said, his voice lowering.

"I see," Jim said. "I have her parents listed as contacts as well, but I felt you were the best person to speak with."

"Is there a problem?" Lev's unease deepened.

"I'm afraid there might be. I need you to come to the funeral home to identify the body."

"Identify the body? Didn't you receive her directly from Brazil?" Lev asked, his mind spinning with confusion, the alcohol doing him no favors.

"I need to show you something," Jim replied, his tone uneasy. "I could have called her parents, but this isn't a usual case. If you can stop by, you'll understand."

Lev hesitated, then agreed. "I'll be there in about fifteen minutes."

After grabbing a bottle of water and some gum from a convenience store to mask the smell of alcohol, he drove down the quiet streets. He hadn't lived in this town long—he'd moved here after meeting Stephanie. It was a small, historical New Jersey town with a train line to the city, the kind of place where everyone knew each other. He'd planned to stay until their lease ran out, deep down he wasn't ready to let go of her.

As he parked in front of the funeral home, the usually bustling lot was deserted. The single-story house, built in the 1940s or '50s, had recently been painted, as though it were trying to compete with the newer facilities by the highway. Lev's heart hammered as he took a deep breath, tasting the remnants of alcohol despite his efforts to mask it. He didn't want to be here, but something in Jim's voice urged him forward.

The silence around him was unsettling, the sound of his footsteps on the stairs echoing too loudly. He paused at the front door, uncertain whether to knock or let himself in. After a moment's hesitation, he tried the handle. It was unlocked. As he stepped inside, a chime sounded in the foyer, announcing his presence.

"I'm up here," Jim's voice called from an upstairs office.

The narrow staircase sagged under his weight as he climbed, each creak amplified in the stillness. He instinctively ducked his head to avoid the low ceiling before stepping into the A-frame attic that served as the office.

Jim stood up, crossing the room to shake Lev's hand. "Hi, Mr. Mathews. Please, have a seat."

"Thanks," Levi replied, taking off his coat and sitting down. He kept his eyes on the desk, unsure of what was to come and dreading the moment when he would have to look at her.

Jim leaned forward, his voice gentle. "I'm very sorry for your loss. I don't know if you know this, but I went to school with Stephanie. I've known her and her family my whole life."

Lev managed a small nod. "Her parents mentioned that."

"That's partly why I wanted to handle her arrangements personally. The other reason is the unusual amount of time her body was in transit. I understand the Brazilian passengers were returned to their families quickly, but the American bodies were held up by customs." Jim adjusted his glasses, scanning a paper in front of him. "Four weeks is a long time without a proper burial. The paperwork indicated she'd been embalmed, but I decided to re-embalm her, just to be sure."

"We appreciate that. Thank you," Lev replied, his voice tight with grief.

Jim hesitated, glancing down at the papers, a shadow of discomfort crossing his face. "A lot of modern funeral homes would have simply arranged the body for viewing. But something didn't feel right, so I took the extra step of examining her body."

Lev noticed Jim's hesitation, the awkward pauses that left an uncomfortable silence hanging between them. Something's wrong, Lev thought, his heart sinking.

Finally, Jim stood. "Let's go downstairs. I think it'll be easier to explain if you see her."

A chill crept through Lev as he followed Jim down the stairs, through a dimly lit hallway, and into a back room that must have once been a kitchen. A nightlight cast a faint glow over the space, enough to see that the stove was gone, replaced by a morgue sink. A metal table sat in the center of the room, a sheet-covered body resting atop it. Jim turned on the fluorescent lights making everything shaded in an unnatural hue making the scene even more dramatic.

"This isn't how we typically handle things here. I've just . . .." Jim's voice fading away.

Lev's stomach twisted, the remnants of alcohol swirling unpleasantly. Mixed with the smell of embalming fluid. He wanted to turn back, but something compelled him to step forward. He forced himself to move closer, his eyes fixed on the body under the sheet, heart pounding.

"When the body was delivered, it was wrapped in an unusual amount of packing material," Jim explained, nodding to a heap of materials in the corner. "I've never seen anything like it. It took me an hour just to unwrap her. I suspected she hadn't been embalmed properly, despite the paperwork saying otherwise."

Lev swallowed hard, his mouth dry. "What . . . what's wrong with her?"

Jim's face grew solemn. "Was there any report of trauma during the landing of Flight 987?"

Lev frowned, shaking his head. "No, they said it was decompression. Hypoxia."

Jim gently pulled back the sheet, revealing Stephanie's face. Lev's breath caught in his throat. The face beneath the fluorescent lights looked more like a mannequin than the woman he'd loved. Her once soft, peach-toned skin was a sickly, plasticky white. Her nose was pushed to the side, the left side of her face caved in. Her left ear was gone, and her features were distorted beyond recognition. Lev's mind reeled, struggling to comprehend what he was seeing.

Jim's voice was barely a whisper. "It appears she was beaten with a blunt object . . . something like a hammer or an ax."

The words seemed to echo in Lev's mind, filling him with a hot, suffocating rage and horror. The air grew thick, almost too heavy to breathe.

"A coroner or an autopsy could tell us more about the cause of these injuries," Jim continued quietly. "Even in a crash, a body wouldn't look like this. And from what I read; the plane didn't crash; the pilot landed."

Lev's gaze was fixed on Stephanie's battered face, his mind a tangle of questions and disbelief. "An . . . autopsy?"

Jim nodded grimly. "There's a problem, though. To perform an accurate autopsy, the organs need to be examined. But Stephanie's organs . . . they're gone. All of them were removed and replaced with bags of sand."

Lev's vision blurred, the world spinning around him. He stumbled backward, heading for the door, and barely made it outside before doubling over the railing and vomiting onto the cold pavement below. He sank to his knees, gasping for air, the night chill biting into his skin.

Jim followed him outside, handing him a paper towel and sitting beside him on the dock.

"You can see now why I called you and not her parents," Jim said softly. "I didn't think they could handle this. I don't know what happened on that plane, but I'm certain she didn't die from decompression."

Lev wiped his mouth, his voice a hoarse whisper. "What . . . what do we do?"

Jim looked him squarely in the eyes. "We need to call the police."

Lev nodded, feeling numb. "Let me break the news to her parents first. They shouldn't find out from the police. I'll tell them in the morning, and then we'll come back to make the call."

Jim patted his shoulder, understanding. "That sounds like the best plan. Are you okay to drive?"

Lev nodded mechanically; his legs shaky as he stood. "I'll call you tomorrow."

With that, he walked down the back stairs, each step feeling heavier than the last. He had come to say goodbye, but instead, he was leaving with more questions and a sickening sense that the truth was far darker than he could have imagined.

CHAPTER 33

The NJ News Courier

Funeral Announcement

It is with deep sorrow that we announce the passing of Stephanie Pratt. Stephanie was a beloved member of our community and will be deeply missed by all who knew her.

Service Details:

Saturday, May 20

1:00 p.m.

Blessed Sacrament Church

1890 Washington Valley Road

Martinsville, New Jersey

We invite all family and friends to join us in celebrating Stephanie's life and to share in the memories and love that she brought to all of us. Your presence will be greatly appreciated during this time of mourning.

In Loving Memory of Stephanie Pratt

Your compassion, strength, and spirit will forever remain in our hearts.

May Stephanie rest in eternal peace.

Officer "Kirb" Kirby
Decker Funeral Home, Sommerville, New Jersey

The overcast skies outside cast a dull, oppressive light into the room, amplifying its somber aura. The funeral of an older man was about to start in the next room. The sharp smell of embalming fluid lingered in the air, filling each breath with a clinical bite. Officer Kirby moved with solemn precision, his name tag catching the fluorescent lights as he photographed Stephanie's body from every angle. Levi stood silently against the counter, watching Kirby's meticulous work, trying to keep his emotions in check. Jim Decker hovered nearby; his gaze fixed intently on the officer.

"I'd say she was bludgeoned to death, but only an autopsy can confirm that," Kirby finally said, turning to Levi. "She was on Flight 987, right?"

Levi nodded, his eyes drifting back to his fiancée's disfigured face, barely recognizable. *How could this have happened?*

"It's been all over the news for weeks. The pilot was the only survivor," Kirby continued, snapping another photo. "Hard to believe."

Levi's response was a weak nod, his mind spinning, numbed by grief and confusion.

Kirby looked at him directly. "Could she have been injured during the landing? Was it rough?"

Levi shook his head. "Not that I've heard. They said the pilot landed safely."

Jim Decker stepped forward. "There's something else. All her internal organs were removed and replaced with bags of sand."

Kirby's eyebrows shot up. "Bags of sand? That's . . . extremely unusual. Why would anyone do that?"

Levi and Jim exchanged glances, each as baffled as the other. Kirby's tone grew serious. "There's enough here for the medical examiner to conduct an autopsy and determine the exact cause of the head trauma."

Levi's voice trembled as he asked, "If the autopsy shows she was beaten to death, what happens next?"

Kirby let out a long sigh. "That's where things get tricky. If this accident had happened on American soil, the NTSB and FBI would have jurisdiction. But it happened in Brazil, so technically, the Brazilians are in charge. The NTSB has authority because it was an American airliner, but according to news reports, the Brazilians didn't allow them to enter the country for an investigation. The NTSB had to close the case based solely on the pilot's testimony."

Levi's eyes widened in disbelief. "So . . . there's nothing we can do? The FBI can't help?"

Kirby shook his head. "Unfortunately, it's a jurisdiction issue. The FBI would only get involved if there was evidence of terrorism. The pilot claimed it was a decompression event and that he got lucky. Without clear evidence to prove otherwise, it's hard to reopen the case, especially if Brazil isn't willing to cooperate." He paused, glancing at Stephanie's covered body. "And the missing organs . . . that's a whole other mystery."

Levi clenched his fists, feeling a surge of frustration. "There has to be something we can do."

Kirby nodded sympathetically. "I understand. Physical evidence is the key here. If we can find something definitive—like blood, DNA evidence, or even the weapon—it would help convince the US Attorney to push for more action. But with so much time passed, and in a foreign country, finding anything is . . . challenging." He looked directly at Levi. "I'll make sure the autopsy is done today. Given the high-profile nature of this case, she'll be seen before the day is out."

Levi watched as Kirby gently covered Stephanie's body with the sheet, a fresh wave of despair pressing down on him.

Kirby continued, "If there was blood evidence or a murder weapon, it might be gone by now. And then there's the black box—the cockpit voice recorder and flight data recorder. Those could confirm or contradict the decompression story. But the plane . . . no one knows what happened to it after it landed. The case was closed, and the media moved on."

A sudden determination rose within Levi. He couldn't let this go. Not like this. "Thank you for your help," he said, his voice steadier than he felt. He walked Kirby to the back door.

"Document everything," Kirby advised before leaving. "Start with the autopsy results. Cross all your t's and dot all your i's. If this ever goes to trial, you'll need every piece of evidence here say rarely holds up in court. I'll reach out to some contacts, see if anyone knows where the investigation stands, and I have an FBI buddy. I'll pass this on to him."

Levi nodded, leaning against the police car's open window, feeling the weight of Kirby's words. "Please tell your FBI friend I'm going to Brazil. I'll search for the black box and whatever else I can find. Someone has to find out what really happened."

Kirby looked at him with a mix of respect and sympathy. "Good luck, Levi. I'll let him know."

As Kirby drove away, Levi stood alone in the parking lot, the oppressive quiet pressing down on him. His fiancée was gone, her body desecrated, her life reduced to a mystery that no one seemed willing—or able—to solve. But he was done standing by. He was going to Brazil, and he was going to find the truth, no matter what it took.

CHAPTER 34

NCC TV NETWORK: BREAKING NEWS

NTSB Investigation Stalled – Flight 987

Don Belman, Anchor

"Good morning, I'm Don Belman with NCC in New York. We have an important update regarding Flight 987.

A frustrated National Transportation Safety Board has been forced to pause their investigation, even after initially determining a decompression incident as the likely cause, based on the account of the sole survivor—the captain who conducted the forced landing. However, the pilot's identity remains withheld and sealed by court order, fueling speculation and raising questions about why such secrecy is necessary.

To date, the investigation has faced significant setbacks due to the Brazilian government's noncompliance, hindering further progress and forcing the NTSB to temporarily suspend efforts. A key issue remains the whereabouts of the plane. With no confirmed wreckage, uncertainty continues to surround its location, leaving officials unable to confirm or deny reports that the plane may have landed intact.

Additionally, the black box—owned by the airline and classified as US property—remains missing. Without it, critical data about the final moments of Flight 987 remains out of reach.

This is a developing story, and NCC will continue to bring you the latest updates. Stay tuned."

Officer "Kirb" Kirby

The Rose Tavern, Bound Brook, New Jersey

It was Sean Kirby's day off, and he found solace in a familiar booth at the Rose, a dive bar on Route 22. He nursed a beer, waiting for his old friend and partner from the police academy, now an FBI agent.

The Rose was his kind of place—an unchanging New Jersey watering hole. The floorboards creaked with the weight of years of spilled drinks and laughter. The booths had peeling vinyl and bare springs that dug into you if you sat wrong. Long scratches scarred the pool tables, and the bar itself was perpetually sticky, no matter how many times it was wiped down. It was a haven for night shift workers, explaining the bustling crowd even at 10:00 a.m.

Kirby spotted his friend walking in and waved him over. Anthony "Ant" Deleon, also known as "Big D," broke into a broad smile as he approached. They embraced with a few hearty backslaps.

"Kirb! How's it going, old man?" Ant's grin was wide. "Last time I saw you, you were doing a strip dance on the pool table at Matt's bachelor party."

Kirby chuckled. "Good party. I made fifty bucks."

"Yeah, people were paying you to put your clothes back on," Ant laughed. "This is my partner, Chrissy Larson."

Kirby shook hands with the younger woman, noting her firm grip and sharp gaze.

Ant glanced around the bar, eyes filling with nostalgia. "I haven't been here in years, and it looks exactly the same. Do they ever repair anything?"

"I hope not," Kirby replied, sliding into the booth. "Can I get you guys a beer?"

"No, believe it or not, we don't drink on duty," Ant said, feigning a serious tone. "So, what's up? You look good. How's the wife?"

"Everything's great. I'm divorced."

"I'm sorry to hear that," Ant said, tone softening.

"I'm not," Kirby laughed, but his expression quickly grew serious. "You remember a few months ago when that jet disappeared over the Amazon?"

"Yeah," Ant nodded.

"Flight 987," Larson added.

Kirby nodded, impressed by her knowledge. "A few days ago, I got a call from the local funeral home. Levi Mathews, the guy from the news, called me."

"The one whose fiancée was on the flight?" Larson's eyes widened.

"Yeah. His fiancée was a flight attendant on that plane," Kirby said.

"That's rough," Larson said, shaking her head sympathetically.

"According to the press, the official cause of death was decompression," Kirby continued. "You know, hypoxia. Supposedly, no oxygen means you just go to sleep—no trauma, no pain."

The two FBI agents nodded in understanding. "Peaceful," they murmured in unison.

Kirby pulled out his phone, bringing up a photo of Steph's face. He braced himself as he showed them; he could still remember the feeling of shock and disgust when he first saw her injuries.

Ant recoiled, his face twisting. He passed the phone to Larson, who stared in horror. "What happened to her?" she whispered.

"Her face . . . her eye . . ." Larson's voice trailed off.

"Her eye isn't missing," Kirby corrected, a chill creeping into his voice. "It's just . . . out of place. She looked like she'd been beaten. And the funeral director found her internal organs had been removed and replaced with bags of sand."

Ant shook his head in disbelief. "You want us to look into this? I'm not sure who has jurisdiction. I thought the case was off-limits because it happened in Brazil."

"That's the problem," Kirby said, lowering his voice. "Levi's planning to go to Brazil to try to gather evidence himself."

Ant looked at Kirby, then Larson. "Send me those photos. I'll show them to my boss and see if we can start poking around. The pilot lived, right?"

"Yeah," Larson added. "The NTSB closed the case, probably because they didn't have enough evidence to pursue anything else. The pilot's story was the only version they got."

Ant frowned. "What's the pilot's name?"

"The airline never released it," Kirby said, frustration tightening his jaw.

"That's strange. The media usually leaks that right away," Ant observed.

Kirby leaned in, his voice barely a whisper. "You ever get that feeling that something's just . . . off? This whole thing feels wrong. When I saw her face, it looked like someone beat her in a rage, like a mafia hit. It was brutal."

Ant nodded slowly, glancing at the image on Kirby's phone. "And that pilot—he just 'happens' to have his oxygen mask around his neck while everyone else dies? Seems too convenient."

Kirby exhaled, feeling some of the tension ease. "I just need to know. Keep me in the loop, all right? I'll tell the funeral director to expect your call, and I'll give Levi your contact info in case he finds anything in Brazil. I don't know what he'll find, but his only real shot is the black box."

Ant put a hand on Kirby's shoulder, a look of determination on his face. "We'll see what we can do, Kirb. This doesn't feel right. We'll dig around."

"Thanks," Kirby said, a small wave of relief washing over him as he watched his friend. "I appreciate it, Ant. Really."

As he watched Ant and Larson leave, Kirby couldn't shake the feeling that he'd just set something much bigger in motion. The truth was buried somewhere, and now, at least, there was a small hope it might come to light.

Kirby picked up his phone and stared at the pictures of Stephanie. Such brutality. The one thing he knew for sure was that whoever did this was filled with rage—there was a disturbing passion in every blow.

CHAPTER 35

NCC TV NETWORK

Seven Weeks: Flight 987 – Forgotten Tragedy, Uncertainty Remains

Jim Malery, Anchor

"Welcome back, I'm Jim Malery. It's been just over six weeks since the disappearance of Flight 987, a flight that vanished over the Amazon rainforest with 180 people on board. While the initial headlines captivated the world, the investigation has since stalled, and public attention has all but disappeared.

In today's era of rapid news cycles and constant information overload, stories that once dominated the headlines fade with alarming speed. Natural disasters, political scandals, and major social movements—each is quickly overshadowed by the next big event. For the families of Flight 987's victims, this shift feels like a betrayal, as unanswered questions and a haunting silence linger.

This phenomenon, often referred to as 'news fatigue' or 'headline churn,' raises troubling questions about the depth of journalistic coverage. Are we too quick to move on, especially when so little has been explained? For the loved ones left behind, the absence of answers is as devastating as the tragedy itself.

We'll continue to follow this story, but for now, the mystery of Flight 987 remains unresolved, and the silence is deafening."

Evan Wheeler
Martinsville, New Jersey

Evan took a sip of his coffee, the morning newspaper spread out before him. His eyes skimmed the headlines, but his mind wandered.

"Did you know that pilot?" Abby asked, leaning over the paper. Despite her recent liver transplant, she was doing well, her recovery progressing just as the doctors had promised.

Evan's focus snapped back to the present. The mention of the pilot transported him back to the airplane. In a flash, he saw the flight attendant standing before him, the oxygen tank around her neck, tears streaming down her face, the yellow cup trembling as she panted. And then his own hand, reaching for the ax . . .

He shook his head, dispelling the haunting vision. These images, so vivid and disturbing, had begun surfacing about a week after Flight 987. He chalked it up to stress.

"Honey?"

Evan blinked, startled. "No, I don't think so. The airline removed his name from all the flight information pages to protect his identity."

"Could he lose his job for this?" she asked, stirring the eggs on the stove.

"Probably, but NTSB ruled it an accident. He's probably flying again," Evan said, biting into his toast, his voice steadier than he felt.

Abby's curiosity wasn't satisfied. "Do you know what happened? I feel like I missed so much being in the hospital."

"I don't," Evan lied, quickly diverting. "What's your day like?"

"Just the usual—parent meetings," Abby replied. "You have a trip today?"

Evan, who had been off due to Abby's surgery, replied, "I'm on call, so we'll see."

"Do you have to call flight service or something? You didn't get to bid on a schedule?" Abby asked, serving scrambled eggs onto their plates.

"No, I just wait for the phone to ring," Evan said, taking another sip of coffee. His hand trembled slightly, and he quickly set down the cup, hoping she hadn't noticed.

Jennifer bounced into the kitchen in her school uniform, her spirits high despite her recent seizure.

"How are you feeling?" Evan asked, setting the paper aside to get a good look at her. It had been three weeks since her last seizure. They were hoping she wouldn't need a transplant after all.

"I'm fine, Dad," she said, rolling her eyes.

"Okay, just checking," Evan said, trying to mask his concern. His teenage daughter was resilient, but he couldn't shake the fear that seemed to linger over them all.

"Dad's going back to work today," Abby mentioned, placing toast in front of Jennifer.

"Where are you going?" Jennifer asked, a common question in the Wheeler household.

"Nowhere exciting, just on call," Evan answered, returning to his paper.

"Okay, whatever," Jennifer said, taking her toast and heading to the sink. She kissed her parent's goodbye and left for school.

Abby loaded the dishwasher, grabbed her keys, and leaned over to kiss Evan, wincing slightly. He reached out to steady her.

"You don't have a liver transplant without feeling a little sore. I'm fine," she said, finishing the kiss. "I have meetings until 6:00, so you'll have to fix dinner. I'll call you later. Love you."

"Love you. Bye," Evan said, watching her leave. He pondered how much their lives had changed in the past few weeks, how normal things felt now. He felt incredibly lucky, no words could fully capture his emotions.

The mail arrived early, adding to the growing pile of bills, but even that couldn't dampen his mood. He headed upstairs for a shower before calling Mark Josef at the pilot flight service office.

Mark answered on the third ring. "Captain Mark Josef, flight service. May I help you?"

Evan smiled, relieved to hear a familiar voice. "Hi, Mark. It's Evan. Evan Wheeler."

A strange silence settled on the line.

"Yes. What can I do for you, Mr. Wheeler?"

The formality stung, and Evan's heart sank a little. "I was calling to see about flying. I'm available to start again."

The silence stretched, heavy and uncomfortable. "I thought I might get in a trip or two before the end of the month."

"Evan, is this some kind of joke?" Mark asked, his voice low.

"No, why?" Evan replied, confusion knotting in his stomach.

"Give me a minute. Let me put you on hold." The line went to soft jazz before Evan could respond.

When Mark returned, his tone was carefully measured. "I have your file here, and the first thing I see is your letter of resignation. You mentioned your family's illnesses were too much and that your mental state made you unable to maintain safe flying."

Evan's blood ran cold. "I . . . I didn't write that . . . I mean, I wrote it, but under duress. I didn't mean it. I want to rescind it. I want to come back to work."

"Unfortunately, HR received the letter, and it's on file. To get your job back, you'd have to go through the rehiring process," Mark said. "I'd like to help, but my hands are tied. Maybe call your union."

Evan felt blindsided, like the ground had fallen out from under him. Flying was his life—how could this be happening? "Okay," he managed, his voice barely a whisper as he hung up.

He sat there, stunned. His mind raced, replaying the conversation with Robert, the assurances that everything would go back to normal. This wasn't supposed to happen. Robert had promised he'd have his life back—his job, his family, his peace. But now it was all slipping away, like sand through his fingers.

There must be some mistake, he thought, panic gnawing at him. I'll call Robert. He'll fix this. He has to.

But then the realization hit him with chilling clarity. He didn't have Robert's number. Their only contact after that meeting at his house had been on the cellphone—the one he'd destroyed and discarded in the jungle. A feeling of dread settled over him, icy and suffocating. He was truly alone.

What am I going to do? Everything he'd done, all the sacrifices, and now he was cut off, abandoned to bear the consequences alone.

Evan hadn't thought about after the flight. For the first time, he allowed himself to feel the anger simmering beneath his shock—the realization of the betrayal, the manipulation, he brought his fists down on the table. Robert had to have written that letter. He had trusted Robert, believed his promises. Now what was he supposed to do? The only work he ever had was flying.

As he sat in the quiet kitchen, Evan felt the last threads of his old life slipping away. He was trapped, tangled in a web.

CHAPTER 36

CBNnews.com

Job Loss and Its Link to PTSD

Recent studies reveal a troubling link between unemployment and severe mental health issues, including depression, anxiety, and even post-traumatic stress disorder (PTSD). The sudden loss of employment often triggers a cascade of emotional responses, from initial shock to prolonged stress and feelings of helplessness.

One striking example comes from studies on airline pilots, a profession known for its high levels of responsibility and identity tied to the job. Research shows that many retired pilots face a steep decline in mental and physical health, with some even dying within months of retirement. Experts attribute this to the sudden loss of structure, purpose, and community that defined their careers.

As more industries face economic uncertainty, mental health professionals urge employers and policymakers to provide support systems to ease the psychological toll of job loss and help individuals transition more effectively. That had been spun long before he'd even realized he was caught.

Levi Mathews

Underground Media Group, New York, New York

Levi tried to make himself comfortable in David Straub's office, but the clutter made it difficult. Papers were strewn everywhere, the wastebasket overflowed, and the stale smell of old coffee lingered in the air. He needed to get into David's head and convince him to help. As the editor of the international desk, David still had the instincts of a reporter, always hungry for a story. For Levi, this was life or death.

His leg bounced nervously. It had been a long time since he'd pitched a story, and he knew he had to get this one right. The door flew open, and David entered, juggling a bagel, coffee, and a stack of papers. He stopped dead when he saw Levi.

"What are you doing here? Never mind. I don't care. Get out!" David's face went cold.

"That's how you say hello after a year?" Levi forced a smile, hoping humor might break the ice. "I'm not leaving. Not yet. You'll want to hear this."

David slammed the door. "What do you want?"

"Long version or short?" Levi asked, trying to keep his tone casual.

"What do you think?" David snapped.

"I want my job back," Levi said, his voice steady.

"No," David replied, opening the door again. "Get out."

"No."

"You quit, and I fired you. Now get out."

Levi took a deep breath. "I need my credentials back."

David slammed the door shut, moving to his desk. "Are you kidding me? Who do you think you are?"

He leaned back, glaring at Levi. "Do I need to remind you why you got fired? Your meltdown almost cost me my job. I've got three kids in college, and you nearly got me fired!"

Levi held up a hand, but he could see it was too late. David was on a roll, his face flushed with anger.

"You cost the company millions in damages and fines. You went on an epic bender in one of the strictest countries, nearly causing an international incident. You got Charlie Stark injured and Yazmin arrested, then stole her story."

Levi felt a pang of guilt but tried to defend himself. "I didn't steal her story. I published it for her."

"Really? It was on your byline, on your website. Everyone knows you stole it!" David's voice was nearly a shout. "I gave you chance after chance, and every time, you screwed up. Not this time. Get out!"

"She was bludgeoned during a decompression," Levi said, desperation creeping into his voice.

David paused, the anger in his eyes softening just slightly. "How do you know she was bludgeoned? And who is 'she'?"

"Steph," Levi said, his voice barely above a whisper. "My fiancée. She was on that plane."

David's expression shifted. "I'm sorry for your loss. Did you get the flowers we sent?"

Levi swallowed, nodding. "Yes, I appreciated them. Thank you."

David leaned back; a bit more open now. "What do you mean, 'bludgeoned'?"

"We got her body back a few days ago. Her face and skull were bashed in." Levi took out his phone and handed it to David, showing him the pictures of Steph.

David winced, turning the phone slightly away from him. "Could it have been from the landing?"

"The police and the undertaker think there's too much damage for that. And all her organs were removed—replaced with sandbags," Levi said, feeling a shudder of anger and disbelief rise up in him again.

David stared at him, the weight of the revelation sinking in. "Why would anyone do that?"

"That's what I need to find out. The police need more evidence to start an investigation. I need my press credentials to get to Brazil, find the plane, and recover the black box."

"That's for the police and FBI to handle, not you," David said, although his tone had softened.

"The Brazilians won't let foreign authorities in. It's like they're covering something up. The NTSB closed the case without finding the black box. It might still be on the plane."

David sighed. "What makes you think they'll let you in?"

Levi leaned forward, his voice low and determined. "No one else has been able to get near the site, but I have to try. This might be the only way I'll ever find out what really happened to Steph."

David studied him for a moment. "Unless you've been busy, you don't speak Portuguese. And the landing site is remote. No one there speaks English."

"Yazmin speaks Portuguese. We could go as a couple. Maybe pose as honeymooners," Levi suggested, though he knew it was a long shot.

David burst into laughter. "Yazmin? She hates you more than anyone here. She'd probably kill you if she saw you."

"If I can convince her, will you get me my credentials back? Maybe even an advance for the story?" Levi asked, feeling a glimmer of hope.

David chuckled, shaking his head. "You want money too? Sure, fine. If you can get Yazmin on board, I'll back you."

"Is she here today?" Levi asked, eager to find her.

"Yup," David said, still smiling in disbelief.

Levi didn't waste any time. He jogged through the maze of cubicles, trying to remember where Yazmin's desk was. A new face stopped him along the way.

"Can I help you, sir?"

"Yazmin DaSilva?" Levi asked.

"Second office on the left, but she's in the breakroom."

Levi took a deep breath as he approached the breakroom, memories of past mornings, and severe hangovers flashing through his mind. Steeling himself, he stepped inside this would be the first time they met since the incident in Iraq. He didn't know how she would react. He knew she would be pissed but not how pissed.

"Yazmin!" he called, forcing a smile.

She turned slowly, her eyes narrowing as they landed on him. "You motherfucker."

Before he could speak, she lifted a stiletto heel, brandishing it like a weapon. "Wait!" he yelled, ducking as she swung.

He turned and sprinted back to David's office, her voice ringing with threats behind him. He burst in, slamming the door and ducking behind the chair as Yazmin stormed in, still holding her shoe.

"I'm going to kill him!" she shouted.

"Whoa, Yazmin!" David yelled, stepping between them.

"I don't want anything from him except his death," she spat, throwing her shoe at Levi. He ducked just in time.

"Let's sit," David said, gesturing for calm.

Yazmin huffed, smoothing her skirt as she sat, her eyes fixed on Levi with a look of pure loathing. Levi took the other chair, inching it slightly away from her.

David sighed. "Levi, apologize."

Levi nodded, swallowing his pride. "Yazmin, I'm sorry you got arrested, and . . . I'm sorry for taking your story. I didn't mean to hurt you."

"That's your apology?" she exploded. "You got me arrested and stole my story, like it was just an inconvenience. I could have been killed and the article would have launched my career into the stratosphere. You care only about yourself. You're a drunk and a liar."

Levi felt a pang of guilt but held back a retort, knowing she was right. He'd been reckless. But this time was different. He just had to make her see that.

David raised a hand to calm her. "Okay, let's not go down this path."

Yazmin took a deep breath, her voice icy. "He owes me money."

"Money?" Levi asked, taken aback.

"Three hundred thousand dollars. The salary I would've earned if I could've published my story," she said, crossing her arms.

David jumped in quickly. "Levi has a new story for you."

"Show her the pictures," David urged.

Levi handed Yazmin his phone, she ripped it out of his hand. He watched as her face shifted from anger to shock. "Who is this?" she asked, her tone softening.

"My fiancée, Steph. She was a flight attendant on Flight 987," Levi said, his voice barely steady.

"I thought it was a decompression," Yazmin murmured, clearly affected.

"It was. But someone beat her to death. Blunt force trauma," Levi said, feeling the familiar ache in his chest.

Yazmin looked down, her anger fading. "I'm sorry, for your loss."

"Thank you," he said thankful she stopped wanting to kill him if for at least a moment.

David took over. "The case is closed. Levi wants to go to Brazil to find evidence and the black box."

Yazmin glanced at him, wary. "And?"

"Levi wants you to go with him as his translator," David said.

Levi leaned forward. "And because you're the best reporter for the job."

She laughed bitterly. "No. I'd be crazy to go anywhere with you again."

"David won't get my credentials unless you go with me. Please?"

David leaned in. "Yazmin, this could be the story of your career."

She looked between them, eyes narrowing. "He'll just screw me over again."

"No, I won't. I just want to know what happened," Levi said, the plea in his voice genuine.

Yazmin stared at him, her expression softening but skeptical. "There is no way in hell I'm going."

David chimed in, "what if Levi sends you what he finds? You could have the exclusive. This could be the story of your dreams."

Levi nodded. "You'll have it. Every detail, every discovery, it's all yours."

Yazmin put her chin on her chest, quiet, thinking. "If you put it in writing that any article published is mine, I will consider it."

"David, are you saying yes to the credentials and the advance?" Levi asked.

David leaned back, "who's going to be your translator?"

Levi shot back, "I know somebody."

"I'll get legal on it," David said picking up the phone.

Outside the building Levi dialed the airline buying a ticket to Miami. He would be there before midnight. He would be at her house the next morning.

CHAPTER 37

Join Us for an Unforgettable Evening in Support of Organ Donation Awareness!

Location: The Alexander Estate, Far Hills, New Jersey

Time: 6:00 p.m. – 10:00 p.m.

Step into elegance at the stunning Alexander mansion in Far Hills, New Jersey, for a night dedicated to saving lives and spreading awareness about the critical need for organ donors. Hosted by Worldwide Airlines CEO Robert Alexander, this exclusive fundraiser promises an evening of connection, inspiration, and hope.

What to Expect:

Live music

Gourmet hors d'oeuvres & wine pairings

Silent auction featuring incredible items & experiences

Hear from organ recipients and donors who share their powerful stories

Every donation and ticket purchase will directly support The Robert Alexander II Organ Donation Fund to help fund organ donation initiatives and education programs. Together, we can make a difference.

Let's create a future where every patient waiting for a life-saving transplant gets the second chance they deserve.

#OrganDonation #SaveLives #AlexanderFundraiser #GivingBack #FarHillsNJ

Robert Alexander III
Far Hills, New Jersey

The night air was warm, and the grand white tent in Robert Alexander's sprawling backyard glowed softly with the light of chandeliers. Guests in evening attire sipped champagne and admired the lavish setup, the scent of roses mingling with the sounds of a string quartet. Robert moved through the crowd with practiced ease, his smile broad, his handshake firm. The media frenzy that once consumed his life was now just a fading memory, and tonight, he was the epitome of charm and sophistication.

As he laughed at a donor's joke, his eyes caught sight of something out of place. There, by the edge of the tent, stood Evan, looking like a homeless person in dirty jeans, a rumpled T-shirt, and a baseball cap pulled low. A flash of cold anger swept over Robert. *What was he doing here?* Their relationship was supposed to be over ended with a finality that left no room for loose ends.

"Excuse me," Robert murmured smoothly to the donor, a practiced smile still plastered on his face. "I think my gardener needs assistance." With a calm that belied the storm brewing inside him, he made his way to where Evan loitered, oblivious to the fury he had ignited.

"Come with me," Robert said through gritted teeth, gripping Evan's elbow firmly. He guided him around the side of the house until they were out of sight of the guests. Without warning, Robert grabbed Evan by the front of his T-shirt and slammed him against the wall of the house, his face inches away, his voice a venomous whisper.

"I should have had you killed when I had the chance," Robert hissed, his eyes blazing with barely controlled rage. "There will be other chances. What the hell are you thinking, coming here?"

Evan's eyes darted around, and though he looked nervous, he didn't back down. "I need money. I need my job back."

Robert's mouth twisted into a cruel smile. He had already anticipated Evan might come begging eventually. He'd even set up a bank account in Evan's daughter's name, a trap ready to be sprung if he ever needed to make it look like Evan was in this for the cash. "You're a fool," Robert whispered, his voice low and deadly. "What's stopping me from getting rid of you right now?"

Evan swallowed hard, his hands twitching by his sides, but he held Robert's gaze. Robert tightened his grip on the T-shirt, feeling a thrill at the power he held over this man, a loose end he hadn't anticipated but could manage with ruthless efficiency. "You have no idea what you've done by coming here. You are so stupid," he added, his voice icy. "Now, get out of my sight before I change my mind."

Evan pulled away, stumbling slightly as he walked off. Robert watched him go, his heart pounding with a mixture of rage and something more dangerous—a thrill at the game that was far from over. He turned to head back to his guests.

But then he heard Evan's voice, louder than before, stopping him in his tracks.

"No," Evan said, voice shaky but determined. "You never told me I would be fired. You never told me I would not be a pilot again. What am I supposed to do? Flying is the only thing I have ever known. You said everything would go back to normal."

Robert turned, looking at Evan with a mixture of disdain and disbelief. "Wow," he said, eyeing Evan up and down. "You really are that stupid. What did you think would happen? You'd just fly your next trip? You need to be as far from an airplane as possible. I'll spell it out for you: any attention on you could lead to an investigation. Ever heard the phrase 'out of sight, out of mind'?"

Evan's hands clenched into fists, and he seemed to steel himself, as if weighing his next words carefully. "No, this is not okay," he said, his voice steadier. "I need help. You . . . you never told me I'd lose everything. Maybe an investigation is exactly what I want."

Robert's expression darkened, his eyes narrowing, a dangerous glint flashing in them. "Are you threatening me?" His tone was sharp, controlled, like a knife held to Evan's throat.

Evan's bravado faltered slightly, but desperation kept him standing his ground. "I'm not asking for much," he said, his voice tight with barely restrained anger and shame. "I just need enough to hold me over until I find another job."

For a moment, Robert just looked at him, taking in the tattered clothes, the pleading eyes. Pathetic, he thought, with a touch of disdain. But a part of him found this pathetic groveling almost amusing, even useful. Evan was desperate enough to be controlled—and stupid enough to think he could push back.

"Here's what you'll do," Robert said, his voice cold as steel. He took a card and a pen out of his inside pocket and wrote down the bank information, handing it to Evan. "Go to my bank and open a memorial account in your daughter's name. I'll deposit the money there. But listen closely, Evan—this is the last time. We can never see each other again. Understand?"

Evan nodded, dazed, his face a mix of relief and humiliation. "We can never talk again," he echoed, barely a whisper.

"Good," Robert said, waving him off as though he were nothing more than an annoying insect. "Now get out of here before I change my mind."

Evan turned and walked away; his shoulders slumped. But Robert could still feel the thrill of control buzzing under his skin as he adjusted his clothes, smoothing out the wrinkles where he had grabbed Evan's shirt. He took a steadying breath, reattaching his mask of charm and poise before returning to his guests.

As he rejoined the crowd, Robert let himself savor the satisfaction of his work. The night continued as if nothing had happened, but he knew better. The game had shifted, and Robert felt a sharp excitement at the thought of what he might have to do next. Evan was a mess of his own making—but he wouldn't let anyone else ruin his perfect world. Not even a desperate fool like Evan.

CHAPTER 38

CBNnews.com

By Dr. Emily Hartman, Mental Health Correspondent

In the wake of traumatic events, individuals often experience a whirlwind of emotions and physical reactions. For some, the immediate aftermath can be overwhelming, leaving them in a state of shock. For others, the effects linger far beyond the event, potentially developing into post-traumatic stress disorder (PTSD). While both conditions stem from traumatic experiences, they are distinctly different in their onset, symptoms, and treatment approaches. Understanding the difference between shock and PTSD is crucial for identifying the appropriate steps toward recovery.

Evan Wheeler

Martinsville, New Jersey

Evan stood under the scalding shower, shivering uncontrollably. The flashback hit him without warning: the interphone chime, the ax in his hand, the flight attendant's terrified eyes as life drained from them. The echo of the chime, the dull thud of metal meeting flesh burned in his memory, each detail as vivid as if it were happening all over again. Suddenly, the shower curtain flew open, and he screamed.

Abby jumped back, startled. "Didn't you hear me? It's so steamy in here. Where is your trip going? I tried to check your schedule, but I couldn't log in to the company portal," she said, oblivious to his distress.

Panting, Evan pressed a hand to his chest, feeling his heart race. "Chicago. I changed my passcode," he said quickly, scrambling to stay composed.

"You've been going to Chicago all week. What's your new passcode?" Abby asked, wiping the mirror with a towel to clear the steam and brushing her bobbed hair.

Evan's mind raced, a pit of dread forming in his stomach. Abby always checked his schedule online. "Oh, I have to change it when I get to the airport," he mumbled, hoping it sounded casual.

"What time will you be back?" she asked, still focused on the mirror.

"Uh . . ." Evan calculated quickly. "Around 5:00, depending on traffic."

"Okay. Will you pick Jen up from drama practice on your way home?"

"I would, but Chicago turns can be tricky with air traffic control holds and delays. I'll call you if I can," he said, feeling the strain of yet another lie, he needed her to believe he was going to Chicago and those were all realistic issues.

"Okay, I'll see if she wants to wait or get a ride. Love you. Gotta go," Abby said, leaving the bathroom.

"Okay, bye," Evan said. The lies felt like stones piling up, each one adding weight to the crushing pressure in his chest, but he was in too deep to stop now. His teeth chattered, and he couldn't catch his breath. He sank to the shower floor, panting. I can't keep this up. Get yourself together. Toughen up.

He turned off the water, dried off, and dressed in his uniform. Usually, he had his shirts professionally laundered, but today he pulled one from the dryer. Wearing the uniform used to give him a sense of control, a reminder of his identity—now it was just a facade.

Yesterday, he spent the day at Starbucks. The day before, the library. Today, he decided on a bar. He could read the help-wanted ads there just as well. He had to find something—anything—to keep this charade from crashing down.

Evan pulled into the bar's parking lot and got out. A car horn startled him. He turned to see his nosy neighbor, Bruce Buckley. The car window rolled down, revealing Bruce's beaming face. "Did you just get home?"

"No, I'm on the way," Evan replied automatically.

"Gonna toss a few back first?" Bruce laughed, winking.

Evan realized his mistake. "Oh, no," he said, forcing a smile. "My wife thinks she left her cellphone here the other night. I'm just picking it up on my way out of town." He was getting used to lying, much to his dismay.

"You should have let me know. I would have been happy to get it. Abby must be feeling a lot better if she's out at bars. Good for her," Bruce said.

"I gotta get going, or I'll be late," Evan said, hoping to shake him off.

"When do you get back?"

"Just a turnaround. I'll be back tonight," Evan said, waving as he entered the bar.

Standing in the doorway, he watched through the dirty windowpane, waiting for Bruce to drive away. He felt eyes on his back and turned. The bar's patrons had stopped to stare at him. He smiled awkwardly—time to go. There had to be a bar in the next town where no one knew him.

Evan drove for an hour before finding a bar where he felt safe. The parking lot was well concealed. Inside, the dim lighting and sparse crowd were comforting. He sat at the bar. "Can I get a Coors?"

The bartender eyed him. "Are you gonna fly today? I can't serve you if you are."

Evan realized he was still wearing his captain's jacket. "I just got off a trip. I'm on my way home."

He took off his jacket and placed it on the seat beside him. The bartender accepted his answer and served his drink. Evan took a long swallow, then opened the newspaper to the help-wanted section. Every job felt foreign. Nothing could replace flying. But if he didn't find something soon, even the small charade he was managing would come crashing down.

"Excuse me, sir," slurred a drunk from a few stools away. "What airline do you work for?"

Evan wasn't in the mood for small talk. "Worldwide," he said, folding the newspaper to signal the end of the conversation.

"Well, you don't have to get snippy. I just asked a simple question," the man mumbled.

Evan took a deep breath and smiled, looking back at his paper.

"Too good for us," the drunk said louder. "This guy thinks he's special."

Just as the man started to rev up, Evan's phone rang. "Hi, honey," he said, cutting the drunk off.

"Hi. Did you change your password?" Abby asked.

The drunk trod over, talking loudly, his breath reeking. Evan turned his back. "Not yet. I just got here. Traffic was heavy."

The drunk kept ranting.

"Are you in a bar?" Abby asked.

Evan paused, thinking fast. "I'm at the food court. Some drunk is causing trouble," he said. "Can I call you back in ten minutes?"

"No, that's okay. Jen couldn't find a ride. She'll be waiting for you after practice."

"Okay, no problem. I'll call you later," Evan said, hanging up.

That was it. The tension coiled in his chest was unbearable. He paid, packed up, and left. No more bars, he thought, his mind numb with dread. He was running out of places to hide—and running out of time.

CHAPTER 39

World Geographic

Hidden Cities

Fordlândia: Henry Ford's Abandoned Rainforest Utopia

Nestled deep within the Amazon rainforest lies the remains of Fordlândia, an ambitious but ill-fated project launched by industrialist Henry Ford in the 1920s. Designed to be a self-sustaining rubber plantation and worker community, Fordlândia was meant to secure Ford Motor Company's tire production without relying on foreign markets.

However, the harsh Amazonian environment and Ford's insistence on rigid work practices doomed the project, leaving behind an eerie ghost town that still stands today. In recent years, Fordlândia has gained attention as a strange tourist destination, with crumbling buildings serving as a stark reminder of the clash between industrial ambition and nature's power.

Levi Mathews

Miramar, Florida

Levi stepped off the plane and made his way to Miramar, his mind churning with everything he needed to say. The Uber pulled up in front of CeCe's house, and he noted the "FOR SALE" sign with a "SOLD" placard dangling beneath it.

A pang of doubt tightened his chest. Should he have called first?

"Are you getting out or what?" the driver asked, glancing back impatiently.

"Yeah. Give me a minute, though—I might need a ride back to the airport." Levi handed over some cash, hoping the driver would wait.

He stepped out and rang the doorbell, watching as the car rolled away. Great. Now there was no backup plan.

After a moment, a teenage girl opened the door, her expression a mix of curiosity and wariness.

"I'm looking for CeCe Cordoso," Levi said, starting to turn, half-expecting to have made a mistake.

"She's in the kitchen. Come in," the girl replied, holding the door open wider. She shut it behind him and pointed down the hallway. "Right back there."

He found CeCe in a bright, airy kitchen bathed in natural light that poured through the large glass doors at the back. The kitchen overlooked a sparkling blue pool, with palm trees swaying in the breeze just beyond it. Beyond the pool, the serene view stretched out to a secluded lagoon, the water shimmering under the Florida sun. It was a peaceful, almost idyllic scene, a stark contrast to the weighty conversation he was about to have.

CeCe was at the kitchen sink, hands buried in potting soil as she transferred a fern into a new pot. When she saw him, her surprise softened into a warm smile.

"Levi! You should've called. I would've picked you up." She held up the fern, her gloves covered in soil. "I'd hug you, but this plant's got other ideas."

Levi gave a quick wave, trying to ease into what he knew would be a difficult conversation. "Don't stop on my account. I'm just glad you're here."

CeCe smiled, patting down the soil and turning on the faucet to water the plant. "So, what's going on? This is a surprise."

His face grew serious as he pulled out his phone. "CeCe, I'm sorry, but I need you to see something. It's . . . hard to look at." His hands trembled slightly as he found the photo. "This is how they brought back Steph's body."

CeCe wiped her hands on a towel, her face shifting from curiosity to concern. She took the phone, and the moment her eyes met the image, her face paled. She swayed slightly, her hand gripping the counter.

"Oh my God. What happened to her?"

Levi's jaw clenched. "The autopsy lists her cause of death as blunt force trauma. She didn't die from decompression like they told us. Somebody did this to her." He paused, his voice thick with conviction. "I owe her the truth, CeCe. I can't just let this go."

CeCe's voice dropped to a whisper. "I . . . I don't understand."

"That's why I'm here. I need your help." Levi leaned in, his eyes pleading. "I think there's evidence on the plane—a black box, something. But I can't get into Brazil alone, not with the restrictions. I need you to come with me, to translate, to help me look. We'd go in as a couple on holiday, nothing that raises flags."

CeCe stared at the photo, still shaken, before looking back at him. "Who would do this?"

Levi nodded; his face grim. "The pilot but without evidence, we're in the dark. My colleagues are working leads here, and I've got a cop who saw her body at the funeral home keeping the FBI in the loop. But I need to do something. I thought maybe if you came with me you could translate."

She took a shaky breath, glancing down at her belly, her hand resting instinctively on her growing bump walking around the corner of the island. "I'll go. Lucas would want me to know what happened too."

Levi's eyes grew big as he realized she was pregnant. "Oh, I'm sorry I had no idea."

"Surprise I'm pregnant," she said her whole face smiling.

"You can't go like that, never mind…I'm so sorry. I didn't know, "Levi said. "I mean congratulations."

"Don't be ridiculous, of course I can go. I'm five months, I'm fine," she said. "I'm not dying I'm pregnant. Yes, I will go with you."

Relief softened Levi's tense expression. "Thank you. And CeCe, if you're really sure, we have to move fast. The next flight to Manaus leaves at 9:00 tonight."

CeCe's lips quirked into a faint smile. "That was pretty optimistic of you to book it already."

Levi shrugged, his face softening. "I didn't know you were pregnant. If I had, I wouldn't have asked."

She looked down, her hand gently rubbing her belly. "Lucas didn't know either. I was going to tell him when he got back." Her voice wavered. "It's a boy."

A bittersweet smile crept onto Levi's face. "Congratulations! Are you sure you're okay traveling? We might have to rough it a little from the information I could find on the area, it's a deserted ghost town on the Amazon. There are no hotels, we will have to camp. I did see however on Google earth a large building just outside of the town, but I couldn't find any information on it. You really don't have to do this"

CeCe met his gaze, her eyes clear and determined. "Lucas and I camped all the time. I'll manage. Let me pack a few things." She paused, eyeing his single backpack. "What exactly did you bring?"

Levi chuckled, holding up his bag. "This. And three phones."

CeCe raised an eyebrow. "Three phones?"

"Yeah. I lose at least two on almost every investigation. Iraq was the worst—lost three before they sent replacements, and then . . ." He stopped, catching himself as her amused expression turned to an eyeroll.

She laughed, shaking her head. "All right, give me a minute to pack. I'll grab a couple of hydration packs and some basics. I'll be down soon."

Levi nodded, watching as she headed upstairs, leaving him alone in the quiet of her soon-to-be-sold home, the reality of their mission settling heavily around him.

CHAPTER 40

When Secrets Take Flight: The Psychological Toll of Double Lives

Living with a deeply held secret can have profound psychological consequences, particularly when that secret involves actions that defy moral or legal boundaries. Studies show that individuals who conceal major guilt-inducing actions often experience heightened anxiety, insomnia, and social withdrawal, especially when their actions conflict with their public persona or family values.

For those who've lost their professional identity—whether through termination, resignation, or forced retirement—the pressure of maintaining appearances can compound feelings of failure and isolation. "The loss of a career can already feel like losing a part of oneself," says Dr. Helen Markham, a forensic psychologist. "But for individuals carrying guilt or shame, the emotional burden can quickly spiral into a full-blown identity crisis, as they attempt to reconcile their actions with the life they're trying to preserve."

Experts warn that without support or resolution, these hidden struggles can lead to self-destructive behaviors or an inability to adapt to a new life—both professionally and personally.

Evan Wheeler
Martinsville, New Jersey

Evan spotted his father-in-law's car in the driveway as he turned the corner. *Fuck.* His stomach tightened as a flashback hit him—the image of blood splatter on the dead passengers slammed into his mind. He clenched the steering wheel, his knuckles turning white, and forced himself to shake off the memory. These ruminations were happening every time he felt the least bit of stress, making it harder to hold himself together. He'd nearly gotten into a car accident earlier that week because of it.

He pulled into the driveway and took a deep breath before grabbing the grocery bags from the passenger seat. As he made his way to the garage door, he paused, giving himself a silent pep talk. Please don't let him be an asshole. Stay calm, stay focused.

Evan struggled with the garage door before finally managing to push through, placing the groceries on the kitchen counter. He looked up and felt his heart sink; his wife and her father sat at the kitchen table, staring at him with expressions so serious it looked like someone had died.

The kitchen, usually bright and welcoming, felt tense and stifling. Bills were stacked in a corner, and the faint smell of antiseptic lingered—a reminder of the countless medications and treatments for his wife and his daughter. Evan could see the weariness in Abby's face, her eyes rimmed with fatigue.

"Hi," he managed, his voice barely above a whisper. "Where's Margret?"

"Take a seat," Jack said, nudging a chair out from the table with his foot.

Evan took off his coat, hanging it on a hook by the garage door. He removed his airline uniform jacket, the weight of the fabric reminding him of the lie he'd been living. He placed it over the back of the chair and sat down slowly, feeling like a child in trouble.

"Where were you today?" Abby asked, her tone devoid of warmth.

"I did a Chicago turn. I told you this morning," he replied, frowning. "What's going on?"

Abby's lips tightened before she spoke. "Jennifer had a mild seizure."

"Oh my God." Evan's voice cracked. "Where is she? Is she all right? What happened?"

"Yes, she's fine," Abby replied, though her voice wavered. "She's upstairs resting. The doctor adjusted her medication." She paused, taking a shaky breath. "I got a call from the school around noon that she was sick, so I called your cellphone. You didn't answer. I kept calling for hours. I even called crew scheduling to see if they could reach you, only to find out that . . . that you don't work for the airline anymore."

The words hit Evan like a punch to the gut. He shifted uncomfortably, feeling the weight of the truth pressing down on him. His mind raced, scrambling for an explanation that wouldn't sound as desperate as he felt.

Abby's eyes filled with hurt and frustration. "Where have you been going every day in your uniform, Evan? This has been going on for weeks."

He swallowed hard, words stumbling out before he could think them through. "I was going to tell you. I wanted to tell you, I just . . . I was looking for another job."

"Why were you fired?" Abby asked, her tone cold.

He took a deep breath, trying to steady himself. "It was . . . because of my attendance. All the times I called in sick to take care of Jen—they counted that against me." He paused, forcing himself to look her in the eye. "I was fired for attendance problems."

Abby's brow furrowed. "I thought you had family leave."

"I did, but they said I didn't fill out the forms correctly, and by the time I realized, it was too late to fix it. I tried calling the union, but all they could do was submit a grievance that could take over a year to resolve." He reached out, touching her shoulder gently. "I didn't want to worry you. I didn't want to add stress to everything you're already dealing with. I thought . . . I thought I was protecting you."

Abby's shoulders slumped as she absorbed his words, and tears began to form in her eyes. "So, what are we going to do now? We owe so much in medical bills, and now we don't even have health insurance. How much do we have in savings?"

Evan sighed, feeling the weight of his lies crushing down on him. "I put all my 401(k) money into our checking account. We're okay for now. And we have supplemental insurance for a bit, so there's still some insurance coverage. I'm looking for another job," all truths.

Jack, who had been sitting silently, finally spoke up. "I know what you're going to do. You're going to come work for me at the dealership. I won't take no for an answer. You can start tomorrow."

Evan's stomach turned at the thought. Working for Jack was his worst nightmare. He didn't get along with his father-in-law, and more than anything, he hated the idea of selling cars. But he knew Jack wouldn't back down.

"You don't have to do that," he said weakly, desperation lacing his voice. "I have an interview next week."

Abby shot him a withering look. "An interview where?"

"It's temporary," he replied, unable to hide the discomfort in his voice. "It's at a cellphone company . . . doing sales."

Jack let out a derisive laugh. "So, you're going to make minimum wage selling phones? You'll be bankrupt in six months." His voice hardened. "I'm offering you a base salary of $60K, plus commission. You'll start Monday."

Evan felt trapped. Every fiber of his being wanted to refuse, but Jack's piercing gaze and Abby's expectant expression left him with no escape.

"He'll be there," Abby said firmly, giving Evan a look that said she was done with his excuses. "I can't believe you even considered turning it down."

Feeling defeated, Evan looked down, nodding slowly. "Thank you, Jack. I . . . I appreciate the offer."

Jack rose from the table, clapping Evan on the shoulder. "Good. I'll see you tomorrow, Son."

Evan forced a smile, his stomach churning. "Yeah. See you tomorrow."

Once Jack left, he turned back to Abby, who was now putting away the groceries with a cold, distant expression. He felt the words of apology forming, but they sounded hollow, even to him.

"I'm sorry I didn't tell you sooner," he said softly.

Abby paused, her back to him. "You lied to me for weeks, Evan. You let me think everything was fine while you were putting on a costume every day." She closed a cupboard door with a sharp click. "I don't even know who you are anymore."

Evan felt his throat tighten, but before he could say anything more, she spoke again, her tone icy. "I'm going to check on Jen. You can start dinner."

"Of course," he replied, trying to keep his voice steady. He watched as she walked away, leaving him alone in the kitchen, a feeling of desperation but also relief. One of his lies was over, he could move on with his life.

CHAPTER 41

World Geographic

Exploring the Uncharted – The Risks of Remote Journeys

Remote expeditions into the Amazon rainforest and other isolated regions often present extreme challenges, from navigating treacherous waterways to unpredictable weather and limited communication. These environments, rich in history and ecological significance, remain largely unexplored but come with inherent risks.

"Once you leave the safety of established routes, you're at the mercy of nature," says Dr. Daniel Ortiz, an expert in remote logistics. "Even with advancements in satellite technology, cell towers, and GPS, many areas still lack reliable infrastructure, leaving travelers vulnerable."

For those venturing into these uncharted territories, the key to survival is preparation, adaptability, and a firm understanding of the unpredictability that comes with the unknown.

Levi Mathews

Amazon River, Brazil

The old wooden boat creaked as it cut through the murky waters of the Amazon. Levi leaned against the worn railing, his fingers brushing over splinters, eyes on the swirling, muddy current below. The thick, humid air pressed down, carrying with it the faint scent of wet earth and decaying plants. A bead of sweat trickled down his temple, but he was too lost in thought to wipe it away.

"I'm sorry about the boat," Levi said, breaking the silence. "I was trying to save money. Back when I was a correspondent, I didn't have to worry about expenses. The company just wanted a story, whatever it took."

CeCe, reclining against her backpack, patted her stomach lightly. "What did you do to get fired?" she asked, her tone casual but her eyes glinting with curiosity.

Levi grinned, a bit of his old charm flickering back. "Which time?"

CeCe chuckled, shifting her head to look up at him. "You can start with the last time."

Levi sighed, a trace of bitterness creeping into his smile. "I was at a small station in New Jersey. My boss was . . . well, he was an ass."

CeCe raised an eyebrow, skeptically. "Everyone thinks their boss is an ass. What did he do?"

Levi glanced over at her, as if measuring how much he should share. "He had this obsession with the teleprompter. Any mistake, he'd lose it. Thing is, reading perfectly from a screen every night? It's mind-numbing."

CeCe's laugh mingled with the boat's creaks. "You're saying your unique style didn't go over well?"

"Pretty much. The night Steph died, I found out live on air from the teleprompter. When I realized it was her flight, I completely lost it. Walked right off the set." Levi paused, a hollow chuckle escaping. "I never went back. I'm not even sure if I quit or was fired."

CeCe took a sip from her thermos, her expression softening. "And since then?"

"Since then, I've been chasing answers. Steph's parents . . . they hated me before. But after everything, we managed to find some common ground. They want closure just as much as I do." He paused, his voice softening. "Steph was the love of my life. She had this laugh . . . it sounded like an old man's wheeze. She hated it, but I thought it was hilarious."

CeCe laughed along, and Levi found himself imitating Steph's laugh, ending with an exaggerated snort. The laughter felt strange, bittersweet, filling the otherwise tense, quiet atmosphere of the Amazon.

"Do you still drink?" CeCe asked gently, glancing sideways at him.

He hesitated, glancing at his bag where he'd stashed a flask, just in case. "No," he replied, hoping she couldn't hear the tightness in his voice. "The night I saw Steph at the funeral home, I was drunk. That was the last time. After that . . . it didn't even feel like an option. I was determined to find out what happened."

CeCe nodded, her eyes scanning the trees as they passed by, vines hanging low over the water. "So, tell me—what happened in the Middle East?"

Levi shifted, uncomfortable. "You probably heard enough about it in the news."

CeCe leaned back, stretching her legs. "I heard bits and pieces, but it's a long boat ride, and I need entertainment."

Levi exhaled, managing a grim smile. "I was assigned to mentor a new correspondent, Yazmin DaSilva, she is going to write this story with the information I find. Anyway, she was green, never been in a combat zone. We were supposed to report on weapons trading in Mosul, but things got out of hand. One night, drunk and overconfident, I dragged her and our bodyguard into a risky part of the city. We got ambushed. Yazmin was captured."

He swallowed, the memory clawing at him. "I ran. Didn't look back. It was cowardly, and I live with that every day. Somehow, Yazmin survived, but . . . yeah. That's the worst part of my career." He glanced over at CeCe, hoping for some understanding.

CeCe held his gaze, her expression unreadable. "Wow," was all she said, her tone neutral but laced with something he couldn't quite place.

Desperate to change the subject. "What does CeCe stand for," Levi asked.

A huge smile lit up her face. "Do you want the truth or what I tell people when they ask."

"Both."

"I tell people that it stands for Caroline Celest," she said.

"And?"

"When my mother was pregnant, she had a craving, or more like an obsession for cupcakes. To the point that she would sit in the bakery parking lot for hours until they opened," CeCe blushed.

"That's your legal name? Cupcake?"

CeCe still blushing nodded her head.

What's wrong with that? It's adorable," Levi said.

"What's wrong with that? Let's see bullying in grammar school, lost credibility as an adult. It's a great name is you're a cartoon character or a stripper."

"I'm not sure a stripper would take the name Cupcake," Levi laughed.

"Are you hungry?" she asked.

"I have a sudden craving for a cupcake," he said.

They shared a few sandwiches, the bread slightly soggy from the humidity. As they ate, Levi finally asked, "How did you and Lucas meet?"

A soft smile crossed CeCe's face. "He was working a flight. I was a gate agent in Miami. We hit it off immediately. A few months later, I was in São Paulo with him." She paused; eyes lost in thought. "We married pretty quickly. It felt right."

Before Levi could respond, the boat began to slow. He looked ahead, spotting the water tower in the distance, its rusted silhouette looming against the dense jungle. CeCe's phone chimed from her bag, a strange intrusion in the wilderness.

"That's weird," CeCe muttered, glancing at Levi with a raised eyebrow. "Cell signal here?"

"Maybe they put a tower out here for the tourists," Levi joked, but unease prickled at the back of his neck.

The captain shouted, gesturing toward the shore, and CeCe translated, "He says we're almost there."

The boat rounded the final bend, and they caught sight of the decaying Fordlândia dock. As the captain navigated them in, Levi and CeCe braced themselves against the sudden lurch as the boat bumped against the dilapidated dock.

Levi helped CeCe steady herself as they disembarked. "Two days," he murmured, glancing at the captain, who held up two fingers in confirmation.

"Let's make it count," CeCe replied, her voice carrying a mix of determination and trepidation.

They watched as the boat receded down the river, leaving them alone on the worn, creaking dock. The silence settled around them, thick and pressing, as they turned toward the path leading into the depths of the forgotten city.

CHAPTER 42

NCC.com

Airline Protocols on Disclosing Crewmember Identities After Accidents

Andre Ellis, Anchor

In the aftermath of aviation accidents, airlines often delay releasing the names of pilots and crew members to prioritize the families' privacy and protect those involved. This global protocol also serves a crucial purpose: preventing retaliation or harm against individuals perceived as responsible for tragic events.

A chilling example occurred in 2004 when a Russian man, grieving the loss of his family in a mid-air collision between a Russian passenger plane and a cargo jet, tracked down and killed the Swiss air traffic controller who was on duty at the time. The incident highlighted the risks of prematurely disclosing identities in emotionally charged situations.

Today, names of pilots and crew are withheld until official investigations are completed, ensuring families are notified first and shielding individuals from public scrutiny or potential danger. Experts agree that while this approach may frustrate those seeking immediate answers, it ultimately protects the integrity of the investigation and those involved in the tragedy.

Robert Alexander, III
Worldwide Airlines Headquarters, New York, New York

The FBI agents sat on the plush, leather sofa in the CEO's outer office. He had kept them waiting for as long as he could, but it was time. He opened his office door and invited them in. He needed to be believed the fact that they were here was a problem. But he was confident that he could keep the rouse that he had no new information pertaining to flight 987 he would be fine. Still, *who got in their ear?*

The agents introduced themselves, shaking hands with Robert before taking seats in front of his sprawling mahogany desk. Robert noted their subtle glances around his office, the awe in their eyes barely concealed. He felt a familiar flicker of satisfaction—this office was as much a symbol of his control as his title was.

"What can I help you with? I understand this is about Flight 987?" Robert began, his voice smooth and measured.

Agent Deleon leaned forward, professional but direct. "There have been some recent developments regarding the flight, and we were hoping you could provide additional information."

Robert's lips tightened briefly, but he forced a smile. "I'd imagine the NTSB could give you more details than I could," he replied coolly, deflecting without giving away any annoyance.

Larson and Deleon exchanged a glance. "We'd like to get straight to the point. We're specifically interested in the pilot—we need his name and his employment records," Larson said, not bothering to mince words.

Robert maintained his composure, folding his hands on his desk. "I'm not at liberty to release employee records just like that. The courts have sealed all documentation for privacy reasons, especially in such a sensitive situation. I'm sure you understand."

Without a word, Deleon pulled out his phone and showed Robert a photo of Stephanie Pratt in her Worldwide Airlines uniform, all smiles and red lipstick. "Do you know who this is?"

Robert examined the photo briefly. "Yes, Stephanie Pratt, the purser on Flight 987. A terrible loss."

Deleon swiped to the next image, a post-mortem photo of Stephanie, bruised and bloodied, unrecognizable handing the phone to Robert.

Robert took the phone and reeled in disgust. He was truly surprised. Santiago had briefly mentioned the flight attendant, but this was worse than he imagined. And the question screaming in his brain. *How did anyone find out? Where was the leak? And why had Jose not mentioned the state of the body?* Keeping his poker face he assumed the body had been shown to her family.

"She didn't die from decompression, as was initially reported. The autopsy confirmed blunt force trauma from a heavy object, likely a hammer or an ax. Namely the cockpit ax. You can see why we need to speak to the pilot."

Robert's expression hardened, but he kept his tone neutral. He couldn't hand Evan over to the police at least not yet. Evan was a loose cannon he would not be able to lie in an interrogation. *Buy time.* "And you're telling me this because . . . ?"

"This has now turned into a murder investigation," Deleon explained, seemingly watching for any flicker of a reaction. "The passengers may have died from decompression, but Ms. Pratt was killed by someone on board. And there's only one surviving witness who could shed light on what happened."

Robert leaned back, fingers tapping softly on his desk. "So, you're suggesting . . . I mean the idea that one of our pilots could be responsible for God I don't even know, mass murder, it's just absurd?"

"We need to speak to the pilot," Deleon clarified. "He may have critical information that could help us piece together what happened to Stephanie Pratt."

After another calculated pause, Robert shrugged, a tight smile playing at his lips. "I'm afraid you'll still need a warrant to access our employee files. Company protocol, you understand."

Deleon handed him the warrant without missing a beat. Robert took it, scanning the paper, his mind racing. He forced himself to look indifferent, but inside, he was recalculating. They were getting too close, but he couldn't let them see that.

"We still are going to need our legal team to go over the paperwork, we'll need a few days to consult with our legal department. You understand, we have stakeholders to consider. I'm sure you can see the weight of this situation and how it might impact our stock."

Larson nodded, but his eyes didn't waver. "We do understand, Mr. Alexander, which is why we're willing to give you some time. For now, all we need is his name."

Robert's fingers tightened momentarily on the edge of his desk, but he nodded. He had no choice had to give them Evans name if for nothing else to appear like the airline is in full cooperation with the investigation. "I appreciate your flexibility. His name is Evan Wheeler. He no longer works for the airline he resigned."

As the agents stood, preparing to leave, Robert cleared his throat. "There's something you should know about Evan Wheeler," he said, affecting a tone of concern. "His daughter died from a rare genetic disease. I believe his remaining family is afflicted as well."

Larson raised an eyebrow. "And you think this is relevant to our investigation?"

Robert shrugged, feigning indifference. "It's just . . . background. It might help you understand his state of mind."

The agents exchanged a final look. "Thank you for the information, Mr. Alexander. We'll be back in two days to pick up Wheeler's employee file."

After they left, Robert let out a slow breath, his hands still steady but his mind churning. He immediately started to turn the narrative to protect himself. *If the FBI interrogates Evan because they believe he killed the passengers, then his ranting of being coerced by the CEO of the airline would just be the rantings of a mad man.* He hadn't seen this coming. He chided himself for not thinking this could happen. Luckily, he still had a few aces up his sleeve.

CHAPTER 43

CBB World News

GUERRILLA PRESENCE IN THE AMAZON – AN ELUSIVE FORCE

The remote Amazon rainforest has long been a stronghold for guerrilla groups, including factions linked to the now-defunct FARC. While their influence has diminished in recent years, these groups are believed to operate discreetly, enforcing control over territories and maintaining uneasy relationships with local communities.

Reports suggest that some guerrilla factions have shifted to acting as enforcers or private security for powerful individuals operating in the region. Others remain ideologically driven, claiming to protect the land and its people from exploitation.

"The Amazon's isolation provides the perfect environment for these groups to thrive," says Dr. Mariana Costa, a security analyst. "Understanding their motivations is difficult, as their alliances often blur the line between protection and profit."

Levi Mathews
Fordlândia, Brazil

"The town should be this way," Levi said, taking a tentative step forward, his gaze sweeping the area. CeCe followed, her steps cautious but steady.

The climb up the hill toward the old water tower was rough, the jungle dense and unyielding. Foliage threatened to swallow the remnants of the long-abandoned town, slowing their progress. Once-paved roads were cracked and consumed by vines, but the sidewalks, in places, still bore remnants of 1920s Americana. Dilapidated Cape Cod houses stood like specters, relics of a forgotten ambition.

"I don't see a plane," Levi murmured, scanning the landscape.

"Maybe it's hidden somewhere, or in the jungle. No one ever said how it landed. For all we know, it could be in the bushes or moved," CeCe suggested, her eyes scanning the thick vegetation.

"Let's keep looking," Levi replied, a nagging thought simmering in the back of his mind. If the plane had landed here, why were there no signs of an emergency landing—no scratches on the concrete, no remnants left behind?

They continued along the main road, Levi's gaze sharpening as he noticed tire skid marks. "This has to be it. Looks like something heavy landed here and skidded. See how it bounces there? It's like the plane didn't stop here on purpose."

"Maybe they moved it. But I doubt they flew it out; it's too risky with jungle on either side. Someone must've parked it nearby," CeCe mused, eyeing the jungle's edge.

"There is a way to fly it out, I think by reving the engines to max, release the brakes then pull up sharply, but you would have to a really good pilot to pull that off. If they dismantled it here, there'd be evidence—scraps, tools, something," Levi pointed out, a mix of curiosity and frustration tightening his jaw. He couldn't shake the feeling that they were missing a critical piece of the story.

They followed the length of the road, observing the skid marks. The path led them to the edge of the jungle, where the dense brush looked recently disturbed. Levi felt his pulse quicken as they pushed through. The notion of the plane landing in the dark, guided only by dim streetlights or headlights, struck him as implausible. Something wasn't adding up.

As they trudged forward, Levi caught sight of a few rusting fire hydrants. They seemed absurdly out of place, stark remnants of a bygone era of civilization in the heart of the jungle.

"Let's take a break," CeCe suggested, gesturing to the shade of an old porch. They climbed over a small chain-link fence and settled onto the steps of one of the least decrepit houses. For a moment, they sat in silence, the hum of the jungle their only company.

"Look," CeCe pointed toward the river, where faint wisps of smoke curled up into the air.

"Someone's campfire," Levi guessed, standing up, adrenaline renewing his energy. They followed the smoke upstream, navigating through muddy embankments and dense underbrush. Levi stumbled, catching himself just in time, and CeCe reached out to steady him.

In a small clearing, they stumbled upon a makeshift encampment. Tattered airline pillows with the WWA logo, overturned beverage carts, and seat cushions littered the area. A child slept on one of the cushions, and adults lounged nearby, casting wary glances in Levi and CeCe's direction.

"What do you know about the locals here?" Levi whispered, noticing a machine gun leaning against a tree.

"Not much, but some areas in the Amazon can be . . . unpredictable," CeCe replied, her gaze cautious.

Levi nodded, deciding to proceed carefully. "We're going to need all the information we can get from them. They know where the plane is—or was or what happened to it."

One of the men spotted them and waved them over. CeCe approached, her Portuguese smooth and warm. "Hello," she greeted. "My name is CeCe, and this is Levi."

The man, toothless but friendly, introduced himself as Olavo. They exchanged a few pleasantries, but CeCe quickly realized the language barrier was deeper than expected. She tried again, but Levi could tell she wasn't getting through.

"Maybe he's just cautious about what he's sharing. Give him an incentive," Levi said, slipping her a hundred-dollar bill.

The man's eyes lit up as CeCe handed him the money, and he nodded vigorously, pointing back toward the path. "Main Street," he managed in broken English.

"We were just there. We're looking for the plane," CeCe pressed, gesturing to airline logo remnants strewed around the camp.

Olavo hesitated, then pointed toward the other side of town. "Army took it," he said, making a swooping gesture with his hand, mimicking a plane taking off. "Brazilian army."

Levi raised an eyebrow, his instincts flaring. "Ask him what he saw that night."

The man played dumb until another $100 was placed in his hand.

CeCe listened intently then translated. "He said an army came and lined their trucks up across from each other, lighting the runway. Then they took the passengers to the hospital on the other side of town."

"I think the pilot said the moon was bright and by chance he found the runway," Lev said. "Ask him where the plane is now."

CeCe put her hand out for Levi to hand her another $100 bill. "He said the military took the plane and left."

He handed Olavo another bill. "Ask him to show us where the hospital is and keep peppering him for details of that night."

They followed Olavo back down the well-worn path to the main street. He pointed to a patch of disturbed earth. "Landed here. Stopped there," he said, gesturing to the jungle's edge.

Levi's mind raced. "If the army lit up the road with trucks, that would explain how the pilot could see the airstrip. None of this is making sense or should I say his whole story is a lie."

"I'm going with that one," CeCe said.

CeCe translated Levi's questions to Olavo, who responded in a mix of Portuguese and hand gestures. "He says the trucks lined both sides of the road. The lights blinked on and off to guide the plane."

Levi snapped photos of the area, tire tracks evident in the dirt. "The only way this works is if the pilot had prearranged it. The pilot's account didn't mention anything about military involvement or landing lights."

"We can't prove that it's his word against ours," CeCe said.

Levi shook his head. "This whole situation was orchestrated. Maybe we'll find some answers at that hospital."

They followed Olavo deeper into the remnants of Fordlândia, toward the hospital he had alluded to earlier. The building loomed ahead, its crumbling structure casting long shadows over the jungle. Tire tracks led the way, evidence of recent movement in an otherwise forgotten place.

"I'm sending this to Yazmin," Levi said. "Maybe she can look into the military involvement.

CHAPTER 44

THE NEW YORK CHRONICLES– Culture Section

**US vs. Them: Understanding a
Twenty-Something-Year-Old**

By Amanda Harper, Culture Correspondent

In the age of TikTok trends and AI breakthroughs, navigating the generational divide has become a full-time job for many Gen X parents and managers. Born between 1965 and 1980, Gen Xers find themselves caught in a cultural whirlwind as they attempt to understand the lives and values of Gen Z—the twenty-somethings redefining work, relationships, and identity in a rapidly changing world.

From debates over "quiet quitting" to the "digital native" approach to problem-solving, Gen Z's unapologetic confidence and strong values can sometimes come across as entitlement to their Gen X counterparts, whose formative years were shaped by economic downturns, latchkey independence, and the rise of grunge. Meanwhile, Gen Z accuses their Gen X mentors of being dismissive of mental health priorities and workplace boundaries.

Sociologists note that while the two generations share a skepticism of authority, their methods of expressing it couldn't be more different. For Gen X, rebellion meant ripping their jeans and blasting Nirvana; for Gen Z, it's starting a hashtag campaign or leaving the corporate world for self-employment.

Experts suggest finding common ground in shared experiences, such as the enduring appeal of '90s nostalgia or a mutual disdain for boomer ideals. "The trick," says generational researcher

Dr. Claire Martinez, "is for Gen X to remember they were once considered the disillusioned disruptors of their time."

Evan Wheeler

Luxury Cars of Plainfield, Plainfield, New Jersey

Evan sat in his car, forehead pressed against the steering wheel, the cold vinyl digging into his skin. He took a deep breath, trying to summon the courage to step out and face his first day at Scotch Plains Used Car Auto Center. How did it come to this, he thought bitterly, a far cry from his days in the cockpit. The cheesy jingle from an old commercial for the dealership played on a loop in his mind, an irritating reminder of how low he'd fallen.

Selling cars isn't the problem, he told himself. Jack, his father-in-law, had made a fortune in this business. But the thought of standing here, at a used-car lot under Jack's watchful gaze, felt like a tight noose around his neck, tightening with each passing second.

He closed his eyes, his mind pulling him back to that flight, to the image of the cabin, an ax in his hand, and—no. A sudden knock on the window jarred him back to reality, his pulse spiking as he looked up to see Jack's unsmiling face.

He opened the door and stepped out, muttering, "Sorry I'm late."

Jack's expression didn't soften. "I didn't think you were ever getting out of the car," he replied, already walking toward the dealership without another word.

Inside, the new-car showroom gleamed under bright lights, all polished chrome and spotless glass—a world away from the cramped, noisy cockpit of an airliner. The stark contrast only deepened the emptiness gnawing at him. He wondered if Jack felt that way too or if he was secretly enjoying watching his son-in-law flounder.

"Wait here," Jack instructed before disappearing into an office.

"Hi, my name's Amber!" came a chirpy voice behind him. Evan turned, heart racing for a moment as he took in her blonde hair and blue eyes. *No. Don't go there.* But the flash of resemblance left him momentarily unsteady, his stomach twisting with the memory.

"You, okay?" she asked, a friendly but cautious smile on her face. "You look like you've seen a ghost."

"Sorry," Evan stammered, managing a weak smile. "Long morning."

Jack reappeared and gestured to Amber. "I see you've met. Amber, this is Evan. Both of you are new here, so you'll start at the used-car lot down the street. Once you've sold a few, we'll talk about moving you up here with the new cars."

Jack's voice had an edge to it—part instruction, part challenge, and part something Evan couldn't quite put his finger on. Was there a trace of disdain there? Or maybe a little satisfaction in seeing him reduced to this?

Outside, Evan walked beside Amber down a narrow dirt path toward the lot, cars speeding by on the adjacent highway. He kept his head down, focusing on the path. One wrong move, and this road could end it all. He shook his head, trying to shove that dark thought aside.

"So, how do you know Mr. Douglas?" Amber asked, looking at him with something that seemed like genuine curiosity.

"He's my father-in-law," Evan replied, keeping his tone as neutral as he could.

"Oh!" She looked impressed. "Cool."

"Yeah. Cool," he muttered, glancing away.

As they reached the used-car lot, Amber launched into a rambling monologue about her art history degree, her plans for grad school in anthropology, and her love of antiques and her entire life story. Evan nodded politely, her words barely registering. He felt disconnected, as though watching his own life from a distance, wondering how he'd ended up here.

The lot was a dreary affair. The carpet was an unsightly shade of green, stained with oil spots from decades past. Desks lined the fake wood-paneled walls, and a door—disguised in the same tacky veneer—seemed barely functional.

Amber quickly resumed texting, leaving Evan to wander the place alone. He found a spot behind a desk to stash his coat and lunch. "Is it always this cold in here?" he asked, trying to break the silence.

"I dunno," she mumbled, not looking up. "Maybe. Anyway, wanna take every other customer? That's what we did last week."

An hour later, Evan's mind had wandered when the bell above the door chimed, announcing a middle-aged couple's arrival. Eager to prove himself, he hurried over. "Hi, I'm Evan. Can I help you?" he asked, a little too enthusiastically.

The man barely glanced at him. "We're just looking," he muttered, taking his wife's hand and heading outside.

Evan watched, them leave without a care and if he was going to be honest with himself, he didn't care.

"Evan!" Jack's voice crackled over a speaker, startling him. He scanned the ceiling, spotting a camera in the corner. "What was that? You just let them leave?"

"I didn't want to pressure them," he replied, knowing it sounded weak.

Jack's silence was filled with a disappointment that stung more than any reprimand. He could imagine the look on Jack's face, the smirk that seemed to say, I knew you wouldn't make it.

Two days and countless "just looking" customers later, Evan was called to Jack's office again. This time, he felt like a kid sent to the principal.

"Sit down, Evan," Jack said, gesturing to the chair across from him. "This morning, with that couple looking for a minivan—what happened?"

"They wanted something we didn't have; I saw the lot across the street had what they were looking for so" he replied.

Jack sighed, leaning forward. "Look, selling cars isn't your thing; I get that. But if you had to choose any job here, what would it be?"

Evan shrugged, feeling cornered. "I'm not sure."

Jack considered him, tapping his fingers against the desk. "All right, let's try something else." He led Evan down the hall to a cluttered room filled with towering stacks of paperwork.

"We need someone to organize these files. It's been neglected for ages," Jack said, pushing the door open.

The smell of stale paper and dust hit Evan like a wall. Finally, thankfully he didn't have to sell cars. This was a challenge he could get behind. "Yeah, I can do this."

Jack watched him, a flicker of something in his eyes—maybe pity, maybe triumph. "Ok then."

CHAPTER 45

CBB WORLD NEWS

Forensic Clues in Abandoned Sites – A Haunting Trail

Abandoned buildings often carry the echoes of their past, but for forensic investigators, they can also hold critical clues to solving modern mysteries. From decaying hospitals to forgotten towns, these locations sometimes harbor evidence that eludes immediate detection.

"Every item, stain, or fragment left behind tells a story," Dr. Helen Marsh, a forensic anthropologist stated. "Even years after abandonment, these sites can reveal truths about crimes or disasters that might otherwise remain unsolved."

However, the challenges are immense—environmental decay, contamination, and the risk of evidence being overlooked. For investigators, the key is preserving and interpreting what little remains to reconstruct events and uncover hidden truths.

Levi Mathews

Fordlândia, Brazil

Levi and CeCe examined the decaying structure in front of them, once a bustling hospital in the 1920s. The building's faded paint and peeling wooden siding stood against the thick, encroaching jungle. The air was thick and damp, carrying an earthy scent mingled with something sharp and metallic. Each step they took up the cracked stone path felt like a step into the past, and yet, the oppressive silence seemed to whisper secrets from a darker chapter in its history.

As they stepped through the main entrance, the wooden frame creaked ominously, and a musty, moldy smell engulfed them. Levi instinctively covered his mouth and nose with his shirt. Inside, decayed leaves and dirt had gathered in corners, and the walls were covered with patches of mildew, veined and black. A fallen beam lay across the reception area, its rotting wood splintered, revealing jagged edges that hinted at years of neglect.

"Be careful," Levi warned, feeling his pulse quicken as his foot disturbed a layer of grime, sending a cloud of dust swirling through the stale air.

"Do you smell that?" CeCe asked, her voice muffled by her hand covering her nose.

Levi nodded, wincing. The odor was more than mildew; it was rancid, a sickly-sweet smell mixed with ammonia that felt thick in the back of his throat.

The hallway stretched in front of them, dimly lit by patches of sunlight filtering through broken windows. Rusted surgical lamps hung from the ceiling at odd angles, their metal frames corroded and splattered with remnants of red stains. Levi's foot slipped slightly as he stepped on a faded bloodstain smeared across the floor, almost indistinguishable from the darkened wood beneath.

"Let's check over here," CeCe suggested, guiding them toward a side room. The door hung loosely on its hinges, squealing as Levi pushed it open, revealing a room filled with toppled metal beds and broken IV stands. A chill crawled down Levi's spine: he couldn't shake the feeling that they were intruding on something best left undisturbed.

They continued down the hallway, their footsteps echoing eerily in the silence. The walls felt closer here, as if pressing in on them. They reached a large room with multiple cots pushed against the walls. The floor was littered with broken glass, cracked syringes, and discarded surgical masks that crackled underfoot.

Levi barely had time to react when CeCe suddenly staggered, her face pale, her hand gripping his arm. "CeCe?" he whispered, catching her as her eyes rolled back, and she slumped forward.

He carried her outside, the fresher air a shock after the stale rot within. Gently, he laid her on the ground, brushing a few damp leaves off her cheek. "Are you okay?" he asked, his heart hammering with residual fear.

CeCe took a long breath, sipping the water he handed her and shivering slightly. "It's just . . . that smell. I think the baby's okay. I can feel him moving," she reassured him, clutching her stomach as if to hold herself together.

Levi squeezed her shoulder. "Stay here. I'll check the rest. Just don't go anywhere."

Steeling himself, he reentered the building, the air seeming heavier, almost resisting his every breath. The pungent odor intensified as he moved deeper, and his stomach churned. In the room he had just left, he spotted dark stains spattered across the floor, some faintly outlined in red—like blood that had been hastily washed away but never truly erased. Levi's pulse quickened; he knew that smell too well. Blood mixed with chemicals, the scent of something horrifically preserved.

He took quick photos of the scene, his fingers trembling. He bagged a rusted scalpel, its blade streaked with dried blood, and a pair of latex gloves, now hardened and cracked from age, speckled with red-brown stains. Each step felt heavier, as though the building itself resented his presence.

Back outside, CeCe waited, her hand resting protectively on her belly, her expression pale but resolute. "Did you find anything?" she asked, her voice barely above a whisper.

Levi nodded, holding up the bagged evidence. "It's bad in there. I think . . . I think they brought the bodies here. Tried something . . . maybe even experimented. There's surgical equipment scattered everywhere." He hesitated, glancing at her, seeing her flinch as if the weight of what he'd said struck her.

CeCe shuddered, looking back toward the looming structure. "What kind of place does this? In a decompression, they would all be dead instantly. But . . . it's like they were . . . kept," she said, a tremor in her voice.

"It's not right. Nothing about this is right," Levi muttered, unable to shake the sense that they were touching something profoundly wrong.

They trudged back toward Olavo's encampment, the ominous silence between them thickening as they replayed what they'd seen. The last rays of sunlight slanted through the trees, casting eerie shadows that seemed to move with them.

At the river's edge, they found Olavo by a small fire, its embers glowing a dull orange. CeCe handed him a crumpled bill and asked him about a place to stay.

"There's a place downriver," she translated for Levi, her voice shaky. "Locals say it's haunted. I guess that's fitting. They say it's a hospital. He said no one ever goes there. People go in but they never go out."

"So, we can go check it out and pray that we can stay there, or we camp out here?"

"Let's go, we can always come back if there is no place to say," CeCe said.

As they turned to leave, a young boy approached CeCe, tugging at her sleeve, holding something small and metallic in his hands. CeCe gasped; it was a shattered smartphone.

Her voice caught as she whispered, "Could this be? It looks like Lucas's phone." She clutched it to her chest, the cracked screen pressing against her hand like a lifeline to something lost.

Levi squeezed her shoulder as she cradled the broken phone, the weight of their journey settling over them like a shroud.

CHAPTER 46

Yazmin Da Silva

Underground Media Group, New York, New York

Yazmin sat in David Straub's office, absently glancing at herself in a compact mirror, catching her own tired reflection. *I look like shit.* The hours had blurred into one another; she hadn't left the building since Levi's last message. It was as though every new piece of information he sent had tightened her focus, keeping her glued to her desk. She thumbed through the photos on her phone, lingering on each unsettling detail, lost in thought.

The door burst open, and David entered, his arms overflowing with papers, a bagel clenched between his teeth. He managed a muffled, "Shut the door," and Yazmin obliged, smirking at the familiar chaos of his arrival. Papers scattered onto his desk, and he took a large bite before dropping the bagel and turning his attention to her. He thrust the bagel in her direction, "want some?"

She didn't have to answer her curled lips and side glance answered for her.

"Were you here all night? And what happened to your hair?" David raised an eyebrow, taking in her rumpled appearance.

Yazmin scoffed, shoving the compact back into her bag. "Levi texted last night, right before I was about to leave, so I stayed."

David chuckled, picking up a few stray papers. "Was the text even coherent?"

She rolled her eyes. "Surprisingly, yes. Look at this," she said, handing him her phone. "This isn't just another 'Levi's drunk again' rant."

David's brows knitted as he scanned through the photos. Yazmin watched him closely, searching for a flicker of interest or even shock. "Go on," he prompted, looking up.

She leaned forward, her voice low. "I spent the night digging through everything. I started with satellite images of the area. There's this huge white blob, like a massive building, but here's the thing—it doesn't officially exist. I used every search engine, even a Brazilian one. There's nothing. Levi sent me pictures of a building another building that used to be the old town's hospital."

David's lips pressed into a thin line, the wheels clearly turning. "Interesting, but so far, it's just a ghost building. Anything concrete?"

"Levi mentioned the inside," Yazmin continued, her voice tightening as she recalled his descriptions. "Medical equipment everywhere. Rubber gloves, surgical scissors, random supplies tossed around. And the floors— stained and trampled. It was a decompression accident; those passengers would've been dead on arrival, or at least brain-dead. So why all the medical equipment? Were they trying to revive the dead?"

David leaned back, mulling it over. The usual bustle of the newsroom beyond his office felt distant as Yazmin watched him absorb the information. "Why wouldn't they use a modern hospital if they were actually trying to save lives?"

She nodded; her gaze intense. "Exactly. And Levi mentioned an over-powering chemical smell. Not just disinfectant—something almost industrial, mixed with stench of rotting blood."

David raised an eyebrow, a hint of skepticism mingling with intrigue. "This doesn't sound like a typical cover-up. It sounds . . . planned. Have you found anything on the pilot?"

"Nothing. His name has been redacted from every official document, and the NTSB, FAA, even Worldwide Airlines—they all closed the investigation. There was like no investigation at all. A federal court sealed it, supposedly for the pilot's 'safety.'" She let out a humorless laugh. "Safety from what?"

David shook his head. "Do you think he's still flying?"

Yazmin shrugged, but her mind was racing. "If he is, he's hidden well. But it doesn't add up. The pilot claims he wandered the jungle until he was found. That would mean he left the passengers . . . where? Just sitting on the plane? Nothing about his story makes sense."

David looked at her thoughtfully, leaning forward. "You've got a few leads here. Start with that building. See if you can get Levi to find out what's in that building. Who owns it? Why doesn't it officially exist? And you need to focus on getting the pilot's name. Listen, don't rush this, Yazmin. The story's gone cold for everyone else; you've got the time to do it right. This could be huge."

She nodded, feeling the weight of his words and the opportunity in front of her. As David turned back to his papers, Yazmin's phone buzzed with another message from Levi. She glanced down, and her pulse quickened. Whatever was happening out there, it was darker than anything she'd ever uncovered. She quickly tapped out a reply, bracing herself for the inevitable dive deeper into the mystery.

Just before she left, she couldn't resist adding one more teaser online, just enough to keep the trail warm without giving away everything. As she hit "post," a sense of purpose settled over her. This was it—her chance to break something big, something that would haunt headlines for years.

CHAPTER 47

X (Twitter) @YazminDaSilvaReports

Why the rush to bury Flight 987 victims? NTSB, FAA, and global agencies sign-off on "official" cause – decompression failure, but never sent a single foreign investigator to Brazil crash site – Brazil refused access. No black box disclosures either. Why the rush? Who benefits from closing investigation so soon? Taking the word of the one, sole survivor as fact? #Flight987 #YazminDaSilva #StayTuned

Levi Mathews

Cattleya Eldorado Longevity Medical Center and Spa, Fordlândia, Brazil

The jungle had swallowed them whole, and as the last traces of sunlight faded, the air thickened with sounds that clawed at their nerves. The shriek of unseen creatures mixed with the buzzing of insects, creating a wall of noise that seemed to close in on them. Strangely the road they were on was newly paved.

"Who paves a road in the middle of a jungle? On the outskirts of a broken downtown?" Levi asked himself out loud.

They kept focus on the stadium lights of the looming building. Something screeched, they looked at each other and without a word they broke into a jog.

"Well, there's the cell tower," Levi muttered, nodding toward the top of the building. A steel and glass high-rise giant at least 10 stories that had no business being in the middle of nowhere.

The building was surrounded by a 20-foot concrete and gold trimmed wall.

"Stop," CeCe said. "Look how the front portion of the hotel has windows, and the back section has none. I don't think I've ever seen such a large structure with no windows at all."

They approached the towering, gilded gate, its cursive initials "JS" catching the light. Behind it, a grand portico and an ornate fountain shimmered beneath the sign: Cattleya Eldorado Longevity Medical Center and Spa.

"A medical center and spa, huh," CeCe whispered. "I know what this is, it's a surgery center where tourist can come and get plastic surgery cheaper than in the states. But how many facelifts can they be doing to fill the place up?"

"That makes a little sense," Lev said. "Medical tourism."

"Yup," CeCe said. "Still, this is a bit much. It doesn't look like it would be cheaper than the states."

Levi pressed the intercom buzzer, trying to sound calm. After a long pause, a man's voice crackled through, laced with irritation. "Yes?"

"My wife is pregnant, and we have nowhere else to go, can we come in?" Levi said, hoping that was enough.

There was a tense silence.

"This is a private hotel and spa," the voice sternly announced.

"Please, my wife is pregnant, and she needs to use the restroom. We can pay in cash."

Another loud unknown animal death reminded him of what was at stake. Finally, the gate clicked and swung open with a rusty hum. They slipped inside, before the man could change his mind. Once inside the gate it was obvious no one was there. A large parking lot was completely empty, and there were no lights coming from any of the windows

Inside, the silence was thick and unnaturally cool. CeCe hurried toward the restroom while Levi approached the front desk. The man behind it wore a name tag that read "Hector," and his expression was cool, controlled.

"We just need a place to stay for the night," Levi began, but Hector's gaze didn't soften. "This is a private facility, sir. Membership by invitation only," Hector said.

Levi's heart sank. "Please. I'll pay whatever you need." He laid out a wad of cash, his hand shaking slightly. The man's eyes flickered, just for a second, and Levi knew he had him.

Hector disappeared into a back office, leaving Levi alone in the unsettling stillness. Every corner of the lobby gleamed, but there was something unnatural about it—the overly polished floors, the empty lounge chairs, the air-conditioning amped up. *Cooling a place like this would cost a fortune.*

When Hector returned, he held a key card, his composure intact. "A thousand dollars per person," he said, his tone businesslike.

Levi laid two thousand dollars in front of him, "we need two nights."

Once they reached their room, Levi noticed the small red lights on the cameras in the hallway, each one trained on a different angle. "Quite a security setup for a hotel," he murmured as Hector unlocked the door.

"We cater to high-profile clients," Hector replied smoothly. "For privacy reasons, the cameras are off in the rooms. Complete confidentiality." He smiled, but it was a smile that didn't reach his eyes. "Let us know if you need anything."

Levi waited until the door closed behind Hector, then turned to CeCe. "He's as weird as this place is."

She nodded, dropping her backpack to the floor and sinking onto the bed. "It's more than just odd. It's almost like they're hiding something. I mean a private club. What's the theme of this club"

"How many procedures could a person be getting to join a club to get them?" He said doing air quotes.

Levi dragged a chair over to one of the cameras and tilted it toward the ceiling. "Just in case," he muttered. He was testing them, hoping to provoke a reaction, he would rather it go unnoticed.

"I'll take a quick shower," CeCe said, heading into the bathroom.

Levi took out his phone, typing a quick message to Yazmin: "Found something strange. Spa/hotel facility, tons of security, feels like a cover. I'll send updates." He glanced at the bathroom door, listening to the sound of running water, and felt a wave of dread settle over him. *There must be a reason the locals are afraid to go here. But what is it.*

As he paced the room, he caught sight of a small vent near the floor and crouched down to inspect it. The faint smell of chemicals drifted up, tinged with a sweet floral scent that reminded him of orchids. It was the same smell he'd caught in the abandoned hospital, without the smell of rotting corpses. The hairs on the back of his neck stood up.

The sound of the shower turning off snapped him back, and CeCe emerged, looking refreshed but wary. "Ready for a little reconnaissance?" she asked, a faint smile playing on her lips, though her eyes betrayed her anxiety.

Levi forced a grin, but the unease gnawed at him. "Let's go. I have a feeling we're only scratching the surface of this place."

They slipped out into the hallway, their footsteps echoing off the polished marble floors as they ventured deeper into the belly of the Cattleya Eldorado, each step heightening the sense that they were walking into something far more sinister than a luxury spa.

CHAPTER 48

THE NEW YORK CHRONICLE

Secrecy Shrouds Revolutionary Medical Breakthroughs

Rumors swirl about groundbreaking medical technologies that could reshape healthcare forever. Speculation includes advancements in gene editing, organ regeneration, and even age reversal. Yet, details remain tightly guarded, sparking both excitement and concern within the scientific community.

While the potential to solve major health challenges is thrilling, critics warn that such secrecy raises ethical questions. Who will control these innovations? Will they be accessible to all, or reserved for the wealthy elite?

Levi Mathews

Cattleya Eldorado Longevity Medical Center and Spa, Fordlândia, Brazil

"We know the hotel is empty, so what are we even looking for?" CeCe whispered, glancing around nervously.

Levi kept his voice low as he jiggled another door handle. Locked. "Good question. I want to find out what's in the other half of this building—the one with no windows. We need to figure out how to get in."

"The entrance must be on the ground floor. Let's start there." She hesitated. "What if he's down here?"

Levi glanced at her, reading the tension in her posture. "We're just two guests looking for a vending machine," he said lightly, even though they both knew the excuse wouldn't hold up under real scrutiny.

Her breathless chuckle didn't fool him. He saw how her eyes darted to the darkened corridor ahead. She was afraid—but she wasn't letting it stop her. That was the thing about CeCe. Fear didn't make her freeze—it made her dig in. And Levi knew, just by looking at her, that this wasn't just about finding a story or chasing down corruption. This was personal. The set of her jaw, the way she squared her shoulders despite the tremor in her breath—she wasn't here for herself. She was here for Lucas.

Levi understood that kind of obsession all too well.

They made their way back to the lobby, expecting to see Hector behind the desk.

"He must be asleep," Levi murmured, glancing toward the front counter.

"What if there are other employees?" CeCe whispered.

They moved cautiously toward the glass doors leading to the pool area, where they'd spotted an access point to the windowless building earlier.

The door swung open without a sound, and a wall of humid air hit them. The thick scent of orchids took over all the air. They were covering nearly every inch of the atrium. CeCe wrinkled her nose, waving a hand before her face and bringing her shirt up to cover her nose.

"There's that smell again," she muttered.

Levi steadied her with a hand on her arm. "Are you okay?"

She nodded, but her expression was tight. "It's overwhelming. But I'm not fainting this time." She exhaled sharply, steeling herself. "I have never been so overcome from the smell of flowers."

They approached a side door leading to the restricted section. Locked. Just as the faint whir of an activating security camera filled the air, Levi cursed under his breath.

"I think the cameras just turned on," he whispered.

CeCe inhaled sharply. "What do we do?"

Levi scanned the area, keeping his voice even. "Let's go back. We're here for food, remember?"

CeCe forced a shaky laugh. "Food. Right."

Just as they turned to retreat, hurried footsteps echoed behind them. Levi's stomach clenched. They weren't alone.

A familiar voice sliced through the thick air. "What are you doing back here?" Hector huffed.

Levi turned slowly, taking in the man's narrowed gaze, the irritation stiffening his posture.

"We're . . . so sorry," CeCe stammered, shifting slightly behind Levi. "We got a little lost looking for a vending machine."

Hector studied them for a moment before jerking his head toward the hotel. "You shouldn't be back here," he said firmly. "I'll bring you something to eat in your room."

Levi didn't argue. There was no point. They let Hector lead them back, his warning about the hotel's motion-activated alarm still hanging in the air.

Hector brought them a tray of cheese, tropical fruit, sandwiches, and pastries. CeCe was mid sandwich her second one.

"The baby is hungry," she mused.

Levi leaned back against the headboard, running a hand through his hair. "You noticed Hector using the same key card at every lock, right?"

CeCe's eyes flicked up to meet his. "You think he has a master key?"

Levi nodded, watching as her focus sharpened.

"Yes," she said. "If we could get that master key, we'd have access to both buildings."

"We need to find the weakest link. There's always a weakest link."

Levi exhaled slowly, already calculating the next move.

And he knew CeCe was doing the same.

CHAPTER 49

THE HARRINGTON POST

PRESS AND FBI: A BALANCING ACT FOR JUSTICE

Recent high-profile cases reveal the growing importance of collaboration between the press and the FBI in solving complex investigations. Journalists and federal agents work hand-in-hand to verify facts, track leads, and inform the public—all while navigating the delicate balance between transparency and confidentiality.

"The media plays a key role in holding law enforcement accountable," says FBI analyst Mark Travers. "But their cooperation is also critical to protect sensitive details that could jeopardize ongoing investigations."

As trust grows between the press and law enforcement, this partnership continues to shape how the public learns the truth while ensuring justice is served.

FBI Agents Deleon and Larson

FBI Field Office New York, New York

The field office was thankfully quiet on this afternoon. Ant craned his neck over the office divider. "Just heard from Kirby," Deleon said, his tone low. "Yazmin DaSilva, the reporter stranded in Iraq by Levi Mathews, is working with him on a new story. Kirby wants us to reach out."

Larson raised her eyebrows, her interest piqued. "Let's give her a call."

Deleon dialed Yazmin's number, putting the call on speakerphone. After a few rings, a voice answered, "This is Yazmin."

"Hi, Ms. DaSilva. This is Special Agent Anthony Deleon from the FBI. Do you have a moment?"

There was a pause on the other end. "What can I do for you, Agent Deleon?"

"We heard from Sergeant Sean Kirby that you're collaborating with Levi Mathews on a story. We'd like to ask a few questions," Deleon said, keeping his tone professional but curious.

Another pause. "I'm a bit busy right now, Agent Deleon. Maybe next week?" Her tone was polite but guarded.

"This is just an informal inquiry," Deleon pressed. "Could we stop by your office? It won't take long."

"I appreciate the interest, but I really can't right now," she replied, a hint of exasperation creeping in.

Deleon glanced at Larson, who gave him a subtle nod. He decided to take a different tack. "We know the pilot's name, Ms. DaSilva."

The line went silent for a long beat. Then Yazmin's voice came through, slightly softer, but intrigued. "All right. Six-thirty at Valeska in the East Village."

Valeska was packed when Deleon and Larson arrived, its cozy interior alive with laughter and the clink of dishes. Yazmin was seated at a corner table, watching the door. She waved them over as they approached.

"Agents," she greeted, extending a hand. After brief introductions, she leaned forward, cutting straight to the chase. "What's the pilot's name?"

Deleon smiled faintly, but didn't answer directly. "First, we'd like to understand what you and Levi have uncovered."

Yazmin's eyes narrowed slightly, assessing them. "I've waited years for a story like this. Handing it over isn't exactly on my agenda."

"We get it," Larson said, her voice smooth and reassuring. "This isn't about taking over your story. We're not going to the press. But we have reason to believe there's a larger cover-up in play here. Think of this as a partnership. You share some intel, we share ours, and we both get closer to the truth."

Yazmin drummed her fingers on the table, glancing around the crowded diner. She seemed to weigh her options, her gaze flicking between the agents. "This could be my big break," she murmured, mostly to herself. Finally, she looked back at them. "Fine. But no leaks. This stays between us."

Deleon nodded, keeping his expression neutral but feeling a slight triumph. "Deal."

Yazmin relaxed a bit, but her eyes were sharp, still scrutinizing them. "You first,"

"You first," Larson shot back

Yazmin exhaled, "all right, you wanted to know what Levi's found?"

The agents leaned in as Yazmin continued, "He's in Brazil with the copilot's widow, CeCe, who's helping him as a translator. They tracked down the supposed landing spot of the missing plane. Instead, they found an abandoned hospital filled with medical equipment. Used gloves, bloody instruments scattered around . . . everything points to a frantic scene."

Deleon raised an eyebrow. "In an abandoned hospital?"

"Yeah. In an old, forgotten town called Fordlândia, near Manaus," Yazmin said, pulling up photos on her phone. She slid it across the table, letting them scroll through images of the ruined structure. "The place stinks of decay and chemicals. Levi suspects they might have experimented on the bodies—or at least tampered with them somehow."

Larson frowned, scrolling through the photos with a grim expression. "And the pilot's story?"

"That's the strangest part. The official report claims he wandered the jungle for days, but Levi's convinced it's a lie. The pilot's story doesn't add up with the evidence Levi's uncovered."

"What exactly is Levi hoping to find?" Deleon asked.

Yazmin glanced down, as if hesitant, then looked back at them with newfound resolve. "Closure. He lost someone on that flight. This isn't just about a story for him—it's personal. And for me . . . well, it's not every day a journalist gets handed a cover-up on this scale."

Larson nodded thoughtfully, handing back the phone. "We understand. And we'll keep our end of the bargain. The pilot's name is Evan Wheeler."

Yazmin's eyes widened, and she scribbled down the name on a napkin. "What do you know about him?"

Deleon and Larson exchanged a look. "We're already digging into his financials," Deleon said carefully. "If there's a motive, we'll find it."

Yazmin stood, tucking her notebook away. "Keep me posted, and I'll do the same." She held out her hand, and Deleon shook it firmly.

As she walked away, Larson looked at Deleon with a small smile. "You think we can trust her?"

"Not completely," Deleon replied, watching Yazmin disappear into the crowd. "But for now, we have a lead. Let's see where it takes us."

CHAPTER 50

MEDICINE WEEKLY

Modern Cloning Breakthroughs Transform Medicine

Scientists have reached a groundbreaking milestone in cloning, successfully replicating complex tissues and organs for the first time. These advancements pave the way for revolutionary treatments, from curing genetic diseases to creating customized organs for transplantation.

"The potential of cloning in medicine is limitless," says Dr. Caroline Finch, a leading researcher in regenerative medicine. "Tailored treatments and reduced organ rejection are just the beginning."

While the promise of personalized medicine excites the scientific community, ethical debates continue to swirl. As cloning technology advances, it raises profound questions about its societal impact and accessibility.

Levi Mathews

Cattleya Eldorado Longevity Medical Center and Spa, Fordlândia, Brazil

When Lev and CeCe entered the lobby, the next morning they saw a teenager in a security uniform leaning against the front desk. When the boy saw them, he stood up straight, trying to appear professional. Hector came out of the office. "Good morning. This is Filipe, our security guard."

They smiled. "Nice to meet you, Filipe," CeCe said in Portuguese. The boy responded with a nod and a smile.

"The chef prepared breakfast for you. Do you remember how to get to the pool?" Hector asked.

"Yes, thank you," CeCe replied.

As they walked away, Lev leaned in and whispered to CeCe, "The kid is our weak link."

They sat down at a table set with fruit, juice, and pastries.

"I'm getting used to this smell, it's like orchids on steroids," CeCe said taking a big bite of a croissant.

"I have an idea," Lev said. "I bet this kid would kill for an iPhone. Let's see if we can trade after breakfast."

"I think that sounds like a pretty good idea. Hurry up and eat; I can't wait to see what's here," CeCe said, taking a sip of juice.

The boy couldn't have been more than eighteen years old. His uniform looked like he'd borrowed it from his father, and he was leaning against the wall, looking completely annoyed and disinterested—just like any other teenager.

CeCe approached him, causing him to stand a little straighter. Hector had already told him they had guests and had slipped him three hundred dollars to keep his mouth shut. Filipe, after all, only had this job because Dr. Santiago owed a favor to his father. He was young, undertrained, and inexperienced—everything Lev and CeCe needed.

"Hi," CeCe said in Portuguese.

"Hi," Filipe said, smiling, revealing a mouth that had never seen a dentist or orthodontist.

"We wanted to know what's around here. Is there anything to do?" CeCe asked, trying to start a conversation.

Filipe looked nervously across the lobby toward Hector, who gave him a reassuring nod.

CeCe positioned herself to block Filipe's view of Hector, focusing his attention entirely on her.

Caught off guard, Filipe replied, "Um, there's a town about a mile from here called Fordlandia."

"Nothing else?" CeCe asked.

"Nope. People usually just hang out by the pool. You know, they're too sick to really do anything else," Filipe said.

"What do you mean, too sick?" CeCe asked, feigning curiosity.

Filipe shifted uncomfortably, unsure if he was allowed to talk about the usual clientele. "After their surgery, they just stay around. Sometimes they come with their husband or wife, and even they just stay at the hotel," he said, glancing nervously around.

"So, this is a hospital?" CeCe asked, looking surprised and confused.

"Well, the front of the building is more like a hotel, but nobody stays here unless they're sick. The back is where the surgeries take place, and where the labs are," Filipe said, growing visibly more uncomfortable.

"Labs?" CeCe questioned.

"Yeah, that's what they tell me, but I've never seen inside. I'm only allowed back there if Hector is with me. I've only been back there a couple of times," Filipe said sluggishly.

"But you have the key?" CeCe asked.

"Yeah," he answered.

"Could you show us that part of the building?" CeCe asked, her tone softening as she reached out, lightly touching his arm.

"No, I could get in trouble," he said, stepping back slightly.

CeCe leaned in closer, her voice soft and almost conspiratorial. "What if I had something to trade? Could I borrow your key for a little while if I give you something really good like an iPhone?" She became more flirtatious, gently touching his hand, making him break out in a nervous sweat.

Filipe hesitated, his mind racing. He knew he shouldn't, that this key card was meant to be guarded carefully. If Hector or Dr. Santiago found out he'd handed it over, there would be consequences—serious ones. But an iPhone . . . He'd wanted one of those for so long, and none of his friends could afford one. Just the thought of having one in his pocket, being the envy of everyone he knew, made him want to ignore the risks. Besides, what could really go wrong?

Still, a small voice in the back of his mind warned him that these guests weren't like the usual ones. They had a sharper look, a way of watching everything around them. He glanced down at the phone, then back at CeCe's face, her smile warm and encouraging. "But if I get caught . . ." he muttered, half to himself.

CeCe picked up on his hesitation immediately. She leaned in closer, her voice dropping to a whisper. "Listen, Filipe. I'm only asking to borrow it for a short time, and nobody has to know. But if you tell anyone . . ." She let the words hang in the air, her gaze turning serious. "I'll tell Hector and Dr. Santiago that you stole my cellphone. They'll believe me over you, and they might even report you to the police. Do you really want to risk that?"

Filipe swallowed, feeling a cold sweat break out on his forehead. She was right. No one would take his side if it came down to his word against hers. He looked down, the weight of the decision pressing on him. He wanted the phone, but he didn't want to lose his job—or worse. But the thought of showing off that phone, of finally having something this cool, overpowered his fear.

He nodded, hardly caring what these people were up to anymore. He just wanted that phone. His friends would be so jealous. Filipe pulled the key from his pocket and handed it to CeCe. She held out the phone but kept her grip on it for a moment longer.

"Remember, this is our secret," she said, her tone firm. "Don't play with the phone where anyone can see you. Later tonight, I'll show you how everything works, by the pool."

CHAPTER 51

THE NORTHEASTERN JOURNAL OF MEDICINE

Modern Cloning Breakthroughs Transform Medicine

Scientists have reached a groundbreaking milestone in cloning, successfully replicating complex tissues and organs for the first time. These advancements pave the way for revolutionary treatments, from curing genetic diseases to creating customized organs for transplantation.

"The potential of cloning in medicine is limitless," says Dr. Caroline Finch, a leading researcher in regenerative medicine. "Tailored treatments and reduced organ rejection are just the beginning."

While the promise of personalized medicine excites the scientific community, ethical debates continue to swirl. As cloning technology advances, it raises profound questions about its societal impact and accessibility.

Levi Mathews

Cattleya Eldorado Longevity Medical Center and Spa, Fordlândia, Brazil

It was almost two in the morning—late enough that Hector should be sound asleep. Levi held his breath, sliding the key card into the lock with trembling fingers, anticipation buzzing through him. A quiet click, and the door opened into a dark, pulsating silence.

The air hit them immediately—warm, humid, with a faintly acrid, medicinal smell and the orchids that made CeCe wrinkle her nose. "Are you okay?" Levi whispered, glancing at her as they stepped inside.

"It's not as strong as that other hospital," she murmured, nodding but clutching his arm a little tighter.

The room stretched before them like an eerie maze, lit by the soft blue glow emanating from towering glass containers that lined the walls and aisles. Shadows twisted along the floor and walls, making everything feel alive, as if the room itself was watching them.

As they ventured further in, Levi noticed the contents of the tanks—dark, shifting shapes, suspended in gelatinous fluid. His heart raced, equal parts horror and morbid fascination. CeCe's fingers dug into his arm as she realized what they were looking at.

"Oh my God . . ." she whispered, voice barely audible. Her eyes were wide, reflecting the unsettling blue glow around them. Inside each tank, human organs floated, connected by thin tubes pulsing with what seemed like artificial lifeblood. Levi approached a tank containing a kidney, perfectly preserved and connected to a tube that disappeared into the depths of the container.

"There's a . . . kidney," he muttered, voice tinged with dread. He scanned the room, noticing the rows upon rows of organs. Across the aisle, he spotted shelves stacked with livers in various stages of development. They moved in silence, unable to speak as the gravity of their discovery settled over them.

Levi spotted a ladder against one of the walls and climbed up, the rungs creaking under his weight. He took his phone out, recording a sweeping video of the tanks that stretched up to the high ceiling. "There are hundreds, maybe thousands," he muttered, more to himself. "This place . . . it's a farm for human organs."

As he climbed down, CeCe walked toward the next row, her hand flying to her mouth as she let out a small, choked gasp. Levi's stomach tightened, and he followed her gaze. In one of the tanks, a nearly fully developed human fetus floated, its tiny hands curled close to its face. Just as he looked, the fetus's foot shifted slightly, as if in a gentle kick.

CeCe's face crumpled, one hand instinctively going to her own belly. Levi's heart twisted. He moved closer, wrapping his arms around her, holding her tight. "Are you okay?" he whispered; his voice thick with concern. He realized in that moment how deeply he felt the need to protect her—not just from physical harm, but from the emotional and mental toll of what they were witnessing.

Yazmin's face appeared in his mind's eye—the look of horror as she was led away. He hadn't done anything to help her, and that guilt still haunted him. Holding CeCe now, he felt a surge of determination to protect her, as if he could make up for his past failure.

She nodded, though silent tears streamed down her cheeks. "There was a woman on the flight who was pregnant do you think it could be hers?" she whispered, her voice shaking.

A chill crept down Levi's spine. A stolen baby. The possibility hit him like a punch to the gut. He tried to hold it together, but his mind spun with the implications. Could it really be a human baby. Had whoever was behind this taken that life and twisted it into this . . . this nightmare of science? His heart hammered painfully, and he felt a swell of anger mixed with helplessness. He couldn't wrap his head around the cruelty of it—the exploitation of such innocence, a child who never had a chance. Or had this person found a way to move beyond growing an embryo in a lab to producing a live baby. The implications were too much to bear. Humanity wasn't ready for this, or at least he wasn't.

Levi gently led her away from the tank, his hand on her shoulder. "I don't know," he murmured, though the weight of the sight pressed down on him. This was beyond anything they had anticipated.

Meanwhile, Outside the Warehouse

Hector bolted upright at the piercing ring of his phone, the shrill sound dragging him from sleep. He grabbed it, barely registering the time. "Hello?" he answered groggily.

"Who's in the lab?" Dr. Santiago's voice cut through, sharp and edged with fury. "And why are the security cameras down."

Hector's heart dropped, cold fear twisting in his stomach. "I . . . I don't think anyone should be in there," he stammered, his mind scrambling.

"Some sensors were triggered in the growth chamber," Santiago said, his voice dangerously calm. "My security team is on route and should arrive within thirty minutes."

Panic exploded within Hector. "No, don't send them! It could just be a glitch—I'll check it out myself and call you back," he said, desperately trying to sound calm, to buy himself some time.

But Santiago was unyielding. "The team is already on their way. Expect them shortly. Contact me after the inspection," he said before hanging up abruptly.

For a long moment, Hector sat frozen, the weight of his betrayal crushing him. Santiago's work, his life's dedication . . . and he'd put it all at risk. All because of a moment of greed. He sprang up, dread clawing at his insides as he raced down the hallway to Filipe's room.

He didn't bother knocking—he shoved the door open, flicking the light on. "Get up!" he yelled; voice raw with barely controlled fury.

Filipe blinked up at him, bleary-eyed and confused. "What's going on?"

Ignoring him, Hector stormed to the dresser, rifling through until his hand closed around a familiar, sleek cellphone—far more expensive than Filipe could have afforded. Rage flared as he realized what had happened. Without a word, he pocketed the phone, his mind racing with suspicion and anger.

"Hey!" Filipe protested, jolting fully awake, panic flashing in his eyes.

Hector's anger bubbled over as he reached into the drawer, pulling out a loaded gun and pointing it at Filipe, his hand shaking. "You gave them your key card?!" he snarled, voice hoarse with rage and fear.

For a brief, terrifying moment, he considered pulling the trigger, his fury clouding his judgment. He had put everything at risk—all of Santiago's work, years of research, and his own reputation. Filipe's eyes went wide, hands raised in surrender.

"I . . . I didn't know they'd go into the lab! I thought they were just tourists!" Filipe stammered, voice trembling, as he processed the danger he was in.

Hector's arm wavered, but he lowered the gun, chest heaving as he struggled to control his breathing. He stared at Filipe, the weight of the mistake sinking in. "Do you know what you've done?" he spat; voice laced with venom. "You've put everything at risk. Santiago's entire life's work . . . and you've destroyed it and destroyed me. They will kill us you stupid boy."

He took a shaky breath, forcing himself to focus. The security team would arrive in minutes—he couldn't let them find Levi and CeCe. He had turned off the security system to hide the couple, it had been risky, but it had happened before. A storm had knocked out the electricity and the generator only covered the lab. He was not going to let this couple destroy everything, he would have he would kill them himself and be the hero who took out the intruders.

CHAPTER 52

NOW MAGAZINE

How Journalists Sparked the FBI's Deep Dive into Watergate

In the early 1970s, what seemed like a routine burglary at the Democratic National Committee headquarters in the Watergate complex unraveled into one of the most defining political scandals in American history. This transformation was driven by the relentless efforts of Washington Post reporters Bob Woodward and Carl Bernstein. Their meticulous investigative reporting uncovered a trail of corruption that reached the highest levels of the Nixon administration, captivating the nation and pressuring the FBI into action.

As Woodward and Bernstein revealed deeper connections between the break-in and White House officials, their groundbreaking work fueled a comprehensive FBI investigation that culminated in the resignation of President Richard Nixon. The Watergate scandal became a landmark moment in American democracy, showcasing the indispensable role of journalism in holding power accountable.

Today, Watergate remains a powerful reminder of how investigative reporting and federal inquiries, when working in tandem, can expose corruption and safeguard democratic principles. In an era of evolving challenges for both journalists and government oversight, the legacy of this collaboration continues to resonate.

Evan Wheeler

Martinsville, New Jersey

Evan Wheeler slid his coffee cup into the dishwasher, the quiet click almost deafening in his still kitchen. He straightened his tie in the bathroom mirror, catching his own reflection just as the doorbell chimed. Two silhouettes loomed through the frosted glass, official and unyielding. His heart stalled. The police.

The doorbell rang again, sharper, demanding action. Evan swallowed, willing his hands steady, and approached the door with measured steps.

"Captain Wheeler," the taller of the two said, flashing his credentials. "We're FBI. I'm Agent Deleon, and this is Agent Larson. We'd like to ask you a few questions about Flight 987."

A prickle of dread crawled up Evan's spine. Robert said no one would ever know my name. "Uh … I was just heading to work. Can this wait?" The crack in his voice betrayed him.

"It'll only take a few minutes," Deleon assured, stepping closer to the threshold, his stare unwavering.

Evan hesitated before stepping aside, the urge to slam the door gnawing at him. "How did you get my name?" His mind whirled. "He said my name was sealed for my safety."

"Your name isn't public, Captain. But we have jurisdiction," Deleon replied, his gaze sharp. "Just to confirm, you were the pilot of Flight 987?"

Evan's mouth agape stunned.

"Who's he?' Larson asked.

Evan looked confused.

"You said they said my name would be sealed." Larson pushed.

A rush of nausea hit him he could be barely think. "The union," Evan stuttered.

Larson clicked her pen, flipping open a notebook. "You're not flying anymore, correct?"

"No," Evan replied too quickly, feeling the lie pulse in his veins. "I . . . I'm grounded."

"Is that permanent?" Larson asked, pen poised.

"Yes . . . No, I mean . . ." He swallowed, his mind scrambling to keep up. Focus. Stay calm.

Deleon's eyes narrowed. "In the NTSB report, you said you blacked out and woke up over the Amazon. How exactly does someone wake up in an oxygen mask?"

Evan blinked, surprised by the question. "Uh, well . . . I must have . . . grabbed the mask when I blacked out, but it didn't go all the way on." He could feel his pulse hammering in his throat. *Just make it sound real.* "My head must've been close enough to get some oxygen. Just enough to . . . wake me."

The agents exchanged glances. Deleon's pen hovered as he made a note. "Can you show us how the mask was positioned?"

Evan nodded, hands shaking as he brought them up to his face, mimicking the motion. "I think . . . like this. My head was low, and as I . . . blacked out, I somehow . . . just got close enough." He could feel the blood roaring in his ears, his thoughts flailing for more details.

Larson's pen scratched on paper. "And the runway? How did you find it in the dark?"

Evan paused, drawing a breath. "When I woke up, I saw my co-pilot . . . I . . . I can't remember his name." His voice cracked as he stumbled over his lie. "I tried calling back to the flight attendants. No one answered. So, I descended to eight thousand feet and . . . saw the runway, lit by the moon. It was bright, almost like daylight," he added, though even he knew the story sounded thin.

Larson's pen didn't stop. "You mentioned in your testimony that you checked the passengers. How did you know they were unconscious? Did you check for pulses?"

Evan's mouth went dry, his mind spinning. "I just . . . looked. And I thought they were all . . . gone."

"You thought?" Larson leaned forward. "Or you knew?"

A wave of dizziness washed over him. He closed his eyes, feeling the weight of it all crashing down. "I . . . I don't remember exactly," he whispered. Just keep it together.

Deleon's voice cut through his fog. "Your daughter recently passed away, correct?"

Evan's eyes flew open, jolted by the shift in topic. "Yes," he murmured, staring down at the carpet.

"Our condolences." Larson's tone softened. "Your wife . . . she's also ill?"

Evan clenched his fists, grounding himself. They don't care. "She's doing better now," he replied, a forced smile tugging at his lips. "Thanks."

The agents rose to leave. "We'll schedule a formal interview for Monday at 11:00. You can bring a lawyer or your union rep."

As the door clicked shut behind them, Evan's gaze drifted to a family photo on the mantle. His wife's eyes sparkled, and their daughter's laughter seemed to echo faintly in his memory. He was losing it, them, everything.

Later, as he hurried into work, Jack's sharp voice stopped him cold.

"Evan," Jack said evenly, "I had the FBI here this morning looking for you."

A rush of panic surged through him. "FBI?" he repeated, hoping to feign ignorance. "Why would they . . . ?"

Jack's gaze held steady, scrutinizing. "Evan . . . I know what you did. I know why you did it." The words hung in the air, heavy with implication.

Evan's heart raced as he nodded, unsure if he was agreeing or conceding. He couldn't bring himself to ask exactly what Jack knew.

CHAPTER 53

Levi Mathews

Cattleya Eldorado Longevity Medical Center and Spa, Fordlândia, Brazil

Levi and CeCe moved cautiously between the towering shelves, their phone screens casting faint glows in the dimly lit lab. The air was thick with the same unnatural smell. Levi raised his phone, snapping pictures in rapid succession.

A thunderous crash shattered the silence, the reverberation bouncing off the high ceiling like an explosion. Levi's heart lurched. He instinctively yanked CeCe behind him, pressing her against the tanks.

A voice, raw with panic, bellowed through the space. "I know you're in here! Come out right now!"

Levi's mind snapped into survival mode. He inched toward the door, his grip firm on CeCe's wrist. A quick glance through the shelving revealed Hector standing near the entrance, his hands trembling as he clutched a gun. The flickering light overhead made his wide, tear-streaked eyes appear even more unhinged.

Levi exhaled slowly. "He has a gun. I think I can talk him down."

CeCe gave him a skeptical glance but didn't argue. Together, they rounded the corner, hands raised in cautious surrender. Levi stepped forward first, keeping his voice steady. "We can explain."

Hector's chest heaved, his face slick with sweat. He looked less like a man in control and more like someone teetering on the edge of total breakdown. His hands shook so badly that Levi feared the gun would go off by accident.

"No, you can't explain!" Hector wailed. "Do you have any idea what you've done?"

Levi stayed still, his pulse hammering in his ears.

"They're coming," Hector sobbed, his voice cracking. "Security. SWAT. They're on their way, and they're going to kill all of us! Everything is ruined! I'm a dead man."

Levi took a slow step forward, his hands still raised. "Hector, calm down. We can get through this. Trust me."

"The only way through this is if I kill you," Hector whispered, his lips trembling. "Then I can look like the hero. It's the only way."

A blur of movement.

Filipe barreled through the entrance, colliding with Hector. The force sent both stumbling. Levi seized the moment, lunging forward. He wrested the gun from Hector's grip. Hector crumpled to the ground, sobbing.

Then Levi heard it—

The unmistakable thump of helicopter blades slicing through the air. The sound sent a jolt of urgency through his system.

He grabbed Hector by the arm, hauling him up. "Get up. We have to move!"

Together, they all sprinted toward the lobby. Levi's mind raced. "Is there a back entrance?"

Hector gasped for breath. "Through the kitchen! Over there."

Levi pushed forward. "And the front gate? It's the only way out?"

Hector nodded frantically.

Levi made a split-second decision. He shoved the gun back into Hector's hands. "Listen to me. Go to the front desk. If they don't find us, it'll look like a glitch. Act normal." He held Hector's gaze, willing him to understand. "When you see us at the gate, activate it. If we escape, they won't know that we've been here, and nothing bad will happen to you. Do you understand?"

Hector's breath hitched. He looked at the gun, then back at Levi. A flicker of something—understanding, desperation, maybe even hope—passed over his face.

Levi turned to CeCe. "We run. Now."

CHAPTER 54

*** BREAKING ***

NCC

Flight 987 – New Questions Surface

Olly Sanchez, Anchor

"Tonight, breaking developments in the investigation of Flight 987, the commercial airliner that vanished in mysterious circumstances. While initial reports suggested mechanical failure, unnamed sources close to the investigation now point to potential discrepancies in the pilot's account of events.

Authorities have reopened key lines of inquiry, and forensic teams are working to reconcile the timeline with physical evidence. Captain Evan Wheeler, who piloted Flight 987, is expected to meet with investigators this week for further questioning.

El Diablo

Central Region Airspace, Amazon, Brazil

The Sikorsky S-97 helicopter cut through the night sky, drawing closer to its target with every passing minute. El Diablo, seated beside the pilot, felt the vibrations of the aircraft as it cruised toward the remote laboratory hidden deep in the Amazon. The emergency alert phone had jolted him awake at precisely 2:00 a.m.—a call he had dreaded for years. It only rang when an intruder breached the lab's secure perimeter.

For years, El Diablo had urged Dr. Santiago to place more security on-site, to treat the project with the caution it demanded. "Religious fanatics, gangs, desperate people—they'll come looking," he had warned. But Santiago, always one to assume control, had dismissed his concerns. He believed the locals, superstitious and fear, would keep them away especially after Hector had spread rumors of the ungodly things that took place inside the fortress.

Tonight, however, those beliefs had failed. Sensors meticulously installed by Santiago had detected a breach in the lab's sterile environment—temperature fluctuations, humidity shifts, even the faintest tremors were enough to trigger an alarm. This intrusion was likely no accident, and if there was one thing El Diablo knew, it was that people who ventured into places like this rarely stumbled in by mistake.

He surveyed his team. They were armed and prepared, faces set in grim determination as they awaited orders. The helicopter was fully fueled, but it would still take ninety minutes to reach the lab, granting any intruder a dangerous head start. El Diablo had fought with Santiago over the decision to base the security team in Manaus, two hours away by air. "It gives intruders a head start," he'd argued, but Santiago had brushed it off, certain he had everything under control.

After his call with Santiago, El Diablo had quickly contacted his operative near Fordlandia, instructing them to control the situation until the team arrived. This operative was a local, well-paid and reliable, someone who could keep an eye on the lab's surroundings and report any movement.

As he waited, El Diablo's thoughts turned to Santiago's obsession with human organ cloning, an ambition that had twisted into something monstrous. Growing up together in the same orphanage in Caracas, El Diablo had once seen Santiago as a brother. They had endured the same hardships, rising out of poverty with a shared resilience. But somewhere along the way, Santiago's drive to change the world had morphed into something darker, leaving behind a trail of blood. El Diablo had questioned him about it more than once, but Santiago, emboldened by a powerful American investor, had been unyielding. "Adjust or resign," he'd said coldly.

In another life, El Diablo might have walked away. But his loyalty to Santiago ran deep—formed in the shared loneliness of their childhood and strengthened over years of survival. Despite his misgivings, he had stayed, watching with a mixture of dread and loyalty as Santiago's vision escalated into mass murder.

As they drew closer to the lab, El Diablo glanced out into the vast darkness of the Amazon below. The jungle spread out endlessly, a dense, unforgiving terrain that swallowed anyone unfamiliar with its perils. He knew that if the intruders had any intention of escaping, the jungle's thick foliage and treacherous terrain would offer them no mercy. The Amazon was as much a barrier as it was a refuge, and that thought provided a cold comfort; there was nowhere for them to run that he couldn't reach.

The pilot signaled their approach, and El Diablo turned to his team, giving the silent command to prepare. He could feel the weight of the moment pressing down on him, a mix of dread and inevitability. Santiago's atrocities were finally catching up to him, and El Diablo knew that tonight might force him to face his own choices—the lines he had crossed and the loyalty that had kept him bound to a man he no longer fully recognized.

With a final nod, El Diablo directed his team into action. The Amazon night stretched dark and still around them, but he knew it wouldn't stay that way for long. They were moments away from confronting whatever horror awaited in that forbidden lab, and El Diablo, for the first time in years, felt the faint stirrings of doubt. But he silenced it, letting the role he had accepted— protector, enforcer—take over.

There would be no turning back now.

CHAPTER 55

The Boston Journal News

June 14, 2005 — Children abandoned at orphanages in Latin America and parts of Europe often inherit the name of the institution itself. A boy left at San Maria's Orphanage, for instance, might become Pedro San Maria. Researchers note that many such orphans later change their surnames as adults, sometimes to obscure their origins, sometimes to reinvent themselves. Tracing these shifts can provide rare insight into a person's past — if you know where to look.

Yazmin Da Silva

Underground Media Group, New York, New York

Yazmin immersed herself in the photos Levi had sent, each one revealing chilling fragments of a disturbing puzzle. The first batch documented the plane's landing site—tire tracks etched deep in the dirt, signs of a large-scale operation, and fences crushed under the weight of heavy trucks. Intriguing, but still missing definitive clues.

Scrolling onward, she studied images of the decrepit hospital on the outskirts of an abandoned ghost town. More truck tracks crisscrossed the area, alongside discarded medical equipment. Levi's notes described an unsettling blend of ammonia, bleach, and decay and the odd sweetness of flowers were hard to understand having no context in this strange tragedy.

Then, real-time updates began arriving from Levi and CeCe's exploration of a warehouse. Yazmin's connection with them was delayed, leaving her unable to communicate directly as the images loaded on her screen. Rows of shelves filled with tanks of viscous liquid came into focus. Inside, floating fragments unmistakably resembled human organs at various stages of development. Yazmin's stomach tightened—someone was cultivating organs, likely for the black market. Her hands stilled on her keyboard when she saw one of the most disturbing images: a human fetus suspended in a tank, its tiny fingers, toes, and limbs shifting involuntarily. It looked like a live sonogram, but horrifyingly real.

Determined to understand the scale of this operation, Yazmin dug deeper. She recalled recent advancements in bioengineering, particularly an article from The New York Times discussing the cultivation of organs from stem cells. But what Levi had captured far surpassed anything she'd read about—fully formed organs, seemingly ready for use. This was on an entirely different level.

She turned to the internet, launching searches from "Brazil medical hospital" to "cloned organs Brazil," but her queries returned nothing relevant. Then a name resurfaced: "El Diablo." Intrigued, she typed it into the search bar and uncovered a profile on Guillermo Flores. A former Venezuelan military man turned mercenary, Flores operated an organization known as Equipo Militar (EM), reputed for their skills and ruthlessness in covert operations. His biography painted the portrait of a man hardened by years of military service, now wielding influence in underground networks.

Digging deeper, Yazmin clicked through articles detailing Flores's exploits and his team's notorious missions. The Journal of Professional Adventurers offered insights into his early life—an orphan raised in a Catholic institution, nicknamed "El Diablo" by a priest. One photo in particular captured her attention: Flores standing beside a man in a lab coat labeled "José Flores." It piqued her curiosity. There was something about that photo that gave her pause.

Following this thread, Yazmin found an obscure link discussing José Flores's celebrated return to Venezuela, hailed as a prodigy from Harvard University set to revolutionize medicine. A few more clicks uncovered articles chronicling José's journey from a Catholic orphanage to Harvard, where he'd received a full scholarship to medical school. Yet, despite his impressive résumé, details about his specialty and achievements were surprisingly scarce. A veil of secrecy seemed to surround his work.

Curious and increasingly suspicious, Yazmin decided to contact Harvard Medical School directly, hoping the registrar's office could verify José Flores' academic background. The response was unsettling. A woman on the line told Yazmin there was no record of a "José Flores" from that period, hesitated, then abruptly hung up. Yazmin stared at the phone, her suspicion deepening. This was no coincidence. She had a hunch that José Flores was operating under an alias.

Her determination solidified, Yazmin booked the first available flight to Boston, driven by a need to uncover the truth about this enigmatic figure and his connection to the illicit organ trade. As she packed her bag, her thoughts raced, each piece of this twisted puzzle falling into place. This story was more than just a career opportunity—it was a chance to expose something horrific, something that could shake the medical and scientific world to its core.

Before heading to the airport, she decided to leverage her social media following for leads. Yazmin posted a cryptic message on Instagram, hinting at a developing story in Brazil and inviting her followers to share any relevant information they might have on "El Diablo" or organ-cloning rumors. Her followers were a mix of investigative minds, conspiracy theorists, and Latin American insiders—she knew they could bring unique insights.

On the flight, Yazmin planned to sift through the comments and messages, hoping the crowd-sourced intel would provide the final pieces to round out her story. Her heart raced as she settled into her seat; anticipation mixed with dread. Whatever awaited her in Boston, she was prepared to face it head-on.

CHAPTER 56

El Diablo

Cattleya Eldorado Longevity Medical Center and Spa, Fordlandia, Brazil

El Diablo moved through the complex with his team, their steps soundless against the cold tile floors. The building had been swept, every room checked, every corridor cleared. Yet something gnawed at him—an unease that coiled deep in his gut. The facility was too quiet, too still. Someone had been here. Someone might still be here.

Pale morning light bled through the lobby's wide windows, the faint glow painting long shadows across the marble floors. The air was thick with the damp chill of the Amazon morning, mixing with the acrid scent of sweat and gun oil. His men, weapons drawn, waited for his orders, their eyes scanning for movement, ears straining for any sound beyond their own breathing.

El Diablo's gaze settled on Hector behind the counter, the man standing unnaturally stiff, his fingers twitching slightly against the polished wood. Suspicion flickered through him like a spark catching dry leaves. Nearby, Filipe hovered, his restless eyes darting from one man to another.

El Diablo strode toward the counter, his movements slow, deliberate. He leveled his gun at Hector's face, the muzzle barely a foot away. His voice was low, edged with ice. "I'll ask you one last time. Were there intruders in this facility?"

Hector didn't flinch, but a bead of sweat traced down his temple. "No one, El Diablo," he said carefully, forcing himself to meet the enforcer's gaze. "I would tell you if there was. I believe the storm last night caused the cameras to go down. And the anomaly in the lab could also be explained by the sudden power outage. It's happened before."

El Diablo didn't move, didn't blink. The weight of his stare bore down on Hector, but something in the man's face—an ever-so-slight flicker of hesitation—pricked at El Diablo's instincts. He'd interrogated enough men to know when someone was lying. Hector was holding something back.

Then, the sharp crack of a gunshot split the morning silence.

Filipe had fired his gun into the floor. The sound sent every man in the room snapping to attention. Weapons raised, eyes scanning for an attack, the team tensed for an ambush that didn't come.

In the split-second of confusion, Hector moved. He ducked behind the counter, his hand pressing the gate control button in a swift, practiced motion. The heavy metal gates groaned as they began to slide open. Out of the corner of his eye, he saw CeCe and Levi slip through the narrow gap. A second later, he released the button, letting the gate slide shut behind them.

"Stand down!" El Diablo's bark cut through the chaos, his command silencing the room.

He turned on Filipe, fury flashing in his eyes, and pointed his gun straight at the young man's chest. "What the hell were you thinking?" His voice was deathly quiet, laced with something more dangerous than rage—controlled wrath.

Filipe's hands shook. He opened his mouth, scrambling for an explanation, but in his panic, his grip on the gun faltered. The weapon slipped from his grasp, hitting the floor with a metallic clang. A second shot rang out as the gun discharged, the bullet ricocheting off the marble and narrowly missing El Diablo's foot.

El Diablo didn't flinch. His eyes were locked on the gate, realization striking like a blow to the chest. The faint rattle of the gate lock confirmed it—Levi and CeCe had a head start, but not for long.

He inhaled slowly, a controlled breath. Failure burned at his pride, but this wasn't over.

"Hector, open the gate now!"

He turned and bolted, his boots pounding against the floor as he ran for the gate. "Everyone, outside! They're running into the jungle!"

His team surged into action, following him through the lobby and out into the open air.

"Move!" El Diablo barked, his voice like a whip. "Don't let them out of your sight!"

The team rushed forward, their boots kicking up damp earth as they stormed after the fugitives. The humid air clung to them, thick as the tension crackling in the air. Guns at the ready, eyes scanning, muscles coiled for pursuit.

El Diablo ran at the front, his mind sharpening with the hunt. He could already picture Levi and CeCe, running blindly into the jungle, thinking they had a chance. But the jungle wasn't a savior—it was a slow, merciless executioner.

They might have made it out of the hotel, but they weren't out of danger.

They wouldn't get far.

Not from him.

CHAPTER 57

Levi and CeCe

Cattleya Eldorado Longevity Medical Center and Spa, Fordlândia, Brazil

Levi and CeCe moved through the gleaming commercial kitchen; their footsteps muffled by the stainless-steel surfaces. The ticking clock added urgency to their movements; the security team's sweep was moments away.

They turned a corner and found the chef holding a knife, looking tense and worried. Levi put a finger to his lips, and the chef, understanding, motioned toward the back.

They found the delivery entrance and a smaller door nearby. With cautious, deliberate movements, they slipped through, making their way toward the front gate. Levi wasn't sure if Filipe and Hector would be able to spot them out in the open.

"Stay here. I'm going to get Hector's attention. Be ready to run," Levi whispered, panting from the oppressive heat and humidity.

"Why can't I go with you?" CeCe asked, sweat dripping from her face.

"There's not enough room for both of us behind the columns. They might see us," Levi replied. "It's going to be okay. Stay here."

Levi moved to the next column, pausing to listen. Inside, voices rose as the men shouted at Hector. Peeking around the corner, Levi caught Filipe's eye and gave a nod before ducking back. He prayed Filipe would signal Hector.

Seconds stretched into an eternity as Levi waited for the gate to open. The security team's sweep was nearing completion, and Levi wasn't sure if their movements included the parking lot. He gave CeCe a reassuring nod; her terror was palpable. Regret gnawed at him for bringing her into this danger.

The gate remained closed. Desperate, Levi craned his neck around the column, trying to catch Hector's or Filipe's attention amidst the chaos inside. Hector's pleas grew more frantic, the voices escalating. *Come on, come on.*

A gunshot cracked the air. Shouts erupted inside, and Hector's scream cut above the noise. The gate began to swing open. Levi waved frantically at CeCe, and they sprinted toward the jungle.

They ran until they thought they were safe, but the sound of the gate opening again spurred them onward. Men shouted behind them, closing in fast. The dense jungle enveloped them, branches clawing at their skin as they pushed forward. Levi had no sense of direction; he could only hope they were heading toward the villagers.

"We have to reach the village. It can't be much farther," Levi gasped, his breath ragged.

The shouts of their pursuers grew louder. At last, through the thick foliage, he could see the glow of the campfire. CeCe cried out and stumbled. He was a few steps ahead and, looking back, saw the men almost upon them, guns drawn.

Every instinct screamed at him to run, to save himself. But memories of abandoning Yazmin in the middle of Baghdad's ghetto flashed through his mind. He couldn't leave CeCe. Not again. In that moment, he resolved that if she died, he would too. He threw himself over her, shielding her with his body, bracing for the end.

Silence.

Levi looked up to see Olavo and the villagers, armed with military-grade weapons, standing between them and El Diablo's team. The mercenaries' guns remained raised, but as they realized the villagers were surrounding them, they hesitated, then slowly lowered their weapons, aware of the villagers' rifles pointed at their backs.

Olavo, the man who had helped them before, faced El Diablo, his rifle trained on the mercenary leader. No one spoke as the villagers confiscated the militia's weapons, stripping them of their firepower with quiet efficiency. One villager pressed his gun to El Diablo's neck, forcing him to release his weapon.

El Diablo and Olavo exchanged a knowing glance. "Good job, Olavo," El Diablo said, his tone hard but tinged with respect. Without another word, he turned and led his team back the way they had come.

"Are you okay? Is the baby okay?" Levi asked, helping CeCe to stand.

"Yes," she replied, exhaling deeply. "We're okay."

Back in the village, Levi and CeCe sat by a campfire as the villagers handed them cups of water. Levi gently rubbed her back, his concern evident. "Are you sure you're all right?"

CeCe gave him a faint smile, her hand resting protectively on her belly. "I'm fine, and the baby's fine. Don't worry."

"I'm sorry I dragged you into this," Levi said softly, guilt etched in his voice. "It was reckless of me."

CeCe looked at him, her expression resolute. "I'm not sorry. I needed to see what happened for myself. I needed to let Lucas rest."

The sound of footsteps drew everyone's attention. The villagers stood; weapons ready. Levi instinctively moved in front of CeCe, shielding her.

"It's me, Papa," Filipe called out, easing the tension. The villagers lowered their guns as he approached.

Filipe handed Levi and CeCe their backpacks. His father pulled him into a tight embrace before letting him sit beside CeCe.

Levi, still piecing everything together, looked at Filipe. "What happened back there?"

Filipe shrugged, a hint of pride in his eyes. "I panicked and pulled the trigger. They pointed their guns at me, but then they saw the gate moving and ran after you."

"What happened to Hector?" Levi inquired.

"I'm not sure," Filipe replied with a shrug. "They took . . . my—uh, I mean, your phone."

"That's okay," CeCe said, giving the boy a warm hug. "When I get back, I'll send you a new phone."

Filipe's face lit up with gratitude.

Exhausted, Levi and CeCe settled by the fire. CeCe leaned against Levi, quickly drifting off to sleep. Levi's hand found his flask in his backpack. He stared at it, the worn leather surface holding echoes of his past. Despite everything, he felt no urge to drink. Somewhere along this journey, things had changed. He'd faced each moment instead of drowning them in alcohol. He'd made a real friend, one he cared about deeply.

Pouring out the contents, he placed the empty flask back in his bag and leaned against the tree. For the first time in a long time, sleep came easily.

* * *

Robert was jolted awake by the ring of his phone.

"What is it?" he grumbled.

"There has been a situation," José Santiago said. "We caught some people in the lab."

"What do you mean? How do you know?"

"My men chased them into the jungle. They got away, but one of them was captured on a helmet cam—Levi Mathews, a journalist. I believe they took photos of the lab. They were inside for at least twenty minutes."

A slow smile spread across Robert's face. "I prepared for this," he replied smoothly. "I'll call you soon."

As he hung up, Robert retrieved a red pouch containing a thumb drive and an FBI contact card. He picked up the phone, his mind whirring with the next phase of his plan.

"Agent Deleon, this is Robert Alexander. I have new information to share. Please call me back as soon as you can. Thank you."

He hung up, setting the pieces of his plan into motion. He would control the narrative and secure his position—no matter the cost.

CHAPTER 58

THE NEW YORK CHRONICLE

"Scientist Vanishes with Breakthrough Cloning Research"

The New York Sentinel, July 23, 1974

Dr. José Santiago (Flores), a once-promising figure in the field of regenerative medicine, is at the center of a shocking scandal that has rocked the global scientific community. Accused of stealing critical test results from the National Institute for Genetic Research, Santiago disappears overnight, leaving his colleagues in a storm of betrayal and unanswered questions.

Witnesses report seeing Santiago in the lab late the night before his abrupt departure, hours after security staff logged out for the evening. By morning, several years' worth of confidential research on human cell cloning—work many believe could revolutionize organ transplantation—has vanished along with him.

Authorities track Santiago to Caracas, Venezuela, where sources claim he is seeking refuge under the protection of powerful, unnamed backers. Speculation swirls that Santiago intends to continue his experiments in secret, outside the jurisdiction of U.S. and international law.

"José always talked about pushing the limits of science, no matter the cost," says a former colleague, who wishes to remain anonymous. "None of us thought he'd go this far."

While federal agents launch an international manhunt, bioethicists warn of the implications of Santiago's actions. "If the stolen data falls into the wrong hands, we could be looking at a new era of unregulated experimentation," says Dr. Alan Hargrove, an ethicist at Harvard University. "It's not just science—it's human-ity that's at risk."

As the world watches this high-stakes drama unfold, one question looms: How far will Dr. Santiago go in his quest to rewrite the rules of medicine?

Yazmin Da Silva

Massachusetts Hall, Harvard University, Cambridge, Massachusetts

Yazmin couldn't believe she was able to find the article that seemingly tied the doctor to all of this. The discovery still buzzed in her mind, a mix of disbelief and vindication. Could it really be this simple, or was she missing something? She glanced at her reflection in the compact mirror, frowning at her smeared lipstick. The cab ride from Logan Airport had dragged on for nearly an hour, each minute weighed down by her growing frustration and anticipation. She'd read the article twice during the ride, her mind racing with the implications of what she'd uncovered.

Now, she was finally here. Harvard's campus looked serene in the early evening light, the last glow of the sunset casting long shadows across the brick buildings. The quiet stillness of the place felt almost mocking, as though the world didn't realize the weight of the information tucked in her bag. If this article was real—and if she could prove it—it could unravel everything.

After consulting the campus directory, she located Dr. John Wembley, director of Stem Cell and Regenerative Biology Studies, at the Camargo Lab. She approached his office and tapped on the door, but silence greeted her. A passing student informed her that Dr. Wembley had left in the afternoon and would be back for an evening lecture at 8:00.

Determined not to waste any time, Yazmin found Dr. Wembley's address, a ten-minute walk away from campus. She navigated through a quiet neighborhood of vintage homes, the air crisp with the smell of decaying leaves and the chill of Massachusetts in spring. As she reached a quaint cottage, she knocked on the door, hoping he was home.

Inside, a dog barked. Moments later, she heard Dr. Wembley's muffled voice, trying to calm the animal. "Quiet, Malloy! Quiet!" The door creaked open, and a miniature pinscher darted out, yapping and jumping at her legs.

"Malloy! Get in here," Dr. Wembley scolded, scooping the dog into his arms. The dog wriggled, still excited, his tail wagging furiously. "What can I do for you?" he asked, adjusting his grip on the energetic pup.

"Dr. Wembley?" she asked, confirming his identity. He was a thin, older man with sandy brown hair, a receding hairline, and round glasses.

"Yes, and you are?"

"My name is Yazmin Da Silva. I'm a reporter working on an article about cloning. Your name kept coming up in my research, and I was hoping to ask you a few questions."

His face grew wary. "It depends on the questions."

"My article is on cloning human organs. Do you know a Dr. José Flores?"

Dr. Wembley's expression hardened. Before she could finish, he began closing the door. Thinking quickly, Yazmin said, "It's about Flight 987." The door paused, and then creaked open again. With a sigh, he motioned her inside. The dog barked at her once more as she entered, and she hesitated before giving it a quick pat.

The cottage's interior was cozy and lived in. Shelves lined with books and knickknacks adorned the far wall, and a flat-screen TV hung over the fireplace. She noticed a faint smell of coffee mingling with the musty scent of old paper—a comforting contrast to the sterile, corporate offices she was used to.

"Sit down. Can I get you some water or something?" he offered, gesturing to a well-worn couch.

"No, thank you." She took a seat as the dog trotted over, hopping onto the couch and nestling among the throw pillows. Dr. Wembley settled into a lounger across from her, his posture guarded.

"You mentioned Flight 987," he said, curiosity now evident in his gaze. "As soon as the details emerged, I had a sinking feeling he was involved."

"So, you know him?" she asked, leaning forward slightly.

He nodded, glancing away for a moment. "Yes. But there's a gag order on this case, so you cannot print my name. If anyone asks, I'll deny talking to you. I could lose my job . . . or worse. Do I have your word I'll remain anonymous?" His eyes met hers, filled with an urgency that made her understand the risk he was taking.

"You have my word," she assured him.

Dr. Wembley sighed, seemingly relieved, and began. "José came to Harvard on a scholarship. He's . . . brilliant. His intelligence is at a genius level. We were part of a study on cloning organs, and I was on the team when he joined."

He paused, his gaze drifting as if recalling a painful memory. "There were ten of us, working together in the lab. We were a close-knit group— except for José. He was ambitious, driven, and often clashed with the rest of us. Despite his genius, he was . . . difficult."

Yazmin could see the bitterness in his eyes as he continued. "Four years later, we were on the verge of a breakthrough. Right before Christmas, we were about to make a significant discovery. We all went home for the holidays, but José . . . he stayed. He had no family or close friends here and couldn't afford to return to Venezuela. At least that' is what he told us; we should have known."

Dr. Wembley's voice grew quieter. "When we returned, we found the lab ransacked. All our notes, samples, data—everything was gone. He even destroyed anything he couldn't carry. It was clear he wanted all the credit for himself."

He shook his head, the memory still raw. "The school launched an investigation, but by then, José had fled to Venezuela. The lawsuits were pointless; Venezuela protected him. They wouldn't extradite him."

Yazmin let his words sink in, feeling the weight of what he'd lost. "When I mentioned 'Flight 987,' it seemed to strike a chord with you. Can you tell me why?"

"At first, I thought it was just a tragic accident. But as the details emerged, I realized it was exactly the kind of thing José would do. He was obsessed with cloning. He used to berate us, saying we were unprofessional and undeserving of the discovery. When I heard about Flight 987, I suspected he might be harvesting the organs for black-market sales. Hearing his name from you just confirms it—José must be cloning those organs."

"During your study, were you close to cloning organs?" Yazmin asked, watching his expression carefully.

"Almost. We managed to get a T-cell from a human heart to multiply, but it stopped after a few divisions. We'd just created a substance like human placenta, hoping it would encourage cell growth. We were set to test it after the break . . . and then he took it all."

Yazmin handed him her phone. "I have pictures of a lab in Brazil. Would you like to see them?"

Dr. Wembley's eyes widened as he scrolled through the images. "Incredible," he murmured, shaking his head. "What he's done is . . . astounding."

"Do you think he did this for money?"

He looked up, his eyes sharp. "José Flores is a narcissist. Fame, recognition—that's what he craves. He wants to be known as the doctor who changed modern medicine."

"These days, he's calling himself José Santiago," she said. "He conspired to commit mass murder . . . to make himself famous?"

Dr. Wembley's voice dropped. "In my opinion, he orchestrated mass murder to secure a supply of uninjured organs for cloning. He wants to dominate the market, to have the world's desperately ill patients coming to him. He'll be seen as a savior, the doctor who 'saves lives.' The money . . . that's secondary to him. What he craves is notoriety."

A shiver ran down Yazmin's spine as she absorbed the enormity of his words. She thanked Dr. Wembley and made her way back to campus, catching the first flight back to New York.

As she waited in the boarding lounge her phone rang. She didn't recognize the number and let it go to voicemail. A minutes later she listened intently to the message:

"Hi, I—I can't say my name, but I work for Worldwide Airlines. I saw your posts about Flight 987. You're asking the right questions. I have documents—ones I was ordered to change by upper management. I kept copies. The official report isn't what really happened."

"I don't trust email, and I don't have long. But I can meet you tomorrow—anytime, anywhere. Just name the place. No calls, no texts. I'll find you. But you need to be careful. They don't want this getting out."

"I'll be waiting for your response. Don't ignore this."

When it rains it pours. She called David. "Hi, David. I've got the motive," she said, her voice steady but tinged with a thrill of revelation. "José Santiago is running a lab where he clones and grows human organs. Then he sells them on the black market. It's a huge, dark industry. Levi sent pictures—I'll forward them to you."

David's voice crackled with shock. "Holy shit. Really? That's diabolical."

"Yeah. And there's more. I've got a whistleblower ready to talk. She said she has airline documents that upper management made her doctor." Yazmin replied, her tone matching his excitement. "This conspiracy is unraveling fast."

David asked, "When do you think you'll have the piece ready?"

"Tomorrow at the latest," Yazmin replied confidently.

"Great. Can you send me the teaser ASAP? I want to get it out there," David pressed.

"I'll write it on my flight," Yazmin said, her mind already racing with the story.

CHAPTER 59

airfinancialsgroup.com

African Airlines Invest in Used Aircraft to Expand Fleets

In a strategic move to improve connectivity and drive growth, several African airlines are increasingly turning to the used airplane market. Carriers like Ethiopian Airlines and Air Peace are leading the charge, purchasing reliable older aircraft to expand routes and serve under-served destinations without the hefty costs of brand-new planes.

This cost-effective strategy comes at a time when global air travel demand is soaring. According to industry data, sales of used aircraft have risen by 15% in the past year, reflecting the growing appeal of this approach. Aviation consultant Mark Egan notes, "These planes are helping African airlines unlock opportunities in regions where connectivity was once a challenge."

By leveraging dependable, high-performing models, African airlines are not only expanding their networks, but also positioning themselves competitively in the international market. This trend is breathing new life into regional aviation, enabling more passengers to access affordable and convenient air travel across the continent.

Levi and CeCe

Eduardo Gomes International Airport, Manaus, Brazil

Olavo's seaplane, hidden under a tarp on a secluded dock, glistened as CeCe and Levi handed him a thick wad of cash. The flight back to Manaus was swift, cutting their travel time in half compared to the boat ride to Fordlândia. It turned out that Olavo and his camp were in fact a domestic nationalist group.

As Olavo taxied into the hangar, Levi noticed a plane parked on the tarmac. It was painted over haphazardly, but the tail still bore the unmistakable WWA logo. A chill ran through him. He glanced over at CeCe, who was leaning back, exhausted. She had been through so much already; he decided not to tell her.

When their taxi dropped them off in front of the hotel, CeCe stepped out, stretching, but Levi remained in the car.

"Aren't you coming in?" she asked, her face creased with concern.

Levi shook his head, his gaze focused on the road leading back to the airport. "I need to check something at the airport. I think I saw our plane as we drove past. Probably isn't, but . . . we've come this far. You get some rest, and I'll be back soon. Then we can grab something to eat before our flight in the morning."

"Are you sure you don't want me to come with you?" she asked, reluctant to part.

He forced a reassuring smile. "You look exhausted. I'll see you in a little bit."

CeCe watched the taxi pull away, a hint of worry lingering in her expression, before turning and heading into the hotel.

Levi's heart thumped as he neared the airport. When the taxi pulled up to the departure lane, he scanned the tarmac, his pulse quickening. There, parked with air stairs attached, was a plane painted white, clearly an attempt to mask its origins. But the tail number was unmistakable: N52UA. It was the one, he found the jet used for flight 987. *Finally.*

After paying the driver, Levi walked into the terminal and found a large window overlooking the tarmac. He snapped several photos, capturing every detail of the aircraft. If he could get inside and find the black box, he might uncover crucial information. According to his quick Google search, the black box on a 757 was in a compartment in the ceiling at the back of the cabin.

Now he had to figure out how to reach the plane unnoticed. It was parked about five hundred feet from the main road, and the air stairs were already in place. *If I run, maybe I won't be noticed. It's not that far.*

Outside, Levi waited for a break in traffic. He hopped over the steel barrier, sliding down the embankment, then bolted across the tarmac, his heart pounding with every step. He reached the air stairs and took them two at a time, glancing over his shoulder to see if anyone had noticed.

At the top, he fumbled with the door, finally managing to get it open with a soft hiss of suction. Quickly, he closed it behind him.

The smell hit him instantly—a sickening blend of decay and blood. He recoiled, covering his nose with his shirt. Blood spattered the walls, floor, ceiling. Bloody handprints smeared the galley curtain. He decided to use video to catch all the details. He felt a chill seep into his bones as he stepped into the first-class cabin, his gaze sweeping over the outlines of where bodies had once sat, the dark stains painting a horrifying picture.

Stephanie. Her name echoed in his mind, grief clawing at his chest as he moved toward the back of the plane. The oxygen compartments were all hanging open, but the yellow masks were missing.

In the bathroom, he noticed one yellow mask still dangling above the sink. His breath caught. She had used that mask. That tiny piece of plastic had been her lifeline in those final moments. The realization washed over him, almost bringing him to his knees. His chest tightened, and tears pricked his eyes as he imagined her fear, her desperate attempt to survive.

As he stood there, lost in his grief, he became aware of voices and footsteps outside. *Shit.* He turned, his press credentials in hand, hoping he could talk his way out of this.

He barely had time to react before the door burst open, and two airport security officers charged up the aisle. "Hi! I'm a journalist," Levi began, holding up his ID. "If you could just wait a second, I can explain—"

One of the officers barked something in Portuguese. Before he could finish, they grabbed him, slamming him against the wall. His press badge slipped from his fingers as they twisted his arms behind his back, handcuffing him. "I'm an American! You're going to be in a lot of trouble!" Levi shouted as they dragged him through the blood-stained cabin, down the stairs, and onto the tarmac.

Inside the airport, he was marched through a series of dimly lit hallways, his phone and wallet confiscated before they threw him into a small holding cell. The steel door clanged shut, leaving him in silence. *Shit. CeCe doesn't know where I am. Nobody knows where I am.* Panic started to bubble up in his chest. He banged on the door, shouting, "Hey! Help me! I'm an American!"

* * *

CeCe woke from her nap, feeling a gentle nudge from the baby. She placed a hand on her belly, a soft smile crossing her face. The clock read six o'clock. Levi should have been back by now.

As she stretched, Levi's backpack tumbled to the floor, and an empty flask rolled out. She froze, staring at it, disbelief washing over her. He had brought a flask.

A sense of sadness and resignation settled over her. Maybe some things never really change. She sat on the bed, debating her options, glancing at the clock again. *There's a flight to Miami at ten. I just want to go home.* She took a deep breath, grabbed a notepad, and wrote Levi a quick note, leaving it under the empty flask on the bed.

CHAPTER 60

WELLMAN WEEKLY

The First Year of Sobriety: The High Risk of Relapse and the Impact on Sober Partners

The first year of sobriety is often described as a tightrope walk—balancing hope and determination against the ever-present risk of relapse. For men recovering from alcohol use disorder, this period is especially perilous, with studies showing relapse rates as high as 40% to 60%. Yet the struggle isn't theirs alone; it profoundly affects their sober partners, who are often navigating their own emotional rollercoaster.

Take Sarah and Mike, for example. When Mike committed to recovery after years of alcohol abuse, Sarah stood by him, offering unwavering support through countless therapy sessions and late-night conversations. But when Mike relapsed three months in, Sarah was devastated. "It felt like everything we worked for crumbled," she recalls. The setback strained their relationship, leaving both grappling with guilt, frustration, and the question of how to rebuild trust.

Stories like theirs underscore the importance of strong, multi-faceted support systems. Comprehensive treatment, couples therapy, and honest communication can be lifelines—not just for individuals in recovery, but for their partners as well. Resources like Al-Anon and counseling programs tailored for loved ones can make a critical difference.

Sobriety is a shared journey, and while the road can be fraught with challenges, it's also paved with opportunities for growth, resilience, and renewal. By working together to navigate the highs and lows, couples can emerge stronger, building a future grounded in trust and sustained recovery.

Levi Mathews

The EuroLux Hotel, Manaus, Brazil

Levi heard keys jangling, followed by the metallic scrape of his cell door unlocking. A policeman waved him over, speaking in rapid Portuguese. Levi was led to a small room where another officer sat at a desk, his expression unreadable. The officer handed Levi his phone, wallet, and passport.

"Did someone bail me out?" Levi asked, sinking into the chair with a mix of confusion and suspicion.

"You are free," the officer replied, his accent thick but clear.

Levi left the police station, his mind racing. Who had arranged this, and why? As he stepped into the humid Manaus evening, he hailed a cab, glancing back at the airport. His heart dropped when he saw the empty tarmac where the plane had been parked. Any chance of finding justice for Stephanie felt like it was over. The evidence he had was at best circumstantial. No black box, no real evidence — it was that simple.

Arriving at the hotel, Levi expected to see CeCe waiting for him, but the room was eerily empty. Her backpack was gone. He took a step inside, and his eyes fell on his old flask on the bed, with a note tucked beneath it. His heart sank as he read:

Levi,

I've decided to head back to Miami. I need to prioritize my well-being and the baby's. I hope you understand. Wishing you all the best. CeCe

He dropped onto the bed, staring at the empty flask in his hands. She thinks I was out drinking. The regret hit him hard, sharper than he expected.

Every step he'd taken toward sobriety seemed to dissolve under the weight of past misunderstandings, and he knew this was his doing. The trust he'd worked so hard to build was fragile—and he was starting to realize how easily it could be shattered, maybe even beyond repair.

A knock on the door pulled him from his thoughts. "CeCe, I can explain," he began, rushing to open the door.

But it wasn't her. Standing there was the man from the jungle—the one who had led the team chasing them. Levi quickly pushed the door closed but the man put his foot in the door and held the gun level with Levi's face. Instinctively, Levi raised his hands and backed into the room.

"Listen, you don't have to do this. I don't know anything," Levi stammered, his mind racing. "I'm going back to the US. You'll never see me again."

The man's face remained impassive. "Sit down," he commanded.

Levi moved back to the bed, lowering himself slowly, his hands still raised.

"I bailed you out. You're welcome," the stranger said, pulling up a chair and sitting across from him.

"Thank you . . . Soooo, you bailed me out to kill me?" Levi managed, trying to keep his voice steady.

The man's lips curved into a faint smile. "I'm not going to kill you if you cooperate. Let's talk. What do you think you saw in that building?"

"Nothing," Levi replied, forcing himself to look calm. "I didn't see anything."

The man leaned forward, gun in hand, unamused. "What do you think you saw in the building?"

Levi swallowed, feeling his pulse quicken. "I . . . I think I saw human organs being grown in tanks. Like they were . . . cloning them."

The man nodded, seemingly pleased. "That's right. Do you know how you grow organs?"

"Cloning," Levi answered, his voice barely a whisper, as if speaking louder would solidify the horror of it.

The man continued, his tone eerily calm. "The doctor who owns that building isn't a murderer. He's a puppet. He discovered how to clone human organs from brain-dead patients. In his mind, he's saving lives."

"Then why say he's a puppet?" Levi asked, his brow furrowing. He didn't trust the man, but he sensed this was his chance to understand the truth.

"Because the doctor's life work is finding cures for people who are almost dead. What happened to that flight wasn't his choice. He was coerced by an American businessman, tricked into it. In his eyes, he's a hero—a compassionate man."

Levi took a shaky breath, the implications weighing heavily on him. "You're talking about the pilot, right? He was involved?"

The man gave a single, slow nod.

"Why are you telling me this? What do you want from me?" Levi asked, his voice wavering.

The man's expression hardened. "The doctor is untouchable. The Venezuelan government will protect him for the rest of his life. Any attempt to expose him would be a waste. I know who you are, and I know this is just a job for you. Think carefully before naming him in one of your articles."

Levi stared back, defiant. "I don't even know his name. So how could I name him?"

The man's smile returned, brief and cold. "Glad we understand each other." He extended his hand, palm up. "Now give me your phone, and I'll be gone."

Levi felt his stomach twist. He'd already sent the photos to the US, but losing the phone meant losing his last bit of evidence from the parked jet. Still, with the gun aimed at him, he had no choice. "It's in my pocket," he muttered, handing it over.

"Thank you, Mr. Mathews. I'm a big fan," the man said with a mockingly polite nod. "Your friend is waiting for the ten o'clock flight to Miami." With that, he turned and left, leaving Levi alone in the suffocating silence.

Levi didn't waste a second. He sprinted out of the hotel, catching a cab back to the airport. His mind was racing with a mix of panic and relief. He had one chance to explain things to CeCe before she left. As he cleared security, he checked his watch—9:30 p.m. The plane must be boarding. He quickened his pace, scanning the crowd until he spotted her at the ticket desk.

"CeCe!" he called, rushing up to her. She looked up, surprise flashing across her face.

"It's not what you think. I wasn't drinking. I got arrested," he blurted, out of breath.

CeCe's eyebrows shot up, confusion and skepticism in her eyes. "Arrested? For what?"

"I found the airplane—the one from the flight. It was parked on the tarmac here, but I had to jump the fence to get to it. I just . . . I had to see it. But the police caught me before I could . . . do anything," he explained, shaking his head as memories of the blood-streaked interiors flooded back. He felt a pang of nausea.

"Did you . . . see anything?" CeCe asked softly, her tone a mix of curiosity and dread.

Levi nodded, looking away, trying to hold himself together. "I'm glad you didn't been see it. It was . . ." He took a deep breath. "I haven't had a drink since . . . since I saw her in the funeral home, CeCe. That flask—it was empty because I poured it out back at the camp. I swear."

"Oh . . . I mean it's none of my business, I'm just tired and I want to go home," she finally murmured at a loss for what to say.

Levi searched her face, desperate to make her understand. "I'm sorry. I know it looked bad. But I haven't touched a drop. Not since Stephanie's funeral."

For a moment, there was silence between them. Finally, CeCe spoke, her voice steady. "I saw this flight wasn't full and thought I'd see if I could get on. Give me your ticket on your phone, and I'll get you on the standby list."

Levi's heart sank. "I don't have my phone," he admitted. "That man—the one who chased us—he took it."

CeCe's face twisted in surprise. "El Diablo?"

Levi nodded. "He's the one who bailed me out. He came to our hotel afterward, pretending it was you at the door. When I opened it, he was there, with a gun. He said the doctor running the lab isn't evil—that he got caught up in a scheme with the pilot. And then . . . he took my phone. He told me where to find you, then just left."

CeCe looked at him, incredulous. "Really, Levi? How many phones is this?"

Levi let out a shaky laugh, relieved to see her smile, however small. "I told you; I was cell phone cursed."

CHAPTER 61

NCC BREAKING NEWS

Black Box from Flight 987 Obtained by Airline Executive

Breaking News – NCC.com

Jason Sawyer, Anchor

Hi, I'm Jason Sawyer In a shocking development in the ongoing investigation into the tragic circumstances of Flight 987, Worldwide Airlines CEO Robert Alexander III has confirmed receipt of the flight's black box from the Brazilian government. The black box reportedly contains the final moments of the ill-fated flight, which could shed light on the mysterious circumstances surrounding the disaster.

Alexander claims to have handed over a transcription of the recording to federal investigators, who are now analyzing the contents. Early speculation points to a rogue pilot acting with a personal agenda, though no official conclusions have been drawn.

Sources close to the investigation suggest that the airline is working closely with authorities to ensure full transparency. However, critics question the timing of this revelation and whether it could be part of an effort to control the narrative and protect the company's reputation.

The FBI has declined to comment on the contents of the black box, but pressure is mounting for answers. Families of the victims continue to demand justice as the case takes another dramatic turn.

Robert Alexander, III

Worldwide Airlines Headquarters, New York, New York

Deleon and Larson fidgeted while waiting for Robert in his office. The opulent surroundings didn't distract them; they were focused on Robert Alexander's promise of game-changing evidence.

The door finally swung open, and Robert walked in, pushing a cart covered with a sheet. He left it by his desk and settled into his chair, a confident smile on his face.

"Good to see you again, gentlemen," Robert greeted them warmly. "Yesterday, I received a package from the Brazilian government. It's the black box from Flight 987."

Deleon and Larson's attention snapped to the cart, eyes widening.

"I had it transcribed," Robert continued, handing Larson a zip drive. "I haven't heard it, but I think everything you need is on there."

"Does anyone else know about this?" Deleon asked, his voice tinged with urgency.

"No, except for the transcriber. I thought it was my duty to inform you of the evidence," Robert said. "With full disclosure, I'm hoping we can work something out."

"I don't quite follow," Larson said, exchanging a glance with Deleon before looking back at Robert.

"Clearly, this was a rogue pilot with an agenda," Robert explained. "He likely did it for the money. But as an active employee, our airline's reputation is at stake. People will question how we hired such a dangerous individual. Why didn't we spot the red flags? My guess is he had family members on the donor list waiting for transplants. He got the organs and the money."

Deleon and Larson exchanged another look, understanding the gravity of the situation. "Okay, what's on the zip drive?" Deleon asked.

"The final thirty minutes of the passengers' and crew's lives. I'm sure it's disturbing; I haven't heard it myself." Robert said, a shadow crossing his face.

"How do you want us to help the airline?" Larson asked, leaning forward.

"I need you to make it clear that the airline did everything in its power and had no part in this tragedy. Our PR department will handle the narrative, but your public statements will be crucial. Emphasize our cooperation with the investigation. Just give us a heads-up before you announce the arrest. Can we handle it that way?" Robert's eyes pleaded for their agreement.

Deleon nodded. "Yeah, I don't see why not."

Robert stood, guiding them to the door. They wheeled the cart to the elevator, curiosity getting the better of them as they peeked under the sheet.

"Case closed," Larson said, his tone carrying a note of finality. "I'll call Yazmin. We can listen to it together. Voicemail. Let's eat—I'm starving."

* * *

As the door clicked shut behind them, Robert's smile faded to a quiet smirk. He had leaked the story about the CEO of Worldwide Airlines receiving the black box from Brazil. The whole plan had played out just as he'd envisioned, like pieces in a game of chess falling neatly into place. Getting away with murder had been easier than he'd ever imagined.

CHAPTER 62

THE JOURNAL

**THE RISKS OF WHISTLEBLOWING: COURAGE
UNDER SCRUTINY**

Whistleblowers shine a light on corruption, fraud, and illegal activities, often at great personal cost. From Edward Snowden's revelations on government surveillance to Frances Haugen exposing Facebook's practices, these individuals risk everything to hold powerful entities accountable.

The stakes are high: a recent study shows that over 65% of whistleblowers face retaliation, ranging from job loss and blacklisting to personal threats and protracted legal battles. Even with protective laws in place, many find themselves in a relentless battle against organizations with vast resources.

This stark reality underscores the urgent need for stronger safeguards and robust support systems to ensure whistleblowers can come forward without jeopardizing their livelihoods or safety. Their courage fuels transparency and justice—but without systemic reform, the risks they face remain unacceptably high.

Yazmin Da Silva

Tik Tok Diner, New York, New York

Yazmin sat in the diner booth, her notebook open, fingers tapping her pen as she waited for the whistleblower. The hum of conversations and clinking silverware surrounded her, but she tuned it out, her focus on the door. Her teaser had hit the news, and her phone buzzed nonstop with calls. She looked up as a young woman with long braids hesitantly entered the restaurant, her eyes scanning the room with a cautious wariness.

Yazmin raised a hand, signaling her over. The woman slid into the booth, her fingers fiddling with the strap of her purse as she glanced around. Yazmin noticed the faint sheen of sweat on her forehead despite the cool air, and the nervous tremor in her hands as she settled across from her. She couldn't have been more than 24-years-old.

"Hi, I'm Yazmin. It's nice to meet you," Yazmin said, keeping her tone gentle.

The young woman's eyes narrowed slightly. "I'm not giving you our names," she said curtly, her voice barely above a whisper, as if afraid someone might overhear.

"Of course. Let's get started," Yazmin replied, signaling the waitress to hold off as she approached.

The woman took a shaky breath, her eyes darting to the exit. "We have information about Flight 987," she began, her voice low and tense. "We're scared of what might happen if anyone finds out it's us. I truly believe our lives are at risk."

Yazmin leaned forward, softening her expression. "Who's 'we'?"

"My father is a mechanic for WWA. He has crucial information too. But we're terrified. They killed an entire plane of passengers. What's two more?" She glanced down, biting her lip, her fingers twisting together under the table.

Yazmin resisted the urge to reach across the table, sensing the woman's fear. "Don't worry, you'll be fully protected," she assured her gently. "The FBI is handling the case, and as a journalist, I don't have to reveal my sources. You'll be safe."

The woman exhaled slowly, her shoulders relaxing just a fraction. "I'm a revenue analyst. I analyze customer trends to set flight prices accurately.

Only two other people have access to this information: my boss and her boss." She paused, her gaze flickering toward the diner's windows. "There were . . . anomalies with Flight 987. They're covering it up. They made me alter the manifest to show passengers of different nationalities when, in fact, every passenger was Brazilian. They even gave me a secret code to edit the document." Her voice wavered. "I made a copy of the original manifest."

Yazmin's eyes widened. "Do you have it with you?"

The woman hesitated, then nodded. "Yes, but I need assurance that our identities remain secret. They went to great lengths to pull this off. We're in danger now." Her voice cracked slightly, and she clutched her bag tightly.

Yazmin's heart pounded, both from the gravity of the information and a rush of protective determination. "I promise, I don't have to reveal my source. I'll give it to the FBI and just hint that I have some inside information. No one will know it's you."

The woman nodded, seeming to steel herself. "There's more," she whispered, casting a wary glance around the room. Her voice dropped to a barely audible murmur. "They switched planes."

Yazmin frowned. "Why is that significant?"

"The airline typically uses a 767 for that flight. But that night, it was a 757. My father checked the master logbook, expecting to see the 767 out of service, but it wasn't."

Yazmin's brow furrowed as she processed this. "That's . . . unusual?"

"Very. Planes are only switched due to mechanical issues," she replied, her tone growing more intense.

Yazmin leaned forward; her pen poised above her notebook. "Anything else?"

The woman's hands trembled as she reached for her glass of water, taking a quick sip. "The ticket pricing for that flight was strange. Normally, a round-trip cost at least $500, but they were selling tickets for under $100—but only from Brazil. They weren't selling any tickets from the US or elsewhere.

And the return date was fixed on April 15. Any attempt to book a return on the 16th was blocked."

Yazmin's mind raced, struggling to piece together the implications. "So, Brazilians could buy a round-trip ticket for under $100, but only if they returned on April 15?"

The woman nodded quickly. "Yes. It was set up to ensure only Brazilians were on that flight on the 15th."

"Why?" Yazmin whispered, more to herself than to the woman.

"It could be because many poorer Brazilians can't afford autopsies and tend to bury their dead within twenty-four hours."

"This way, no one would notice their organs were missing," Yazmin said.

The woman's face recoiled in disbelief, "their organs were missing?" she echoed, her voice trembling. "That makes sense. They stole the passengers' organs." She shuddered, hugging herself. "But . . . why?"

Yazmin felt a pang of empathy for the woman, but she needed to push forward. "I'll tell you but keep this to yourself for now. My article will be published tomorrow." She took a deep breath, then leaned in, her voice steady but soft. "The passengers were killed for their organs—to be cloned and sold on the black market."

The woman's hand flew to her mouth. "Oh my God," she whispered, her eyes wide with horror as she sank back into the booth.

Yazmin pressed on, sensing the urgency. "Will you give me the manifest? I need it to prove I'm not fabricating this. It would give my article so much weight."

The woman looked down, hesitating, her fingers clenched tightly around her purse strap. "I don't think so," she said finally, her voice firm but tinged with regret.

Yazmin softened her tone, hoping to appeal to her sense of justice. "Why share this if you don't want it known?" she asked gently. "You can remain anonymous. Your name and job won't be public."

The woman shook her head, her gaze dropping to the table. "No, the details are too specific. They'd figure it out," she murmured. After a moment, she looked up, her expression resolute.

"Please, I can guarantee your safety," Yazmin pressed.

She slid out of the booth, gathering her things. "Let me think about it."

"When you're ready let me know, you know how to reach me," Yazmin said.

The woman nodded once, a faint glimmer of relief in her eyes. Then, with a final glance around the diner, she turned and walked away, disappearing into the evening bustle outside.

Yazmin took a deep breath, her mind swirling with everything she'd just learned. As she gathered her notes, the weight of what she was about to reveal settled heavily on her shoulders.

CHAPTER 63

NCC Breaking News

Breaking News: 987 Black Box Found

Walt Booker, Anchor

"Good evening, I'm Walt Booker, and you're in the Situation Room. Breaking news just in—NCC can now confirm, repeat, now confirm, that the black box from Flight 987 is in the hands of the FBI and the pilot has been named as Evan Wheeler. This crucial piece of evidence, potentially shedding light on the mysterious happenings, was reportedly delivered in a high-security transfer.

How it got there, and the circumstances of its recovery remain unclear, but this marks a major turning point in the investigation. Our correspondent Yazmin Da Silva is standing by with a full report, which we'll bring you right after the break. Could this be the breakthrough investigators have been waiting for? Stay with us for expert analysis and more details as this story unfolds."

Levi, CeCe, David, Yazmin, and Agents Deleon and Larson

FBI Field Office, New York, New York

David had called everyone to the conference room. The air was thick with anticipation, the weight of the past weeks pressing down on every person at the table.

Levi and CeCe sat side by side, an unspoken bond between them after everything they'd been through. FBI agents Deleon and Larson were in their usual spots, unreadable but poised for action. Yazmin, her phone vibrating with constant updates, kept her voice low as she finished a hushed conversation before setting it down. "My editor just signed off," she said, tapping the screen. "The story's prepped."

Larson pulled a small zip drive from her pocket and held it up between two fingers. "This is the zip drive Robert gave us yesterday," she said, her tone neutral but with an edge of suspicion.

"Convenient," David said, his expression unreadable. "I think he may be more involved than we think."

The room went silent.

Larson plugged the drive into her laptop. A folder appeared on the screen, displaying a list of files. She clicked on the main document.

A transcript loaded.

"It's from the Brazilian government," she confirmed. "The lab is still working on the data from the black box."

Deleon leaned forward. "The lab could take weeks. But the zip drive should show his actions."

Levi let out a breath he hadn't realized he was holding. It was happening.

Everyone stared at the laptop in the middle of the conference table.

Nothing happened.

"No way, the file is empty," Larson said, removing the zip drive and reinserting it, frustration creeping into her voice.

A tense silence filled the room, broken only by CeCe letting out a quiet curse under her breath. She leaned forward, gripping the edge of the table. "We were counting on this."

Yazmin muttered something under her breath, already checking her email. "I'm dropping the story."

"I'll call the lab, see if they're finding anything on the black box," Larson muttered. "Maybe it's just this zip drive."

Deleon exhaled sharply, already pushing back from the table. "We still have plenty to arrest him with. A lot of circumstantial evidence, but more than enough for a grand jury. Let's go get him."

Yazmin closed her laptop, already standing. "I'm coming with you."

Deleon didn't argue. She had been part of this from the beginning.

"I'll follow," she added, grabbing her keys.

"I'll ride with you," Levi said.

She shot him a look, smirking. "You can take the video."

They moved fast, everyone filing out of the conference room with purpose. The time for waiting was over.

CHAPTER 64

Breaking News: Explosive Investigative Report Exposes Aviation Scandal

Allen Ellington, Anchor

"Good evening. A shocking investigative report from NCC journalist Yazmin Da Silva has just been released, exposing a dark conspiracy tied to the disappearance of Flight 987. The report alleges that the tragic flight was not a mere accident but part of a sinister scheme involving organ trafficking, corporate corruption, and a deliberate cover-up at the highest levels of the aviation industry."

Key findings from the report include:

- **Evidence linking Flight 987's altered manifests to a secretive black-market medical operation.**
- **Financial records suggesting key airline executives were complicit in the scheme.**
- **Newly uncovered witness testimonies contradicting official statements regarding the crash.**

Authorities have yet to comment on these bombshell allegations, but sources indicate that the FBI is actively pursuing new leads.

And now, in a dramatic turn of events, we have just received word that **police have surrounded the home of Captain Evan Wheeler.** *Officers are executing a search warrant, and we are awaiting confirmation on whether Wheeler is inside. Law* *enforcement sources say this is directly tied to the revelations in Yazmin Da Silva's report.*

We'll bring you live updates as the situation unfolds. For now, all eyes are on this breaking development. Anderson, we'll keep you updated as more details emerge."

Evan Wheeler
Wawa Convenience Store, Bound Brook, New Jersey

Evan stepped into the Wawa to grab a quick sandwich, his mind a frantic blur. The man behind the counter was transfixed by the TV, eyes glued to the breaking news. Evan's gaze followed—and froze. His own face stared back at him from the screen, alongside his crew badge photo.

The air left his lungs, and he stumbled back, gripping the counter for support. Panic surged through him, his pulse roaring in his ears. He turned abruptly, ducking his head, and bolted out of the store. His hands shook so hard that he could barely get the key into the lock. Throwing the car into reverse, he backed out recklessly. A blaring horn jolted him, but he didn't stop. His breath came in rapid, shallow gasps. You're okay, you're okay. He didn't see you, he muttered to himself, fighting to force calm over the terror clawing inside.

What am I going to do? I need to think. His gaze darted wildly as he sped down the road until he spotted an overgrown driveway, hidden from the street by thick bushes. Veering into it, he killed the engine, his hands gripping the steering wheel like a lifeline. He squeezed his eyes shut, clamping his hands over his face as he tried to quiet the storm inside his head, the weight of his situation pressing down like a lead blanket.

This is it. They know. It's over.

Images of Abby and Jennifer flashed through his mind, guilt twisting like a knife in his gut. He swallowed hard, forcing his thoughts to clear. Think, Evan. His eyes darted to the trunk, and he had a sudden, desperate idea.

Caracas. He had his uniform in the back; if he could make it to Newark and fly to Miami, he could connect to Caracas. *The doctor owes me. He'll help me disappear. No one would think to look for him there.*

Moving quickly, he got out and opened the trunk, revealing his neatly folded pilot uniform, ID, and flight bag—a twisted reminder of the life he was leaving behind. Shoving down the last traces of hesitation, he pulled on the uniform, the familiar fabric settling over him like armor against the chaos of his thoughts. He adjusted the ID around his neck.

Rage simmered beneath his calm facade as he climbed back into the driver's seat. *Robert had turned him in; it could only be Robert. I was always going to pay the price, part of his plan. I'm so stupid.*

He only had one obstacle left: getting through security. He'd done this thousands of times. Forcing himself to act natural, he practiced a neutral expression. As he approached the guard, he was asked, "Where are you off to today?" Unable to think, he blurted, "I don't know." *None truer words.*

At Newark, he kept his head low, his gaze fixed ahead as he passed a group of passengers watching the live NCC feed. Multiple TV screens broadcast his treachery. Yazmin Da Silva, the journalist, was there—her face and his own side by side. She was reporting live from his house, where police cars surrounded his front yard. Flashing lights painted the scene red and blue, casting ominous shadows. They were seconds from breaking down the door.

Heart pounding, he yanked his cap lower, trying to shield his face from view. *Don't panic. Act natural.* He moved with purpose, blending into the bustle of the terminal, careful to avoid eye contact. The tension wrapped around his chest like a vice, each step tightening its hold. A voice cut through his focus, startling him. "Hey, buddy. Know where the smoking area is?"

Evan's head snapped around, his heart nearly leaping out of his chest. A passenger was looking at him expectantly. His mind spun for an answer, any answer. "No," he said sharply, his voice rough and final.

The man blinked, taken aback, then nodded and wandered off, muttering under his breath.

When he finally reached the gate for Miami, his stomach dropped—the jet bridge was pulling away. Too late. His chest tightened. He'd counted on that flight. Now what? His eyes darted across the terminal. Think, damn it, think. He scanned the area, searching for another option. Another flight? Or maybe . . .

A deserted plane caught his eye, waiting at a quiet gate across the terminal. The next Miami flight wasn't scheduled to leave for hours. Moving deliberately, he strode toward the gate, entering the passcode to unlock the jet bridge door. His pulse thundered as he stepped inside. If anybody sees me, I'm just a pilot going to work.

In the cockpit, the familiar controls awaited him, grounding him in the moment. He took the pilot's seat, running through the preflight checks by memory, his fingers moving with automatic precision. He checked the fuel gauge; it was filled enough to make Miami, with just enough to stretch to Cuba. If he could get this plane off the ground, he'd head straight there.

The engines rumbled to life, vibrating through his seat, a sound he'd heard a thousand times—but this time, it was different. This time, it meant escape. Or disaster.

His thoughts drifted, unbidden, to Abby and Jennifer. Leaving them cut deep, but he forced the emotion down. They'll be better off without me. They didn't sign up for this, he told himself, swallowing the lump in his throat. This is the right thing. For them.

Evan took a deep breath, trying to calm the tremor in his hands. He looked out the cockpit window toward the terminal and noticed a uniformed employee staring back at him, hurrying toward the gate with a colleague. Their eyes locked onto him. A jolt of adrenaline shot through his limbs. Move. Now.

He hurried to the aircraft door, shutting and arming it. If anyone tried to open it, they'd be knocked back by the emergency slide, making it an undesirable choice. Back in the cockpit, he saw the two employees pointing toward him. Running through the last of the checks, he fired up the engines, their roar filling the cabin and vibrating through his seat, grounding him even as his mind spiraled.

There was no turning back now.

CHAPTER 65

NCC TV NETWORK – BREAKING NEWS

Breaking News: Law Enforcement Authorities Seek Flight 987 Captain

Allen Ellington, Anchor

"Welcome back to NCC, where we're following breaking news. Police have surrounded the home of Captain Evan Wheeler, the pilot of the ill-fated Flight 987. We're going live now to our correspondent Yazmin Da Silva, who is on the scene. Yazmin, what's the latest?"

Yazmin Da Silva

"Allen, I'm here at Captain Wheeler's home, where law enforcement has surrounded the property. Police are actively serving a warrant and are now forcing entry into the residence. Sources close to the investigation say this warrant is tied to new evidence uncovered from the Flight 987 black box—evidence that may implicate Wheeler in the tragedy."

Neighbors have gathered outside, watching the tense situation unfold. Police appear to be preparing to take Captain Wheeler into custody, though it's unclear at this time if he is inside the home.

The shocking development raises serious questions: What charges could Wheeler face, and how does this tie into the mysterious crash of Flight 987? We'll bring you updates as this story develops. Back to you, Anderson."

FBI, New Jersey State Police, Bridgewater Police
Martinsville, New Jersey

Deleon parked the unmarked car behind a police cruiser. Levi pulled up just behind him.

"You guys stay here, keep your heads down," Larson instructed, her tone leaving no room for argument.

Yazmin, mid-conversation with a NCC producer, nodded. "Here we go," she said, ending the call and stepping out of the car. Levi followed closely. She handed him her phone, her eyes sharp. "You know what to do. Don't screw this up for me this time."

Levi took the phone, meeting her gaze with a nod of understanding.

Deleon and Larson moved swiftly, crouching behind the police car positioned in front of Evan's house. They watched as officers stealthily approached the front door. The lead officer signaled, and with a unified force, they charged the door, splintering it with a battering ram. The team stormed inside, methodically sweeping each room. The house was eerily quiet, devoid of life.

"All clear!" one officer called out; the disappointment palpable in his voice.

Deleon exchanged a look with Larson. "I just talked to the dealership, he's not there either," he muttered, frustration seeping through.

"Damn it," Larson cursed under her breath.

"He's a flight risk—literally," Deleon said, urgency edging into his tone. "He's headed for Newark. Call the Port Authority Police."

Deleon's eyes widened. "Lights and sirens," he barked, adrenaline kicking in. He had a twenty-minute lead on them. "We're moving now!" He turned to Yazmin and Levi, urgency in his tone. "Try to keep up!"

Yazmin and Levi scrambled back to their car, Levi firing up the engine with a grim sense of urgency. The convoy sped toward Newark, lights flashing as they entered Route 78. The traffic was heavy, but the police cleared the lanes with ease.

Yazmin's fingers flew over her phone, sending updates to the NCC producer, her mind racing as fast as the car. Levi focused on the road, his grip tight on the wheel, thoughts swirling about what they might find at the airport.

In the back of their minds, a shared realization took root—this was their last chance to catch Evan before he vanished into thin air.

CHAPTER 66

NCC TV NETWORK – BREAKING NEWS

Breaking News: Evan Wheeler Not Found at Home, No Arrests Made

Allen Ellington, Anchor

"Good evening. We begin tonight with breaking news in the ongoing investigation into Flight 987. FBI agents and local authorities have surrounded the home of Captain Evan Wheeler, but in a shocking development, we are now learning that **Wheeler is not inside.**

Sources confirm that police executed a search warrant at his residence, expecting to take him into custody. However, law enforcement officials now state that Wheeler **remains at large**, *and his current whereabouts are unknown. Authorities have launched an active search, urging the public to report any information regarding his location. As this situation unfolds, questions are mounting about whether Wheeler may have already fled."*

Breaking Now: Unauthorized Aircraft Movement at Newark Airport

"And now, just moments ago, we are receiving reports from Newark Liberty International Airport of an unauthorized aircraft movement. FAA officials confirm that an aircraft belonging to WWA Airlines—a company directly tied to the Flight 987 investigation—has begun taxiing on the runway **without proper clearance.**

Security footage and eyewitness reports indicate that this aircraft may have been **stolen.** *Air traffic control has attempted* *contact, but as of now, the pilot has not responded. Law enforcement sources tell NCC that investigators are working urgently to determine whether* **this incident is connected to Evan Wheeler.** *Could the missing pilot now be airborne?*

Authorities have not yet confirmed the identity of the individual operating the aircraft, but emergency response teams are mobilizing, and federal agencies are actively monitoring the situation.

We'll continue to follow this breaking story as it develops. Anderson, we'll bring you the latest updates as more details emerge."

Robert Alexander, III

Worldwide Airlines Headquarters, New York, New York

Robert sat in the dim glow of his penthouse office, a glass of scotch in hand, savoring the smoky warmth as he watched the television across the room. The NCC banner flashed red with breaking news.

"FBI SWARMS PILOT EVAN WHEELER'S HOME— ARREST IMMINENT."

Robert's lips curled into a satisfied smile. Everything was falling into place, just as he had planned. **Every move had been orchestrated to lead to this moment—Evan taking the fall, the authorities following the perfect trail of breadcrumbs.**

The only thing that irritated him was the timing. **This was supposed to happen later, once all the loose ends were tied up.** Now, things were moving faster than he wanted. But it didn't matter. The outcome would be the same. **Evan would be the scapegoat, and Robert would remain untouchable.**

His phone buzzed on the desk. **Santiago.**

Robert smirked, already knowing what the call was about. He let it ring twice before answering. "I assume you're watching."

"I heard the black box was delivered," Santiago's voice was sharp, cutting straight to the point.

Robert exhaled slowly, swirling his scotch. "That's what they're saying."

"Is it the real data?" Jose asked.

Robert chuckled, walking toward the window. The city below pulsed with energy, a stark contrast to the chaos unfolding in Evan's world. "It doesn't matter."

Santiago's frustration bled through the line. "Of course it matters! If the real data gets out—"

"It won't." Robert's tone was calm, controlled. "He's so naive. He'll confess, but no one will believe him. The idea that the CEO of the airline was involved. Laughable. The ravings of a mad man, a person cornered grasping at straws. The media's already shaping the story. He's about to get arrested."

Silence. Then, a slow exhale from Santiago. "You are confident."

Robert's grip tightened around his glass. He turned back to the TV, where the camera zoomed in on Evan's front door, the SWAT team preparing to breach.

"Of course, I am."

Then Santiago muttered, "Of course you are." The call cut off.

Robert placed the phone down, watching the screen as the first officer moved in. The door was seconds from being forced open.

Just as he took another sip of scotch, a new **breaking news alert** flashed across the screen.

BREAKING NEWS: REPORTS OF A STOLEN AIRCRAFT COMING IN—LIVE FROM NEWARK AIRPORT.

The TV cut to shaky footage of a WWA airplane, taxiing aimlessly across the tarmac.

Robert's smirk vanished. He leaned forward, gripping the edge of his desk, his eyes narrowing as he processed what he was seeing.

His grip on the glass tightened. This wasn't supposed to happen.

CHAPTER 67

NCC TV NETWORK – BREAKING NEWS

Commercial Jet Stolen: Breaking

Allen Ellington Anchor

"We have shocking, potentially dangerous breaking news coming out of Newark Airport in New Jersey. Authorities are reporting that a commercial jet has just been stolen from the gate area. Early indications suggest that a pilot—yes, a licensed pilot— may have taken the aircraft in what appears to be a desperate attempt to escape the police.

It's unclear at this time whether any passengers were onboard or if there is an immediate risk to public safety. We're getting live footage of the plane taxiing on the runway—let's take a look.

The big questions now: Where is the plane heading, and how are authorities responding to this unprecedented situation? Stay with us as we bring you the latest on this rapidly unfolding story."

Paul Cento

Newark Airport Control Tower, Newark, New Jersey

The Newark Aircraft Control Tower was charged with tension as Paul Cento, the afternoon shift manager, stepped in. All the controllers were out of their seats, staring wide-eyed at the chaos unfolding on the runway. "What are you guys looking at?" he asked, noting the anxiety etched on every face.

An ATC agent's voice cut through the air: "Worldwide, acknowledge. Worldwide, you are on an active taxiway. Acknowledge."

"Someone just stole a 737," someone muttered, disbelief thick in their tone. The weight of the statement settled heavily in the room.

Paul's gaze stayed locked on the rogue jet. The 737 lurched across the taxiway in clumsy, jerky movements, like a giant, unpredictable animal thrashing in a confined space. It swerved dangerously close to trucks and signage, veering off course with no clear direction. His face tightened as he watched.

"Did you close the ramp?" he asked, his tone sharp.

"Yes," came the response, clipped and tense.

"What about the airspace?" Paul's voice was tight, pushing for action.

"Working on it," an agent replied, before pivoting to the radio, voice strained. "Worldwide, come in. You need to stop!"

Paul's attention snapped back to the runway. The rogue jet jerked sideways, almost clipping a catering truck. The entire room collectively gasped, some wincing as the plane narrowly avoided a collision. One controller whispered a curse under their breath, the tension palpable.

"He almost hit the catering truck," Paul murmured, unable to look away.

"Ramps closed. We're diverting incoming flights to Syracuse, Buffalo, and Boston," another controller reported, struggling to keep their focus amidst the tension.

"It's like he's hunting for a runway," someone noted, voice tight with disbelief. "He just crossed the grass to get to one."

The jet rocked unevenly as it bounced over the grassy strip, moving like a runaway train with no clear control. Paul clenched his jaw, watching it swerve dangerously close to an Alaska Airlines plane waiting halfway down the runway.

United 506 waited to cross where the Worldwide jet was lining up. Paul clicked on the mic. "United 506, pull onto the runway and hold."

Moments later, the radio crackled with the United captain's response. "Control, you're telling us to block him. That's Evan Wheeler in there—Flight 987's pilot, desperate and on the run. It's all over the news. I'm not risking my plane."

Paul felt a pang of frustration but understood the captain's hesitation. "United 506, cleared to continue to the ramp," he replied, his voice strained.

"Yeah, no shit," United came back, the tension in his voice mirroring the room's.

"He's going for it!" an agent shouted as the jet lined up on the runway, its engines roaring, vibrating the ground beneath it.

The room fell into a tense silence, the controllers watching the jet, every movement loaded with potential disaster. Paul winced, his eyes fixed on the 737 as it began to pick up speed, hurtling down the runway in a desperate, reckless bid for takeoff.

"Wow, he did it," Paul breathed, a mixture of awe and dread in his tone. He turned to the radio operator. "Call departure. Tell them we're going to keep him on our radio."

CHAPTER 68

NCC TV NETWORK – BREAKING NEWS
Flight 987 Fugitive Pilot Takes Control of Stolen Jet
Allen Ellington, Anchor

"Breaking news out of Newark, New Jersey: Captain Evan Wheeler, the pilot at the center of the Flight 987 investigation, has now been implicated in another shocking aviation incident. Authorities have confirmed that Wheeler has stolen a commercial aircraft from Newark Airport in what appears to be a desperate and dangerous act.

Details are still coming in, but sources say the stolen jet is a narrow-body aircraft capable of carrying dozens of passengers, raising serious concerns about public safety. Law enforcement and aviation officials are scrambling to respond, and Newark Airport has reportedly gone into lockdown.

This is the kind of story you just can't make up, folks. Where is Wheeler heading, and can authorities stop him before it's too late? Stay with us as we bring you live updates on this rapidly unfolding situation."

Evan Wheeler
Newark Airport, Newark, New Jersey
Evan's pulse quickened as urgent calls from the control tower crackled through the radio, but his focus remained sharp. His cellphone buzzed

incessantly on the console, but he ignored it, muttering, "I can't come to the phone right now. Leave a message, and I'll call you back," as he concentrated on the cockpit instruments and the runway unfolding ahead of him.

The aircraft jolted violently as it crossed the rough terrain of the grass median, but Evan's hands stayed steady on the controls, feeling relaxed. The yoke had a hypnotic pull, a strange sense of peace that filled him as he aligned the 737 on the runway. He knew the airspace was shut down; he'd have the path to himself.

His gaze flicked to the United plane partially blocking the runway. A flicker of adrenaline surged, but he kept his hands firm on the throttle. Smart move, he thought, preparing for the gamble. He pushed the throttle to full power, feeling the yoke meld with his grip. The other aircraft accelerated out of the way just in time, and his plane lifted off, skimming past with inches to spare.

The ground fell away, and with it, everything else. Evan climbed to five thousand feet. For the first time in a long time, he felt free.

Paul's voice came through, tight with frustration. "WWA, remain on this frequency. What are you doing? You could have killed those people on the United plane. Go around for landing."

"Nope, I'm not going to do that," Evan replied coolly. Not landing.

"Where do you think you're going? You'll be arrested wherever you land," Paul pressed, his voice edged with desperation.

In the control tower, Deleon and Larson burst in, followed by New Jersey State Police, Levi, and Yazmin. The room was packed, the air growing warm and stifling with all the bodies crammed together. Beads of sweat glistened on brows as tension mixed with the heat.

"This is what I want," Evan's voice carried a grim resolve. "I want everyone to know the truth. I want it live on air. I want to talk to Yazmin DaSilva on air right now."

"Did he take off?" Larson demanded, eyes wide with shock.

"Yes," Paul confirmed, his gaze locked on the radar screen, tracking Evan's jet as it climbed. His shoulders slumped in resignation. "He wants to be live on NCC with Yazmin DaSilva."

All eyes turned to Yazmin. The room buzzed with a low murmur, voices overlapping as everyone absorbed the gravity of the situation. Yazmin's mouth fell open in shock, her eyes wide as she processed Evan's demand. But her surprise quickly hardened into resolve as she grabbed her phone. "Okay, I'll get him on."

Deleon held up a hand, signaling her to wait.

Paul cleared his throat, raising his voice to be heard over the noise. "I think we should do it," he said finally. "Call NCC. He has nothing to lose. Maybe if he gets what he wants, we can talk him down."

Larson exchanged a look with Deleon, then nodded, her gaze shifting back to Yazmin. "Get NCC on the line, Yazmin. Let's see if we can bring him in safely."

The noise in the room continued to swell, controllers, agents, and state police murmuring to each other, tense energy crackling in the crowded space.

Deleon leaned in; his voice barely audible over the commotion. "Did they scramble the jets?"

"Yes, out of Andrews," Paul replied, his eyes glued to the radar blip that represented Evan's plane, now steady in its climb.

Larson grabbed a headset, gesturing for quiet, and spoke into the mic, keeping her voice steady. "Evan, it's Larson. You don't want to go down like this. We can come up with a better solution, a better outcome. You know how this is going to end. We don't want anyone to get hurt."

There was a pause, the radio crackling in the silence that had fallen over the crowded room.

"Are you calling NCC?" Evan's voice finally came through, taut with controlled anger. "I'll land after I tell my side of this story."

Larson glanced at Paul, then back at the radio. "We're getting them patched through now. How do we know you'll keep your word and land after?"

Evan's response was flat, emotionless. "I have no place left to go."

In the control tower, no one spoke. They all watched the radar and monitors, every eye following Evan's jet as it climbed further into the open sky, carrying both his desperation and his final demands. The hum of equipment and soft rustle of movement filled the silence, as if even the air held its breath, waiting.

CHAPTER 69

NCC TV NETWORK – BREAKING NEWS

Breaking: Stolen Airplane at Newark Int'l

Allen Elington, Anchor

"We have breaking news—Captain Evan Wheeler, the fugitive pilot at the center of this unfolding crisis, is now demanding a live, on-air interview with our correspondent Yazmin Da Silva. Wheeler, who is still in control of the stolen aircraft, appears to be using this interview as a platform to make his case—or perhaps issue new demands.

Hold on . . . I'm being told we're attempting to reach Yazmin right now. Stand by. Okay, I've just been informed that Yazmin is currently in her car, and we have her live on her cellphone.

'Yazmin, can you tell us what's happening and how you're preparing for this extraordinary request?'

What will Wheeler say, and could this conversation escalate an already dangerous situation? Stay with us for live updates as this story develops."

Evan Wheeler

New Jersey Airspace

Evan's phone rang, its buzz sharp against the background hum of the cockpit. He put it on speaker, hearing the familiar static of a live news broadcast. The cold presence of the fighter jets shadowed his plane, visible on his periphery.

"The fighters just got here. Tell them I see them," Evan said, his voice strained but controlled. "Am I live on the air?"

"Yes," a producer confirmed.

"Hi, Evan. It's Yazmin DaSilva. Go ahead and say what you want to say."

Evan took a deep breath, his voice cracking as he began. "I'm not a monster. I didn't do this on my own. I was tricked. My daughter died, and my wife and other daughter were dying. They both need organ transplants." He choked back a sob, his throat tightening. "If they're listening, I love you both so much. I couldn't live my life without you. I did this to save your lives."

He paused, feeling the weight of his confession press against his chest. "When Robert Alexander, the CEO of Worldwide Airlines, met me in the ICU waiting room, he told me he could get the organs my family needed. At first, I refused. I'm not a murderer. Even during my Air Force days, I delivered cargo—I never saw combat, and I never wanted to hurt anyone. But then Jennifer had a grand mal seizure. She was in intensive care next to her mother, who was in a coma. The plan he laid out made sense in a twisted way. He said I'd be giving thousands of people desperate for transplants a chance . . . and I would get my family the organs they needed. A decompression, he said, would be peaceful." Evan's voice faltered. "I made a terrible mistake. I killed all those people, and I'm so sorry. Abby and Jen, I hate that you'll carry this for the rest of your lives. I did this for you, and it was wrong."

Evan's voice softened, raw with regret. "But I want everyone to know—I didn't plan this alone. Robert Alexander and Dr. José Santiago were behind it all. This plan was thought out over months, maybe years. I just . . . turned off the oxygen. Afterward, I was supposed to land on a remote airstrip in the Amazon. When I did, it was like a military operation—trucks with floodlights lighting up the runway. They took the bodies away with catering trucks. I don't know where they took them. They put me in a hotel a mile away, kept me hidden. This was all part of a vast plot to harvest organs from the brain-dead passengers of Flight 987. Santiago, a doctor I never met, was pioneering a way to clone organs. That's all I know."

"Go on," Yazmin urged gently, her voice carrying both sympathy and disbelief.

"How could an airline pilot pull off something like this alone? Where would I get poison? We stopped in Caracas, not to refuel—that was just a cover story. That's where they handed me the poison to kill the first officer. Robert had everything planned. He gave me a cellphone loaded with instructions—latitude, longitude, step-by-step directions. I followed them. Then he told me to destroy the phone, to throw it into the jungle. I bet it's still there." Evan exhaled shakily, the enormity of his actions settling in his gut like a stone. "I thought . . . I thought I was helping my family. Helping others. I was wrong. So, so wrong."

There was a long silence. Then, Yazmin's voice came through, soft yet probing. "Is there anything else you want to tell us?"

Evan's voice was barely a whisper. "No. Just that I'm so sorry. I'm sorry for all those people. Abby, Jennifer . . . please remember how much I love you."

The call ended abruptly. Evan took off his headset and silenced the cockpit's radio speaker, sealing himself in quiet. He turned the plane toward the Atlantic Ocean, climbing higher, feeling the weight lift as he broke free of the coastline. The fighter jets flanked him at a distance, unwilling to fire over water.

At thirty-five thousand feet, Evan engaged the autopilot to maintain heading, altitude, and speed. Reaching above the co-pilot's seat, he switched the pressurization from auto to manual, setting the pressure altitude to sea level. As the air in the cabin began to thin, he leaned back, a strange calm washing over him.

CHAPTER 70

NCC TV NETWORK – BREAKING NEWS
Live: NCC Talking to Pilot of Stolen Jet
Allen Ellington, Anchor

"If you're just joining us, we have breaking news unfolding right now. Evan Wheeler, the pilot at the center of the Flight 987 tragedy, has stolen a 737 from Newark Airport. Wheeler had specifically requested to speak live on air to Yazmin Da Silva, the journalist who first cracked this story. And in an unprecedented act he confessed to the plot to kill and steal the organs of all the passengers on board Flight 987. And Accused the Worldwide Airline CEO Robert Alexander as the mastermind of the entire plot. We are waiting for a response from Alexander."

NCC News
New York, New York

"We have Evan Wheelers Wife Abby Wheeler on the phone."

Bree Keeler, Anchor

"Good day, I'm Bree Keeler with continuing coverage on the tragic events involving Captain Evan Wheeler. The situation is still developing following yesterday's shocking confession and apparent suicide of Captain Wheeler, who implicated the CEO of Worldwide Airlines in a sinister plot involving the suffocation of passengers to harvest organs for transplants.

"We now have an exclusive live interview with Evan Wheeler's wife, Abby Wheeler, who has bravely agreed to speak with us. Abby, thank you for joining us during this incredibly difficult time."

Abby Wheeler (visibly distraught, tears in her eyes)

"Thank you for having me. I just . . . I need people to know that my husband couldn't have done this alone. He acted out of desperation, out of fear of losing us."

Bree Keeler, Anchor

"Abby, first of all, we are deeply sorry for your loss. Can you tell us more about what you believe led to yesterday's tragic events?"

Abby Wheeler (voice trembling)

"You know, Evan was a good man, a good father. People don't want to hear that, but it's the truth. He . . . he was manipulated by Robert Alexander, the CEO of Worldwide Airlines. Robert knew Evan was vulnerable. Less than a year ago, we lost our oldest daughter, Danni." Her eyes flickered with the memory, an image flashing in her mind: a white sheet pulled over Danni's still form. A coldness swept over her. "And then my youngest daughter and I were diagnosed with the same illness. We were on the transplant list, waiting. But time was running out."

Bree Keeler, Anchor

"He was afraid of losing you both. And what I'm about to say is difficult but taking 188 lives . . . that's unimaginable. You understand that, right?"

Abby Wheeler (nodding, wiping her tears)

"I do. It's . . . horrifying. But Evan was a pilot, not a criminal master-mind. He was coerced, pulled into this by someone with far more power. Robert Alexander orchestrated everything. Evan was desperate. If I hadn't been in a coma, maybe I could have stopped him. Maybe I could have reminded him . . ." Her voice faltered, thick with guilt.

Bree Keeler, Anchor

"Abby, these are serious allegations. What do you hope to accomplish by coming forward now?"

Abby Wheeler (finding resolve)

"I'll spend the rest of my life fighting to expose the truth. For my husband, for the victims, for everyone affected by this tragedy. Evan wasn't a monster. He was a victim too. I didn't know what he was involved in until it was too late. But I will not stop until the real villain, Robert Alexander, is held accountable."

Bree Keeler, Anchor

"I understand. But in the end, Evan pulled the trigger. He committed one of the most devastating crimes in aviation history. That responsibility... it's his, isn't it?"

Abby Wheeler (taking a deep breath)

"Yes. And to the families of the victims, I am so deeply sorry. Nothing I say will bring back your loved ones, but I promise to seek justice. Sometimes, people do terrible things out of desperation and fear. Evan was manipulated, and I'll make sure the world knows who the real mastermind is."

Bree Keeler, Anchor (leans in, voice softer but cutting)

"Abby, if you had known what Evan was planning, knowing it was the only way to save your life and your daughter's, would you have allowed it?"

The question hung in the air, a chilling silence settling over the studio. The room felt colder; even the low hum of equipment seemed to fade away. Abby's fingers clenched, and for a heartbeat, the world fell away. She saw Danni's covered form again, remembered the hollow ache of that loss. Her lips parted, the answer heavy and raw.

Finally, she whispered, "No."

Bree Keeler, Anchor

"Thank you, Abby, for your courage and honesty."

Abby Wheeler

"Thank you for giving me the chance to tell the truth."

Bree Keeler, Anchor

"That was Abby Wheeler, wife of Captain Evan Wheeler, with a powerful message and serious allegations. We will continue to follow this developing story and bring you the latest updates. I'm Bree Keeler; this is NCC."

NCC TV – BREAKING NEWS
Live: NCC Talking to Pilot of Stolen Jet
Walt Booker, Anchor

"I'm Walt Booker, and you're in the situation room. We have breaking news that a warrant has been issued for Robert Thomas Alexander III in response to Evan Wheeler's, the captain of Flight 987, claim that Robert was in fact the mastermind of the scheme to sell and clone human organs using the passengers on Flight 987. Stand by as we wait live outside Worldwide Airlines headquarters in New York City. Yazmin DaSilva, who broke this story, is waiting outside of the building. Here's Yazmin."

"Hi Walt, my sources have told me that Robert Alexander is being arrested for his involvement in the cloning plot. Here he comes."

Yazmin thrust the microphone into Robert's face. "Do you have anything to say?"

"The rantings of a crazed mass murderer should not be used against me," Robert said as he was put into the police car.

MSNCB Breaking News
The Final Victim of Flight 987
Brian Willis

"We are following the plight of Flight 987. Two years after the plight of Flight 987, the victim list continue to grow. Venezuelan Dr. José Santiago, the doctor who invented a way to clone human organs, is being blamed for the hundreds of victims who received his cloned organs. Doctors are frantically trying to figure out

why those cloned organs have continued to grow inside their hosts. The organs are continuing to grow, so large that they are invading the bodies, causing death. In some cases, you can see the organs as large lumps under the skin of the victims. One disturbing video shows a liver bursting out of the abdomen of one of the patients. People are urged to go to the hospital as quickly as possible."

Robert Alexander III
Worldwide Airlines Headquarters, New York, New York

Robert Alexander sat in his plush office on the top floor of the Worldwide Airlines (WWA) building, savoring a glass of aged scotch. The panoramic view of the city stretched before him, a reminder of his success, his dominance. He'd crafted a scheme so meticulous, so brilliantly executed, it seemed foolproof. Every detail had been manipulated; every loose end tied. The authorities had been deftly misled, all fingers pointing to the pilot of Flight 987, Evan Wheeler. The FBI had even received the black box and transcripts from him; he was certain he'd covered every base.

But now, a chill crept into his confidence. Evan Wheeler's confession had gone public. He could picture the pilot, desperate and half-crazed, throwing his name out there like a lifeline. "Doesn't matter," Robert whispered, tightening his grip on the glass, fingers whitening against the cold crystal. They'd find no evidence linking him to the crime—just the wild accusations of a man who had everything to lose. Yet, a slight tremor ran through his hand as he took another sip. He could feel the walls inching closer, an invisible pressure bearing down on him.

A sharp knock on the door pulled him from his thoughts. He set the glass down, barely managing to keep his expression neutral. The door swung open, and in walked two police officers flanked by FBI agents. "Mr. Alexander, you're under arrest for mass murder," one of them announced, their tone as unyielding as the steel cuffs in their hands.

Robert forced a tight smile, adjusting his tie as if this were just another business meeting. "This will all be cleared up in no time," he assured himself. "Probably be out in time for dinner." He straightened his jacket, maintaining his composure as they led him from the office, down the polished halls of the company he'd built. He could feel eyes on him, his employees watching as he descended from his ivory tower to the grim ground floor below.

Outside, the press surged forward, cameras flashing in an unrelenting assault. Microphones were thrust in his face, their questions blurring into an indistinct roar. But through the chaos, one face caught his eye—Yazmin DaSilva, the journalist who had broken the story. Her gaze bore into him, steely and victorious, a look that made his skin prickle. He averted his eyes, feeling, for the first time, a tremor of doubt gnawing at his confidence.

At the police station in midtown, they placed him in a cold, fluorescent-lit interrogation room. The sparse furniture and harsh lighting were a jarring contrast to his office's luxury. The silence felt thick, pressing in from all sides. He drummed his fingers on the table, feeling sweat gather at his collar, waiting for his lawyer to arrive and put an end to this charade. But as the minutes dragged on, unease crept into his chest, a slow, insidious tightening.

Finally, his lawyer entered, nodding curtly, and the interrogation began.

"Mr. Alexander let's discuss your involvement in the events surrounding Flight 987," Agent Larson said, her gaze unblinking.

He leaned back, feigning calm, a smirk flickering at the edges of his lips. "I had nothing to do with it. The black box speaks for itself. I was as shocked as anyone to hear what Captain Wheeler did."

Larson's expression remained flat. She lifted a plastic evidence bag, holding it up for him to see. Inside was a battered, mangled iPhone. "Recognize this?" she asked.

His smirk faltered, replaced by a barely perceptible twitch in his jaw. "No," he replied, but his voice had lost its edge.

The FBI agent played a recording from the phone, and Robert's own voice filled the room—calmly reading off coordinates, directions. Each word echoed back at him, tightening the coil of dread in his gut. His pulse thudded in his ears, and he swallowed hard, fighting to maintain his composure as the walls seemed to close in.

"We also have a receipt for this iPhone, Mr. Alexander," the agent continued, savoring the moment. "Would you care to guess whose name is on it?"

The room spun. His well-crafted facade was unraveling thread by thread. He forced himself to remain still, but he could feel his hands beginning to tremble, a bead of sweat tracing a cold path down his temple. His lawyer interjected quickly, "This interview is over," but even that felt hollow, a futile attempt to seal a crack in a dam about to burst.

As they led him from the room, back toward the holding cell, the reality of his situation hit him with brutal clarity. His meticulously constructed empire, his reputation, his carefully guarded freedom—they were slipping through his fingers like sand. He could see Yazmin's face in his mind, that look of quiet triumph, her victory complete.

Sitting alone in his cell, the fluorescent light casting harsh shadows, Robert Alexander realized, perhaps for the first time, that he was utterly alone. And there would be no escape this time.

"Authorities Close in on Controversial Scientist"

Global Daily News, Breaking Report

Brazilian authorities are closing in on Dr. José Santiago, the controversial figure behind the revolutionary yet highly contentious organ cloning research at the Cattleya Eldorado Longevity Medical Center in Fordlândia. Reports suggest police are moments away from raiding Santiago's lab following allegations of malpractice and unauthorized human experimentation.

Sources inside the lab describe a chaotic scene, with ruptured tanks and overgrown, unstable cloned organs spilling into the facility. The breakthrough that once promised to extend human lifespans is now at the center of an international scandal, with multiple deaths linked to Santiago's unregulated procedures.

Colleagues close to the scientist say he has been under immense pressure in recent weeks, facing mounting accusations and grow- ing public outrage. Santiago, who once declared his goal was to "redefine medicine as we know it," now finds himself on the verge of ruin.

As the situation develops, questions swirl about the legacy of a man who dared to push the boundaries of science but may have crossed an irreversible ethical line.

Dr. José Santiago
Cattleya Eldorado Longevity Medical Center and Spa, Fordlândia, Brazil

Dr. José Santiago stood in the center of his laboratory, pacing, surrounded by cold, sterile glass tanks filled with organs meant to revolutionize medicine. Dim light reflected off the liquid inside, casting eerie shadows on the walls. His hands trembled as he adjusted the controls on one of the tanks, though his mind was far from the task at hand. He had once envisioned himself as the father of organ cloning, a pioneer on the brink of reshaping modern medicine. Now, he faced the ruin of everything he'd worked for.

He glanced at the tanks, each one a grim testament to his obsession. The organs, intended to save countless lives, were now growing out of control. The chemical baths, crucial for stabilizing the cloning process, had not been given enough time to perfect. Robert Alexander, his business partner, had insisted they launch immediately, driven by greed and impatience. That haste had spiraled into the catastrophe unfolding around him.

At first, the signs of failure had been subtle—hardly a cause for con- cern. But then, tanks had started to rupture, unable to contain the overgrown organs. Thick fluid from the broken tanks pooled across the floor, sickly and foul. Santiago's eyes lingered on the latest casualty—a tank meant to nurture a liver, now shattered, with the organ grotesquely swollen beyond recognition.

Reports had trickled in from patients who had received the cloned organs. What should have been life-saving transplants had turned into ticking time bombs, as the organs continued growing inside their hosts, suffocating them from within. One particularly harrowing case involved the grandson of the president of Venezuela, who had received a cloned heart. The child had died in agony, the heart expanding until it crushed his lungs.

The door to the lab burst open, and Santiago's assistant, Hector, rushed in, his face pale with fear. "Dr. Santiago, the police are here. They're coming to arrest you."

Santiago's heart hammered in his chest. He had always known his work skirted the edges of legality, but he had never imagined it would come to this. He could already see the headlines: "Pioneer of Organ Cloning Falls from Grace."

He turned back to the tanks, his mind racing. There was no way out. The weight of his failure pressed down on him, suffocating. Reaching into his coat pocket, he pulled out a small vial of sodium pentothal—the same drug he had once used for patients as a merciful end, preserving their organs. Now, it would serve a different purpose.

Hector stepped closer, voice trembling. "Dr. Santiago, you don't have to do this. We can fight this."

Santiago shook his head slowly. "It's over, Hector. My work . . . it was supposed to save lives, not end them. Make sure the officials get the black box from my office."

Hector nodded, resignation in his eyes.

With hands steadier than they had been in days, Santiago uncapped the vial and filled a syringe, the liquid glinting under the lab's harsh lights. As he injected the drug, a strange calm washed over him. His vision blurred, the room around him fading to darkness. The last thing he saw were the tanks—the organs still growing, grotesque shadows playing on the walls.

As he sank to the floor, a fleeting thought surfaced: the legacy he had dreamed of, now shattered beyond repair. His last breath was a whisper, a silent apology to the world and a plea for forgiveness that would go unheard.

Hector knelt beside him, tears streaming down his face. Outside, the police approached, their footsteps echoing through the hall. Inside the lab, all was silent. Dr. José Santiago, the man who had hoped to change the world, was gone, leaving behind only a legacy of ambition turned tragedy.